11/2016

THE RAINS

THE
RAINS

GREGG HURWITZ

TOR
TEEN

A TOM DOHERTY ASSOCIATES BOOK • NEW YORK

THE RAINS

Copyright © 2016 by Gregg Hurwitz

A Tor Teen Book
Published by Tom Doherty Associates
175 Fifth Avenue
New York, NY 10010

www.tor-forge.com

Tor® is a registered trademark of Macmillan Publishing Group, LLC.

The Library of Congress Cataloging-in-Publication Data is available
upon request.

ISBN 978-0-7653-8267-2 (hardcover)
ISBN 978-1-4668-8851-7 (e-book)

Our books may be purchased in bulk for promotional, educational, or business
use. Please contact your local bookseller or the Macmillan Corporate and
Premium Sales Department at 1-800-221-7945, extension 5442, or
by e-mail at MacmillanSpecialMarkets@macmillan.com.

First Edition: October 2016

Printed in the United States of America

0 9 8 7 6 5 4 3 2 1

TO PHILIP EISNER

A great friend and writer,
fellow traveler through the darkness . . .

. . . and the light

The document you are reading does not—cannot—exist. If you're reading this, your life is at risk. Or I should say, your life is at even greater risk than it was already. I'm sorry to burden you with this. I don't wish you the kind of harm that came to me and the others from Creek's Cause. This is what I've managed to piece together since it all began. I wrote it down knowing that words are more powerful than bullets—and certainly more dangerous. All is probably lost already.

But maybe, just maybe, these pages will give you a chance.

I hope you're up to it.

The day after the day after tomorrow,
in a state nestled among others . . .

THE RAINS

ENTRY 1   It was past midnight. I was still working in the barn when I heard the rolling door lurch open. I started and lost my grip on a block of hay. It tumbled off the baling hooks.

It was creepy out here with the wind whipping across the roof, fluttering loose shingles. Bits of hay strobed through the shafts of light from the dangling overheads, and the old beams groaned beneath the load of the loft. I was plenty tough, sure, but I was also a high-school sophomore and still got spooked more often than I'd want to admit.

I turned to the door, my fists clenched around the wooden handles of the baling hooks. Each hook is a wicked metal curve that protrudes about a foot from between the knuckles of my hand. The barn door, now open, looked out onto darkness. The wind lashed in, cutting through my jeans and flannel shirt, carrying a reek that overpowered the scent of hay. It smelled as if someone were cooking rotten flesh.

I clutched those baling hooks like a second-rate Wolverine, cleared my throat, and stepped toward the door, doing my best to deepen my voice. "Who's there?"

Patrick swung into sight, his pump-action shotgun pointed at the floor. "Chance," he said, "thank God you're okay."

My older brother's broad chest rose and fell, his black cowboy hat seated back on his head. He'd been running, or he was scared.

But Patrick didn't get scared.

"Of course I'm okay," I said. "What are you talking about?" I let the baling hooks drop so they dangled around my wrists from the nylon loops on the handles. Covering my nose with a sleeve, I stepped outside. "What's that *smell*?"

The wind was blowing west from McCafferty's place or maybe even the Franklins' beyond.

"I don't know," Patrick said. "But that's the least of it. Come with me. Now."

I turned to set down my gear on the pallet jack, but Patrick grabbed my shoulder.

"You might want to bring the hooks," he said.

ENTRY 2   I should probably introduce myself at this point. My name is Chance Rain, and I'm fifteen. Fifteen in Creek's Cause isn't like fifteen in a lot of other places. We work hard here and start young. I can till a field and deliver a calf and drive a truck. I can work a bulldozer, break a mustang, and if you put me behind a hunting rifle, odds are I'll bring home dinner.

I'm also really good at training dogs.

That's what my aunt and uncle put me in charge of when they saw I was neither as strong nor as tough as my older brother.

No one was.

In the place where you're from, Patrick would be the star quarterback or the homecoming king. Here we don't have homecoming, but we do have the Harvest King, which Patrick won by a landslide. And of course his girlfriend, Alexandra, won Harvest Queen.

Alex with her hair the color of wheat and her wide smile and eyes like sea glass.

Patrick is seventeen, so Alex is between us in age, though I'm on the wrong end of that seesaw. Besides, to look at Patrick you wouldn't think he was just two years older than me. Don't get me wrong—years of field work have built me up pretty good, but at six-two, Patrick stands half a head taller than me and has grown-man strength. He wanted to stop wrestling me years ago, because there was never any question about the outcome, but I still wanted to try now and then.

Sometimes trying's all you got.

It's hard to remember now before the Dusting, but things were normal here once. Our town of three thousand had dances and graduations and weddings and funerals. Every summer a fair swept through, the carnies taking over the baseball diamond with their twirly-whirly rides and rigged games. When someone's house got blown away in a tornado, people pitched in to help rebuild it. There were disputes and affairs, and every few years someone got shot hunting and had to get rushed to Stark Peak, the closest thing to a city around here, an hour and a half by car when the weather cooperated. We had a hospital in town, better than you'd think—we had to, what with the arms caught in threshers and ranch hands thrown from horses—but Stark Peak's where you'd head if you needed brain surgery or your face put back together. Two years ago the three Braaten brothers took their mean streaks and a juiced-up Camaro on a joyride, and only one crawled out of the wreckage alive. You can bet Ben Braaten and his broken skull got hauled to Stark Peak in a hurry.

Our tiny town was behind on a lot. The whole valley didn't get any cell-phone coverage. There was a rumor that AT&T was gonna come put in a tower, but what with our measly population they didn't seem in a big hurry. Our parents said that made it peaceful here. I thought that made it boring, especially when compared to all the stuff we saw on TV. The hardest part was knowing there was a whole, vast world out there, far from us. Some kids left and went off to New York or L.A. to pursue big dreams, and I was always a bit envious, but I shook their hands and wished them well and meant it.

Patrick and I didn't have the same choices as a lot of other kids.

When I was six and Patrick eight, our parents went to Stark Peak for their anniversary. From what we learned later, there was steak and red wine and maybe a few martinis, too. On their way to the theater, Dad ran an intersection and his trusty Chrysler got T-boned by a muni bus.

At the funeral the caskets had to stay closed, and I could only imagine what Mom and Dad looked like beneath those shiny maple lids. When Stark Peak PD released their personals, I waited until late at night, snuck downstairs, and snooped through them. The face of Dad's beloved Timex was cracked. I ran my thumb across the picture on his driver's license. Mom's fancy black clutch purse reeked of lilac from her cracked-open perfume bottle. It was the smell of her, but too strong, sickly sweet, and it hit on memories buried in my chest, making them ring like the struck bars of a xylophone. When I opened the purse, a stream of pebbled windshield glass spilled out. Some of it was red.

Breathing the lilac air, I remember staring at those bloody bits scattered on the floorboards around my bare feet, all those pieces that could never be put back together. I blanked out after that, but I must have been crying, because the next thing I remember was Patrick appearing from nowhere, my face pressed to his arm when he hugged me, and his voice quiet in my ear: "I got it from here, little brother."

I always felt safe when Patrick was there. I never once saw him cry after my parents died. It was like he ran the math in his head, calm and steady as always, and decided that one of us had to hold it together for both of us, and since he was the big brother, that responsibility fell to him.

Sue-Anne and Jim, my aunt and uncle, took us in. They lived just four miles away, but it was the beginning of a new life. Even though I wanted time to stay frozen like it was on Dad's shattered Timex, it couldn't, and so Patrick and I and Jim and Sue-Anne started over.

They didn't have any kids, but they did the best they could.

They tried their hardest to figure out teacher conferences and the Tooth Fairy and buying the right kind of toys at Christmas. They weren't cut out to be parents but they did their damnedest, and at the end of the day that's all that really matters. Patrick and I loved them for it, and they loved us right back.

That doesn't mean my brother and I didn't have to grow up in a hurry. There was plenty of work to be done around the ranch and more bellies to fill. Jim had a couple hundred heads of cattle, and he bred Rhodesian ridgebacks and shipped them off across the country as guard dogs at two thousand a pop. Sue-Anne made sure to have hot food on the table three times a day, and she read to us every night. I vanished into those stories—the *Odyssey*, *Huck Finn*, *The Arabian Nights*. As we got older, Patrick grew tired of it all, but I kept on, raiding the bookshelf, reading myself to sleep with a flashlight under the covers. I think I hid inside those fictional worlds because they kept me from thinking about how much I'd lost in the real one.

By his early teens, Patrick was clearly a force to be reckoned with. He and I didn't look much alike—strangers were usually surprised to find out we were brothers. Not that I was ugly or weak or anything, but Patrick . . . well, he was Patrick. He got my dad's wide shoulders and good looks, and he could ride herd and rope cattle alongside the best ranch hand, chewing a piece of straw and never breaking a sweat. The girls lost their mind over who got to wear his cowboy hat during lunchtime.

Until Alex. Then it was only her.

I didn't like math so much, but I loved English and science. I didn't have Patrick's skills as a cattleman, but I wasn't afraid of hard work. I was pretty good behind a hunting rifle, almost as good as Uncle Jim himself, but the one thing I was better at than anyone was raising those puppies. Ridgebacks are lion hunters from Africa, the most fearless and loyal creatures you'll ever meet. Whenever we had a new litter, I'd play with the pups, training them up from day one. By the time they hit two months, they'd follow me anywhere, and by the time they were half a year old, I could put them on a sit-stay and they wouldn't move if you tried to drag them from their spot. It was hard fitting in all the work around school, but somehow I managed, and if there's one thing Dad taught me, it's that the Rains don't complain.

When it came time to stack the hay, Patrick always finished his part early and offered to help me on my share, but I made sure I finished it myself. Even if it was at the end of a long day. Even if it meant I had to stay up past midnight, working alone in the barn.

Which was what I was doing after the Dusting, the first time I'd seen Patrick nervous for as far back as my memory could stretch.

Considering everything that had been going on lately, I couldn't blame him.

But hang on. Let me start where it makes sense, one week ago. Not that *any* of it makes sense, but if I lay out some of what I learned later, maybe you'll be able to keep up.

I do need you to keep up.

Your life depends on it.

ENTRY 3   It began with a hard, slanting rain. And soon there was fire, too, but it wasn't fire. Not really. It was the pieces of Asteroid 9918 Darwinia breaking up above Earth, flaming as they entered the atmosphere.

It exploded twenty-four kilometers up, a bright flash that turned night into day. There was a boom above Creek's Cause and a wave of heat that evaporated the drops right out of the air. Jack Kaner's garret window blew out, and the rickety shed behind Grandpa Donovan's house fell over. The surge of warmth dried the pastures and the irrigated soil.

Fist-size fragments kicked up the powdered dirt in the field lying fallow behind Hank McCafferty's place, embedding themselves deep below the earth. A late winter had pushed back harvest, and so the fields were still full. McCafferty had been working sweet corn and barley through the fall, but this one empty plot, depleted by a recent planting, had been layered with manure to set up a double crop of alfalfa and oats for the next summer.

The soil was rich, primed for roots to take hold.

Or something else.

One of the meteorites struck Pollywog Lake at the base of the rocky ridge and burned off a foot of water. Another rocketed straight through Grandpa Donovan's cow, leaving a Frisbee-width channel through the meat as clean as a drill. The cow staggered halfway across the marshy back meadow before realizing it was dead and falling over. The coyotes ate well that night.

We came out of our farmhouses and ranch homes, stared at the sky in puzzlement, then went back inside, finishing the dinner dishes, watching TV, getting ready for bed. Living in a land of tornadoes and deadly storms, we were used to Mother Earth's moods.

We'd learn soon enough that Mother Earth had nothing to do with this.

Creek's Cause was originally called Craik's Cause, after James Craik, George Washington's personal physician. Sometime in the early 1800s, someone screwed up transcribing a map, and the wrong name took hold. But to this day we shared a pride in the purpose for which our town was named. After all, Craik had kept Washington healthy through the Revolutionary War and the following years, remaining at the first president's side until he finally died on that damp December night.

Standing there in the sudden heat of the night air, blinking against the afterimpressions of those bursts of flame in the sky, we couldn't have known that more than two hundred years later the opening salvo of a new revolutionary war had been fired.

And that my brother and I would find ourselves on the front lines.

The rains continued through the night, pounding the earth, turning our roofs into waterfalls. At the edge of town, Hogan's Creek overflowed its banks, drowning the Widow Latrell's snow peas until minnows swam shimmering figure eights through the vines.

Since McCafferty's farm was on higher ground, his crops weren't deluged. Narrow, bright green shoots poked up from the moist soil of his fallow field, thickening into stalks by the third day. At the top of each was a small bud encased in a leafy sheath. McCafferty lifted his trucker's cap to scratch his head at them, vowing to borrow Charles Franklin's undercutter to tear those strange-looking weeds from his land, but Franklin was not a generous man, and besides, there was corn to harvest, and so it waited another day and then another.

The rains finally stopped, but the stalks kept growing. The townsfolk went to check out the crazy growths rising from the soil where the meteorites had blazed deep into the ground. Patrick and I even stopped by one day after school to join the gawkers. By the end of the workweek, the stalks were taller than Hank himself. On the seventh day they towered over ten feet.

And then they died.

Just like that, they turned brittle and brown. The pods, which had grown to the size of corncobs, seemed to wither.

Some of the neighbors stood around, spitting tobacco into the dirt and saying it was indeed the damnedest thing, but there was nothing to do until McCafferty finished his harvest and tamped down his pride enough to ask Franklin for the loan of that undercutter.

McCafferty was at the bottle that night again after dinner. I can picture the scene like I was there—him in his rickety rocker on his rickety porch, the cool night filled with the sweet-rot smell of old wood. He had put his true love in the ground three summers ago, and you could see the grief in the creases of his face. His newer, younger wife fought like hell with his two kids, turning his house into a battleground, and he hid in the fields by day and in the bars by night. On this night he was rocking and sipping, letting a sweet bourbon burn away memories of his dear departed Lucille, when over the sound of the nightly bedtime squabble upstairs he heard a faint pop-ping noise.

At first he probably thought it was a clearing of his ears or the drink playing tricks on him. Then it came again, riding the breeze from the fields, a gentle popping like feather pillows ripping open.

A moment later he tasted a bitter dust coating his mouth. He spit a gob over the railing, reached through his screen door, grabbed his shotgun, and lumbered down the steps toward the fields. From an upstairs window, his son watched the power-ful beam of a flashlight zigzag across the ground, carving up the darkness.

The bitter taste grew stronger in McCafferty's mouth, as if a waft of pollen had thickened the air. He reached the brink of his fallow field, and what he saw brought him up short, his mouth gaping, his boots sinking in the soft mud.

A dried-out pod imploded, releasing a puff of tiny parti-cles into the air. And then the seven-foot stalk beneath it collapsed, disintegrating into a heap of dust above the soil. He watched as the neighboring pod burst, its stalk crumbling into nothingness. And then the next. And the next. It was like a haunted-house trick—a ghost vanishing, leaving only a sheet fluttering to the ground. The weeds collapsed, row after row, sinking down into the earth they'd mysteriously appeared from.

At last the pollen grew too strong, and he coughed into a fist and headed back to his bottle, hoping the bourbon would clear his throat.

Early the next morning, McCafferty awoke and threw off the sheets. His belly was distended. Not ribs-and-coleslaw-at-a-Fourth-of-July-party swollen, but bulging like a pregnant woman five months in. His wife stirred at his side, pulling the pillow over her head. Ignoring the cramps, he trudged to the closet and dressed as he did every morning. The overalls stretched across his bulging gut, but he managed to wiggle them up and snap the straps into place. He had work to do, and the hired hands weren't gonna pay themselves.

As the sun climbed the sky, the pain in his stomach worsened. He sat on the motionless tractor, mopping his forehead. He could still taste that bitter pollen, feel it in the lining of his gut, even sense it creeping up the back of his throat into his head.

He knocked off early, a luxury he had not indulged in since his wedding day, and dragged himself upstairs and into a cold shower. His bloated stomach pushed out so far that his arms could barely encircle it. Streaks fissured the skin on his sides just like the stretch marks that had appeared at Lucille's hips during her pregnancies. The cramping came constantly now, throbbing knots of pain.

The water beat at him, and he felt himself grow foggy. He leaned against the wall of the shower stall, his vision smearing the tiles, and he sensed that pollen in his skull, burrowing into his brain.

He remembered nothing else.

He did not remember stepping from the shower.

Or his wife calling up to him that dinner was on the table.

Or the screams of his children as he descended naked to the first floor, the added weight of his belly creaking each stair.

He couldn't hear his wife shouting, asking what was wrong, was he in pain, that they had to get him to a doctor.

He was unaware as he stumbled out into the night and scanned the dusk-dimmed horizon, searching out the highest point.

The water tower at the edge of Franklin's land.

Without thought or sensation, McCafferty ambled across

the fields, walking straight over crops, husks cutting at his legs and arms, sticks stabbing his bare feet. By the time he reached the tower, his ribboned skin was leaving a trail of blood in his wake.

With nicked-up limbs, he pulled himself off the ground and onto the ladder. He made his painstaking ascent. From time to time, a blood-slick hand or a tattered foot slipped from a rung, but he kept on until he reached the top.

He crawled to the middle of the giant tank's roof, his elbows and knees knocking the metal, sending out deep echoes. And then he rolled onto his back, pointing that giant belly at the moon. His eyes remained dark, unseeing.

His chest heaved and heaved and then was still.

For a long time, he lay there, motionless.

There came a churning sound from deep within his gut. It grew louder and louder.

And then his body split open.

The massive pod of his gut simply erupted, sending up a cloud of fine, red-tinted particles. They rose into the wind, scattering through the air, riding the current toward his house and the town beyond.

What happened to Hank McCafferty was terrible.

What was coming for us was far, far worse.

ENTRY 4   It was later that same night when Patrick came to get me in the barn.

Gripping the baling hooks at my sides, I stepped through the rolled-back door into the night. My brother's face was turned to the east. That bitter breeze kept blowing in across the fields.

"What's going on?" I asked.

Patrick raised a hand for silence.

A shift of the wind brought distant noises. Hammering sounds. And then, barely audible, the squeals of children.

"McCafferty's place?" I asked.

"Sounds like it."

"Do we wake Uncle Jim?"

Patrick turned his gaze at me. "And if it's just the kids messing around, playing a game? You wanna be the one to tell Jim sorry for dragging him outta bed, knowing the workday he's got tomorrow?"

I spit to clear the bitter taste from my mouth. "Then why do we need the shotgun?"

Patrick headed along the side of our ranch house toward the McCafferty place. "'Cuz what if we see a buck along the way?"

I didn't smile.

As we passed the rows of cozy crates lining the outside wall, our seven remaining ridgies stirred, a few of the boys sniffing the air and starting to growl. All at once they went crazy, snapping at the scent on the wind and howling. When they were riled up, you could hear the hound in them.

"Quiet," Patrick hissed. "Quiet!" Then to me, "Make them shut up before they wake Jim and Sue-Anne."

I said, "Hush," and the dogs fell silent, though Cassius whimpered with impatience.

Weeds grew tough and fast out here, so Uncle Jim let a few hungry goats roam the acre beyond our doorstep to keep the view. A few bleated as we passed them by and cut through the pasture. Some of the cows stirred as we drifted by. As we neared the McCafferty place, the cries got louder and my mouth dryer. The air tasted so vile I choked on it.

"You think something's *burning?*"

Patrick shook his head. "No. That's something else."

A dot of yellow illuminated the McCafferty porch, the light glowing next to the front screen. The door was laid open, the house's interior black as pitch.

We heard the kids clearly now through that screen door. This was no game. They weren't squealing.

They were screaming.

A slow, steady banging echoed out at us.

Maybe Hank was drunk again, trying to kick down the kids' door. Maybe there was an escapee from the state pen one county over. Maybe a homicidal psychopath had hitchhiked to our quiet little town and decided to have some fun.

The terrible banging continued from inside the house.

I whispered, "Should we go back and get Uncle Jim?"

"And leave JoJo and Rocky to whatever's happening?" Patrick said.

The question required no answer. I shrank back behind Patrick. Despite the cold, I could see sweat sparkling on the nape of his neck. He quickened his pace. When we were about twenty yards away, he stopped and called out, "Whoever's causing trouble in there, I got a shotgun!"

The banging ceased at once.

The McCafferty kids inside—JoJo and Rocky—stopped screaming, but we could still hear them sobbing. Patrick and I stood side by side, his shotgun raised, my grip growing tighter on the baling hooks.

JoJo's wails tailed off into silence.

From inside the house came a creak. Then another. Someone descending the stairs?

The footsteps continued, maddeningly slow, growing nearer.

Then we sensed a dark form behind the mesh of the screen. Just standing there. Staring ahead. We couldn't make out anything more than a silhouette of shoulders and a head, shadow against darkness.

Breaths clouded through the screen, quick puffs of mist in the cold night air. A sound carried out to us—shallow pants, as if from someone who had just learned to breathe.

Patrick jacked the pump of the Winchester, the *shuck-shuck* loud enough to make my scalp crawl.

The breaths continued. The wind blew cold and steady.

It went down so fast we could barely register it.

The screen banged open. A woman in a nightgown flew out, a clawed hand jerking up to shatter the porch light, the front of the house falling into darkness. Bare feet hammered across the boards, and then the form leapt over the railing, moonlit, limbs spread like a cat's. She landed on all fours, bounded up onto her feet, and scampered toward the grain silo.

A hatch opened on rusty hinges, then banged shut.

Patrick and I stood there in the night for a moment, breathing. My undershirt clung to me, and I realized I'd sweated right through it. Slowly, Patrick lowered his shoulders.

"What . . . *was* that thing?" I said.

"A woman, I expect. We better check it out."

My heart did something weird in my chest. "Shouldn't we check on JoJo and Rocky instead?"

"And let her escape?" Patrick said. "We got her cornered in the silo. What if she gets out and circles behind us? Or heads back for Jim and Sue-Anne?"

He started walking through the gloom toward the grain silo. He was my brother. I had to follow.

Plus, being alone with that thing out here didn't sound much better.

The side hatch was loose, swaying in the wind. The latches clicked against the metal wall.

Patrick readied the shotgun with one hand as he reached for the handle. His fingers might have been steady, but my whole body was shaking.

The hatch creaked open, and Patrick stepped back, pointing the shotgun barrel at the black square. We waited for something to fly out at us.

But nothing came.

We blinked, let our eyes acclimate to the darkness.

Uneven mounds of barley rose head-high.

The woman stood at the far side of the silo behind one of the mounds, facing away so we could make out only a shoulder and the back of a head.

She half turned, and we caught a silhouette. Her skin looked pale, and her nightgown was torn and ragged at the shoulder, as if chewed.

Patrick lowered the shotgun. "Mrs. McCafferty?" he said. "Are you all right?"

She twitched a few times, her head jerking to the side. Moonlight from the open hatch cast her in an otherworldly glow.

"Did someone hurt you?" Patrick asked. "Is something in there with you?"

He lifted one leg and started to step into the hatch, ducking down to get the Stetson through. I grabbed his shoulder. "Patrick," I said. "No."

"I have to make sure she's okay," he said, shaking me off.

He entered, stepping over the arm of the sweep auger. It was like a giant clock hand that rotated around the floor, sweeping the barley toward a center vertical auger that carried the grain up through the roof and into a chute for loading trucks. It wasn't moving now, shut down for the day.

I armed sweat from my forehead and watched my brother approach Mrs. McCafferty. I could see directly over his shoulder. She remained partly turned toward us, twitching and slightly hunched. Her rhythmic breathing continued, bellows without the wheeze.

"Mrs. McCafferty?" Patrick said. "Whatever happened to you, it's over now. You're okay."

She turned and looked at us.

For a moment I didn't believe what I was seeing.

In place of eyes, two tunnels ran straight through her skull. The beam of illumination from the flashlight cast twin glowing dots on the silo wall behind her. There was no blood at all on her face.

Those cored-out holes seemed to look right at us.

And then she lunged.

Patrick stumbled back, his ankle catching on the thick metal auger arm, and he went down, his hat tumbling off. She scrambled over the mound, her bare feet fighting for traction, rivulets of grain spilling beneath her heels. Her face was blank, devoid of any emotion, even as she reached the top of the mound and leapt for Patrick, limbs spread as they'd been when she'd sprung over the porch railing.

The sound of the shotgun inside the silo was deafening. The blast hit her in the stomach, knocking her back onto the mound of grain and embedding her in the side like a snow angel, arms thrown wide. The echo kept on, cycling in the metal walls and in my own head, crashing like cymbals.

Patrick pulled himself up, his face bloodless. He staggered over to the open hatch.

My mouth was working but could find no words. Although I couldn't hear anything yet, I saw his lips moving.

And then the percussive crash lessened and his words came clear. "Chance. *Chance*. We gotta get help. We gotta get the sheriff."

I tried to nod.

Behind him, I sensed movement.

Mrs. McCafferty, pulling herself stiffly up out of the mound of barley. Her torso and head rose as one. A few strands of hair swept across the back of her head, making the light through her eyeholes flicker. And then she tilted forward onto her feet, grain showering off her like sand.

She was right there, visible over Patrick's shoulder.

I didn't have time to yell, so I grabbed him to yank him through the hatch. I caught both his arms, the shotgun flying to land on the ground beyond me. I tugged his head through when she grabbed him from behind and ripped him into the silo with enough force to throw me off my feet. My forehead banged the hatch, and I fell into the soft mud outside the silo.

Somewhere Patrick was yelling, his shouts amplified inside the giant metal drum.

I willed myself not to black out. Grabbing the sill of the hatch, I pulled myself to my feet and forced myself to look.

Bleeding freely from her gut, Mrs. McCafferty had pinned Patrick to the floor on his stomach. He looked stunned and semiconscious; he must have struck the floor hard, or he would have overpowered her. She was crouched on his back like some feral animal, one knee between his shoulder blades. She ripped out a hank of her own long hair, and it came free with a plug of skin riding the end. Using her hair as rope, she started to bind Patrick's wrists at the small of his back.

Drooling blood, my brother blinked at me languidly.

I started to climb in after him, but he was yelling for me to stay out.

"No!" I yelled. "I'm not leaving you!"

Terrified, I swung one leg through the hatch, straddling the metal lip.

That's when his words finally registered: *"Turn on the sweep auger!"*

Mrs. McCafferty's clawlike hands secured the hair in a knot, Patrick's wrists cinched tight.

Then her head snapped up, those eyeless eyes pinning me to my spot.

I jerked back out of the hatch, stumbling to keep my feet beneath me. Mrs. McCafferty popped upright so quickly it seemed like she'd been jerked by a string. Then she flew toward me.

Panicked, I reached for the mounted box next to me, flipped open the guard lid, and hammered the big red button that turned it on.

The sweep auger roared to life inside the silo.

Mrs. McCafferty stopped midway between Patrick and me, her head cocked at the sudden commotion.

The auger began its rotation around the floor, the drive hooks raking through the mounds of barley, then skittering across the bare spots that provided no friction. Husk particles whirled up, filling the space inside.

Patrick rolled onto his knees, then stood, fighting his hands free. Dust clouded the air, bits of barley beating against him, blinding him. I raised an arm against the onslaught to block my eyes.

The metal arm rotated around the floor, a giant clock arm sweeping toward Patrick.

I yelled as loud as I could into the roar, "Jump, Patrick!"

Blindly, he leapt up, bringing his knees high as the drive hooks whipped beneath him. He caught a heel on the edge and fell, safe for now on the silo's floor as the arm swung away into its next rotation.

Mrs. McCafferty started for me again. Sheets of barley rippled underfoot, slowing her progress. But still she came.

I fought my instinct to slam the hatch door; I couldn't lock Patrick in there with her. Particles flecked my face, my eyes. My boots felt rooted to the ground.

Through the holes bored in her head, I could see my brother find his feet again, shaking his hands free of the restraint Mrs. McCafferty had fashioned from her ripped-out hair. Shielding his eyes from the flurry of hulls and spikelets, he took his bearings.

He'd never get to me in time.

Mrs. McCafferty reached for me, both hands tensed to yank me through the hatch.

But just as her fingers brushed my chest, she was ripped backward, her arms flying up over her head, her legs snared on the thick drive hooks of the sweep auger. The sturdy arm whipped her around the circumference of the silo, sucking her in toward the vertical auger in the middle.

Her lower half met the junction first. The drive belt squealed as the powerful teeth ground flesh and bone. She was still alive, clawing haplessly at the floor, her fingernails snapping.

Finally able to see, Patrick whisked his cowboy hat off the floor and jumped over the arm again as it flew at him. He sprinted for me and dove through the hatch.

We heard Mrs. McCafferty shriek as she was siphoned up into the vertical auger, too narrow for a human form. A crimson spray painted the swarming barley hulls and metal walls, and then Patrick's muscular arm reached past me and slammed the hatch door shut.

He banged the big red button with the heel of his hand, and all of a sudden there was quiet in the world again. We both leaned against the closed hatch door, breathing hard.

We stayed like that for a long time.

Then Patrick bent over, picked up his shotgun, and headed for the house. "The kids," he said.

ENTRY 5   Patrick and I stood side by side outside the kids' bedroom upstairs. The door was locked. At the edge by the knob, fingernail marks marred the wood. The bottom panels were splintered from where Mrs. McCafferty had tried to kick them in.

"Hey, JoJo? Rocky?" my brother called. "It's Patrick and Chance. Everything's clear out here now. You're safe."

Silence.

"Hey, guys," I said. "It's me."

Rocky finally answered, "Chance?"

I was closer with the McCafferty kids than Patrick was. They came over to play with the dogs. I even let them watch the litters being born if it wasn't a school night. Rocky was ten years old, JoJo only eight, so they couldn't afford being up late if they had school the next day.

"Yep," I said. "Come on out now and let us help you."

"Our stepmom," Rocky said through the door. "She tried to kill us. Except . . ." His voice quavered.

I said, "Except it wasn't your stepmom."

A moment later we heard the click of the door unlocking. It swung in to reveal two tearstained faces. Rocky held a baseball bat, and JoJo clutched Bunny, her worn yellow stuffed animal, to her chest.

At the sight of me, JoJo held up her arms like a little kid wanting to be picked up. I let the baling hooks drop so they dangled from my forearms on their nylon loops, freeing my hands. When I lifted her, she clung to me and started crying again, her long brown hair brushing against my face.

Rocky peered up the hall behind us. "Where is she now?"

Patrick said, "You don't have to worry about her anymore."

Rocky nodded, clearly trying not to cry. "Good."

JoJo's face was hot where it touched my neck. She pulled back and looked at me. "Our daddy," she said. "He wasn't our daddy either. Not when he left."

"When did he leave?" Patrick asked.

"Earlier tonight."

"Where'd he go?" I asked.

JoJo lifted her arm and pointed through her bedroom window. Past the Franklins' place, the water tower rose beneath the moonlight.

———

"He was hurt bad," Rocky said as we headed downstairs. Black curls fringed his round face. Though he'd gone pale, circles flushed his cheeks. He looked even younger than his ten years.

Patrick chose his words carefully. "Like your stepmom?"

"No, not like her," JoJo said. "His stomach was swole up, and he was all weird and stumbly."

"And naked," Rocky added.

Patrick looked like he wasn't sure what to make of that, and I wasn't either.

"Our stepmom, she went into shock after Dad left," Rocky said. "She sat on the kitchen floor and couldn't talk. She just cried and shivered. We didn't know what to do. Then when night came on, she . . . she *changed*."

As we passed through the kitchen, Patrick plucked the phone receiver from the wall and held it to his ear. Then he tapped the switch-hook a few times, gave me a little shake of his head, and hung the phone back up.

My stomach pulsed with alarm. Mrs. McCafferty must have cut the phone line, though it seemed crazy to me that she'd have thought to do something like that. By the time we saw her, it didn't seem like she was thinking at all.

"We're gonna head back to our place and rouse Jim and Sue-Anne," Patrick said. "We've got to get some help."

"I want him," JoJo said. She still hadn't come out of my arms. "I want my dad."

"I understand that, Junebug," I said, hoping her favorite nickname would calm her. "But we need to let the sheriff know what happened here."

The sheriff happened to be Alex's father, an added complication that neither Patrick nor I wanted to dwell on right now. Timothy Blanton had been a single father for five years, ever since his wife had driven off to the West Coast one crisp autumn morning, never to return. He was as strict as you'd imagine a single father/sheriff might be, and while Patrick was respectful to him, there wasn't a lot of affection between them. There'd be even less once we told him about shooting Mrs. McCafferty in the gut, then shredding her in a sweep auger.

Shotgun in hand, Patrick stepped through the screen door onto the porch and scanned the darkness. The night wind gusted in our faces. JoJo sniffed the bitter air and wrinkled her nose.

"But he was hurt," Rocky said. "What if he needs our help *now*? Your place is the opposite way. Can we help him first?"

JoJo started crying. "I want my dad," she said again.

I looked at Patrick, and he nodded. "Okay. We'll do a quick loop to look for him in case he's in trouble, then head home and call the sheriff."

I set JoJo down, careful not to snag her sweater on the baling hooks. "Keep behind us," I said.

We headed off the porch and forged ahead into the crops.

We came to that cleared field and noticed the little piles where the stalks had once been, the crumbled remains like ash.

I remembered the news frenzy following Asteroid 9918 Darwinia's disintegration. All the statistics and gossip about what had landed where.

At the sight, Patrick made a noise deep in his throat, and then we continued on. Sweet corn rose on either side of us, the husks scraping our sleeves. On alert, we rasped through the darkness toward the Franklins' land, Patrick and I keeping the lead.

"What *was* that in the silo?" I whispered.

"I don't know," Patrick said. "But it wasn't Mrs. McCafferty. Not anymore."

"We killed her."

"No," he said. "You saw her. She was already dead."

"Then what *was* she? And don't say the Z-word."

"I have no idea," Patrick said. "It's like she was sick with some crazy disease. Rabies or whatever."

"Rabies doesn't put tunnels through your head."

"A new strain, then," Patrick said. "Or some other killer virus."

"But what disease does *that*?" I said. "It's like something had . . . I don't know, taken her over."

Just saying it out loud made the back of my neck prickle. Our boots crunched the hard earth.

Patrick cleared his throat. "She was more like a . . . a . . . what's the name for it? In biology? The opposite of a parasite?"

"A host," I said.

We let the word hang there. Behind us we could hear JoJo sniffling and Rocky murmuring, "It's all right. It's all right."

We reached the edge of the field, breaking through the stalks onto open ground.

"What was she trying to do?" I whispered. "The . . . *host*?

Ripping out her hair, pinning you down, tying your wrists? Was she gonna eat you?"

"No," Patrick said. "She was trying to take me captive."

"For *what?*"

Instead of answering, Patrick halted abruptly. Touched his hand to the earth. When he lifted it to the moonlight, his fingertips were smudged with something dark.

Blood.

The kids emerged from the corn, nearly stumbling into us from behind. Patrick stood quickly and lowered his hand so they wouldn't see his stained fingertips.

"What?" Rocky said.

"Just catching my breath," Patrick said.

The blood trail continued forward, nearly impossible to make out in the darkness. Patrick's eyes traced the direction it went, his head slowly tilting up. I looked where he was looking. A stream of particles flowed above us, luminous in the moonlight, like the trail of a magic carpet.

We traced the stream across the starry sky to its source.

The top of the water tower.

———

The giant tower rose like a spider on stilts. We stood at the base of the metal ladder leading up and up. I realized that my knee was jittering and told it to stop. The stream of particles looked to be growing thinner, a fire burning itself out.

"What do you think it is?" Rocky asked.

"I don't know," I said. "Maybe your dad went up there, started a fire or something?"

"Please help him," JoJo said. "Please bring him home."

Patrick set his hands on a rung, the shotgun making a clang against the side rail.

"Shouldn't I come up and get your back?" I asked.

"Yes," he said.

I turned to the kids. "Stay here—*right here*. If you see any-thing or anyone, give a shout."

Rocky nodded and drew his little sister in protectively.

Patrick was already twenty or so rungs above me, his pro-gress punctuated by the steady knock of the shotgun against metal. I started up after him.

I will confess: I don't love heights. This water tower was 150 feet high, which wasn't so bad, except for the fact that the ladder rose in the space between the legs of the tower, unattached to anything else. It felt like scaling a magical beanstalk, the earth falling away, my fists and toes finding holds in thin air.

Patrick finally reached the tank itself, and he climbed the metal rungs welded to the side. I followed him, focusing on each handhold, not daring to look anywhere else.

I heard a final clank of the shotgun as Patrick got to the top, and then there was silence.

"Patrick?" I called up, panic finding its way into my voice. "Everything okay?"

His voice floated down from the darkness. "No," he said.

I quickened my pace to the top and crawled onto the flat roof of the tank, still not risking a look up from my feet until I was a few paces off the edge. My legs felt wobbly, though whether that was from the altitude or the sight before me, I didn't know.

There on his back lay what was left of Hank McCafferty.

His torso and stomach were gone. In their place was a cra-ter. He'd been hollowed out, the cage of his ribs thrusting up in the eroded space. Deep in the gleaming cavern, I could make out the line of his spinal cord. That strange pollen streamed forth from the hole, his remains turning to particles and pay-ing out like a ribbon riding the wind.

It took me two tries to speak. My voice came out reedy. "What the hell is that stuff?" I asked.

"I don't know," Patrick said. "We need help. We need to tell someone."

I followed the pollen's course to the distant lights of town and felt something inside me go cold.

That's when we heard Rocky and JoJo screaming.

ENTRY 6   I was closest to the ladder, so I was the first man down. Patrick clanked down above me, urging me to move faster, his boots skimming my fingers as I pulled them off the rungs. My descent was so fast that it felt like falling. I couldn't tell how far we'd come or how much farther we had to go.

Below, the kids' screams grew louder, louder, and I risked a glance down. Forty or so feet below, Rocky and JoJo sprinted by, around the base of the water tower. A figure flashed past, chasing them, nightgown fluttering like a ghost in its wake.

Mrs. Franklin?

Patrick's tread crunched my fingers. I yelped and whipped that hand free, holding on with the other. I reeled away from the ladder. The ground spun dizzyingly below. My sweaty grip nearly slipped, but I swung around and clamped back onto the rungs.

"Move!" Patrick was shouting. *"Movemovemovemovemove!"*

I did, not looking down again until my heel jammed into the dirt and I tumbled onto my back.

I blinked away the pain. A menacing silhouette leaned over me. It was Mr. Franklin, an outline of solid black against the blackness. Except I could see right through the holes where his eyes used to be, the stars shining through the tunnels in his head.

Quick breaths misted the air by his mouth. He leaned

over, his head twitching, those large farmer's hands reaching for me.

I opened my mouth to scream when he was wiped suddenly from view. Patrick had barreled off the ladder and knocked him over. Patrick rolled to his feet, planted a boot in the middle of Franklin's chest, and unloaded the shotgun right into the man's head.

The boom made me recoil there in the mud. It echoed off the hills of Ponderosa Pass.

Terror had left my skin clammy. I pulled myself to my feet.

Mr. Franklin's body lay inert. His head was mostly gone.

After the experience with Mrs. McCafferty coming back to life after the gut shot, Patrick had taken no chances, going straight for the head.

A high-pitched scream snapped us out of our daze. Rocky and JoJo sprinted around one of the legs of the water tower, Mrs. Franklin right behind them, a streak of white.

Patrick chambered another shell and stepped into the path of the kids. Rocky split in one direction, JoJo the other. They brushed the outsides of Patrick's legs as he fired a blast through Mrs. Franklin's face.

She flew back and landed, her dress hiked up, exposing her pale, smooth thighs.

The kids cowered behind Patrick. Rocky sobbed. JoJo clutched Bunny and didn't make a sound, just stared at the woman's legs.

Patrick's shoulders rose and fell. Sweat glossed his neck. Though I was standing, I felt like I was falling, my foundation tumbling away. Seeing Mrs. McCafferty get tangled in the auger had been horrifying. This was worse. Standing there beneath the water tower over the corpses of our neighbors was one of those nothing-will-ever-be-the-same moments. In the space of an hour, Patrick and I had killed three grown-ups. And the stream of pollen just kept pouring out of Hank McCafferty overhead. I couldn't help but think it had something to do with what was going on.

That whatever we'd run into hadn't even gotten started.

I walked over and straightened out Mrs. Franklin's dress so it covered her legs. I don't know why it mattered to me. But it did.

Then I leaned over and threw up. Patrick eased to my side, put a hand on my shoulder. I wiped my mouth.

"Sorry," I said. "Sorry."

I turned back to the kids. JoJo hugged Bunny to her chest, shivering violently despite her thick sweater. "Did you find our dad?"

Patrick nodded. He didn't say anything, but it was enough. The kids' eyes were glazed over with shock.

I thought about my mom's clutch purse spilling blood-stained pebbles of windshield glass. How Patrick had slept on the floor next to my bed those first days after the car crash because I kept waking up screaming.

I crouched, bringing myself to eye level with JoJo, and rested my hands on her shoulders. "Why don't you stay with us now?" I said.

This was no time to linger on loss. We had to get safely home and start figuring out just what in the hell was going on.

She managed a nod.

Bracing myself, I tightened my grip on the baling hooks and turned for the cornfields. Something caught my eye, a dark stream against the stars.

The river of pollen was blowing directly over our house.

ENTRY 7   We moved silently through the stalks and across pastures until the distant lights of our porch were yellow blurs in the darkness. Again Patrick and I were leading the way ahead of the kids. We followed the particles floating overhead.

They looked almost like fireflies in the moonlight. I felt something twist inside my chest.

"That pollen stuff," Patrick said. "What do you think it is?"

"Some kind of airborne . . . blood mist?" I shook my head. "It all sounds friggin' nuts."

"Maybe we're overthinking it," Patrick said. "It could just be how people decompose when they're infected with what-ever it is. Instead of rotting away, I mean."

"But the wind carried it right to where we found Mrs. McCafferty." I couldn't bring myself to mention that it was headed for our house, too, and town beyond. "That seems like a pretty big coincidence."

"So you're saying people are breathing it in, getting infected by it?"

I shrugged.

"What *does* that?" Patrick asked. "You're the one who pays attention in science."

I racked my brain. "Viruses, bacteria—" I cut off abruptly, heat rushing to my face.

"What?"

"Spores," I said.

"Spores?"

"Remember what you said about parasites and hosts?" I asked. "Well, there's this movie that Dr. Chatterjee showed in biology. About this kind of fungus. It's like a parasite."

I remembered the class: Dr. Chatterjee, walking his wobbly walk up and down the aisles with his leg braces, lecturing us in his singsong accent. He'd been our family doctor for years, treating Patrick and me since we were in diapers. Eventually his multiple sclerosis made it too hard for him to hold a syringe steady, so he'd retired to teach high-school science. He had to have a helper—usually me—write for him on the dryerase board and input grades into the computer, but he needed no assistance when it came to being a great teacher. He also worked as the town coroner. I guess his hand tremors were less of a concern when it came to dealing with dead people.

"Okay," Patrick said. "And what does this fungus do?"

I glanced back, made sure we were out of earshot of the kids. "It attacks ants," I said.

"Ants?"

"It infects their brains, makes them fall out of trees. Then the infected ant—"

"The host."

"Yeah. The host climbs the stem of the tallest plant nearby and clamps down its mandibles on the top of it. Know what it's called? The *death grip*. The fungus eats the ant and then releases spores that drift all over the place and infect more ants."

There was a pause, and I suddenly felt self-conscious for remembering this stuff. I was mostly in advanced classes, one or two grades ahead. Patrick had once told me that I seemed more at home in books than outside of them. He hadn't meant it as an insult—he'd intended it as a compliment after I'd brought home another solid report card—but it had burned like one. I guess I still felt a touch of embarrassment talking about school stuff with him. Patrick, who was most in his element atop a horse at full gallop.

I glanced over and saw that his face wasn't judgmental but thoughtful.

"So it makes them march to their death," he said. "Like Mr. McCafferty."

It struck me then that maybe some of the odd bits I remembered from stories and textbooks and documentaries might actually be useful out here in the real world. Which meant that maybe at some point I might be as useful as Patrick out here, too.

"That's right," I said.

"If this stuff is like that fungus, then why didn't Mrs. McCafferty do the same thing as her husband? And the Franklins? If they were infected by some human version of that parasite or whatever, why didn't they climb up to the highest spot they could find and . . . *explode*?"

"I don't know. It makes no sense." Picturing that dark shadow looming over me at the base of the water tower, I shuddered. "What was Mr. Franklin gonna do to me?"

"It was weird," Patrick said. "He was just walking calmly, not trying to run you down. Different from his wife or Mrs. McCafferty. I saw him from the ladder. He was walking with his head angled down, like he was looking for something."

"Without any eyes," I said.

"That's right. But if he *did* have eyes, they would've been pointed at the ground. You happened to land right in his path. That's the only reason he noticed you and started to come after you. At least that's what it looked like."

"So the spores, maybe they affect men and women differently," I said.

"The women try to catch people and the men walk around and look at stuff? What for?"

I shrugged. JoJo ambled forward and hugged my side, even as we kept walking. I laid an arm across her back, careful not to hurt her with the baling hook. She was murmuring to herself, what sounded like a nursery rhyme. After a few steps, she let go and drifted back with her brother.

We walked in silence for a time. The only sound was our boots crunching against the dirt. We emerged from the corn into the scrubby, tree-studded land between our place and the McCaffertys'. As we edged through a row of Gambel oak, the lights of our porch started to resolve.

"Even if they weren't human anymore," I said quietly to Patrick, "it still feels like we've killed people, you know?"

"If you were like *that*, would you want to keep living?" Patrick asked. "Would you want to know your body was still running around, terrorizing other people?"

I pictured myself doing awful things without knowing I was doing them. "No," I said. "No way."

"These spores float over everything," Patrick said. "Like a crop dusting."

"That's right," I said. "A dusting."

"Then why aren't *we* Hosts?" Patrick gestured back to Rocky and JoJo. "Or them? We breathed the same air as Mrs. Mc-Cafferty and the Franklins. If the spores turn people, why hasn't it turned *us*?"

"Maybe we're immune."

"Or maybe," Patrick said, "we're *already* infected and it's just a matter of time."

I looked down at the backs of my hands, fish-white in the darkness. Was something already creeping beneath my skin, transforming me? I felt each breath, cool in my throat, filling my lungs.

The changing wind brought the barking of the dogs. An angry ruckus, full of snaps and snarls. As we drew nearer, the lights clicked on in our house, our living room lighting up as clear as day, a beacon in the darkness. Relief spread through me, a warmth in my chest. We were about a hundred yards away from home and safety.

Uncle Jim came into view inside, heading for the front door. "Thank God," I said.

Uncle Jim opened the door and stepped out onto the porch. I started to jog forward, but Patrick grabbed my arm. "Hang on," he whispered.

Something in his voice scared me into stillness.

We stopped behind the big old ash tree with the rope swing. I rested my hand on the trunk, feeling beneath my palm the carving that Alex had made last year with Patrick's folding knife: *A.B.+P.R.* in a heart. I remembered watching her work the blade into the bark, her brow furrowed with concentration, her teeth pinching that full lower lip. As usual I was the third wheel, grinding a stick into an anthill and doing my best not to notice the way Alex's shirt rode up when she leaned forward, revealing a strip of tan skin at her lower back.

After all the things that had happened, the memory seemed like a glimpse into another world.

I felt JoJo clutching my side again, but I couldn't move to comfort her. I was rooted to the ground, my eyes fixed on Uncle Jim.

He stood perfectly still in the middle of the porch, lit from the glow of the house.

"What's he *doing?*" Rocky whispered, and Patrick hushed him.

We watched Uncle Jim do nothing.

And then he shuddered.

Not a shiver from the cold but a full-body shudder as if an electric current had passed through him. Then he was still once again.

A few seconds went by.

Fear clawed up my throat, and I swallowed it down.

"I'm gonna go to him," I whispered to Patrick. "He's fine."

I started forward, but Patrick's hand clamped down on my arm. I shook him loose and stepped into the open.

My brother's voice came at me quietly from behind. "Chance," he said. "Wait. Just wait."

The grief in his voice made my denial melt away, and I halted. The wind blew through my jacket. The bitterness was still in the air, riding the back of my tongue. I felt a pressure behind my face. I didn't keep on, but I didn't retreat behind the tree either.

Uncle Jim had no way to see me in the darkness.

He was just standing there, frozen.

Then a blackness crept across his eyes until they looked like two giant pupils filling the space between the lids.

And then the blackness crumbled away like ash. The breeze lifted the bits of residue out of his head.

The lights of the house behind him showed in those two spots.

I tried to swallow, but my throat felt like sand. We watched as he stepped off the porch. He walked about fifty feet from the house, then halted. His head lowered, a smooth motion like a security camera autoswiveling. Then he walked a few steps, made a right-angle turn, walked a few more, and did it again. He walked a little bit longer each time, though the turns remained crisp. He seemed to be charting a rectangular grid, spiraling out from the center point. It made no sense at all, and yet there was some terrible cold logic to it, a logic I could not grasp.

Seeing him like that, all stiff as if under a hex, felt worse than if we'd come home and found him split open like

Mr. Franklin. I realized I'd cupped my hand over my mouth, maybe to keep from crying out.

Uncle Jim, who'd played marbles with me when I was a kid. Uncle Jim, who made the best paper airplanes and taught me how to sail them across the barn from the hayloft. Uncle Jim, who'd helped me with my algebra homework, puzzling through the equations at my side.

He continued charting his course over the land in front of our house, his vacant eyes lowered. I remembered what Patrick had said about Mr. Franklin, how it seemed he'd been looking for something on the ground. Uncle Jim stumbled over a rock but then righted himself and kept on course.

I turned around and saw that Patrick was breathing hard, his grip firm on the shotgun. JoJo and Rocky had drawn back into the brush behind us, ready to run.

"We have to go to him," I said to Patrick. "We can't leave him like that."

"I know," Patrick said.

I stepped out and jogged for Uncle Jim, ignoring Patrick's shouts for me to wait up. As I neared, I sprinted even faster. I had to see up close, to know it was true, because part of me wouldn't believe it.

I got within talking distance, and Uncle Jim finally halted. His head tilted up, and then I was looking at his face and through it at the same time. Everything else seemed the same—the scuffed cowboy boots, his faded Wranglers, that worn Carhartt jacket. I felt an impulse to run to him and hug him—to shut my eyes and pretend he was okay.

But then his hands went to his buckle. He yanked his belt free of the loops on his jeans and came at me. At first I thought he was going to whip me. Then I remembered Mrs. McCafferty and her hank of long hair, and I realized he was going to restrain me.

And then do *what*?

My hands whitened around the baling hooks. The curved metal spikes stuck out from between the knuckles of my fists.

"Please don't," I said. "Uncle Jim? Please don't. Don't make me."

His face lost to shadow, he kept on, readying the leather strap with his hands.

I raised my weaponed fists. "Please don't."

I could hear Patrick running to catch up. He wouldn't be here in time.

Uncle Jim's boots kept on, tramping across the mud, closer and closer.

I was crying. *"Don't."*

And then he was on me.

I sidestepped him and swung the baling hook. It embedded itself in his throat. He made a terrible gurgling sound and sank to his knees. I shook the spike free of his neck as Patrick finally arrived, his face flushed from his sprint.

Uncle Jim got one boot under him, then another. He stood, blood streaming from his neck, soaking the front of his jacket. As Patrick raised the shotgun, I turned my head, not wanting to see.

I heard the boom.

I heard the sound of a body hitting the dirt.

Then I heard the creak of our screen door, way over by the house.

I turned back in time to see Sue-Anne glide onto the porch. She halted beneath the light, a swirl of moths wreathing her head. For a moment she remained there, peaceful and still.

Then that full-body shudder racked her body.

I'd been waiting for it. That made it even worse.

Her chest jerked a few times.

We watched her eyes turn black and disintegrate. We watched those tunnels swivel across the landscape and lock onto us. Her spine curled, and she leapt from the porch, landing on all fours, then springing up onto her bare feet. She sprinted at us faster than she should have been able to, her muscles strained to the breaking point. She was thirty feet away. I blinked, and then it was twenty.

Her hair flew about her face, her lips stretched thin with effort. She had tugged the sash free from her bathrobe, and it flapped wildly behind her.

Patrick chambered another shell.

ENTRY 8   We didn't want to take the time to dig graves, so we laid Jim and Sue-Anne side by side on their bed in the master upstairs. It was a messy business, but after everything they'd done for us, we owed them that. We set up Rocky and JoJo in the living room watching TV so they wouldn't have to see the terrible state of our aunt and uncle.

My brother and I stood by the footboard, looking at them lying there. Patrick had draped empty pillowcases over their heads to hide the damage, but already blood was spotting through. It was an awful scene, made more awful by how normal it might have been, the two of them reclining beside each other as if ready for bed.

At least they were together.

Our family had never been big on praying, but Patrick clasped his hands at his belt and cleared his throat. "They were good folks who took care of us when they didn't have to." He paused. I heard him breathing wetly but didn't dare turn to look at him, because I was worried I'd start crying. "And they didn't just love each other but they *liked* each other, too, always laughing together and still slow-dancing sometimes. As far as I've seen, that's pretty rare in a couple who's been married that long. They set a good example for us, and I hope me and Alex are lucky enough to feel that way no matter how long we're together, and I hope Chance finds that with someone someday, too." He was quiet for a bit longer, and when he spoke again, his voice was strained. "They were lucky to have each other, and we were lucky to have them."

I reached out and touched the bump of Sue-Anne's foot. My chest gave a little, and I bit my lip, hard. Patrick lifted Uncle Jim's cowboy hat from the bedpost and rested it over the pillowcase-covered head, cocking the brim the way Uncle Jim always did. We turned off the lights and closed the door behind us, not knowing when we'd come back.

Standing in the hall, we could hear the TV playing downstairs. I said, "We've been breathing the same spores as Mrs. McCafferty and the Franklins and Jim and Sue-Anne. So some people must be more susceptible to them. Or maybe adults turn quicker and it takes longer for kids to change."

We looked at each other, and I knew we were thinking the same thing. Either of us could transform at any minute. I was watching my brother for that telltale full-body shudder, and he was watching me for the same.

Patrick broke off the mini-staredown, reaching past me for the phone in the tiny alcove off the hall. He dialed and waited. I could hear the ringing, though the sound was muffled against his cheek, and then I heard Alex's message.

You've reached me, Alex, and my dad, Sheriff Blanton. Dad, say hi.

Hi.

Real personable, Dad. Way to intimidate your constituency. Anyways, leave a message here for us. If it's an emergency, then you wouldn't be calling here, would you? You'd be calling Dad at the office. So we'll just pretend this whole thing never happened.

Alex.

Okay, okay.

Beep.

Patrick hung up and redialed. With the phone wedged between his shoulder and cheek, he drummed his fingers against the wall, his impatience starting to show. His other hand fished his pendant necklace out of his shirt.

It was a sterling silver jigsaw-puzzle piece strung on ball chain like a dog tag. The puzzle piece fit together with the one around Alex's neck, though hers was on a fancier necklace. She'd bought the set at the mall in Stark Peak. I remember the day she gave Patrick's to him. I was inside reading *Beowulf* at my desk. I happened to look up and see them through the window. They were having a picnic outside. She opened the little jewelry box, presenting the fitting pieces to him like an engagement ring. They cracked up a bit about the whole fake proposal, and then she cocked her head like she did.

I could hear her voice through my open window.

"So, Big Rain," she'd said, "what would you do to prove your love for me?"

Their old game. I'd seen them play it more times than I could count.

Patrick's cowboy hat shadowed him across the eyes, but I could see his smile at the nickname.

She sidled up close to him, pendant in hand. "Would you cross raging rivers?"

"I would."

She kept on, joking and dead serious at the same time. "Would you climb mountains?"

The Stetson dipped in a nod. His lips pursed, amused. "If they were between me and you, those mountains I would climb."

Her face was flushed, and she was looking at his mouth. "Would you crawl through *mud* for me?"

"If mud needed crawling through to get to you, I would."

Finally she reached up and hooked his pendant around his neck. Before she was done, they started kissing.

I closed the blinds. I was embarrassed and guilty to be spying on this private moment between them.

Or maybe it was something else.

Now in the alcove upstairs, waiting for someone to pick up, Patrick pressed the shiny puzzle piece to his lips. I don't think he even realized he was doing it.

When Alex's recorded voice came on again, he hung up and called the sheriff's office. No answer there either. Patrick set down the phone a little harder than necessary.

"Pack a bag with some stuff," he said. "We're going to get Alex."

Alex's house was in town, a ten-minute drive.

"Why do I need to pack up?" I asked.

"Just in case," Patrick said.

A few minutes later, with a change of clothes stuffed into my backpack, I met Patrick in the kitchen. He was stuffing cans of food into his heavy-duty hiking pack.

I set my own bag on the counter next to his and loaded in some dog food. He looked across at me, then said, "Good idea."

"There's gotta be some . . . what's it called?" I reached for the term and finally retrieved it. "*Infection radius* for the Dusting. Town's so much farther from the water tower. The spores probably haven't reached there yet. Sheriff Blanton's gotta be fine. We'll round up a bunch of adults who aren't affected, and they'll help us."

I wasn't sure if I was trying to convince Patrick or myself.

We pulled Rocky and JoJo from the television and stepped outside again. I tried not to notice the smears on the porch from when we'd dragged Uncle Jim and Sue-Anne inside.

One of the goats tilted his head toward me, a tuft of yellow weed hanging from his mouth. His rectangular pupils stared up at me, asking questions I couldn't answer. We breezed past him.

The ridgebacks smelled us coming and paced in their big metal crates, rattling the sides. I flipped the latches, and all seven of them poured out, surrounding us with snouts and fur, nuzzling into us and wagging their tails so hard that their rear ends shook. The kids let Cassius and his father, Zeus, lick their palms. With a snap of my fingers, I put the dogs on a sit-stay. Cassius was still a pup, but a big one—seventy pounds at just five months. He was what they called a "black mask" ridgie, with dark coloring across his nose and the band of his eyes. His forehead stayed wrinkled up with concern, and I stroked his head until he relaxed.

I looked to Patrick and said, "We'll need to take the flat-bed to fit the dogs."

"No," Patrick said. "We want to head into town quietly." He distributed shotgun shells into the various pockets of his jacket. "We have no idea what's waiting for us."

We made uneven time, slowing for the kids. After twenty minutes Patrick took my backpack so I could piggyback JoJo. Rocky matched our pace and didn't complain. I followed Patrick's lead just like always. He kept us off the main road, cutting through fields and forests, splashing across Hogan's Creek on the set of boulders behind the Widow Latrell's. The dogs kept close. Zeus, my biggest boy, forged ahead of us, 110 pounds of muscle on alert.

I noticed that Patrick was steering us around houses as well as roads. In the distance, the lit windows of the Latrell farm-house flickered into view through the dense pine trunks as we passed.

I wondered about what was happening behind those lit windows and what state Mrs. Latrell was in. I pictured Mrs. McCafferty inside the grain silo, turning slowly to give us her profile over one shoulder, shallow breaths clouding the cold air. No matter how I tried, I couldn't scrape that image out of my mind.

We continued on for what seemed like forever, keeping to the forest and fields. The Blantons' house waited at the edge of town. It was nicely kept, with its white picket fence, wrap-around porch, and Cape Cod shutters. We drew up to the property, peering around the detached garage. No lights on in the house.

There was something so much cleaner about the houses in town, owned by folks whose jobs didn't require them to toil in fields or slop hogs. Blanton came from money, or so everyone said. That seemed to be another thing he didn't like so much about Patrick and me: We didn't.

He'd never thought Patrick was good enough for his daughter. He wanted a bigger, better future for her. Not with some orphaned kid who worked a ranch and probably would for the rest of his life. More than once we'd overheard him telling Alex, "Rain only goes one direction: *down*." But that didn't discourage her. No, it just gave a *Romeo and Juliet* gleam to their relationship, like those wedding pictures at the mall they shoot through some kind of filter so the couple looks all dreamy and out of focus.

The house sat still now, with its proud blue-slate paint and white trim, its porch swing swaying gently in the night breeze. Everything just as it might be on another night, on any night.

"Maybe they're still asleep," I said. "Maybe they don't know anything's wrong."

At my side Cassius and Princess whined uneasily, and I hushed them.

"Stay here," Patrick said to the kids. Then to me, "Make the dogs stay with them."

I gave the command, and they sat. I looked Zeus in his

yellow-brown eyes. I always thought of him as my warrior, his face marred with scars from play-fighting with the others or driving coyotes off our property. Having fathered five litters in his seven years, he occupied the top of the hierarchy, the others falling in behind him whenever he gave a directed stare or showed his teeth.

"On guard," I said, and his ears flattened back against his skull. Then I looked at Rocky. "You see anything, tell him to S-P-E-A-K, and he'll bark like crazy. You guys are our look-outs. Got it?"

He nodded, but his face was pale with fear.

I followed Patrick across the open front yard. We took a turn around the house, peering in windows. Behind us an empty hammock squeaked at the swivels. Patrick went up on tiptoes to peer into Alex's bedroom, and I saw his back stiffen.

"What?" I whispered.

He gestured for me to look. Her bed was empty, the sheets smeared to one side, half on the floor.

As if she'd been dragged off the mattress.

The rest of her room looked normal enough, her closet door ajar, a big leopard-print beanbag in the corner, a vintage steamer trunk pushed up against the footboard of the sleigh bed.

Behind us the hammock squeaked and squeaked.

Patrick stepped away from the window, shotgun in hand. My own hands cramped around the baling hooks. A sprinkler leaked at our feet, turning the flower bed to mush.

We eased across to the next window. Sheriff Blanton's bed was empty, the duvet thrown to one side.

Two ghostly faces peered at us from the far wall. I lurched backward, the realization hitting only a moment later—it was our own reflections thrown back at us from a mirror.

I needed a moment to catch my breath, but Patrick was

already moving to check the other windows. The house appeared to be empty. We hit the tall fence at the edge of the house and circled back in the direction we'd come. Patrick walked briskly, his body tense. I had to pause in front of Alex's window to tug my boot out of the mud caused by that leaky sprinkler.

Through the pane I heard a faint rattle.

With mounting dread I turned my head and looked through the window.

Nothing.

Then the lid of the steamer trunk jumped, the latch jangling.

I started. It banged again, even louder, the metal loop rattling against the hasp.

My mouth had gone dry. I looked up, but Patrick had already vanished around the corner.

The next bang nearly sent me airborne. Patrick reappeared at the edge of the house, staring back at me. I could barely make out his face in the gloom. He mouthed *What?* and I gestured furiously for him to get back over here.

A moment later we stood shoulder to shoulder at the window. The steamer trunk lid lifted, an inch of black showing at the seam. A hand flashed into view, four fingers curling over the lip, pale in the shadows. Then they pulled back into darkness, the lid banging shut again.

Patrick was breathing hard. "The hell was that?" he whispered hoarsely.

I shook my head.

The trunk made a noise like a heartbeat. *Thump-thump.*

We were frozen, our breath fogging the glass. Then Patrick said what I was dreading he might: "We have to go in."

He set his palms flat against the pane and shoved gently upward. The sash window rose, squeaking in its tracks. He swung one leg over the sill, then eased himself through.

I gleaned that this was something he'd done before.

Gathering what courage I could, I followed.

Side by side in Alex's room, we stared at the steamer trunk.

Thump-thump.

We drew near. Patrick readied the shotgun in one hand, seating the butt firmly against his shoulder. With his other hand, he reached for the latch. His fingers trembled. I'd never seen them tremble before, not even after Mom and Dad died.

His fingertips reached the latch. Curled beneath it.

Then he flung it up over the metal loop, freeing the lid and skipping back with the shotgun raised.

A form exploded up out of the trunk, screaming, long hair fanning out. Two hands drew back and swiped the air, moving as one piece. Long nails whisked so close to my face that I felt the wind against my cheeks. Metal glinted around the wrists.

I waited for the boom of the shotgun, but Patrick wasn't firing. The person lunged forward to attack again, her face falling into a band of moonlight from the window.

"Alex?" I said.

All the tension went out of her body. Her shoulders curled in, and her hands fell to her waist. Handcuffs cinched her wrists.

"Oh, my God," she said. "Chance?" Her gaze immediately moved past me. She squinted into the darkness, and then her lips parted. "Patrick," she said. She moved by me and hooked her arms up around his neck. He lowered the shotgun to his side and held her.

"What happened?" Patrick asked. "Who did this to you?"

"My dad."

"Where is he now?"

A clicking sound rose, barely audible at first but growing louder.

It was coming from the closet.

ENTRY 9   From the darkness of the walk-in closet, two spots glowed a bluish white.

Eyes.

Or—I realized somewhere through the wave of panic crashing over me—eye*holes.*

The sound continued, a wet, irregular, throaty clicking.

I swallowed. We turned slowly to face the closet head-on.

The glow illuminated the interior, enough for us to see Sheriff Blanton standing stiffly between the racks of hanging clothes, his head tilted slightly back to face the ceiling.

The glow faded, and the clicking stopped. His chin dipped down, and then those empty tunnels stared at us. It was as though he'd been sleeping and we'd woken him up.

Sheriff Blanton leapt from the closet.

Patrick stumbled back, trying to raise the shotgun, but Alex's cuffed hands were still tangled around his neck. The two of them fell down, clearing the way to me.

The sheriff jumped over their bodies, one hand grabbing a second set of cuffs from his belt, the other reaching for my throat.

There was barely time to react.

I dropped, and as his hands clenched the air where my head had been, I whipped the hook at him, the point sinking into the meat of his thigh.

It was a deep blow—I felt the shock tremor of the tip

striking bone—and he froze, staring down as blood soaked out through his khaki uniform pants.

For a moment everything stopped.

Then the shotgun exploded. In the confined space of the room, the sound rattled my teeth.

Patrick had managed to untangle himself from Alex. Not wanting to injure me or her, he'd fired straight up into the ceiling.

Sheriff Blanton tore himself free, ripping his leg off the hook. Patrick was on his feet now, the gun leveled, but before he could fire, the sheriff bounded across the floor and sprang at the window. He balled up, going sideways through the panes, glass shattering all around his curled form.

He hit the ground, rolled through the mud, and popped up onto all fours like a wolf. We crowded around the window, watching with disbelief. Sheriff Blanton galloped for the high fence, somehow transitioning from all fours to his legs without slowing. Then he jumped.

His haunches pulled up as he rose, his heels skimming the top of the fence. For an instant he was in clear view, silhouetted against the moonlit sky.

Patrick had the Winchester raised, the sheriff in his sights.

Alex slammed her palm down on the top of the shotgun as Patrick fired. The shot blew up a cluster of marigolds in the garden.

Her father was gone.

She whirled on Patrick. "What are you doing?"

"You saw his face, Alex. His *eyes*. That thing handcuffed you and shoved you into a steamer trunk."

Tears streamed down her cheeks. "That *thing* is still my dad."

Blood dripped from the baling hook in my hand, tapping onto the floor. Alex's green eyes lowered to the curved steel protruding from my fist. She took in a gulp of air. I felt my face burn as if I'd done something wrong, even though I knew that I'd had to do it.

From the front of the house, we could hear the dogs barking ferociously. I sprinted out of the room, Alex and Patrick following me. Bursting through the front door, I jumped over the porch steps, running for the detached garage.

Around the corner, Rocky and JoJo huddled against the wall. The dogs had formed a protective ring surrounding them, Zeus snapping at the air, barking so hard that flecks of saliva sprayed from his mouth. I settled the dogs.

Only then did we realize that Alex's hands were still cuffed. She shuddered and Patrick wrapped his arms around her.

"My dad keeps a spare key in his nightstand drawer," she said.

"I'll get it," I said.

"Will you grab her a jacket and some clothes, too?" Patrick said.

I nodded and headed for the dark house.

Behind me I heard Alex ask, "Where are we going?"

"We're heading into town," Patrick said. "We have to get out of range."

"Of what?"

I was glad I didn't have to explain that one.

I walked through the halls of the Blanton house, the floorboards groaning beneath my feet. Cold winters and hot summers warped the wood, making our town a creaky place. Any other time that felt homey.

I found the sheriff's spare key in his nightstand. Nestled in the drawer beside it was a framed picture of Blanton's ex-wife. I lifted it to the light. The shot showed Katie Blanton at a backyard barbecue. Her blouse was unbuttoned at the top, not too much but enough to show a sliver of tan skin beneath her collarbones. She held a beer and was laughing, her teeth flashing in the sun.

She looked a lot like Alex.

As I lowered the picture back into the drawer, I saw what the frame had been covering. The sheriff's holstered revolver. It was heavier than I thought it would be. I clipped it onto my jeans and headed into Alex's room.

I'd been too scared to notice before, but it smelled really good, like shampoo and citrusy perfume. In the corner leaned a hockey stick—Alex was a tough-as-nails forward with a wicked slapshot. Standing in her room with those scents washing over me, I felt as though I'd stepped into some other dimension.

I put the baling hooks on her bed and went to her walk-in closet, looking for a jacket. I found one, looped it over my arm, and started emptying her drawers into her hockey gear bag. Shirts. Jeans. Socks. I opened the next drawer and froze.

Bras.

They were black, white, or skin-colored. Embarrassed, I shoveled them into the gear bag, doing my best to look away, down at the floor. My eye caught on two big boot prints in the carpet.

Sheriff Blanton had to have been standing here for a long time to leave footprints as clear and deep as that. I pictured him motionless with his eyes glowing and his head tilted up, like he was meditating or something. That clicking sound returned, a memory echo, and I shuddered.

What had he been doing?

"Chance?"

Mortified, I looked up to see Alex leaning in her doorway. I pivoted my head to the bra still grasped in my hand. I released it. It fell into the bag.

"Um . . . ," I said.

Her lips pursed—not a smile, not tonight, but maybe something close. She came toward me and held out her cuffed hands. I dropped the bag.

Standing this close, I had a hard time focusing on the tiny key. It was hard to believe she was still just sixteen. I remembered the full-faced kid she'd been, all braces and laughter. How, before Mom and Dad died, me, her, and Patrick used to pile into the hammock, all three of us, and stare up at the stars. We'd name the constellations or make new ones up. *Orion. Aries. Girl Walking Her Puppy. Angry Hobo. Giant Broccoli.* Then one week it was like a breeze blew through Alex's house and everything changed. She started to wear undershirts beneath her blouses. Some new sparkly lotion made her cheeks glitter here and there in the sunlight. We started taking turns on the hammock. Patrick would sit in the tall grass and watch her sway, and I couldn't for the life of me figure out what was so fascinating about that.

Until I did.

As I struggled to unlock her cuffs now, she flicked her head to get her long hair off her face.

"Chance," she said, cupping her hands over mine. "It's okay."

She thought my hands were shaking from fear. But that wasn't it.

I concentrated on fitting the key into place. The cuffs fell away, and she rubbed at her raw wrists. I picked her bag up off the floor, and it gaped wide, the bras showing inside. She gave a little smirk.

"Why don't I take it from here," she said, tugging the bag from my hands.

"I was just grabbing whatever—"

"I know," she said. "And thank you."

She finished in the closet and headed into the bathroom for a few more things. When she was done packing up, she slung the gear bag over her shoulders like a backpack, then paused.

She walked over and plucked her hockey stick from the corner of the room.

I picked my baling hooks up off her bed.

We looked at each other a moment, then headed out.

We walked down her stone front path. On the far side of the white picket fence, Patrick waited with the kids and dogs. Alex reached down to unhook the latch on the thigh-high gate, and we stepped through. There was something so civilized in the gesture, given everything that was going on.

She closed the gate and looked back at her house. Her eyes shimmered. She lifted her hockey stick off the ground, gave it an expert twirl, and brushed past us.

"To town, then," she said.

We pressed on, avoiding streets and houses, taking a winding route through the trees. From time to time, Cassius snuck forward and licked my palms. JoJo got tired, and I carried her again, and when my arms started aching, Alex took over. At last we came up over the wooded hill behind Main Street and saw the warm glow of streetlamps through the tree trunks ahead.

Our two-traffic-light town was little more than a few square blocks of stores and restaurants. In the center a big church sat behind a grassy square filled with benches and squirrels. The high school at the edge of town was large for the town's population, because Creek's Cause was lousy with kids. Most ranch-and-farm communities need hands and backs, and folks here have kids early and often. It wasn't unusual to see families of six or seven roll into church on a Sunday morning. What with all the cattle and crops, it was easy enough to fill mouths, and the sprawling countryside provided more space than anyone knew what to do with.

As we wove through the pines toward the familiar lights, we heard the movement of people in action, machinery whirring, doors opening and closing. Everybody was probably preparing to face the threat, like when an F2 tornado blew through last July and the town gathered in the church basement with food and supplies, battening down the hatches. I felt a flicker of relief that we'd lived through the worst and had finally arrived back in the world as we knew it.

We stepped out of the woods and scrambled down the gentle slope onto the tar-and-gravel roof of the general store. Creek's Cause spread out below us.

For an instant, everything looked perfect. Folks in motion, working together, hauling wheelbarrows, moving back and forth across the square.

Then it all came into horrific focus. It was like some elaborate windup toy, everything running according to a precise but mysterious order, driven by invisible cogs and wheels.

The adults of our town toiled down below, too many to take in with a sweep of the eye. The men were walking their squared-off spirals or loading guns into wheelbarrows. They'd rolled back the rear door of the Bob n' Bit Hardware store to reveal the stoked-up blacksmith forge where Bob Bitley hammered out his old-timey mailboxes and weather vanes. They were feeding handguns and hunting rifles into the roaring flame, melting the weapons into useless metal.

The women restrained screaming children, binding their arms and legs. Some of the men paused in their tasks to help. In the middle of the road, Don Braaten had pinned Janie Woodrow, the girl who sat next to me in Dr. Chatterjee's biology class, to the asphalt. Still wearing his splattered overalls from the slaughterhouse, he was on top of her, mashing her cheek to the dotted yellow line. His knee pressed into her back as he wound duct tape around her wrists. Beside him the Durant brothers worked a pair of jackhammers into the road, sparks flying around their muscular forearms. Another Host had scaled a telephone pole outside the two-story hospital and was going after the junction box with an electric saw.

Over on the lawn, a number of PTA moms were on their hands and knees, laying out various items—zip ties and belts, lengths of rope and neckties. The church buzzed like a hive, bound children being dragged inside. Six-year-old Sam Miller's grandparents carried him like a sack up the broad stone steps, gripping him by his wrists and ankles. Other kids bucked and fought, but they stood no chance. The Hosts were everywhere, tunnels of light bored through their heads, toiling away like brainless slaves.

The Dusting hadn't affected some of the adults.

It had gotten *all* of them.

ENTRY 10   We stood there on the roof of the general store with the woods to our backs, looking down at our town. Rocky lowered his head and cried hoarsely, doing his best to hold it in. The dogs whinnied like horses, brushing up against our legs.

The horizon glowed with the faintest tinge of dawn. On the one hand, I couldn't believe it had taken us all night to reach town. But on the other, it felt like the night had lasted a lifetime. Fog shrouded the road running east, out to our place and the water tower. A bull of a man emerged from the wisps, leaning forward, shoulders straining beneath a red flannel shirt. It took a moment for me to recognize Afa Similai, a Tongan farmhand who sometimes helped McCafferty during harvests. His eyes were gone, and his thick black dreads swayed from side to side, making the light tunneling through his head flicker. He strained, his hands behind his back, pulling something.

As he trudged forward, the object he was hauling melted from the fog behind him. A bright yellow pallet jack.

Our bright yellow pallet jack. The very one I'd used earlier tonight to move the bales of hay in the barn.

As the pallet jack rolled forward, I saw that the back was loaded up with fifteen or so crates. Uncle Jim's dog crates, the ones we used to kennel the ridgebacks.

My dry lips moved—I was about to ask what the hell they

wanted dog crates for—but then I remembered that steamer trunk in Alex's bedroom. The one she'd been locked inside.

They needed cages to hold the kids.

Afa continued across the square into the church. The front courtyard was littered with trunks and cages of many sizes, all of them big enough to hold a child.

Patrick's and Alex's expressions made it clear that they'd seen it, too. Instinctively, I reached out for JoJo's hand, and she clutched my fingers, hard. Rocky grabbed the union of our hands as well. He'd been pretty tough all night, but he was still only ten.

I realized that I had a responsibility now to help protect them, just as Patrick had always protected me. Down below, the Hosts continued their busy-bee work, converting Creek's Cause into a prison camp.

"I guess there's our answer," Patrick whispered, sweeping a hand to indicate the town. "The spores transform the adults, but kids aren't affected."

I couldn't find my voice to respond. I kept hoping that I'd blink and it would all go back to normal.

The Host on the telephone pole descended, lumbered a quarter mile past the square, and began to walk those expanding spirals we were now familiar with. On the road the abandoned jackhammers rattled against the asphalt. It took a moment for me to pick up the Durant brothers at the farthest reach of town, spread out from each other, heads lowered, making their ninety-degree turns. It seemed that every time a man finished a task, he went to a new starting point to walk his pattern. I looked across the landscape, dotted with men as far as the eye could see, all of them moving in similar fashion. For all we knew, they continued beyond in the darkness, their bizarre footwork covering the whole county.

Patrick finally broke us out of our spell. "We better pull back," he whispered. "Before any of them notice us."

But I wasn't watching him. My eyes were on Zeus, who was facing the other way, his big head oriented on the woods behind us. His upper lip wrinkled back from his fangs, his growl so low I could feel it in my bones. Cassius turned next, and then all seven dogs were focused on the tree line, heads lowered, teeth bared.

We watched, breathless. A faint sound carried to us, like the murmur of distant bees. It took a moment for me to place it.

Shallow panting.

A twig snapped. A branch bobbed, the pine needles rustling. And then a wall of Hosts became visible between the trunks, moving toward us.

Our schoolteachers.

Principal Delarusso, still dressed from the PTA meeting in her crisp skirt suit and string of pearls. Coach Hanson in her Adidas sweats, the ever-present whistle swaying on its lanyard. Mrs. Wolfgram from geometry honors, oversize glasses guarding the blank holes where her eyes used to be. And many more than my gaze could fix on.

They advanced.

I looked at the dogs. "Release," I said.

Zeus lunged first, grabbing Coach's arm and torquing her to the ground. Cassius barked as the others charged in.

"Give me your gun," Patrick said. "The shotgun's no good from here."

I slapped Sheriff Blanton's revolver into his hand. He fired it at Coach. The hammer clicked down dry. No bullets.

I'd been in such a hurry back at Alex's house, I hadn't thought to look.

Patrick stared at the revolver and then tossed it back at me. I holstered it and swept up JoJo. We backed up, the gravel popping beneath our shoes. The dogs contained the teachers for the moment, but more kept pouring through the tree line, outnumbering them. Many were dressed from the meeting. Others wore pajamas. Some had no clothes on at all.

We took another step back, but we were out of room, our heels at the lip of the roof. Wolfgram kicked Cassius, and he yelped, skidding into my shins, almost knocking me over the edge. He popped up onto his legs again, snarling.

The teachers were on the roof now, coming at us.

I spun, looking out across the town square. Every last Host below had halted, each one's focus drawn to the commotion. Countless hollow stares fixed on the skirmish atop the general store. It is difficult to describe the terror I felt standing there exposed on the rooftop before the whole town, burning under the heat of all those empty gazes.

We turned back toward the advancing teachers. They lurched forward, tangling with the dogs. Zeus's jaws locked on Principal Delarusso's leg. He sawed his weight back and forth, head shaking, teeth shearing. Atticus and Tanner had gotten ahold of the school librarian, ripping his pajama bottoms right off. Patrick pumped the shotgun and raised it, but there was no point. There were too many of them. And any shotgun blast would kill at least some of our ridgies, too.

"Guys," Alex said. "We don't run for it now, we're gonna find ourselves crated up and carted off."

She dropped to her butt, then swung herself off the edge of the roof, falling to the sidewalk. She landed hard, yanked down by the heavy bag around her shoulders. The hockey stick clattered to the pavement.

A jangle of bells announced the opening of the door beneath our feet. Don Weiss stepped out from the general store onto the sidewalk behind Alex. He was still wearing his shop apron. As she started pulling herself up, he reached for her.

Patrick shouted down, "Alex! Behind you!"

Alex snatched up her hockey stick, pivoted, and swung it hard up into Don's face. The head of the stick caught him just beneath the jaw. Even from up above, we could hear the crack of bone before his head snapped around and he went airborne.

Weiss crashed to the sidewalk and lay there, his limbs twitching, his jaw unhinged.

Alex spun the hockey stick in her hands, then slotted it through her gear bag over one shoulder, like a samurai sheathing his sword. She held up her arms. "Drop JoJo to me."

I took in the melee between dogs and teachers, the front line drawing ever closer. Patrick struck Principal Delarusso in the face with the butt of the shotgun. Rocky weaved back and forth as Mrs. Wolfgram tried to grab him. We were down to seconds.

Letting the baling hooks clatter to the rooftop, I went down on my knees, took JoJo's sweaty hands, and lowered her over the edge. She dangled, her tearstained face looking up at me. "Don't drop me," she said.

I dropped her.

Mrs. Wolfgram had Rocky by the dark locks of his hair. I wrenched him free, kicking her in the gut with all my might. She flew back, and I grabbed Rocky's arm and yanked him off the edge. I held his hand as he twisted to and fro in the air, until he shouted, "I got it!" and I let go.

He landed on his feet.

Patrick was waist-deep in the fight. Swinging, elbowing, and jabbing with the shotgun butt. "Patrick!" I yelled. "Let's go!"

Coach broke through Princess and Tanner and dove, hitting me with a football tackle. She knocked me toward the edge. I skidded painfully across the gravel. There was no time to stop—I was going over.

At the last minute, one of my flailing hands caught the handle of a baling hook. As I flew off the building, the hook scrabbled along the rooftop, then caught in the gutter. Hanging on with one hand, I swung way out from the roof, the hook bending the gutter but somehow miraculously holding. Below I caught a whirling view of Don Weiss rising up from the pavement and beelining for Alex and JoJo. His twitching head was angled wrong on his neck.

I lunged for the other hook still up on the roof. It was too far to reach, but my fingers snagged the nylon loop attached to the handle. Spinning wildly, I managed to drag the second hook with me, and it flew by my face, nicking my cheek just as the gutter gave way under my weight. My momentum carried me beneath the overhang, and I fell back, cartwheeling my arms. My heels jarred the sidewalk, and then my shoulder blades and tailbone hammered the ground. I lay there looking up, waiting for the wall of pain to hit.

Before it could, I saw my brother take flight, an apparition streaking overhead, graceful as a big cat. He broke his fall with his feet, tumbled over one shoulder, and came up in a shooting position, blasting a shell through Don Weiss's face as he closed in on Alex. Patrick's cowboy hat never even shifted on his head.

Forcing myself up, I gave a whistle through my fingers. A moment later Cassius scrambled around the hillside by the edge of the store, tumbling over himself, skidding out across loose dirt. He took up at my side. I yelled for the other dogs, but they didn't come. Far up on the hill, I caught streaks of low movement between the tree trunks, the other ridgebacks scattering. They were disoriented and couldn't find us. Between the severe shadows thrown by the streetlights, I could make out Zeus's loping run into the forest. I shouted again, but they kept on, the others following him until they vanished. Though I was relieved they were safe, I felt something in my chest give way. I wanted all my dogs with me. Blood dripped from my cheek, hot and sticky.

Beside me I heard Alex clear her throat, a faint noise that sounded a lot like fear. When I turned in line with her and the others, I found myself staring at countless eyeless faces all across the square. The Hosts ramped into motion, heading toward us from every direction.

"Oh, no," JoJo said, scaling my legs, climbing into my arms. "Oh, no."

Gene Durant trudged back over to the rattling jackhammer, picked it up, and sank it through the craggy hole in the road that he and his brother had created earlier. A pulse flickered across the streetlights, and then everything went dark.

The power—out.

Now we could discern only shadowy figures with holes for eyes. They were all around us.

Patrick moved first, breaking for the alley behind Bob n' Bit Hardware, where the Hosts seemed to be sparsest. "Follow me!" he shouted.

We ran.

The hardware shop still blazed with the light of the forge. As we neared it, the Widow Latrell sprang out, but Patrick turned and kicked her, his boot pistoning into her frail chest. She flew back into the forge. Sparks exploded up, clinging to the other Hosts around the fire, their arms loaded with guns from the wheelbarrow. Latrell's limbs rowed mechanically, trying to pull her free even as the orange flame engulfed her. JoJo buried her face in my shoulder, and we kept running, but not before I saw fire bubble the flesh of Latrell's neck.

Carrying JoJo slowed me down. I fell farther behind the

others. We cut up the alley, and Alex screamed and pointed overhead. I looked up. A woman took flight from the rooftop of the One Cup Cafe, her arms spread like a bat's wings. I weaved at the last second and heard her hit the ground behind us. Rocky was breathing hard, half wheezes, half sobs. Cassius trotted at my side, but even at his size he was more puppy than dog. He managed a few snarls but couldn't provide the kind of muscle Zeus or Tanner would have.

Patrick cleared a path for us through the tight alley, smashing Hosts with the butt of the shotgun, preserving ammo. Feet pounded across the rooftops on either side of us, Hosts stalking our movement overhead.

One leapt and struck Alex on the way down. She spilled, losing her grip on her hockey stick. The Host rose, looming over her. Even from behind I could tell that it was Mrs. Wolfgram. She held a length of rope coiled around both clawlike hands. I could see straight through the back of her head.

Mrs. Wolfgram pounced.

Before she could land, she was knocked violently to the side, hammering into a brick wall and crumpling to the ground. Patrick stood over Alex now, gripping the shotgun like a baseball bat.

He held out his hand for her.

Alex reached up and cupped her fingers around Patrick's, and he lifted her to her feet as though she was weightless. Her momentum carried her forward into him so that both hands pressed to his chest, and then their faces were close and she was looking at him with her lips slightly parted.

Over by the wall, Mrs. Wolfgram jerked herself to her feet, her limbs broken and angled in all the wrong directions. Patrick swung the shotgun up past Alex and said, "Cover your ears."

Her hands rose to the sides of her head. The barrel flared.

Mrs. Wolfgram smacked back against the brick wall, a chalk outline gone vertical, then slid wetly to the ground and lay still.

Alex had kept her eyes on Patrick's the entire time. I couldn't blame her. It was the coolest thing I'd ever seen.

The footfalls on the roofs overhead quickened. Shallow breaths reverberated down at us off the walls. We huddled a moment, our eyes flashing around, reading the shadows.

"We gotta get to the square," Patrick said.

"But there are so many there," Rocky said.

"At least we can see them. We're gonna cut right through the center and head for the high school."

"The school," I said. "Why the—"

Dark forms flashed off the roofs, striking the ground behind us, bouncing low on their haunches, then rising.

We bolted.

Exploding out of the alley, I felt vulnerable all over again. The rising sun cast the square in an otherworldly light, everything washed in sepia tones like in an old photograph. Hosts everywhere paused from their work, then started for us.

We charted a path across the middle of the square, hurdling benches. I set JoJo down so I could use the baling hooks when I needed them. I swiped at Hosts as they neared. They were fast, pushing their muscles to their limits. Principal Delarusso pulled even with me, sprinting faster than a fifty-year-old body should allow, that string of pearls bouncing around her neck. A run in her stocking snaked up from her shin, widening as it rose, her protruding kneecap somehow obscene. She hurled herself at me, hitting me high before I could get a hook up to protect myself. The blow sent us into a rolling tumble. I glimpsed Patrick and the others ahead, their legs vanishing through the closing ranks of Hosts.

I was caught.

Delarusso flung me over, one bony knee poking me in the chest, tensed hands pinning my arms to either side. Her strength was incredible, and I had a fleeting thought of those possessed ants, their mandibles clamping with enough new-found strength to hold their entire bodies up in the air. Delarusso's head pulled down over mine, and I found myself looking clear up through her eyes to the lightening sky above.

A streak flew overhead and wiped her from view. I rolled to my feet to see Alex finishing her follow-through, her torso twisted with the strength of her swing. She whipped the hockey stick in a full circle, staggering several Hosts back on their heels, then yelled, "Chance—c'mon!"

She cleared a route and I forged after her. We broke through the pack. Then we were dodging stragglers, knocking them over, cutting hard to fake others out. Hosts poured from the church. Most of the adults from the county had congregated there. I couldn't even imagine what was happening inside.

Up ahead with the kids, Patrick waved at us from the Piggly Wiggly. He stood on the front mat of the supermarket's automated doors, but they weren't opening, not after Gene Durant cut the power. Cassius's fur stood up, even beyond the ridge, and he was barking furiously. Patrick stepped back, lifted the shotgun, and fired at the glass doors. The big panes wobbled and scarred, but the pellets weren't enough to break through.

I recalled Jack Kaner bragging about the new heavy-duty clear Lexan doors he'd installed after the F2 tornado ripped through last July, shattering the old ones. *Bullet-resistant* doors.

We ran toward Patrick as he slotted another shell into the shotgun. A few spiral-walkers kept on pacing their patterns in the big parking lot, not looking up to notice as we ran past. We reached Patrick, panting hard, and he said, "Don't turn around."

So of course I did.

An army of Hosts descended on us, already at the perimeter of the parking lot. More poured around either side of the building from the back, blocking off any exit path.

JoJo smashed Bunny to the hollow of her throat and squeezed her eyes shut.

Patrick said, "Get behind me."

He stepped to the front of our little vanguard, but I'd heard the resignation in his voice. It was gonna end here like this.

As the horde closed in on us, we held our ground—because we had nothing else to do.

ENTRY 11   They flew at us, some sprinting stiffly, others bounding on all fours, blank-faced and panting. The eye sockets tunneling through their heads gave us glimpses of the waves of Hosts behind them. They would overpower us and haul us to the church and put us in cages.

And then what?

The thought of what was coming tightened the skin across the back of my neck. A flurry of images overwhelmed me, scenes from every horror movie I'd ever seen. Probes and scalpels, boiling cauldrons and bloody chains. The baling hooks swung at my sides, scraping my jeans.

The mass drew nearer, nearer.

I listened to the *flick-flick-flick* of the hooks against denim. One of the points snagged in the fabric.

The point!

I turned and jammed the tip of the baling hook into the seam between the sliding doors. I yanked with all my might. The doors peeled back, barely wide enough to slither through.

I shouted through clenched teeth, "JoJo! Rocky! Go!"

They darted through the gap, Cassius scrambling after them. My biceps were cramping, but I held on, gripping one baling hook's handle with both hands, the other hook dangling from my wrist. Alex squeezed through the gap next, spilling onto the supermarket floor.

The horde was twenty feet away. Now ten. Ahead of the pack, Coach Hanson scrabbled forward on three limbs, one leg stuck out to the side, a splinter of bone thrust up through her thigh.

Patrick ducked beneath me to blade through the gap, but he was too wide. His chest jammed in the opening. The Hosts were almost on us. I wrenched the hook as hard as I could, prying the doors apart another inch, and Patrick tumbled through. I fell in behind him, feeling dozens of hands brushing my back. The doors banged shut around my ankle. I turned, looking back into the press of flesh filling the giant glass door. At the bottom, Coach's breaths fogged the pane, her hands cradling my boot at the heel and toe, like a mom helping a child slip off a sneaker.

Cassius stood protectively over me, the fur raised along his scruff, barking at the glass. I ripped my foot back as hard as I could, and the doors slammed shut. Faces and hands smeared the panes, blotting out the light.

My chest jerked up and down. For a minute it seemed I wasn't going to catch my breath ever again.

"They can use tools," Patrick said. "Let's move before they figure it out."

I rolled out from beneath Cassius. He was upset now, his tail tucked between his legs. We ran through the dark aisles, heading for the rear of the building. Rocky clipped a grapefruit pyramid, sending the fruit rolling across the tiles. Being in here now was surreal, the aisles dark and empty.

We rushed through the swinging doors behind the butcher's counter and through the car-wash curtain that never made any sense to me. The rear room, a concrete box rimmed with freezers, was cold enough that I could feel the chill coming up through my boots. Boxes and pallets and a broken meat grinder.

We doubled over, hands on our knees, breathing hard. It felt like when Coach Hanson made us run the mile during PE, screaming at us over her stopwatch, her face nearly as red as her Cardinals hat. I thought about her back there at the sliding doors, her broken leg stuck out to one side, not feeling the pain. Driven by a single focus: getting at us.

I shuddered, and it wasn't from the cold.

Patrick put his hand on the dead bolt leading to the loading bay in back. Alex set her hand gently on his and said, "Don't."

He paused.

"The kids are too tired." She gestured vaguely toward Rocky and JoJo. I realized I was standing behind them and hoped she wasn't including me among "the kids." She looked back at Patrick. "Give them a sec to catch their breath."

A shattering sound carried across the aisles, followed with what sounded like bodies slapping the floor.

Patrick threw the dead bolt.

The loading bay was empty—whatever Hosts had been back here must have been drawn to the front. We jumped off the dock, landing on the asphalt. Patrick headed into the row of Dumpsters. We single-filed behind him, squeezing through the narrow space. Cassius scrambled to press into the side of my leg.

Patrick halted and held up his hand.

Ahead of him a shadow fell across the mouth of the makeshift alley between Dumpsters. I put my hand on Cassius's back, willing him not to whine. The shadow tick-tocked back and forth, and a moment later a body crossed into the narrow view ahead.

Eddie Lu, one of the baggers, headed across the row of Dumpsters, his head angled toward the ground. Eddie graduated Creek's Cause High last year. He still wore his hipster beanie and Piggly Wiggly apron. In front of me, JoJo opened her mouth, and I clamped my hand over it.

Eddie walked directly in front of us, never glancing over. He passed so close to Patrick that Patrick could've reached out and poked his shoulder. Eddie moved across our brief field of vision and disappeared. We heard his shoes scuff the ground as he made a sharp right angle at the corner of the Dumpster, and then his footsteps continued along the far side. We held our breath.

We listened to his shoes moving on the other side of the Dumpster. The scuffing sound came again as he pivoted to head back behind us.

Patrick gestured us forward, Alex right on his heels, me bringing up the rear behind the kids. We eased through the thin corridor between metal bins. Just past the trash area rose the chain-link that let onto our high school's baseball field. At the bottom of the fence, the Braaten boys had cut a slit for sneaking through to play hooky during fishing season. Patrick pried up the flap of chain-link, ducked under, and held it for us.

We tiptoed forward.

Behind us we heard that scuffing noise once again as Eddie reached the lane between the Dumpsters. I turned and looked over my shoulder. Less than ten feet away, his dark silhouette faced up the corridor in which we were neatly lined. He started after us.

The eyeholes and vacant expression were made more awful by Eddie's casual cap, the familiar ankh tattoo on his inner wrist, his yin-yang necklace. We'd seen a lot of Hosts, but none even close to our age. He was one of us.

I'd just tensed to sprint when I realized that Eddie hadn't noticed us. His head was still oriented toward the ground. With a series of furious hand gestures, I conveyed as much to Alex, and she nodded and crept forward as silently as possible.

We kept on that way, a train of bodies filtering through the space between Dumpsters, Eddie bringing up the rear on a slight delay. Without slowing, Alex dropped to her hands and knees and slithered through the gap in the fence. Rocky crawled through next. I could feel Eddie gaining on me from behind. I didn't know how much longer I had before my heel would catch his field of vision and he'd spring onto my back, taking me down. I didn't dare turn around. I just moved toward that slit in the fence, trying not to let my shoulders scrape the metal sides of the Dumpsters.

I ushered JoJo before me, struggling somehow to rush her and not rush her at the same time. She barely had to crouch to get through the fence, Bunny dragging in the dirt. Cassius followed her, and then it was just me with Eddie in the tight corridor.

I could hear his shallow breaths, practically feel them against my back. My hands cramped around the handles of the baling hooks. I forced myself to release them, letting them dangle from my wrists by their loops. Fighting down my panic, I bent over, stretched my arms into the gap, and slid through. Patrick caught my hands as I knew he would and whisked me through the gap. Alex lowered the chain-link section as gently as she could, closing it like a curtain. It made the faintest click.

Eddie reached the fence, his eye tunnels aimed just in front of his toes. We stood right on the far side of the chain-link. All he had to do was tilt his head up an inch and he'd see us.

But instead he turned on his heel—a neat pivot like you see in the army when some junior officer is dismissed—and continued his course along the fence line. I exhaled.

We moved backward, keeping our eyes on him even as he continued his right-angle swivels through the trash zone. The dew-wet grass of right field shot up beneath the cuffs of my jeans, tickling my ankles. At last I felt the dirt of the infield beneath my boots and turned to face Creek's Cause High. I realized now why Patrick had pointed us here. After a few school shootings swept through the heartland, the town council had voted to make the grounds as secure and contained as possible.

It was the only place in town that was completely fenced off.

Who'd have ever thought high school would be our last safe haven?

We spread out, breathing easier as we headed toward the dark, sprawling building. The football stadium loomed to the left. We reached the math-and-science wing first, Mrs. Wolfgram's classroom at the near end. Cupping my hands like a scuba mask, I put my face to the window. The rows of empty desks inside looked emptier now. Proofs scribbled on the dry-erase board. Faded charts breaking down geometric 3-D shapes and surface areas. A dangling wooden octahedron made from eight equilateral triangles, an extra-credit project built by Janie Woodrow or, more likely, her overly involved mother. I thought about how competitive Janie always was, wearing down the teachers to turn her A-minuses into straight A's, and how much I resented and envied that at the same time. A memory flashed at me, Don Braaten pinning Janie down in the middle of the road, his grown-man knee crushing into her back, her cheek smashed to the asphalt. Had there been tears? We were too far away to see, but Janie tended to cry easily.

I used to make fun of her for her color-coded Post-its, her collection of mechanical pencils, her flawless handwriting, and now I regretted every unkind word.

To my side, Patrick jiggled the handle of a service door. Locked.

"Should we break a window?" he asked.

"Too much noise," Alex said. "What if they're in there?"

Morning was coming on, leaving us visible here outside the building. Inside, everything was connected—classrooms, gym, cafeteria. A necessity for our harsh winters. If we could only get in there.

"Wait," I said. "The back door by Dr. Chatterjee's room might be unlocked. He has trouble with the key and dead bolt because of, you know, his hands."

Dr. Chatterjee often stayed late to grade papers. Rather than make his way through the school's warren of corridors and doors to the front exit, he sometimes left out a back door so he could circle easily to the parking lot. Because of his weakened grip, he couldn't use a key, so he tended to leave the door unlocked behind him. It was worth a shot.

JoJo's tiny hand rose, pointing. "Look," she said.

A few Piggly Wiggly stockers had appeared along with Eddie Lu at the edge of the baseball field. It was only a matter of time before one of them noticed us standing here in the open and breached the fence.

I rushed along the building, put my hand on the doorknob, and took a deep breath. The others crowded at my shoulders. I clenched and turned.

The door creaked open.

We piled in and closed the door. Alex reached over and locked it behind us. We slipped through the open hallway, ducking into Chatterjee's room to take cover. The familiar scent of formaldehyde washed over us. Never before had I been so relieved to be in a classroom.

Patrick clicked the light switch quickly to check the electricity, but nothing happened. He shrugged. "Worth a shot."

Cassius stuck his head in the trash can and came up with an apple core. No matter what else is going on, dogs will be dogs.

"Drop it," I said.

He opened his jaw and let the core drop back into the trash with a thunk. From the look in his brown eyes, you'd have thought I'd kicked him in the ribs.

Patrick peeked around the jamb into the hall for a while, then signaled us to come. We moved out into the dark corridor, the swinging door blowing a Ziploc bag across the floor, chased by a trampled brown paper lunch sack. The rows of battered lockers, that dirty-sneaker smell, the dented recycle bins. Flyers curling from bulletin boards announced various events in bubble letters: *Blood Drive Week! Buy Your Tickets for the Harvest Dance! Auditions for Sartre's* No Exit! A varsity jacket was stuffed above the lockers where someone had forgotten it. For some reason the sight of that stupid jacket without its owner tore open something inside me, and I had to fight to keep my composure. How many kids were missing? How many adults were missing as well, even inside their own bodies? It felt too huge to contemplate. Here in the safety of the school where I'd spent so much of my life, it all seemed unreal and impossibly close at the same time.

Patrick's voice cut in on my thoughts. "Let's make sure all the other doors and windows are locked," he said. "Secure the school as a base."

That was Patrick, grace under pressure, burying the horrific present beneath What Had to Be Done. I thought about his reassuring hand on my shoulder when he'd found me downstairs, crying over the bloody spill of windshield glass from Mom's purse. I remember wondering if I'd ever be that grown up.

I wondered it again now. I bit down on my lower lip and put my hand on JoJo's shoulder, as Patrick had put his on mine. If I couldn't be as brave as him, at least I could fake it.

We moved as a group, going corridor by corridor, floor by

floor, checking that everything was secure. We spread out to get the job done faster but stayed within eyeshot—or at least within shouting distance. Everything looked to be empty. We moved as quietly as we could. We reached the humanities wing and disappeared through different doorways. In Mr. Tomasi's English classroom, alone, I paused by my desk. I ran my fingers across the graffiti scratched into the wood, some bad joke by a student who'd sat there before me—LURNING SUKS. I wondered where that kid was now. Trapped in one of our dog crates in the bowels of the church?

I crossed to the windows and made sure all the latches were thrown. They were. Through the tall chain-link fence hemming in the school's front lawn, I could see a few men in the neighborhood walking their bizarre spirals. I stood watching them, pins and needles pricking my skin. It felt as though I'd landed on Mars and was staring out at an exotic landscape populated with alien beings.

Turning for the door, I weaved between the empty chairs, giving my desk a little tap with my knuckles as I passed. I suppose it was a good-bye to all the learning I'd done in that plastic chair, all the great books we'd talked about, the homework I'd read aloud from nervously but with bits of pride shining through whenever Mr. Tomasi nodded his shaggy head.

I stepped out into the hall at the same time Patrick and Alex emerged from their respective classrooms. We waited for Rocky and JoJo to come out from their room with Cassius, the delay making us nervous. I was just about to head after them when Cassius padded out, his tail wagging, the kids behind him. We all flashed one another thumbs-ups and gestured at the next set of rooms we would tackle.

I headed through the open door into shop class, the biggest of the rooms, filled with slumbering machines. It was creepy, the air thick with the scent of grease and sawdust.

Half-finished projects lay on shelves to the side. Pig-shaped cutting boards, the hind legs still trapped in wood. An unsanded back scratcher. A model of a jalopy missing a roof and two wheels. They'd never be finished. They'd just lie there, incomplete, collecting dust. Heading for the windows, I passed between the belt sander and the band saw. That's when I heard it.

The faintest clank.

Inside the room with me.

I froze, one boot inches above the dusty floor.

It came again. *Clank-clank.*

I bit my lip, lowered my weight. Was it one of the machines, shuddering with a dying jolt of electricity?

I leaned around the band saw. The vertical blade cut my view in half, but I could still make out a man hunched over the workbench across the room. Though his back was turned, I could see his hand to the side, hovering over various tools, deciding which one to grab. Wrench . . . Phillips head . . . clawhammer.

The hand closed around the clawhammer.

The man straightened up and started to turn, his legs swinging stiffly. I dropped behind the base of the band saw, my knees rising to touch my chin. I heard another clank and realized that the sound came from leg braces.

Dr. Chatterjee.

The footsteps neared. *Clank-clank. Clank-clank.*

I debated shouting for Patrick, but if there were other Hosts all around us, that would only alert them. I braced myself, hoping Chatterjee would change course. My baling hooks were at the ready, but I hadn't killed anyone yet and prayed that I wouldn't have to now. Sweat stung my eyes. My heartbeat came so loud I thought he might hear it.

Clank-clank. Clank-clank.

A worn loafer set down in view—*clank*—and I knew his next step would bring me into full sight. I set my feet and sprang.

But my boot skidded on a slick of sawdust, and I fell forward, dropping the baling hooks, my palms jarring the floor. I rolled over onto my back, arms raised over my face. Dr. Chatterjee stood nearly on top of me, the hammer swaying at his side.

With my wrists I jerked at the baling hooks' nylon loops, trying to tug the handles into my palms. They bounced off my fingers. I couldn't look away, not even as Dr. Chatterjee leaned over me. For an instant the faint light from outside hit his wire-rimmed eyeglasses at the perfect angle, turning the lenses to mirrored circles. I knew that once he moved another inch, the glint would vanish and I would see what lay beneath.

I steeled myself for those tunnels, two circular views through to the ceiling above, and I wondered if this would be the last thing I'd ever see.

Dr. Chatterjee looked down at me.

With real eyes.

I let out a garbled sound, choking on a gasp.

His gentle voice descended on me with that great lilting accent. "Chance? Is that you?"

It took two tries before I could find any words. "Dr. Chatterjee," I said. "Wait—you're a grown-up. Why aren't you infected?"

He held out a trembling hand to pull me up to my feet. "That isn't the question," he said. "It's the *answer*."

ENTRY 12   We all headed down the long school hallway clustered together, Dr. Chatterjee moving at a decent pace despite his leg orthotics. I was still breathing hard, relieved that I hadn't had my skull caved in by my favorite teacher.

"White matter!" Dr. Chatterjee announced excitedly. "It's the key."

"Like *brain* white matter?" I asked.

"Shouldn't we keep our voices down?" Patrick said.

Dr. Chatterjee waved him off. "It's safe in here. Now, look." He unclipped an electronic unit swaying from his belt like a holstered gun. We all crowded around to see it in the dim hall.

"Wait," Rocky said. "That's the carbon monoxide detector thing, right?"

We looked at him, surprised.

"What?" he said. "I was emergency room captain in Mrs. Rauch's class last year."

"That's right," Dr. Chatterjee said. "It detects carbon monoxide, natural gas, other hazardous leaks. But check this out." He clicked a button, backlighting the screen, which blinked code red. Beneath it two words flashed: UNIDENTIFIED PARTICULATE.

His face, shiny with sweat, held equal parts worry and excitement. "So my hypothesis is that this airborne particulate enters the human body—"

"Tell him about the spores," Patrick said to me.

Dr. Chatterjee stiffened. "What spores?"

"Like the zombie ants," I said.

His lips quivered a little. He scratched at the side of his face, the stubble giving off a rasping sound. It occurred to me that I'd never seen him not perfectly clean-shaven. "What do you mean, Chance?"

"Well, we saw Hank McCafferty—" I caught myself, feeling a surge of remorse. I glanced nervously at Rocky and JoJo.

Rocky's eyes glimmered, but he kept his chin up. "It's okay," he said. "I want to know."

I took a deep breath. Then I continued, filling in Dr. Chatterjee, starting with when Patrick had interrupted me in the barn. The acrid smell on the wind. The hammering noises and screams carrying over from the McCafferty place. When I got to the part about Mrs. McCafferty in the grain silo, JoJo buried her and Bunny's faces in her brother's chest. I described climbing to the top of the water tower and the sight waiting for us, Hank blown wide open, releasing spores to the wind.

Rocky held his sister tight. He didn't sob, but tears spilled down his cheeks. Alex put her arms around him from behind, holding him even as he held JoJo. My face burned as I related details of Hank's death—I knew as well as anyone that a child should never have to know too much about that— but I also realized that everything was different now.

We couldn't lose track of our emotions, certainly, but we couldn't give in to them the way we used to. Maybe Rocky and JoJo would need this information someday. Dr. Chatterjee certainly needed it now.

I finished telling him about the scene at the water tower and said, "Like those ants in that video you showed us. With the parasite?"

He took off his glasses and polished the lenses on his rumpled button-down shirt, though they did not look in need of polishing. "*Ophiocordyceps unilateralis*," he said quietly. "The pieces are starting to fit together."

"How?" Patrick said.

"Those adults out there"—Chatterjee pointed a trembling finger through the doorway of the nearest classroom to the windows and beyond—"have been infected." He shook the detector, the words blinking out at us again: UNIDENTIFIED PARTICULATE. "This parasite attacked their white matter."

"So why didn't it attack ours?" Alex asked.

"You're teenagers," he said. "You have less."

Patrick drew back his head. "We *do*?"

"Of course. Kids have a lesser-developed frontal cortex."

"Rub it in," Alex said.

"Look," Chatterjee said. His hands shaped the air as they did when he was in teacher mode. He seemed to forget that one of them was gripping a clawhammer. "Every year from childhood on, white matter wraps around more and more of the nerve cells of the brain—that process is called my-elination."

"What *is* white matter?" Rocky asked.

As the sun inched up, squares of light from the windows stretched across the classroom floor opposite us. Some of the male Hosts had drawn closer to the school, spiraling their way around the front parking lot. One man in a scuffed denim jacket drew closer to the fence, his shoulder rat-a-tat-tatting along the chain-link, the sound sending electricity up my spine. Dr. Chatterjee took Rocky by the arm, drawing him out of sight past the doorway, the rest of us following. Sensing that something was wrong, Cassius leaned into my leg, his black-mask face pointed up, no doubt reading the stress coming off me.

"White matter transmits information from different parts of the body back to the cerebral cortex," Chatterjee said, the hammer wagging by his face. "Which helps with executive function—decision making, attention, planning, motivation. Think of the myelination of axons as creating information pathways, connections that allow communication between all the parts of the brain. That's what maturity *is*, really. Teenagers grow more white matter every year. But the *last* part of the brain to be myelinated is the frontal lobe."

"So you're basically saying we're all stupid," Alex said.

Chatterjee shook his head. "I'm saying that part of being a kid, a teenager, is that you literally don't have the capacity yet to think fully about the consequences of your actions."

Alex cut in: "Where have I heard *that* before?"

Patrick had leaned back around the doorjamb to spy on the Hosts outside. Chatterjee yanked him back, as if proving his point, while barely slowing down. "That's why teenagers can be impulsive, angry, lovesick, higher in risk taking—"

"Well," Patrick said. "We'll need risk taking now."

"That's absolutely true. But if what Chance is saying is correct, then this airborne parasite invades its host and gains control by spreading through the white matter, seizing control of the frontal cortex." He waved the clawhammer in a circle. "From there it takes over the brain and the nervous system, manipulating the host like a puppet. It can run the human body as if it's a machine, operating the muscles without regard for pain or injury."

I thought about Uncle Jim's death shudder. All those men we'd seen out there, walking their mindless spirals. Coach Hanson scrabbling forward to get us, not even caring about the bone sticking out of her leg.

I suddenly understood. "So if the parasite is spread through white matter, the frontal cortex—the puppet master—has to be covered with white matter for it to become infected. Or else the spores have no pathways to get to our brain's control centers."

"That's right!" Dr. Chatterjee said. "Which means the thing that makes it harder for teenagers to formulate mature decisions is the same thing that saved you. And saved me."

Suddenly I felt much younger than my fifteen years. There it was, tightening around my spinal cord, that same sensation I'd felt as a six-year-old waking up to Sheriff Blanton standing on our porch, shifting awkwardly from boot to boot, hat in his hands, bad news on his face. That feeling of bone-deep aloneness, as if I'd been set adrift, a boat left to navigate across the rocky slate of the ocean. If what Dr. Chatterjee was saying was true, then the people least equipped to make good decisions were the only ones around Creek's Cause left to make them.

Like me.

But Patrick was still focused on Chatterjee. "Why'd it save *you*?"

"Do you know what causes multiple sclerosis?" Chatterjee asked.

We all shook our heads.

"White-matter lesions." He smiled. "I have enough holes in my brain that the parasite couldn't take me over either." Turning, he started back up the hallway, wobbling past the cracked-porcelain bank of water fountains. I hurried to keep up, Cassius scampering along at my side. With his big strides, Patrick had no problem regaining the lead.

"Your weakness is your strength," Patrick said.

"That's right, Patrick," Chatterjee agreed. Then he looked at us all. "Just like your weakness is yours. As Alex said, you're willing to take risks. Now you'll have plenty of opportunity to do so."

I thought of Eddie Lu out there wandering around the Dumpsters in his beanie and apron. "Wait," I said. "But this means . . . as we get older . . ."

Chatterjee's eyes moistened behind his round glasses. "If the spores are still in the air, yes."

"What?" JoJo asked. "What's that mean?"

"It means we'll turn into *them*," Rocky said angrily, waving a hand at the wall and the Hosts beyond.

It took a moment for the realization to work its way across JoJo's face, and then her forehead furrowed and she started crying. I wanted to comfort her, but the shock was still ringing through me, too. Of all of us, she'd be safe the longest. I'd get there well before her, the white matter spreading through my brain until one day it hit a tipping point. One more cell would grow, bridging some microscopic connection—just enough to allow the parasite to reach its nasty little claws around my frontal cortex, encasing it and taking me over.

But first I'd lose Patrick.

And Alex.

It was like life had always been, I guess, but accelerated. Aging brings us closer to death—any idiot knows that. I'd just always thought I'd have a longer runway. I was fifteen, sure, but at times I still felt like I was just a kid. Even if the future laid out before me wasn't glamorous or grand, it still always seemed to stretch out, decade after decade, farther than I could see. I didn't want the end of the road to be visible. Not yet.

I pictured having to watch that death shudder hit Patrick. And *alter* him. My big brother, my rock, the most solid thing I'd ever known.

And that was only if we got lucky. If the Hosts didn't take him first. Or me.

JoJo's cries grew louder.

Patrick said, "We gotta be quiet. We don't know who's in here."

JoJo crammed Bunny's ear into her mouth and chewed on the ragged tip.

"Don't worry," Chatterjee said, ambling ahead of us past the glass trophy cabinet toward the gymnasium. "We've checked the entire school. It's secure."

"Who's *we*?" Patrick said.

Dr. Chatterjee struck the double doors with the heels of his hands, and Alex gave a little gulp of shock. We froze at the threshold. Dozens of sets of eyes stared back at us.

Huddled in groups across the bleachers and the basketball court were about half the kids of Creek's Cause.

The others who had made it.

ENTRY 13　　　Our friends and schoolmates were in terrible shape. Both of the Mendez twins, JoJo's closest friends, were missing patches of their hair. Little Jenny White wore a torn and bloody dress, and one of her shoes was gone. I couldn't remember her age, but she couldn't have been older than ten. A few seniors were there, including Ben Braaten, his face sporting that jigsaw scar from the car crash that had killed his two brothers. I saw several of my classmates. Eve Jenkins, who sat next to me in American history, had claw marks across her face. It looked like they'd been caused by fingernails.

A bunch of the emergency cots had been rolled out from the storage room, just like after last year's flood, when two dozen families had taken up residence here for the better part of a month while their houses were repaired. The retractable bleachers, pulled out now like they were for pep rallies and basketball games, served as a base camp for some of the kids. The benches were covered with sleeping bags, backpacks, first-aid kits, and a few scattered pillows for those lucky enough to have grabbed them before they fled. A row of makeshift weapons—knives, fire axes, baseball bats—lined the lowest bench. Now I understood Chatterjee's foraging among hammers and wrenches in the shop class. High casement windows atop the bleachers let in weak shafts of dusty light. A free-standing dry-erase board had been wheeled to the front of the polished court, facing the cots. Coach McGill's zone defense diagrams had been mostly erased and written over them was a list of hundreds of names.

A roll call of all the kids of Creek's Cause.

The survivors must have made a list of their team members and classmates, young neighbors and relatives. About a hundred of the names on the unofficial census had been crossed off.

While we'd been scrambling from horror to horror, they'd been hard at work organizing here tonight. Almost as hard at work as the Hosts had been.

Dr. Chatterjee walked to the board, his steps echoing through the gym. He picked up the marker and crossed out *Patrick Rain, Chance Rain, Alexandra Blanton, Rocky McCafferty, JoJo McCafferty*. The tip made a squeak with each line.

None of us had spoken. We were too stunned. I couldn't take my eyes off the hundreds of names that *weren't* crossed off. All those kids missing, taken by Hosts. Andre Swisher from track. Talia Randall, the picture-perfect cheer captain. Blake Dubois, one of the special-needs kids. I pictured Blake with his warm smile, his stick-thin legs propped on the footrests of his wheelchair. He wouldn't have stood a chance.

"We weren't sure we'd find any more kids," Chatterjee said. "The town is pretty much locked down by the Hosts. You live the farthest out, so I suppose it makes sense that it took you longer to get here."

Alex peered out through her tangled bangs. "Plus, we had a few detours on the way."

Patrick finally broke our silence, turning to face the others. "We got work to do," he said. "More of us could still be locked up or hiding in houses." His shadow against the floorboard was well defined, right down to the Stetson. "Why aren't we out there helping them?"

A number of the older kids averted their eyes.

"Dick and Jaydon went out," Ben Braaten said. "And never came back."

Patrick stared at him. He and Ben had never gotten along, not since the fistfight behind Jack Kaner's barn in their freshman year. This was a while before the car crash, and Ben and his brothers thought it would be funny to empty my backpack into Hogan's Creek. I hadn't thought it was very funny, and Patrick hadn't either. The brawl went twenty minutes and wound up a draw—the only fight I'd known Patrick not to win. Both of them were bigger now, and every time they were near each other, it seemed like they were itching to go at it again and answer the question left hanging by the last round.

"The Hosts are taking the kids to the church." Patrick raised the shotgun, laid it over his shoulder. "We should scout it, see if we can free them."

Ben waved a hand. A line of scar tissue twisted his upper lip, so you could never tell whether he was smirking or not. "You want to kill yourself, have at it."

Britney Durant, Gene's daughter and Alex's best friend, cocked her head, her jaw shifting from side to side. A rainbow ribbon took up her chestnut hair in a ponytail. She said, "Ben, don't be such a—"

"We need a plan," Dr. Chatterjee said, cutting her off. "But first we need to regroup, think everything through carefully."

I remembered what he'd said in the hall about impulsiveness and decision making and put a hand on my brother's shoulder. "Let's take a second, Patrick," I said quietly.

He looked over at me, gave a little nod. At times I was the only person Patrick would listen to.

"Check in your weapons, please," Chatterjee said, gesturing to the lowest bench. We stepped into the gym, Cassius staying next to me like he'd been trained. As Patrick, Alex, and I laid down our weapons, JoJo ran to the Mendez girls, and they did a three-way huddle-embrace. The rest of our little band spread out, greeting our friends, bumping knuckles and waving. It was comforting, but I also felt a weird embarrassment. One of the McGraw boys from my PE class was balled up in a corner sobbing. Leonora Rose, who I'd known since forever, squeezed me in a tight hug. Others crowded in on me with a million questions.

Chubby Chet Rogers leaned toward me, his cheeks flushed with concern. "Did you see my little brother?"

Someone else said, "My mom—was my mom in the square?"

All those dread-filled faces, hands grabbing at me, trying to get my attention. Fighting through claustrophobia, I shook my head. "Sorry. Sorry, I didn't. I don't know." The kids finally eased off and left me alone, going back to their groups. Gossip swirled all around, bitter with desperation.

"I heard Tommy's dad put him in a duffel bag."

"Sheila saw Patrice slung over her mommy's shoulder in a burlap sack. She said she could see her in there *squirming*."

Through the press of bodies, I saw Alex resting her hands on Britney's shoulders, talking to her. Britney was crying. I figured Alex had told her about seeing her dad and uncle in the square, working the jackhammers, taking down the power grid. They were Hosts like everyone else's parents. For the first time in my life, I was grateful that my mom and dad weren't around. Seeing Uncle Jim and Aunt Sue-Anne had been painful enough. At least I never had to see *this* happen to my parents.

I reached the bleachers and realized I was standing next to Eve Jenkins. She said hi quietly and turned her right cheek away from me, the one with the scrapes.

Patrick had always thought that she had a crush on me, though I wasn't sure. She'd do things like borrow my science textbook, then stop by our house later with it, apologizing that she'd forgotten to give it back. Patrick said it was an excuse to see me, but I wondered if she was just absentminded. She was pretty in a simple kind of way—dark hair with straight bangs, round face, a dimple in one cheek when she smiled. Even though she was also older than me, next to Alex she still looked like a kid.

Then again, I supposed I still looked like a kid, too.

Up in the bleachers, JoJo and Rocky were sitting behind the Mendez twins, helping them put their hair up in pigtails to cover the patches that had been yanked out.

Eve's eyes were still lowered, her face turned slightly away. I figured maybe I should take a page from JoJo and Rocky's book.

"Hey," I said to her. "You okay?"

Her eyes were watering. "It's nothing."

"Fingernails?"

She nodded, maybe because she knew she'd start crying if she spoke.

"Can I clean it for you?" I asked.

She firmed her trembling lips. Then she turned her face fully to me for the first time. Her brown eyes held tiny flecks of yellow. "My mom," she said. And that was all she could get out.

I took some Neosporin from one of the first-aid kits on the bleachers and put it on a soft gauze pad. I rested one hand on her warm cheek, and she closed her eyes. When the pad dabbed her cuts, she flinched, squeezing the wrist of my hand on her cheek. I didn't pause, and she didn't stop me. Cassius walked over and nudged her, and she lowered her other hand. He licked her palm. Once I'd finished, Eve took a shuddering breath and opened her eyes.

"Thank you," she said.

We were interrupted by a loud rapping sound. We turned

to see Alex tapping the dry-erase board with her hockey stick to get everyone's attention. Patrick was up front with her, Dr. Chatterjee to the side. The gym fell silent.

Britney stood beside Alex, her face red from crying. They were holding hands, but now Alex let go and stepped in front of the board.

"Okay, guys," Alex said. "Let's talk about where we are with everything. Have you tried a phone?"

"Of course we tried a phone," Ben Braaten said. He wasn't as tall as Patrick, but he was thicker, with beefy biceps and big square wrists. His flannel shirt tugged up in the front, snared around something shoved in the waistband of his jeans. As he swaggered closer, I saw that it was a bolt gun used to stun cattle before the kill. It made sense, since his dad worked at a slaughterhouse. An image from earlier came to me—Don Braaten in his bloodstained overalls, pinning Janie Woodrow to the road.

Cassius gave a low growl, and a moment later Ben breezed by me, bumping my shoulder. He ran a hand over his bristling crew cut. The rippled flesh from a skin graft at his hairline never ceased to fascinate me, not because it was ugly—it wasn't—but because it always looked to me like some other-worldly mark. When his drunken older brothers had crashed the Camaro, Ben alone had emerged from the fiery hull, and the scar on his forehead seemed like the thumbprint of an angel or a devil branded into his flesh, marking him to survive.

He crossed his arms, confronting Alex and Patrick. "Phone lines are cut. Internet's out. Power's out. We got the emergency generator, but we figure it's best to use it as little as possible, keep the lights off so we don't draw the—What'd you call 'em? Hosts? We gotta go through the entire school before we power on the generator, make sure all the light switches and fans are off, anything that'll alert them. We were just about to get started. So thanks for the quick thinking, Alexandra, but we got it covered."

"Oh, yeah," Patrick said, gesturing around. "Looks like you've got everything solved, Ben. No need for any new ideas."

"We've managed just fine so far without big bad Patrick Rain. We got a system in place, and that's the only reason you're looking at a hundred survivors. We don't need some blonde waltzing in here giving orders."

Patrick's mouth tensed. "I didn't hear her give any orders."

"What? She can't speak up for herself? She needs you to look out for her like you've looked out for your kid brother since your parents croaked?"

Patrick set down the shotgun and took a step forward. Ben smiled that twisted smile and raised his fists. "Okay, then."

Dr. Chatterjee tried to get between Patrick and Ben, but he was too slow; Patrick had already breezed by. "Hang on," Chatterjee said. "This is the last thing we need right now."

Patrick and Ben had almost closed in on each other when a scream from outside lofted in through the high windows. The two of them froze. JoJo covered her ears, squeezed her eyes shut. It came again, a child's cry.

And then suddenly it cut off.

Marina Mendez scampered up the bleachers to the top bench and put her face to the window. "They got Angie B.," she said.

The silence that followed was broken by a few of the younger kids sobbing. Slowly, I became aware of Patrick and Ben close to me, still locked in their standoff. Patrick stepped back from Ben, holding his hands to the sides. "I'm sorry," he said. Then he turned to Dr. Chatterjee and the other kids. "I was being stupid."

Alex glared at Ben. "Have you tried the TV?" she asked.

"Cable lines are cut," Ben said.

"How 'bout the crappy old one with the rabbit ears in the teachers' lounge?" Alex said. "You think of that?"

Ben reddened a little. "Who cares about the TV?"

"I do. Because with a TV we can see how far this thing's spread." Alex reached over her shoulder, grabbing the handle of her hockey stick and whipping it free of the backpack. It looked like she was unsheathing a sword. "I'll go get it," she said. "You stay here and act important."

She turned and pushed out through the swinging doors. Patrick started after her, but Britney wiped her face and said, "It's okay, Patrick. You stay and help figure things out here. I'll go with her."

He hesitated a moment, then nodded. Britney grabbed a baseball bat and jogged out after her best friend, her ponytail bouncing from side to side, the bright ribbon flashing into view.

"Okay," Chatterjee said. "Chance, will you come up here and explain to everyone what you explained to me?"

I walked to the front, sensing all those sets of eyes on me, a familiar self-consciousness welling in my chest. I felt better when Cassius padded over and sat next to me. I cleared my throat. "Look, I'm not sure about this, but there's some stuff I thought might be right, maybe."

"Chance," Patrick said. "Just tell them."

So I did. I went through what we'd managed to work out about the spores and the Hosts. Saying it out loud again, I realized just how much we still *didn't* know. I felt like an impostor standing up there acting like I was some kind of expert. It didn't help that Ben stood in the front, arms crossed. A few times Patrick urged me to speak louder so the kids in the back could hear, too. It was hard, but I got through it.

As soon as I was done, the questions started pouring in.

Eve asked, "Why do some of them swell up and explode and others chase kids around and look at the ground and stuff?"

"I have no idea," I said.

"In some species it's not uncommon to see differentiated roles," Dr. Chatterjee said, stepping in to help me. "Like ants and bees have drones, workers, and queens. Or it could be that the first-generation Hosts serve to spread the infection and the second-generation Hosts . . ." He paused. "Act differently."

Little Jenny White raised her hand next. "I stabbed Mrs. Johnson through the stomach. And she lived."

Her cheeks were flushed, and her chin trembled. Nine years old or so, standing there in a bloody dress, talking about putting a knife through her neighbor's gut. A week ago it would have been unthinkable. A *day* ago it would have been unthinkable.

When Jenny spoke again, her voice was hoarse. "So how do you kill them?"

"We think it's their brains that are effected," I said. "So you gotta shoot them in the head."

Marina Mendez piped up from her post by the window atop the bleachers. "Just like z—"

"Don't say it," Rocky cut in.

Dezi Siegler, one of Ben's buddies, called out from the back, "But we don't have any guns. Except your brother. And you."

"Yeah," Leonora Rose said. "Does other stuff work? Like if you *bash* them in the skull?"

Ben tugged the bolt gun from his jeans and held it up over his head. He tugged the trigger. Compressed air hissed, and there came the thunderous smack of the steel rod firing. "This worked just fine," he said.

The raised gun caught a beam of light from the high window. The end was coated in blood.

"But I thought that was just a *stun* gun," Eve said.

"For cattle." Ben thumbed another air cartridge into place. "But compared to a cow skull, a human's is like an eggshell.

It'll put a Host on the ground in seconds flat." A smile blossomed on his face. "Trust me."

The doors boomed open behind us, making me jump. Alex entered with the small TV tucked under one arm, hockey stick clenched in her other hand. Her hair fell across her face, and she jerked her head, clearing it from her eyes. "Look what the blonde found," she said.

Britney came in at her heels. I had to say, seeing them up there with their makeshift weapons, they looked pretty tough. Britney might not have been an athlete like Alex, but she was on the cheer team, her muscles shaped from being a base, propping up the pyramids and throwing the fliers. These were Creek's Cause girls, not the willowy types you saw on TV who looked like they needed a cheeseburger.

Alex walked over, set down the unit on the lowest bleacher bench, and let her bag slip off her shoulder and thud on the floor.

"That's all well and good," Ben said. "But what are you gonna plug it into? Like I said, we can't turn on the generator until—"

From her bag Alex pulled a twelve-volt battery with an outlet plug, the one Mrs. Yee used in physics when she talked about circuits and joules and made a lightbulb glow. Alex plugged in the TV, looked across her shoulder, and gave Ben a smirk.

He sucked his teeth and glanced away.

All the kids gathered in the court, sitting cross-legged, staring hopefully at the screen. Marina alone stayed in her perch high on the bleachers, staring out the window, as if she still couldn't believe the world she was looking at. Taking a deep breath, Alex pushed the button. The TV went on with a popping sound. The little screen filled with static.

As Alex fussed with the rabbit ears, I stared across the rows of stressed-out faces. In the dimness of the gym, I could see the TV's glow flickering in all those sets of eyes like a pilot light. Like hope.

Everyone sat there as if it were some kind of movie night.

A signal caught on the screen, a blurry image scrolling vertically like the self-dumping hoppers in a grain lift machine. Another tweak of the rabbit ears and the image stilled. It was some dumb talk show, the host overseeing a competition between housewives who'd done their own makeovers. Alex started clicking the plastic knob, changing the channels. An ad for a new kind of car wax. A close-up of a weeping woman in soap-opera-soft lighting. A newscaster giving a live early-morning traffic report, the sound fuzzed by the bad signal.

Everything looked to be normal.

When Alex turned off the TV, you could sense the relief in the room, the first stirrings of optimism.

"Okay," Patrick said. "So we can assume that the spores from McCafferty haven't spread out of the valley."

"Not yet," Eve said.

That sent a ripple of concern across the basketball court.

"Let's focus first," Chatterjee said, "on what we *know* to be true." He ticked off the first point on his slender forefinger. "The adults are affected, but not the kids. Can we zero in on an age?"

A silence as we all regarded one another. Marina called down from the bleachers, "I see Stevie Saunders and Hanna Everston across the street. How old are they?"

Answers rang out.

"Stevie's twenty-three,"

"I think Hanna is, too."

"No, she's just twenty."

"Twenty, then," Dr. Chatterjee said, his voice heavy with dread.

My insides felt heavy, too. I pictured that hipster beanie, the Piggly Wiggly apron. When I spoke, my voice sounded thin against the gym walls. "We saw Eddie Lu. I think he's just nineteen."

"He is." A younger kid raised his hand as if he were in class. Chatterjee nodded at him. "He's my cousin. His birthday was this summer. We had a pool party."

"Oh, my God," Marina said. She covered her mouth, turning away from the window so fast that her pigtails whipped her cheeks.

"What?" Patrick said.

Marina said, "Talia Randall's out there."

Britney stiffened at the mention of her cheer captain. "She is? Is she . . . ?"

Marina's face looked down at us all. She didn't say anything.

"Oh, my God," Britney said.

Alex said, "Wasn't her birthday just last month?"

Britney nodded. Her lips parted in shock. Her face, suddenly wan. Sweat sparkled across her temple. I didn't understand what was going on.

"How old did she turn?" I asked, trying to catch up.

"Eighteen," Alex said, keeping her gaze pegged on Britney.

Britney's trembling hand rose to the back of her head. She tugged the rainbow ribbon free, and her hair fell about her face, crowding her cheeks, her eyes. Her pale, sweaty face stared out from beneath the straggly locks.

"We did a thing in class yesterday," Britney said faintly. "But today . . ."

Her fingers loosened, the ribbon unfurling from her fist. The colorful letters running down its length became visible. Even though they were sideways, I could read them clear as day.

PARTY ON, BIRTHDAY PRINCESS!

"Today's my actual . . ." Britney's voice faded away.

Alex stepped forward and took her hand. "It's gonna be okay. There's no way it works that precisely. You're gonna be—"

"Do you know," Dr. Chatterjee spoke slowly, shaping each word, "what time of day you were born?"

Britney opened her mouth to answer. Her glossy lips stayed like that, wobbling in an oval.

And then she shuddered.

Alex took an unsteady step back. "No," she said. *"No, no, no."*

Patrick came up behind Alex, and she stepped back again, bumping into him. He hugged her with one arm from behind but I noticed he kept his other hand free.

The one holding the shotgun.

Blackness stole across Britney's eyes, darkening the whites until they looked like giant pupils.

The faintest crackling sound came, like the sound of insects feasting, as Britney's eyeballs turned to dried bits of ash.

Alex was sobbing, bent forward, her shoulders shaking. She was screaming, but I couldn't hear her.

The ash fell away, leaving two tunnels through Britney's head.

ENTRY 14   Britney seemed to hang forward, her weight shifted onto the balls of her feet, hair dangling across her features, an electronic doll waiting to animate.

The kids were all standing now, backing away. A few broke for the doors. Cassius barked once, and I hushed him firmly. Up on the bleachers, Marina screamed. Alex clutched Patrick's arm, shaking her head, her eyes rimmed red. They were about five feet away from Britney. Sprinting kids strobed across my field of vision, turning the scene into a stop-action—Alex's hand lurching to cover her mouth, the shotgun jerkily rising in Patrick's grip. It seemed we were the only four still points in the gym, the kids swarming all around like bees.

"We have to be quiet!" Dr. Chatterjee said. It was the first time I'd ever heard his voice raised. He was staggering away from Alex, nearly tripping over his orthotics. "If we're too loud, we'll bring more of them here!"

A ripple coursed beneath the skin of Britney's face. Nothing moved, but there was a change in the substance of her flesh, as if some invisible spark had been struck. She tilted back more fully onto her feet. She lifted her head.

Those blank tunnels aimed directly at Alex. Best friend facing best friend.

Patrick remained behind Alex, his chest to her back, one arm slung protectively across her. Alex's head was just in front of his, their bodies aligned so they were both peering down the length of the shotgun at Britney.

Thank God Patrick had thought quickly and grabbed the Winchester off the bleachers at the first sign of trouble.

Alex's hand pressed over her mouth, holding in a scream. She was still shaking her head—*no, no, no.*

Britney's shoulders drew back, her spine straightening. Then her head pulled back, too, twitching. Her body tensed to lunge.

Still Patrick hadn't fired. Was he afraid the shotgun boom would alert the Hosts?

A loud smack of metal on metal reverberated through the gym. Britney corkscrewed up onto her toes, her spine twisting. She fell away and revealed Ben Braaten standing behind her, stun gun raised, sleek metal rod dripping fresh blood.

Britney crumpled onto the floor.

Only when I heard her limbs hit the shiny floorboards did I realize that the gym had gone completely quiet.

Alex doubled over, clutching her stomach. Her cries came soft and low, as if something had broken open inside her. Patrick held her tighter as she sank to the floor.

A puddle spread beneath Britney's head.

Ben finally lowered the stun gun, wiped it back and forth on his thigh, and shoved it into the front of his jeans. Remorse flickered across his face. "I'm sorry," he said. "But someone had to."

"Chance," Dr. Chatterjee said in a voice strained with stress. "Go see if any Hosts are heading toward us."

I darted up the bleacher steps as quietly as possible and put my face to the window. In the neighborhood across the parking lot, a bunch of male Hosts had stopped, frozen, their heads oriented toward the gym.

I jerked away, my heart pounding. The other kids stared up at me. I put my finger to my lips, and they got even quieter. Cassius put his front paws on the bottom bench of the bleachers, trying to figure out if he could climb up to me. I snapped my fingers, and he hopped down and gave me a hangdog pout.

We all stayed like that for a minute or two. A sneaker chirped on the floor. Someone stifled a cough. It felt weird to be staring down at all those scared faces. From up here that dark puddle beneath Britney's head looked like a shiny halo.

I turned again and eased my eyes up over the sill. The men were still looking this way, wolves on alert. All at once, they lowered their heads and continued along, walking their patterns. A breath hissed out through my teeth.

"We're okay," I said as I made my way back down.

"I have to clean up Britney," Alex said. "I have to take her somewhere."

A clatter of falling objects sounded from the storage room. Ben emerged, carrying an empty duffel bag. I recognized it as the bag that stored the soccer goal nets and spikes during the winter. With his other hand, Ben steered a mop in a yellow bucket on wheels.

He dropped the duffel next to Britney and flopped her limp body into it. Then he rose, lifted the dripping mop from the bucket, and tossed it at Patrick. Patrick caught the handle in front of his chest.

Crouching, Ben hoisted the hefty duffel bag and headed out, muscles straining beneath his shirt. Already the bag had started to spot.

Ben disappeared, and Patrick mopped up. Alex stayed on the floor, her face slack, staring at nothing. Patrick finished, squeezing pink water from the mop. When he wheeled the bucket across to the storage closet, one of the wheels gave off the faintest squeak.

Everyone stayed silent, out of either respect or shock.

A moment later Ben returned, the front of his shirt covered in blood. More blood than made sense. What had he done with Britney's body? As everyone stared at him, he cuffed his flannel sleeves back from his thick forearms, twice each. "So," he said. "I guess we figured out the age cutoff."

I glanced over at Patrick and saw him swallow. Hard. He caught my eye, then looked away fast.

His eighteenth birthday was next week.

Dr. Chatterjee worked his way back across the court. He paused behind Alex and rested a hand on her shoulder. "I'm sorry," he said. Continuing on, he flipped over the dry-erase board to reveal the blank back side.

Then he regarded the rest of us. "Everyone line up by age," he said. "Youngest in the front. I'm gonna write all your names and birthdays in order here. So we know."

After some jostling and confusion, we formed a single row. Everything proceeded in orderly fashion, pretty amazing given what was going on. Maybe we were just happy to have something easy to do. Marina took her spot ahead of Maria, having been born a few minutes before her. Dr. Chatterjee listened to everyone, then jotted his or her information up on the board in his neat hand. The line moved slowly forward. I tried to choke down my fear, to keep my gaze ahead at Rocky's black curls, at JoJo and the Mendez twins, but every step of the way I sensed Patrick back there toward the end of the line. I didn't want to know *how* near the end he was.

Finally I couldn't fight the urge anymore, and I turned and looked back along the long line of kids, past Ben and Alex and Eve.

Patrick was the second kid from the end.

The last in line was Chet Rogers, his big ruddy face downcast. His arms trembled, and his left knee jackhammered. He twisted one sweaty hand in the other.

Whereas Patrick was trying to fight off his fear and doing a pretty good job of it. I don't think anyone except me could tell how rattled he was, but I knew him the way only brothers know each other. The way he knew me.

His jaw looked tight. His mouth thin and firm. For a moment I thought he was holding it together for me like he always did. But then I noticed that he wasn't looking at me. He was looking at Alex.

And she was looking back at him. I didn't think it was possible for her to seem more upset than she had when Britney died, but she held herself now as if her body were hollow, as if her insides had crumbled away.

I knew she felt that way because I felt that way myself.

Eve traced where I was looking and stepped forward in line. "I'm *so* sorry, Chance," she said.

"I'm fine," I said, and turned back around quickly so she couldn't see me bite my lip. I reached down, and sure enough, Cassius was there, his black muzzle pointed up at me. I scratched at his scruff beneath the collar the way he always loved, and he tilted into me. "Good boy," I said. "Good, good boy." It was all I could do to hold myself together.

Finally I arrived at the front of the line. I had to fight to keep my voice from cracking when I spoke to Dr. Chatterjee. "July fourth," I said. "Not sure what time."

"Thank you, Chance," he said. "I seem to recall you were born in the morning."

I went and took my seat on the bleachers with the others. After a while Alex came and sat next to me.

"Hey, Blanton," I said.

"Hey, Little Rain."

It made me smile, which I'm sure was her intent. "I hate when you call me that," I said.

She leaned over, gave me a playful bump with her shoulder. "Yup." But it was sad, too. There was nothing more to say, really. It was just a way of reaching out, of connecting. We were united in that moment as the two people who cared the most about Patrick. And about what was gonna happen to him.

A while later—though we tried not to notice how *much* later—my brother joined us on the bleachers. Together we listened to Chet give his birthday in a trembling voice.

Ben hopped up onto one of the middle bleachers and started pacing across it. The front of his shirt was stiff with dried blood from where he'd wiped his hands. "Look," he said, "the first thing to figure out is who's in charge. And I think it's pretty clear who's protected us the best so far." The heel of his hand rested on the stun gun tucked in his waistband.

"Dr. Chatterjee's in charge," I said.

Ben cast his broken gaze over at me. "Dr. Chatterjee," he said, "can't hold a gun. Not with that grip."

A lot of the kids looked taken aback. We'd heard students be rude to teachers before, but we'd never seen one be so *dismissive* before.

Ben's mood had changed since he'd returned from taking care of Britney's body. He seemed more cocky, his eyes gleaming with some secret confidence.

Dr. Chatterjee took off his glasses again, calmly polishing them. "Is that what you think leadership is about, Mr. Braaten?" he asked.

"Not generally," Ben said. "But now more than ever."

"How about wisdom? Experience?"

"You may have noticed that age ain't exactly being rewarded in the new order." Ben scanned the kids' faces. "Like I said, I'm willing to do what has to be done to keep you guys safe."

"You wouldn't send help for Dick and Jaydon," Eve said, "when they went to help the others. So which of us are you keeping safe?"

"The majority of you."

"Which is fine," Patrick said. "Until you're not part of the majority."

Rocky spoke up. "I think our leader should be Dr. Chatterjee," he said. "And whoever's oldest."

We looked up at that board, Chet Rogers's name at the very bottom. His birthday four days from now.

And Patrick's name written right above.

Chet made a nervous noise. I thought maybe he was going to say something, but he drew into himself. He crossed his arms over his chest as if he were hugging himself. His eyes stayed lowered as he tried to smooth out his breathing, but he was wheezing pretty good. I remembered how his mother and the school nurse always seemed to hover nearby, fearful of an attack. A kid with asthma in farm country was at no small risk. If he had an episode now, I'd have to run to the nurse's office to fetch his oxygen mask.

But Ben paid Chet little mind. "If we're going for stability," Ben said to Eve, "why would we choose leaders who are next in line to die?"

Patrick stood up abruptly. "Let's cut to it. Do we agree that everyone gets a vote?"

Most everybody nodded.

"Okay. How many vote that Dr. Chatterjee's in charge?"

About three-fourths of the hands went up.

"That's settled, then," Patrick said, with a glance at Ben. "Now let's get back to figuring out just what the hell to do."

"Fine," Ben said. He cast a look across the faces of the kids. "But think about it. When the next Host shows up, who do you want between you and it? Me or Chatterjee?"

"For now, Mr. Braaten, we will let that remain a rhetorical question," Dr. Chatterjee said, "and get back to the facts as we're learning them. Eighteen appears to be the age at which people . . . transform." His forehead furrowed as he puzzled this out. "Once that chronological point is crossed, it's as if a switch is thrown, making the person susceptible to spores in the air."

"How do you know the spores aren't *already* inside us all?" Eve asked. "Just hanging out, waiting to spread?"

Dr. Chatterjee blinked a few times. "Well," he said, "I suppose I don't."

"No," Chet said, still rocking himself. "You're right."

"How do you know?" Chatterjee asked. "Chet? How do you know?"

"I . . . um, I saw my neighbor—Mr. Gaeta? Right after it happened. He was chasing a kid down the middle of our street, and a car . . ." Chet gasped a few times. "I saw his brains when they . . . spilled out. And they were black. Like covered with *oil*. And then next . . ." His breathing quickened, and for a moment I thought he might hyperventilate. "The car plowed into the kid he'd been chasing." He took in a gulp of air. "Luis Millan."

At this a wail went up from the back of the gym. Probably one of Luis's cousins. We were all shocked.

"His head was . . ." Chet's hand hovered by his forehead. "And his . . . brain . . . I could see . . . it looked normal. It *wasn't* all black and oily. Not yet. So no, I don't think the stuff was in there. I think it waits in the air until the second we turn eighteen. Your brain's ready, and then that next breath costs you . . . everything." He stared at his trembling hands. "Like Britney."

Alex pulled the cuffs of her sweater down over her fists. She jackknifed over, her feet up on the bleacher bench in front of her, her arms pressed between her thighs and her chest. Patrick sat beside her, rubbing her back.

Again I looked across at my brother's name and birthday

written up on the board. Then down at the wet smudge from the mop where Britney had fallen.

I didn't mean to speak, at least not that loudly, but there was my voice, carrying across the gym. "How could they know?"

"How do they know *any* of it?" Ben said. "They know to burn the guns. They know to cut the power. And the phone lines. The grown-ups—it's like they're still in there somewhere, but just the bad parts."

Beside me, Alex shook off a shudder.

I said, "What I mean is, how could the parasite know *exactly* when Britney turned eighteen?"

Rocky said, "Well, Dr. C. said the white matter—"

"I know, I know," I said. "But everyone develops at different rates. I mean, we're humans. It's not like we're trees and you can just cut us open and count the rings inside. I know that doctors can make guesses based on teeth and bone development and stuff, but it's not like we have some internal meter or something. Besides, nothing can tell when we actually enter the world. I mean, as opposed to conception or being in the womb or whatever."

"If there *is* a meter of some kind," Eve said, "maybe it starts the instant air first hits the lungs?"

"But there *isn't* one." I looked over at Dr. Chatterjee. "Isn't that right?"

"Not a meter, exactly," he said. "But there is something. Structures on the tips of chromosomes called telomeres. They're repetitive nucleotide sequences that get shortened every time DNA duplicates. Recently there's been some research indicating that these provide estimates for how long an organism has been alive and how long it has until it dies. They've been doing promising work with warblers on Cousin Island—"

"But those are *estimates*," I said.

"As our technology advances," Chatterjee said, "we are find-ing them to be alarmingly accurate as indicators of life expec-tancy."

"Fine," I said. "But we can't tell how old a person is to the *day*. To the *minute*."

"Well . . ." Ben stood up, his weight creaking the bleacher. "*We* can't."

I felt a tingling under my scalp. "What do you mean?"

"I mean we're dealing with more than spores and parasites," Ben said. He hopped down the benches, one after another, then stood at the bottom and looked up at me, Alex, and Patrick. "When I was out there taking care of Britney's body, guess who I bumped into? Ezekiel. Looks like our ol' janitor was sleeping off a hangover in the football stadium again, woke up with the commotion." Ben took a moment to wipe his hands across the front of his shirt, mimicking the gesture that had left those bloody streaks. "So I handled him, too." With a glance at Chatterjee, he added, "Maybe not as well as our elected leader here could've."

"Why on earth didn't you say something?" Chatterjee asked.

"Didn't want to overstep my bounds. But seeing as our leadership is casting about for answers, I figure I'd better speak up now." Ben started for the doors, waving at us to follow. "You three and the good doctor better come with me." He turned back to look at us, the crimped skin of his forehead shiny even in the diffuse light of the high windows. "You're gonna wanna see this."

ENTRY 15   We halted in the corridor of the humanities wing, bumping into one another. I tried to swallow, but my throat gave only a dry click. The sight before us had brought us up short.

A pale arm thrust across the threshold of Mr. Tomasi's classroom. Limp fingers touched the floor as if reaching for something.

And they were twitching.

"Wait," Patrick said. "He's still *alive?*"

"If you can call it that," Ben said.

A dark snake of blood streamed parallel to the arm, polished and gleaming, mirroring back the pinhole ceiling tiles above. The duffel bag containing Britney had been dumped by the lockers; Ben had probably dropped it there when he'd run into Ezekiel.

Alex's voice cut through my shock. "This whole time we've been in the gym? You left a Host out here still *alive?*"

"Oh, don't worry," Ben said. "He ain't going nowhere. You'll see." He strode forward, but none of us moved.

We'd seen a lot, but that didn't mean we were used to it.

Aside from Ben, who led the way with a big-game hunter's delight. "C'mon, then," he said. "He's not gonna get you. Not anymore."

Patrick broke us out of our statue formation. Alex, Chatterjee, and I followed. I'd had Cassius stay back with JoJo, who'd started crying at the thought of being left without me and Patrick. The big pup had tucked up to her side, and she'd rested her face on his tan fur, her head rising and falling as he breathed. Seventy pounds of Rhodesian ridgeback was a pretty good comfort.

I could have used some comfort myself. Though it was day, the hall was surprisingly dim, and I realized I'd never been inside the school with the lights off. Another first.

As we neared the doorway, Ezekiel drew slowly into view. Arm. Shoulder. Then the head nodded to the side, facing away, those two tunnels bored through the back of the skull, framed by mouse-brown hair.

We confronted the body, that twitching hand.

The palm slid a few inches on the tile, making a squeaking sound, and Chatterjee gave a little yelp. Ezekiel repeated the motion, as if he were trying to paddle.

"So check it out," Ben said, stepping across the body. He grabbed the legs, rotated Ezekiel around, and pulled him out into the hall like a rolled-up carpet.

Ezekiel's head knocked the doorjamb, his arms drifting up over his head as if he'd jumped off a cliff. A deep indentation cratered the flesh above his left eyehole where the stun gun had caved in his skull and penetrated his brain. A black slick showed beneath, a smear of infected white matter. One cheek twitched. His Adam's apple lurched, and clicking sounds emerged, as if something were trying to talk through his voice box but had no idea how to operate it.

I thought about Dr. Chatterjee's description of the parasite wrapped around the frontal cortex—how it had its figurative hands on the control levers of the human body—and I shuddered. I heard Alex gasp. Chatterjee's hand was up, covering his mouth. Patrick alone didn't flinch as he stared down at the thing that used to be Ezekiel.

Ben kept pulling him by the ankles, the body shushing

across the tile, the head leaving behind a six-inch swath of blood. Once Ezekiel was well into the hall, Ben dropped his legs with a thump. Then he kicked the limbs wide, posing the guy so it looked like he was doing a jumping jack.

Patrick stood back a few feet with the rest of us. Watching Ben drag Ezekiel around like a sack of trash, I felt something clench in my stomach. I was intimidated by Ben, and that feeling was made worse when I glanced over at Patrick and could tell that he was, too. It wasn't just Ben's ruthlessness that was scary. It was the fact that he actually seemed in his element.

He looked up at us, the scar tissue pulling into different arrangements on his face. "You're not gonna see from back there."

We eased forward. Alex hesitated a moment over by the duffel bag containing what remained of her best friend. Patrick rested a hand on her lower back, steering her with us.

We ringed the twitching body.

I'd not yet seen a Host up close. The eyeholes were bizarrely clean, the insides rimmed with vessels and brain matter but not dripping or bleeding at all. It was almost as if they'd been bored by a laser that cauterized as it went.

Setting his feet on either side of the flung-wide arm, Ben crouched by Ezekiel's face and beckoned us to come in even closer. I'd seen too many horror movies to not be freaked out. But I wasn't willing to let Ben see me scared, so I bit the inside of my cheek and bent in a little more.

Ben took a slender Maglite out of his pocket and clicked it on. He tilted the flashlight's beam across Ezekiel's face, and what I saw made my nerves jump.

The eyeholes weren't holes at all. Each had a transparent membrane stretched across the surface like Saran Wrap. It looked like the liquid sheet covering the little plastic ring on a bubble wand after you dip it in the soapy solution.

Ben grabbed a handful of Ezekiel's hair and tugged his head up off the floor so we could see through to the second membranes stretched across the backs of the tunnels.

"God in heaven," Chatterjee said. "What in the world is that?"

"Dunno," Ben said, breathing heavily from all his exertion. "But watch this."

He let the head clunk back to the floor. Then he tapped the membrane with a forefinger. The membrane turned on like a computer screen but stayed transparent at the same time, so we were looking through an image and at it at the same time.

It showed the gray early-morning sky broken by a few clouds, their shapes rendered with lines, sort of like you see on a blueprint. The picture—if you could call it that—twitched a few times, fuzzed with static like the TV back in the gym. Somewhere beneath my shock, it occurred to me that this interference might be because of the damage to the brain caused by the stun gun. Were the clouds in the image *drifting?* Before I could process any of this, the angle shifted, scanning across the sky.

It wasn't a still picture. It was footage.

As the view tilted downward, the football stadium's bleachers scrolled into sight, marked with those same odd structural outlines. It was as though some software program were tracing every edge and contour of the visual field. The point of view rose higher, about six feet off the field, and then the angle tilted forward severely so we were looking at the grass.

"What are we *seeing?*" Patrick asked.

The footage continued at a rapid clip, the line of the end zone coming into sight. A ninety-degree right turn spun the field on its axis, and the point of view moved forward, turf sweeping by, each blade of grass delineated by those digital-looking lines. Every now and then, the toe of a boot poked into range at the bottom.

My burning lungs told me I'd been holding my breath. I only realized that I knew the answer as I heard myself say it out loud: "We're seeing what Ezekiel saw after he turned into a Host. This is the *inside* view." My heartbeat made itself known against my ribs. "He's being played like an avatar in a video game."

Chatterjee blew out a breath. "It's as though the virus was . . . *engineered*."

For the first time, I noticed that the footage also played on the rear membrane, but upside down and reversed. Ms. Yee had taught us how pinhole cameras used to work, and it looked like a version of that.

I refocused on the front membrane. Ezekiel's path continued in jerky fast-forward. Another turn and the ten-yard line flew by. The footage zipped forward at a dizzyingly swift rate, made even more dizzying by the close-up sight of the ground underfoot. Once the field had been covered by the gradually widening spiral, the point of view entered the bleachers, scanning them, then reversing back to solid ground. Like the male Hosts we'd seen in town, it seemed Ezekiel broke from the spiral pattern only when he encountered an obstacle or a redundancy. Then he straightened out, headed for new terrain, and started over from a different center position.

"They're not just walking in patterns," Ben said. "They're covering *all* the ground. Searching strategically."

"For what?" Alex asked.

"For *us*," Ben said.

"Wouldn't it be more effective to keep their heads up and scan for movement?" Alex said. "I mean, if you're on the lookout for kids, it seems pretty dumb to keep your eyes glued to the ground—or your non-eyes or whatever."

I hadn't looked away from the membrane. Slowly, it dawned on me what Ezekiel had been doing. The realization made my throat go so dry that I had to swallow before I could talk. "They're Mappers," I said.

Everyone looked at me.

"What do you mean?" Ben asked.

Ezekiel's lips fluttered as if he were about to say something, but all that came out was an odd vowel sound. The fast-forward stream kept zipping across the membrane covering his eyehole.

"They're mapping the terrain," Dr. Chatterjee said.

Ben's laugh was high-pitched, nervous. "For what?"

I pried my eyes off the sight beneath me, looking at Patrick. "Do you remember Sheriff Blanton?"

Alex spoke before Patrick could reply. "What about my dad?"

I said, "When we came in, he was in your closet with his head tilted back toward the ceiling."

"Like he was catching a signal," Patrick said.

"What if he wasn't receiving?" I said. "What if he was *transmitting*? Sending data."

"Data?" Ben said. "What data?"

"*This*," I said, pointing at the miniature feed playing in Ezekiel's eye membrane.

We watched all that terrain continue to be vacuumed up and outlined as Ezekiel chewed up turf. It was hard to tell where he was heading until he bumped into a wall. The angle crept along the wall, coming to a locked door. Ezekiel's hand rose into range, clutching his massive janitor's ring of keys. He tried maybe fifteen keys in the lock, though considering the sped-up view, this took only a few seconds to watch. And then a key fit, the door swung wide, and the scene scrolled through a classroom. It moved through various floors and classrooms, the school's interior being mapped like the football field.

The whole time Ezekiel's cheek twitched, his Adam's apple undulating. Aside from that, his face stayed expressionless.

"Wait a minute," Ben said. "So you think this thing's turning people into computers?"

Dr. Chatterjee said, "As organisms we're not unlike computers to begin with. I mean to say they're not unlike *us*. Maybe that's why the eyeholes go all the way through. Maybe they need to access—or plug into—all parts of the brain."

I could feel the heat of Ben's gaze fixed on me, but I couldn't look away from the footage fast-forwarding across Ezekiel's eye membrane. It flew into the humanities wing, entering various classrooms and spiraling through them. I felt a chill as the point of view neared Mr. Tomasi's room, passing the very spot where we stood. It zipped through Tomasi's room, spiraling out to the perimeter in seconds. As it zipped toward the door, a familiar meaty hand swung into the frame holding a stun gun, the gleaming barrel filling up the screen. A bolt of lightning fizzled across the membrane, the spark so bright it made us jump. The next view was straight up at the ceiling, each tile delineated with those weird blueprint lines, though they were now even more scrambled and staticky than before. Soon enough the ceiling slid into a blur, passing through the doorway into the hall, and then we were looking up at ourselves looking down at us.

Live footage.

"I asked you a question, Chance," Ben was saying.

"Sorry," I said. I couldn't lift my eyes. I could barely even speak. "What?"

Ben's image, even fuzzily captured in the bubble membrane, looked annoyed. "I said, 'Transmitting to *who?*'"

Before I could answer, a sudden movement in Ezekiel's eye startled me so badly I jerked back onto my heels.

A virtual eyeball rolled into the membrane, replacing the

view of us. Squirming and veiny, it stared up from the space where a real eyeball was supposed to be.

Alex screamed. I might have as well.

Not Ben, though.

Ben had his stun gun out in a flash. He fired it directly through Ezekiel's forehead into the brain. All light vanished from the membrane, taking that horrific eyeball with it.

ENTRY 16   "What the hell *was* that?"

"And what does it want?"

"Where is it?"

"Are there more?"

"Did it see us?"

"I don't know."

The tense voices washed over my back. We were still right outside Mr. Tomasi's classroom, but I was at my locker, twirling the combination dial.

"Does it know how to get here?"

"Well, it is a friggin' *Mapper*, Ben."

"But why would it think we'd stick around? Wouldn't it think we'd be long gone?"

"That's true," Chatterjee said. "If it saw us, then it knows that *we* saw it see us."

"Plus, the signal looked all weak and screwed up," Patrick said. "Maybe it wasn't transmitting clearly."

"Either way," Alex said, "we'll have to watch out even more."

"Meaning what?"

My combination lock clicked open, the battered metal door swinging on its rusty hinges.

Taped to the inside, a photo of me, Patrick, and Alex at the creek. We'd propped a camera on a rock and set the timer before huddling together, Patrick in the middle, one arm around each of our necks. Our only concern that day had been finding flat rocks to skip.

"Ezekiel used keys," Alex said. "We saw him use keys."

"Big deal," Ben said. "They're using all kinds of things."

"The big deal is, lots of teachers have keys to the outside fences," Alex said. "And it's clear the Mappers want to record everything."

"Ezekiel already got the school," Ben said. "We just saw it."

"But he didn't finish. And we don't know what he transmitted."

"Better safe than sorry," Patrick said. "They might come back to finish the job."

"We need to switch the locks and post lookouts," Alex said.

I flipped through various textbooks in my locker. A pencil box. An old apple, soft and brown. In the back I found what I was looking for: my composition notebook from English. I ran my hand over the battered black-and-white static design of the cover. The corners were worn, dog-eared, the pages nearly filled. I set it aside and reached for the one beneath it, still blank. The one I was gonna use when I ran out of room in the old one.

Behind me Dr. Chatterjee said, "We have a lot to keep track of."

"Yeah, we do," I said, elbowing my locker closed as I turned. At the clang, the others looked over at me. I gripped the new notebook. "We need to start writing all this down."

———

In the quiet dark of the gym, surrounded by sleeping bodies, I stared down at my neat, slanted handwriting.

It was past midnight. I was still working in the barn when I heard the rolling door lurch open. I started and lost my grip on a block of hay. It tumbled off the baling hooks.

Once we'd gotten back to the gym, we'd circled up the kids and reported what we knew. Or at least what we thought we knew.

At the mention of the eyeball, terror rippled across the room, stiffening the spines of the kids. Now we weren't just talking about parasites and altered adults. We were talking about aliens, advanced technologies, government conspiracies. The room buzzed with theories.

It quickly became clear that our questions would find no answers right now, so Dr. Chatterjee took charge, focusing our efforts. We'd sprung into action, setting schedules for lookouts, checking that all lights and appliances were in the off position, then getting the backup generator up and running. The generator was supposed to supply three weeks of power, but with everything turned off aside from the water heater, refrigerators, and freezers, we were hoping to stretch out that time frame much longer. Patrick and Ben ran sneak missions to the chained-shut perimeter gates, switching the school's locks for thick padlocks from our PE lockers.

After my lookout shift watching the northeast quadrant from a perch atop Mr. Tomasi's desk, I spent the afternoon and evening talking to as many kids as possible to start piecing together the story of what had happened—what *was* happening—to Creek's Cause. Everyone seemed to have a different bit of information. Through bouts of tears, JoJo and Rocky bravely described the events of the last week around their house. Dr. Chatterjee and I sat down and figured out how a parasite like *Ophiocordyceps unilateralis* might have worked its way through Hank McCafferty's distended gut into the frontal cortex of every adult in our county.

By the time midnight rolled around, my hand was cramped from writing and I had caught up to myself here, now, in the gym.

I clicked off the Maglite I'd checked out of the supply station that Eve Jenkins had been given the job of running out of the storage room. Then I leaned back on my cot, staring up at the high ceiling. Pennants overhead announced various sports titles. It had seemed so important last year when our baseball team won regionals.

I turned my head, looking at the cots lined neatly in rows. Most kids were sleeping, but a few were crying, some more quietly than others. Patrick was on lookout atop the bleachers, his big form barely visible against the casement window, watching over everything like a guardian angel. Less than a week until he turned eighteen. If we didn't get help or if the spores didn't magically dissipate, he'd turn into something unrecognizable. The thought stole the breath from my lungs.

He was my best friend. He was my only family. He was the only person left who'd known me since I was born, who'd held me when I was a baby.

What would you do if you only had seven days left with your favorite person in the world?

Cassius lay beneath my bed, sleep-breathing with a faint whistle, but that only reminded me of my other pups and made me feel more alone. I thought of Zeus out there somewhere. I'd been eight when he was born; I'd known him half my life. I'd delivered him myself, the biggest boy in the first litter that Uncle Jim had let me take care of. Zeus's first act had been to yawn a puppy yawn in my face, his pink tongue curling. I pictured him now, grown and powerful, running through the forest, the other ridgebacks at his side. Were they hungry? Were they cold? Cassius whimpered in his sleep. Did he miss his father as much as I did?

Tears slid down my temples. With everything going on, I was crying over my missing dogs? And yet they seemed the only thing safe to focus on right now. When I thought of Mom and Dad or Uncle Jim and Sue-Anne or what was waiting for Patrick, I wanted to come apart.

Springs creaked on the cot next to me as Alex sat down, her hair twisted up in a threadbare gym towel. Fortunately, the locker rooms were right off the nearest hall, so we had easy access to toilets, sinks, and showers. Chatterjee had set a two-minute limit on hot showers to save energy, and Alex had been one of the first to jump on the offer. She smelled like soap and some girly shampoo, and if I hadn't felt so embarrassed for crying, I might have been distracted. I wiped at my cheeks, hoping she couldn't see my face in the darkness.

She lay back and shot a sigh at the ceiling. With Patrick on lookout and the kids around us asleep, it was almost like we were alone. That made me uncomfortable, but I wasn't sure why.

"I thought it was bad when my mom left," she said. "Every day when school got out, I used to run to the oak tree out front. And I'd sit on that low branch—the one that dips down, you know?"

"Yeah," I said.

Everyone knew that branch.

"And I'd wait and pray that her little Jeep would turn in to the parking lot. And she'd pull up and flash that huge smile and say, 'I was just kidding, honey. I'd never leave you behind. I'd never leave you—'" Her voice cracked, and she covered her mouth. "I guess I couldn't believe I'd never see that smile again."

You can see it anytime you want, I thought. *You just have to look in the mirror.*

But I didn't say anything, because that wasn't the point, and besides, there was something precious and rare in her telling me this. Like it was some jewel she'd uncovered in the sand and handed to me.

"And now I just feel dumb for thinking that my mom leaving was so bad. Like it was some huge earth-changing thing. Big deal, right? Compared to this. I mean, pretty much all the grown-ups we know are changed into robots. And so many of our friends are captured. God knows what's being done to them right now."

I rubbed my eyes hard, remembering Sam Miller being carried into the church by his grandparents, his little body swinging between them.

When Alex spoke again, her voice was a hoarse whisper. "Nothing'll ever be the same."

Someone coughed across the gym, and another kid turned in his sleep, murmuring from a nightmare. I looked over at Patrick, faintly backlit up there against the pane, steady as a gargoyle.

"When my parents died," I said, "I thought nothing would ever be the same. And it wasn't." I sensed her head turning toward me. "But that just meant I had to figure out a new way."

"To what?"

"To live, I guess."

The sheets rustled as she nodded. "I suppose we all do now."

We lay like that for a time in the darkness, breathing.

"Patrick never talks about stuff like this," she said. "And there's a kind of strength in that. But there's also a kind of strength in not being afraid to talk about it."

My first instinct was to defend Patrick, to point out that he wasn't afraid of anything. But I kept my mouth shut. Maybe it's because I enjoyed how it felt, this secret compliment.

A wet slurp landed on the side of my face. Cassius, licking off the trails of my tears. He whimpered at me insistently. I knew that whimper.

It meant he had to go to the bathroom.

And I'd trained him from the instant he was born only to

go outside. Which meant that now I had to risk my life so my dog could pee.

That really sucked.

He hadn't gone all day. I hadn't even thought about it. I wondered how many other things I had yet to consider.

I sat up with a groan, like an old person. "I gotta go," I said. "Take him out."

"*Out* out?" Alex asked.

"Uh-huh."

"How you gonna do that?"

"I have no idea," I said.

Cassius and I threaded quietly through the cots and across the court. Ben guarded the double doors, sitting on a metal folding chair like some kind of security guard. The set of his jaw showed just how much he dug the position of authority.

"Where you going?" he asked.

"Front lawn."

"Front lawn? Now? What for?"

I gestured at Cassius. "He's gotta go."

"He can use the bathroom."

"I don't know how to break this to you, Ben, but dogs don't generally use toilets."

His face shifted, and for a moment I worried that I'd joked too hard. But instead he held out his hand. "Flashlight."

"How am I supposed to—"

"I don't care how you do anything. I'm not having you put the group at risk if a Host sees you out there. And a flashlight means you could be spotted from far away."

I slapped the Maglite into his palm.

He leaned over me. "Don't make a noise. And make sure your dog doesn't either."

He shoved the doors open and made me walk under his armpit to get out. I headed down the hall, hesitating by the front doors. Since setting foot inside the school, I hadn't been back outside. It felt safe in here, sheltered and protected.

"You heard the jerk," I told Cassius. "Not a sound."

I pushed the doors open, and we eased out, the night breeze chilling my neck, my hands. Though we kept on the lawn close to the building, I shot nervous glances through the front gates to the parking lot and the street beyond. A few Mappers moved along. I couldn't make out anything more than their shadowy forms, but I recognized the posture, the pattern of their steps.

One of them stopped and tilted his head back. His eyes, aimed at the heavens, began to glow. I watched, fascinated and horrified. If our theory was right, he was uploading data. Sending along the terrain he'd scanned to whoever that squirming virtual eye belonged to. The breeze wafted over the sound of throaty clicking, the same sound Sheriff Blanton had been making in Alex's closet. It struck me that it sounded a bit like a fax machine trying for a connection or the noises I'd heard Internet dial-ups make in old movies.

Finally the Mapper lowered his head and continued on his course.

I urged Cassius onto the dewy lawn, and he darted along with his nose to the ground, sniffing.

"Come *on*," I whispered. "Just go already."

He moved closer to the edge of the lawn, toward the fence line.

"Hey, stop. Cassius. *Cassius.*"

I was gonna tug him back toward the building, but try telling a dog where to go to the bathroom. At last he lifted his leg and started peeing right on the fence.

As I looked up, a Host emerged from the darkness, the hollowed-out face right there on the far side of the chain-link.

My insides froze. I opened my mouth to yell but somehow managed to stop the noise in my throat.

The Host was Mr. Tomasi, his elbow-patched corduroy blazer looking frayed, his eyeholes focused on the ground in front of him.

He swept past me, close enough that I could smell a lingering trace of his cologne. His loafer moved right through the spot where Cassius was peeing, but he kept on, never so much as raising his head.

I watched until he vanished back into the darkness, and at some point I remembered to close my mouth.

I looked down at Cassius, and he looked up at me, his forehead furrowed.

"Let's not do that again," I said.

We headed back up the broad stone steps to the front doors. When we stepped inside, a hand set down on my shoulder, hard, startling me.

Ben had snuck over from his post in the gym to spy on us.

"If you'd screwed up," he said, tapping my chest with his stun gun, "I'd have killed you myself."

I believed him.

ENTRY 17   *I'm snuggled in the sheets, and Sue-Anne sits next to me, leaning against the headboard, reading from* To Kill a Mockingbird. *Patrick is down with Uncle Jim in the garage, helping him change out the brake pads on his truck. He's eight and gets a whole other set of privileges, including coming up to bed later.*

I lie as still as possible, hoping that if I'm good, she'll read one more chapter, that she'll keep going forever. But she doesn't. She finishes the page and closes the book, and my heart sinks. It is my third month in their house, and this quiet time with her is my favorite time of all. Tonight I will figure out how to fall asleep alone. Tomorrow I will get up early to help on the ranch before school. Everything is different.

Sue-Anne leans over, kisses my forehead.

The words burn in my chest, and before I can catch them, they are out of my mouth. "I hate them," I say.

On her way out the door, she pauses. "I don't understand."

"My parents."

She takes a moment, her lips pouched out like she's thinking real hard. "Why do you say that, Chance?"

"They didn't have to get drunk and get in a stupid car crash. They had me and Patrick at home. They never even thought about us that night."

She doesn't say anything. She just nods—not like in agreement but to show she's listening. I know I'm acting like a baby, but I can't help it. Everything's burning—my chest, my face, my eyes.

"And I don't want to—" My breath catches in my throat, and I have to stop for a second. I'm ashamed to admit it, but I say it anyways. *"And I don't want to grow up yet."*

She nods again, and her eyes are wistful, and I realize that even though I've known her my whole life, maybe I don't know her much at all. When she speaks, her tone is as soft and kind as I've ever heard it. "Sometimes what we want *isn't what we* need." *I look up at her, confused. "What does that mean?" I say.*

A commotion jarred me out of the dream memory.

Hushed whispers and quiet footfalls. But it wasn't the noise that was alarming so much as the panic running through the room. I opened my eyes, disoriented by the tall ceiling, the bright light streaming through the high windows, the movement all around me. On a slight delay, reality flooded in.

The gym. With the survivors. Uncle Jim and Sue-Anne dead. Kids snatched. Hosts everywhere. Our town overrun.

I sat up and followed the current of hushed anxiety. It had direction to it, pointing at Patrick in the lookout post atop the bleachers. With Alex at his side, he was ducked beneath the windowsill, his eyes wide.

His stare found me among the kids, and he gestured for me to get up there. I didn't like the expression on his face.

Keeping hunched over, I crept across the floor, then up the bleachers, wincing every time they creaked. At last I reached him. Beside him, Alex was breathing hard, her chest rising and falling as if trying to tamp something down.

"What's going on?" I whispered.

Patrick pointed above his head. As slowly as I could, I raised myself up and peered over the sill.

Mappers lined the front fence. They stood shoulder to shoulder, blank faces peering through the chain-link. Their heads were nodding up and down in unison.

I dropped from sight, putting my back to the wall, and blew out a breath.

"Your mouth's bleeding," Patrick said.

I'd bitten down on my lip hard enough to draw blood.

Below, the other kids looked up at us expectantly. Chet Rogers chewed on the collar of his shirt nervously, his breaths starting to get that asthma rasp. Dr. Chatterjee leaned on the dry-erase board, light glinting off his eyeglasses. Ben Braaten cracked the double doors to peer out into the corridor, his shoulders raised. For once, even *he* looked nervous.

"What are they *doing*?" Patrick whispered.

I shook my head with bewilderment.

After I'd caught my breath, I inched back up to take another look. They were still there, maybe forty of them, their heads rocking robotically. At once they stopped. They turned and walked in single file down the length of the fence, then turned once more to face the building and started moving their heads again. Their eyeholes scanned the front lawn, scouring the contours of the building. Then I understood.

"They're mapping the grounds," I said, addressing the gym in a loud whisper. "Through the fence."

"Why don't they just break in?" Chet asked. "They've used jackhammers and stuff."

"Maybe they want to leave as much of the infrastructure standing as possible," Dr. Chatterjee said.

"For what?" Ben asked.

I thought of that squirming virtual eye rolling into place in Ezekiel's head. "The question isn't 'For *what*?'" I said. "It's, 'For *who*?'"

Patrick, Alex, and I rose again, bringing our noses level with the sill. The Hosts finished wagging their heads and then broke apart, branching off into the neighboring streets, their faces lowered as usual.

I exhaled, and everyone else, reading our expressions, seemed to as well.

"Well," Dr. Chatterjee said, "let's get to the day, then."

Logistics consumed the morning. The lookouts rotated, reporting back to Ben. A few of the kids took a shift in the cafeteria. Dr. Chatterjee told them to burn through the perishables first, so they served up runny eggs, cartons of milk, and OJ. I fed Cassius and took him out to the flower bed by the sheltered picnic area so he could go to the bathroom. In the gym Patrick cranked open the casement windows, letting the stale air out. The fresh breeze was a relief, what with the hundred or so bodies in close proximity. Alex turned on the TV, which still showed business as usual elsewhere in the world. Dr. Chatterjee continued to check the carbon monoxide detector at intervals, jotting the "unidentified particulate" readings on the dry-erase board.

Patrick walked over and stared at the board. I came up behind him and looked at the readings over his shoulder. They hadn't dropped at all. In fact, they hadn't even varied, the percentage remaining dead steady since Chatterjee had first started gathering data yesterday. My stomach roiled.

"You okay?" I asked.

"It's only been a day," Patrick said. "The spores have to dissipate at some point."

Finally he turned, tried for a casual smile. He didn't say what we were both thinking: *Yeah, but will they be gone six days from now?*

By the edge of the bleachers, JoJo gave a cry of delight. She crawled under the risers and retrieved—of all things—a Frisbee. She called out to her brother, and they started tossing the disk back and forth. Even here, even now, kids were kids.

A movement at my side broke me from my thoughts, and I

glanced over. Alex had drawn level with me. Eyeing the readings, she took in a shaky breath.

She looked over at me, her expression changing. Then she started jogging toward the bleachers.

"Alexandra," Patrick said. "Hang on."

But she hopped up on the first bench. "Hey!" she called out, careful not to yell too loud, mindful of the open windows. "Everyone listen up."

She waited a moment as the others stopped what they were doing.

"I don't know about you guys," she said, "but I don't want to just wait around here and do nothing."

"What do you propose, then?" Dr. Chatterjee asked.

Alex gestured at the TV, showing a fake-tanned weather reporter gesturing at a map. "We have to get outside the infection zone."

"You won't make it a block." Ben's voice carried over to us from the base of the bleachers. He was sitting on the floor in a fall of light from the windows, turned away so only his profile was visible. His legs were kicked wide, his shoulders drooping. His hands were doing something on the floor, but from this angle I couldn't tell what.

"Even if you could, where you gonna go?" Eve asked.

Alex tilted her head, indicating the SPTV logo beneath the still-yammering weather reporter. "Stark Peak is closest."

Ben gave a nasty laugh. "You're gonna risk escaping town, getting all the way across the valley and up over Ponderosa Pass?"

He had a point. Ponderosa Pass was nearly fifty miles away.

"Hell, yeah," Alex said. "It's a different weather system over the mountain range. Let's hope that the spores stay here in the valley, socked in like fog."

"It beats waiting holed up here anyways," Patrick said. "The

Hosts are doing two things: Mapping the terrain. And collecting all the kids. We still don't know why. But we know they're doing it *for* someone."

"For whoever that eye belongs to," Chet said, his voice wrenched high with fear.

"Which means," Patrick said, talking over the muffled outcry caused by Chet's comment, "that someone needs to go get help. Because whatever's coming hasn't even gotten started yet."

"We're safer here," Ben said.

"They were at the gate this morning," Patrick said. "At some point one of them will catch wind that we're in here. They'll get in eventually."

Ben shifted, the floor between his legs coming visible, and I saw at last what he'd been up to. He'd been pulling the wings off dying flies. They wiggled against the floorboards like little beans. He plucked up another one lazing across the seam between floor and wall. "If they do," he said, pinching off one translucent wing, then the other, "I'll take care of it."

"How about the other kids out there?" Alex said. "Shouldn't we get help for them?"

"It's too late for them already," Ben said. "We gotta protect what we have."

"Until what?"

"The other cities'll catch word soon enough. Send the army and scientists or whatever. Until then we just have to stay alive." Ben looked at Patrick. "Course, some of us have more time than others."

Over on the bleachers, Chet stifled a sob.

"That could be weeks," Alex said. "Remember last July? The tornado? How long did it take for Stark Peak to send two lousy fire engines?"

Ben let the fly's body drop among the others. He walked

over, turned off the TV, and shoved it under the bleachers. "We need to conserve electricity. Turn off anything that uses energy we don't absolutely need for survival. Buy time. Like I said, most of us can afford to wait."

"We don't make decisions solely based on what's best for most of us," Dr. Chatterjee said.

"You're right," Ben said. "I can't tell you what to do." He pointed his shiny face over at us. "You wanna get caught like Dick and Jaydon or kill yourself, be my guest."

"And what's *your* plan?" Patrick said. "If help doesn't magically arrive soon?"

"The cafeteria freezers are stocked with food. We live with crops and cattle all around us if it gets to that. One nighttime sneak to bring back a few cows could feed us for months. We got everything we need right here in Creek's Cause." Ben stood up, grinding his boot on the wriggling fly parts. "So let's call it like it is, Patrick. You're just freaking out because you've got less time than everyone else. Aside from Chet, that is."

"We're *all* on a clock here," Patrick said. "You've got what? Six more months than me?"

"That's a lot of months for those spores to go away. Or for help to get here."

"Or for something else to get here first," Patrick said.

At this the kids bristled.

Patrick looked out across all those faces. "Is anyone willing to go with us?"

A low pulse of fear started up in my stomach. That "us" included me for sure, and I knew that if Patrick asked, no matter how scared I was, I had his back. The kids looked away, one after another. I couldn't really blame them.

"How 'bout you, Chet?" Patrick asked.

"No way," Chet said. "No way I'm going out there."

"You have even less time than I do."

"I know. But if you saw what my dad did to my little brother . . ." He started wheezing a bit and shook his head. "I'm sorry, Patrick. Not with them out there. I just can't do it. I'll take my chances that the air'll get better."

"No one else?" Patrick's voice echoed around the hard walls of the gym.

He turned and looked at Alex and me. I felt my stomach lurch as if I'd walked off a ledge and was endlessly plummeting.

His eyes met mine. He said, "We leave at nightfall."

———

The day passed in a crawl, sunlight inching across the gym floor until it hit the far wall and started to climb. At last dusk textured the air, and Dr. Chatterjee ordered the high casement windows cinched shut against the cold.

Alex sat on her cot wearing Patrick's black cowboy hat, her face tilted down. Her hair fell like a curtain across her cheek, blocking her eyes from view. She was taping her fingers carefully, like she did before hockey games, neat protective strips between the knuckles, biting each piece off the roll. Her hockey stick lay across her thighs.

She looked pretty bad-ass.

I was watching her while pretending not to watch her at the same time, so when Patrick spoke right behind me, I nearly jumped off my cot. I set down my composition notebook and said, "What?"

He laid his shotgun across one shoulder. "I said, 'Get what you need from the supply station.'"

I headed over to where Eve Jenkins sat at a desk she'd pulled over in front of the open door to the storage room. She'd done a great job organizing everything inside, bats and crowbars lining one wall, knives stashed against the others. Bins held flashlights and compasses and pocketknives. Most of the food remained in the cafeteria, but she kept energy bars, granola mix, and apples in a crate for the lookouts.

When she saw me coming, she smiled and straightened up a bit. I looked past her into the room. "Wow, this is pretty cool."

"It's nothing," she said. "Just organizing stuff. I'm sure anyone could've done it."

"You know, you are allowed to just say thanks."

She blushed a little. "Thanks. What do you need, Chance?"

My baling hooks, hung on a peg in the back, gleamed as if calling to me. I nodded at them.

She said, "I figured you were gonna ask for a hunting rifle, but we just have the one from Leonora Rose, and there's no ammo."

"Too big anyways," I said.

"I heard you were a crack shot with a rifle."

I shrugged. "I have okay aim," I said. "But I need something for up close."

She blanched slightly, then lifted the baling hooks from the peg and brought them over.

I gripped them again, the wood firm and comforting in my hands. "Guess I'm gonna need a flashlight, a folding knife, some matches, and a couple of energy bars. Everything else we'll figure out along the way."

She shifted her weight uncomfortably. "Ben says you can only take what you brought. He said we gotta preserve supplies and weapons for the lookouts."

Ben had decided he was running security, and no one had *un*decided it for him since.

Her lips pressed together, that pretty dimple making a tiny crescent in her right cheek. "But . . . ," she continued, "I think Ben's sort of a jerk. And Dr. Chatterjee never agreed to the rule. So." She gave a quick look at the double doors where Ben's chair sat empty, then grabbed the supplies and slid them across the desk to me. "Here you go."

"Thanks, Eve."

When I turned away, she said my name. I looked at her over my shoulder.

"Make sure you come back," she said. A wisp of glossy dark hair drifted down over her face, and she blew it away.

I realized she was prettier than I'd thought.

"Do my best," I said.

JoJo ran over and clamped onto my side, hugging me. She was crying. "Don't leave, Chance. Please don't."

I bent over and kissed her head. "I have to," I said.

She pried herself from me, ran off, and hid beneath the bleachers. Rocky sat on one of the middle benches. I caught his eye, gestured to the space where JoJo had disappeared: *Take care of your sister.* He nodded, but I could tell he was scared, too.

I turned away. Over in the middle of the cots, Patrick and Alex were sitting together. He held his hands over hers and they were leaning in, his hat cocked back on her head so their foreheads could touch. He must've felt me looking at him because he stood up, and then Alex saw me, too, and rose to her feet. A moment later Cassius's head reared into view beside them.

Patrick lifted the shotgun, balancing it on the ledge of his collarbone. The hockey stick spun expertly in Alex's hands. Patrick reached over, plucked his Stetson from Alex's head, and seated it firmly on his own. With a baling hook, I gestured toward the door.

As we headed out, I could feel the eyes of everyone in the gym on us. We were the brave few. Or the soon-to-be-dead few.

We reached the double doors, pushed them open, and headed

down the corridor. Cassius trotted at our side, his head raised, tongue lolling. He probably thought we were going for a stroll.

By the front of the school, Ben stood lookout, that stun gun shoved into the waist of his jeans. As we neared, he spun the keys around his finger like a cowboy showing off his revolver.

Patrick halted, studied him. "You're *enjoying* all this, aren't you?"

Ben considered for a moment. "I'm used to death, Patrick. I grew up around a slaughterhouse. It gave me an up-close look at, you know, the cycle of life. And I knew exactly how *my* life was gonna play out. How many hours I'd work when I was twenty or thirty or forty. How much overtime I'd pull on weekends during culling season. What kind of crappy place I'd live in when I got older and what bar I'd drink at." He swallowed, and I could see in his face the same longing I sometimes felt, the dreams he didn't allow himself to have. "I get to protect people now. Make choices that actually matter. *I* get to actually matter."

His eyes glimmered wetly. Again I thought back to that car crash that had taken his brothers and wondered what he'd lost in the flames. Or found.

"So yeah . . ." Ben turned to slot the key into the lock. He opened the big door for us, the air billowing in, cold and unforgiving. "The end of the world is pretty much the best thing that ever happened to me."

ENTRY 18   The three of us crammed beneath a stand of oak, the velvety leaves tickling our necks and the backs of our arms. Cassius remained outside the tangle, lying flat on the dirt, his snout resting between his paws. We'd taken a high vantage on a hill, town square sprawling before us. It had quieted down a lot since we'd last seen it, the Mappers dispersing to scan new terrain. In fact, I couldn't see a single Host on the vast lawn or the bordering streets. Aside from movement in the church windows and the glow of the forge from Bob n' Bit Hardware, there was no sign of life at all. Jackhammered chunks of asphalt lay like boulders on the street. A power cable dangled from the roof of the One Cup Cafe, striking the sidewalk and sending up sprays of sparks. The pallet jack dragged into town by Afa Similai remained in the front courtyard of the church, but the dog crates were missing from it, as were the other trunks and cages I'd spotted there earlier.

We'd doglegged through the neighborhood by the school, drifting through wisps of fog, making painfully slow headway. We'd kept close to the houses, moving through yards, hiding behind trash cans and parked cars. More than once we'd had to hold our breath and keep our heads ducked as packs of Hosts drifted by. Cassius obeyed my hand gestures perfectly, all those cold morning hours of training paying off. Patrick and Alex debated grabbing a truck but decided the noise of an engine would be too risky here in town. If we drew a throng of Hosts, we'd be as stuck as a car in a herd of sheep.

The square now was as desolate as I'd ever seen it.

Alex leaned over, her hair brushing my face. "Where *are* they all?" she whispered.

I said, "Maybe once they've mapped an area, they move on."

Cassius's head lifted, his ears flattening against his skull.

The clack of a screen door drew our focus to the line of shops. A kid sprinted out of the One Cup Cafe and through the fountain of sparks. He looked tiny, dwarfed by the hugeness of the square. He sliced between two parked cars, zigzagging across the open grass. Even way up here, we could hear his panicked breaths. He hurdled a bench and ran for the road. Patches of fog blurred his outline.

Patrick said, "Is that . . . ?"

"Andre Swisher," I said.

Suddenly there were faces in the windows of the houses and storefronts. We watched, breathless. Various doors banged open all around the square, a haunted-house orchestration, Hosts filling doorways and the mouths of alleys. Way across in the hospital, a woman in an untied gown pried open the ER doors and halted in the threshold, her stance wide, her arms spread to hold the doors at bay. For an instant they all just stood there, watching with their non-eyes.

Then they flashed into motion.

Andre screamed, switching direction once and then again, but the Hosts bounded toward him, cinching the noose. They were female, moving fast enough to burst their muscles. Though there were only seven or eight of them, they shot at him from every direction, streaking across the square. Sam Miller's grandma leapt over a car, landing on all fours, then rocketing forward.

Patrick tensed, bringing one knee under him like a sprinter at the starting line, but Alex put her hand on his back, firm, and said, "You go down there, you'll die. We can't help him right now."

Cassius whined faintly, and I hushed him.

Andre tugged frantically at a car handle—locked. Hosts closed in. He ran to a pickup slant-parked behind the chunks of broken asphalt and vaulted in. His fist smashed down the lock. His hand darted below the dash, and his shoulder flexed—the keys must've been left in the ignition—but nothing happened. Either the Hosts had disabled the truck or when its owner transformed, he'd walked away, leaving the engine running until the gas ran out.

The female Hosts mobbed the pickup. Through a break between them, we caught a glimpse of Andre's panicked face, his mouth stretched wide in a scream we couldn't hear.

Sam Miller's grandma drew back an arm, the flesh sagging beneath the bone, and drove her fist through the window. Hands crowded the jagged orifice as they pulled Andre out. They flung him violently chest-down on the road. A mother who worked as a volunteer at the library tore her blouse right off. Wearing nothing but a long skirt and a black bra, she used her shirt to bind him.

They hoisted him up and ran to the church, his muffled cries growing fainter and fainter. They disappeared inside, leaving the square as peaceful as it had been just a few minutes before.

None of us said anything. There was nothing to say. It was one of the most awful things I'd ever seen.

Our breath misted in the darkness, three puffs in a row.

"Even though the Mappers are scary," Alex said, "at least you stand a chance if they don't look up and see you. But the females, all they do is chase. They're the worst."

She was right. They were quick and fierce and terrible.

"We need to get a look inside that church," Patrick said. "See if there's any way we can help those kids."

It was what I'd most dreaded he'd say.

We kept to the hillside, moving among the trees, Cassius a few feet ahead of us, a canine early-warning system. The backpack tugged at my shoulders, filled with our supplies, including extra shells for Patrick's shotgun and my notebook. It took forever, but we finally worked our way down toward the back of the church and peered out from the edge of the parking lot. To one side the pews lay in a jumble like a giant stack of firewood. The Hosts had removed them all from the church. To make room for *what*?

A flatbed truck parked by the rear door blocked most of our view of the building, but we could still make out the stained-glass windows on either side of the altar, glowing with light from within. Over the breeze we heard moans and sobs, footfalls and dragging sounds.

My mouth went dry.

We waited for a while, watching and listening, but nothing changed. Then Patrick said, "Now or never, I guess," and crept out from cover.

I looked across at Alex. I could read the fear in her eyes, but she tightened her grip on the hockey stick and stepped from the tree line. Cassius and I stayed at her heels.

We hurried across the parking lot, passing the flatbed and jumping over the boxwood hedges beneath the window. I put my hand on Cassius's neck and pushed him down into the dirt with us. The whine of machinery vibrated the wall at my shoulders.

Cautiously, we rose and peered through the window. Due to the stained glass, everything looked murky, drenched in blues and reds, but then I found a white piece in the mosaic and the view inside became clear.

I wish it hadn't.

In place of the pews were rows of cages, crates, and pens, stretching from wall to wall, filling the whole interior. Every last one filled with a kid.

Hundreds of them.

Inside a repurposed chicken coop, Lyssa Unger, one of the cheerleaders, lay curled in the fetal position. Now loaded into one of our dog crates, Andre Swisher sobbed hoarsely, his muscular arms trembling. Blake Dubois had been crammed into a flat battery cage used to house hens, his discarded wheelchair flipped over beside it, one tire spinning lazily in a draft.

Dozens of Hosts moved through the aisles like the guards in some awful death camp. Most of them distributed white plastic coffee mugs from the church kitchen. I sourced the whining noise to an industrial meat grinder at the edge of the altar. Wearing his smeared butcher's apron, Ken Everston fed the grinder, grabbing items piled at his feet. Corncobs. Raw meat. Dog food. A whole turkey still in the plastic wrapper. A constant stream of beige sludge emerged from the machine, the other Hosts passing the white mugs beneath it, filling them for the children.

They were fattening them up? Or just keeping them alive? To what end?

My gorge reared up, pressing at the back of my throat.

What made it even more scary was how organized it all was. The Hosts—or whoever was controlling them—kept moving pieces around the chessboard, executing a grand plan we couldn't keep up with. They'd temporarily abandoned their roles to carry out various tasks. They'd done this before, of course, like when they'd melted down the guns and taken out the power lines, but I hadn't seen this many working with such machinelike precision in one place before. It was as though their programming had been rewritten all at once, putting them in service of a new goal. Seeing them in action was as awe-inspiring as it was fearsome.

There were way too many Hosts in the church for us to launch some kind of rescue mission. We'd be overpowered immediately.

Beside me Alex stiffened. In a tiny voice, she said, "Dad?"

There he was. Sheriff Blanton, patrolling the church like a foreman. The other Hosts stepped aside before him, falling into line, making clear who was in charge.

He walked over to the basement door and swung it open. A moment later Afa Similai emerged from below, his dreadlocks swaying around his empty eye sockets. His muscles protruded as if carved from granite; Afa lifted the battery cage holding Blake. Blake slid to one end of the cage, crying out. Afa thundered to the front of the church and exited, returning a moment later to grab another crated kid.

We watched this for a time, doing our best to remember to breathe. After Afa had retrieved five kids, he didn't come back from the front of the church. We waited nervously for him to reappear, but that door stayed shut.

Alex's gaze stayed locked on her father. Sheriff Blanton led several Hosts up to the meat grinder, each of them carrying food—a pineapple, dry pasta, a jar of pickles. It would all go into the gruel. He patrolled around the church, passing right in front of our window. As his boots thumped past us, Alex pressed her hand to her mouth, tears spilling over the bumps of her knuckles. His shadow rolled across her face and then was gone.

Cassius gave a low growl, fur standing up on his shoulders. He swung his head toward the side of the building.

"What?" I whispered. "What is it, boy?"

From around the corner came the rattling of wheels.

My muscles tensed. "Let's go," I said. *"Now."*

We hurdled the boxwood hedge, making it to the far side of the flatbed truck just before Afa came into view. He was hauling the pallet jack. Shooting a look over my shoulder, I saw that it was stacked with cages. Fortunately, Afa was bent forward, straining against the weight of the pallet, so he didn't see us as we vanished into the tree line.

Breathing hard, we watched him roll the pallet jack to the side of the big truck. Several more big male Hosts trailed behind him. They hoisted the crates up onto the flatbed. Seeing the kids loaded up like produce was almost too much to bear. Cheeks pressed into wire. Fingers curled around bars. Sobs and pleading.

When he was done, Afa grabbed the pallet jack and started back the way he'd come. One of the Hosts climbed into the truck and drove off, exhaust steaming from the tailpipe. The flatbed vanished, and a moment later another pulled in. They were running shifts, moving the kids somewhere.

The driver left the flatbed idling and walked into the church, probably to help with the next load. The other Hosts remained at the far end of the truck, staring at the church, waiting for Afa and the driver to reemerge.

Patrick drew back farther into the trees. "Let's go," he said.

Something stopped me in my tracks. I thought of Lyssa Unger curled in the fetal position. Blake crammed into that battery cage, his kicked-over wheelchair left behind. Wherever he was going, he'd be even more helpless than the others. Anger clawed its way up my throat.

I put Cassius on a sit-stay and broke from the tree line, sneaking up behind the truck. The male Hosts were right there on the far side, facing away, but any fear I had was overpowered by anger.

I swung one of the baling hooks into the rear tire. It punctured the rubber softly, giving off a hiss. The guards didn't turn around. Keeping a careful eye on them, I walked silently backward into the woods.

Hands reached out, grabbing me from behind, and I almost yelled.

Patrick.

"That was dumb," he said.

Annoyed, he nudged me along through the tree trunks.

He was right, of course. Taking out one tire wouldn't solve anything, but maybe it would slow them down a little.

Right now it was the best I could do.

We carved through the woods, staying off the main roads until we were well outside town. I had an urge to whistle for my missing dogs, but I didn't, worried what else might come crashing through the trees to answer my call. If we got anywhere near the other ridgebacks, I figured Cassius would let me know.

We crested a rise. Through a break in the pines, we could see Jack Kaner's place below, the weathered barn thrusting up from the fields. Long tunnels of tarp covered some of his vegetable crops, insulating them from the cold. To the south, the highway snaked through the landscape, a dark strip splitting the darkness.

Alex gestured toward the barn. "Ever since he got rid of his horses, Mr. Kaner parks his truck in there by the stables. I came once with my dad when someone spray-painted graffiti on the side of the barn."

"I heard that was Andre Swisher," Patrick said.

I thought about Andre running around the square like a trapped rat as the women—the Chasers—closed in. How they'd circled the pickup and dragged him out through the shattered window.

"Do you think it's safe to drive now?" I asked. "The noise and headlights might draw them."

"It's fifty miles just to Ponderosa Pass," Patrick said. "Then up and over to Stark Peak. No way we make that on foot." He scanned the highway ahead, the wide plain of the valley unfurled like a giant map. "More open space out here. Less chance we get penned in."

We worked our way down the steep hillside toward the barn, our flashlights stabbing the dark. We stumbled over roots, sent pebbles and dirt cascading. We were as quiet as we could be, but probably not as quiet as we thought we were.

At last we came out onto level ground about a mile from the barn, walls of corn spreading before us. In the plots behind the corn, rows of curved tarp lay over beds of lettuce and other produce that Kaner sold in his market. The "caterpillar tunnels" were built by stretching tarp over arcs of bent PVC piping, so they were segmented like the bugs. Each one was as long as a football field. A corner of tarp had pulled free from its rebar stake, snapping in the wind. The air smelled of rich soil, rot, and greens. A scarecrow jutted up, pitchfork in hand, and in the distance the Kaner house sat dark and quiet.

Cassius hesitated, his growl no longer a puppy growl but a rumble in his chest.

"It's okay, boy," I whispered. "Come on."

As we eased out into the field, more scarecrows came into sight all around us. A whole patch of them. And then we realized.

They weren't scarecrows.

ENTRY 19   First the heads moved, rotating to face us, moonlight streaming through the skulls. Then the shoulders pivoted. They turned as one, the bodies separate and yet coordinated, like a flock of birds changing direction.

A bunch of them in ragged crop-picker overalls and flannels. Weather-beaten cheeks, bronzed skin, lanky builds. Jack Kaner used migrant workers and paid them a decent wage, though he rotated them through like crops. Sometimes there were a dozen. Sometimes more.

From the corner of my eye, I caught more movement. Turning, I came aware of shadowed forms spread through the fields, ovals of countless faces hidden among the cornstalks.

They'd frozen at our approach, letting us creep right into their midst.

My chest jerked in breaths. Instinctively, we'd fallen into a fighting formation, facing outward, our backs nearly touching. Cassius barked and barked.

The Hosts exploded into motion, flying at us, stalks rustling. The nearest one leapt. I saw Patrick's arms move, and then the boom of the shotgun thundered through the air. With a swipe of her hockey stick, Alex snapped a Chaser's head to the side. Cassius launched himself at the next Host, locking his jaws around the throat. The Host fell back, arms grabbing to pry his jaws loose.

"Into the corn!" Patrick said. "Stick together!"

Cassius lifted his dark muzzle from the Host and led the charge. We ran right over the Host's body, breath hissing through his torn throat as our boots trampled his chest.

We plunged into the field. Leaves tore at my cheeks. Ears of corn knocked against my shoulders, my chest. Stalks snapped underfoot. I kept Alex's back in sight, but it was hard, the view chaotic and jumbled. Arms and leaves flew at us from all sides like brushes at a car wash. The panting breaths and flashes of limbs all around made the very field seem alive.

A face and shoulder shot into sight, knocking Alex two steps to the side. I swung a baling hook in the Host's direction, felt it penetrate flesh, jerked it free. We kept on, stumbling behind Patrick and Cassius.

The sounds grew louder, closing from behind and coming at us from both sides. I realized we were probably going to die here in the fields behind Jack Kaner's barn. Patrick bowled a Host over, the stalks bending low for an instant. Before they snapped back up, I made out a caterpillar tunnel to our right.

"This way!" I shouted. "Follow me!"

Alex and Patrick fell behind me as I bulled through lanes of corn, swiping with the baling hooks, using them like machetes. The mouth of the caterpillar tunnel came up quicker than I'd expected, and I had to duck to avoid getting clipped on the forehead by the top of the arch.

I skidded in across moist dirt, the others piling in behind me. The inside of the tunnel looked like a giant intestine, the translucent white poly tarp fluttering and lifelike. It stretched five feet tall, so a worker could walk down the middle with only a slight hunch. The trapped heat pressed into our skin.

Keeping a low profile, I crawled a ways into the tunnel, the heels of my hands mashing kale and chard into the mud. A snapping sound turned my head. I froze to watch the outlines of the corn rows through the translucent tarp. Patrick banged into me from behind. A cornstalk bent forward and tapped the outside of the poly.

I dropped flat on my stomach, my cheek pressed into a knot of cucumber vine. Rustling sounds told me that Alex and Patrick had also gone flat. I could only pray that my brother could keep Cassius quiet. Patrick started to raise the shotgun, but I looked back at him over my shoulder and put my finger to my lips.

In the place where the corn had dipped forward, a form emerged. Its shadow, backlit by the moon, fell onto the tunnel right next to me. A head with two holes through it, grotesquely stretching up the curved wall of the tarp. As the Host lumbered forward, the shadow evolved, shoulders and torso and waist, until the entire outline seemed to hover over us.

Wind whipped across the mouth of the tunnel, giving off a low wail. We waited, trying not to move, trying to not even breathe. The smell of fertilizer burned my nostrils.

More crackling came from outside, and then other shadows played over the tarp all around us. Behind me I heard Cassius growl, but Patrick hushed him quietly and he listened.

The figures shuffled by, just outside the tunnel, their shadows flickering past the half hoops of PVC piping, riding the bumps of the segments.

The last Host finally ambled away. I stayed still until I could no longer make out the crunch of his boots in the rich soil. Then I sat up. Patrick and Alex looked at me, their faces drained of blood in the ghostly light of the tarp-filtered moon.

I said, "*That* was close."

A Chaser shot through the wall on the other side, long nails tearing a dagger slit in the tarp. A tilted face, eyeless, covered by tangles of hair. She lunged forward, grabbing Alex's ankles.

Alex screamed and hacked at the skinny arms with her hockey stick, knocking them away.

The Chaser's waist hung up on the tarp as she tried to pull herself through. Her head twitched; raspy breaths leaked through her cracked lips. Patrick rolled over and yanked a rebar spike out of the ground, the segment of tarp flapping up. Then he rolled back and drove the stake through the Chaser's skull. She shuddered and went limp.

The freed segment of tarp snapped in the wind, straining the other spikes. Patrick hadn't made a noise with the shotgun, but this wasn't much better.

We ran.

Hunched over, barreling up the length of the caterpillar tunnel. The shadows reappeared, zooming in from our left. Three, then five, then eight. On the other side, there was no moon to backlight the Hosts and give us warning, but I had to imagine they were swooping in from that direction as well.

The Hosts started diving at the tarp, trying to break through. They dented the walls, which collapsed or puffed back into place. Stooped over, we sprinted through the gauntlet, heading for the barn on the far end. It was our only hope.

Patrick shouted something, and I looked back. The tunnel had been flattened behind us, but now the rear end of the tarp caught the wind. It rose, ripping segment after segment free, the destruction catching up to us. It felt like being inside a snake that was being skinned. Spikes flew, PVC pipes sprang free, and then the walls around us lifted up and away, leaving us running between Hosts on either side, fully exposed.

The tarp floated off toward the hillside, riding the wind like a magic carpet.

Some of the Hosts had run ahead, knocking free a few of the spikes from the tunnel next to us. As they turned for us, I veered between two of them and dove for the raised lip of the neighboring tunnel. I rolled inside and came up with blood dripping from my arms and chest.

Not blood. I'd smashed through a row of tomatoes.

Alex and Patrick sailed through the gap, and then we were running again, trying not to slip on the smashed tomatoes underfoot. On the left side, shadows zoomed along parallel to us, skimming across the poly. I made out Cassius's bounding form among them, snapping and barking.

The Hosts' numbers grew again, and they started pelting the poly with their bodies. This tunnel was going to give way just like the first one.

I halted and started burrowing through the far side.

"What are you doing?" Alex screamed.

"I have a plan!"

I rolled free of the tunnel's right wall and saw with relief that there were no Hosts over here. Patrick and Alex appeared through the translucent poly, yelling at me, shadows massing at their backs. "We gotta go, Chance!"

Falling to my knees, I tore up the nearest stakes. Then I scuttled along the length of the tunnel, yanking rebar stakes free as I went.

When I risked a glance up, I saw the Hosts smeared against the far wall of the tarp, all distorted faces and fingers worming through rips. We were almost out of time.

Grabbing the edge of the tarp I'd just freed, I lifted it as high as I could, feeling the wind blast across my back.

At last it caught.

The lifting wall brought me face-to-face with Alex and Patrick. They watched with stunned amazement as the tarp flopped over, the sky opening above their heads. Rebar went airborne all around me, dirt peppering my face like shrapnel. The floating tarp wrapped around the mass of Hosts, blasting them back into the corn, clearing the row.

Only Cassius, low to the ground, remained, staring at us, as befuddled as a dog can get.

The tarp lurched and bulged like a living blob.

The barn was fifty yards away.

An arm tore free of the tarp, thrust up at the moon.

Shoulder to shoulder, we sprinted for the big rolling door. My footsteps jarred the dirt, my view of the barn rocking side to side. I could hear movement behind us, getting closer. That awful quick panting at our backs.

My breath fired through my lungs. Patrick bolted out ahead, shotgun swinging at his side. He slammed into the door first, then started rolling it open. We hurtled toward him. The gap wasn't big enough for us to fit through, but there was no time to slow. Alex bladed sideways and skimmed by. I followed her lead, the door clipping my shoulder. I spilled onto the floor, somersaulting over in time to see Patrick slide inside after us. As he put his weight to the door, the gap filled with mouths and eyeholes, countless Chasers clamoring to get in.

The hefty door slammed shut, smashing a woman's frail wrist. Patrick strained against the handle to keep it closed, cords standing out in his neck. "The truck!" he shouted. "Get in the truck!"

Jack Kaner, bless him, had an extended-cab Chevy Silverado pickup with diesel V8, four-wheel drive, and dually tires. A no-screwing-around farm vehicle, parked across from the stall doors like a mirage. I ran for the driver's seat, gave a quick prayer, and reached for the ignition. The keys were there. Cassius leapt over the tailgate as he was trained, and Alex swung into the passenger side, but I was accelerating before she could get the door shut. Patrick drove himself against the barn door, but he was losing the battle, his boots skidding across fallen hay.

As we neared, he let go. The barn door flew wide with the

force of dozens of bodies, banging at the end of its tracks. Hosts tumbled over from the sudden lack of resistance. Aiming the cab at the opening, I sped past Patrick, who hooked the tailgate with his hand and swung himself into the bed like he always did when we repaired fence posts on Uncle Jim's ranch.

I plowed into the Hosts, their heads snapping against the hood. Some churned under the powerful wheels; others flew off to the sides. For a moment the tires gummed up, and I was afraid the sheer mass of them would stop us. In the band of the rearview mirror, Patrick flashed in and out of sight, hammering the butt of the shotgun down into faces, Cassius snapping and clawing right along with him.

The V8 roared, and then we shot free. I drove straight across the field, throwing back rooster tails of mud and lettuce. A Host emerged from the cornstalks, and I smacked him with the grille, sending him bumping over the windshield and then up into the night sky.

The Silverado hammered across the roadside channel and then screeched sideways onto the highway as I braked. The engine shuddered, smoke wisping up from the tires.

We'd made it.

Alex shot me a look that might have held admiration. I waited for Patrick to hop down from the bed. As he came around the driver's side, I slid over the console into the backseat, relinquishing the wheel.

He climbed in and stepped heavy on the gas, heading for the shadowy rise of Ponderosa Pass. Jack Kaner's farm faded behind us.

"Nice job, Chance," Alex said.

Patrick shot her a look of his own and kept driving.

ENTRY 20   Our excitement built as we neared the base of Ponderosa Pass. Maybe we were reaching the end of the infection zone, or maybe we had to get up and over to Stark Peak, but either way it felt good to be making progress. Deserted cars cropped up here and there on the road, spaced out far enough that we could steer around them. The highway was desolate under normal circumstances but looked even more so now. Few folks had been on the open road far from town two nights ago when the spores had blown across the plain.

The high beams gave us early warning of Hosts on the highway. We drove past a few stragglers. Twice we saw a horde up ahead, but Patrick had plenty of time to veer into a field and cut around them. A mile or so from the base of the pass, we came upon a dark gas station, the pump area littered with abandoned cars.

Patrick eased the truck in, aimed for the open road. He kept it idling and hopped out. I started to follow, but he shot me a wink and said, "I got it from here, little brother."

He headed over to check the pumps. Cassius sprang from the truck bed, keeping pace at his side. Patrick coasted between cars, his head dipping from view as he peered through windows. Then he ducked behind a minivan and didn't come back up.

Alex's fingers tightened around the door handle. Through gritted teeth she said, "*Chance.*"

I braced myself to go with her, but then Patrick's head

popped into sight again. He gave a wave and jogged over. Beside me Alex blew out a breath.

With a scraping of claws, Cassius jumped into the pickup's bed. Patrick slid into the driver's seat, locking the door behind him. "The power's out here, too. Which means the pumps won't work." He shot a nervous glance over at the dark windows of the store. "I'm sure they have a backup generator somewhere for emergencies. The problem is getting to it."

I leaned between the seats and peeked at the dial. "We have a quarter tank. Will that get us there?"

"It'll get us up but not over," Patrick said. "Last thing we need is to be stranded on the pass."

"I suppose we could coast down."

"How about getting back?"

"Hey, dummies," Alex said. She pointed to the cab of a semi truck parked off to the side of the gas station. "Ever heard of siphoning?"

Seconds later we were idling next to the semi. Alex unscrewed an air hose from a nearby pump, ripped the nozzle off, then unscrewed the gas cap on the cab and stuck one end in. She sucked the hose a few times, spit out a mouthful of diesel fuel, and sank the streaming end into the Silverado's waiting tank.

She wiped her chin on her shirt and gave a little smirk at our expressions.

A few minutes later, we were back on the road with a full tank.

The country thickened up with brush, then trees, and soon the mountains resolved from the darkness. Leaning between Alex and Patrick, I marveled at the green peaks, granite showing through like old castles or giant's teeth. The pass had never looked so beautiful before.

Soon we'd be in Stark Peak, where Patrick would be safe.

We'd find police stations and scientific experts and put matters where they belonged—back in the hands of grown-ups.

We barreled toward the mountains, our headlights boring through the darkness, when all of a sudden a jumbled rise of green and brown appeared where none should be.

Patrick stomped on the brakes. The seat-belt strap cut into my lap, and my arms braced against the headrests for the collision. As the locked tires screeched, trying to halt the two-and-a-half-ton Silverado, I caught streaked glimpses of the view ahead. A pile of fallen trees barricaded the road haphazardly, rising twenty or thirty feet. One of the biggest trees had smashed across the rear of an old-fashioned station wagon. A Host tilted through the shattered windshield, his face raised so our headlights shone right through his sightless eyes.

We were going to smash right into him.

The Silverado skidded, skidded, and finally stopped, the grille almost kissing the hood of the station wagon.

For a moment we sat there, staring at the Host as he stared back at us, the smoke from our brake pads and tires drifting past us, joining the streamers of fog.

We lifted our eyes to the cause of the landslide. Farther up the pass, an eighteen-wheeler had careened off the road, smashing into a shelf of trees. The last falling pine had caught the station wagon, trapping the driver even as he transformed.

There would be no getting our Silverado through the barricade. We'd have to progress on foot, which put Stark Peak farther away.

Right now we had a bigger problem, underscored by the rasp of the Host's hands as he tried to pull himself through the mouth of the shattered windshield. He'd snapped off most of his nails, lifting them right out of the beds. Judging by the bloody scratches in the hood, he'd been trying to claw free for a while. The steering wheel had broken from the impact, one curved edge gouging him between the ribs, holding him in place. But it looked like he might tear himself free soon.

The headrest behind the Host and the passenger seat hung in tatters. He'd also tried to pull himself toward the back of the station wagon. Why?

We climbed down and fanned out around the car. Cassius started to bark, backing up and stomping the ground like a bull. I hushed him.

"What do we do?" I asked.

Patrick hopped onto the hood of the station wagon. The Host's focus shifted, his bloody hands grasping for Patrick's ankle. Setting his boot on the nape of the Host's neck, Patrick pinned the twitching face against the metal. Then he drew the butt of the shotgun back over his shoulder and hammered it down, pulverizing the Host's head.

Patrick jumped down. "We're on foot from here," he said. "At least until we find another car on the far side of the barricade."

"I'll pull the truck off the highway," Alex said. "Stash it for our drive home."

She held up her hand, and Patrick hit it with the keys.

A thin voice called out from behind us. "Wait! Don't leave me!"

I whirled around, catching movement in the station wagon's backseat. A hand held up, the palm facing us. Another palm rose barely into view and then a boy's face, squinting into the glare of our headlights.

"Please help me out," he said. "And hurry. There are tons of them around here."

"How long have you been trapped in there?" Patrick asked.

"I lost track," the boy said. "My seat belt got pinned in the crash. And then my dad, he just *changed*. He . . . he could almost get me."

To keep out of reach, the kid must've stayed balled up on the seat, cramming himself down into the footwell as much as his seat belt would allow.

My eyes moved past the body to the tattered headrest and passenger seat. What had it been like for him hiding here, mere feet from a Host bent on destroying him? A Host who was also his dad?

"I'll get you out of there," Patrick said.

He nodded at Alex, who jogged back to the truck behind us. As I watched her go, a blocky form glinted in the darkness a good ways from the side of the road. A commuter bus lay on its side, half sunk in the marshy reeds. Decaled on the back, the giant logo from the Lawrenceville Cannery. Lawrenceville was little more than a cluster of lean-to houses around the factory perched on the highest shoulder of Ponderosa Pass, so they bused in most of their work staff from the valley. The windows were tinted. There was no telling who was inside.

Patrick said, "Go check out that bus, Chance."

Thumbing up a folding knife, he leaned into the windshield past the dead Host and started sawing off the kid's seat belt. The rear of the station wagon looked caved in and claustrophobic, but the kid seemed to be uninjured.

Alex pulled the Silverado around onto the reeds in front of the rocky brink of the pass. When the headlights swept the bus, the dark windows reflected back the glare, giving up nothing. My boots sank into the reeds as I walked over. Using the tires for holds, I climbed up onto the side of the bus and crouched for a moment, my baling hooks ready. Below, Cassius took up a guard posture, aiming his snout at the darkness.

Toward the front of the bus, the door lay open, pointing at the stars. My breath hitched in my chest. I clicked on my flashlight and shone it between my feet through the windows. This close, the beam penetrated the tinted glass, giving a murky view of the interior. Bags and purses lay jumbled against the far windows at the bottom, their contents strewn all over the place. Slowly, I walked across the panes, shining my light on the shattered glass and the trash below. A wallet. A baseball cap. A few coolers knocked open. Shoes and lipstick tubes. There'd been a lot of workers in there when the driver had transformed, tipping it over.

Which meant that now there were a lot of workers out here.

One of the windows fissured beneath my weight. I jumped to the next. That one spiderwebbed as well, so I hopscotched onto the metal beside the panes. I continued along, my flashlight stabbing across the empty rows of seats.

Finally I reached the end and slid off the bus. Alex joined me and Cassius as we headed back. Patrick was still leaning through the windshield of the station wagon, working on the kid's belt.

The kid's breaths came as panicked wheezes.

"What's your name?" Patrick asked, using that voice he reserved for calming down sheep tangled in barbed wire.

The boy's lips trembled. "Nick."

With a snap the belt fell away. Patrick grabbed Nick's hands and pulled him out carefully through the windshield. As he slid past the corpse of his father, the boy squeezed his eyes shut.

"It's okay," Patrick said. "Don't look. I'll tell you when you're clear. Just keep talking to me."

"Okay. Okay." Nick's side rubbed against his father's body, the stiff hand trailing along his back. He stifled a cry.

"Hey," Patrick said. "Hey. How old are you?"

"I'm thirteen," Nick said, barely managing his words. "A freshman at Stark Peak High."

"A Monarch?" Patrick said. "Monarchs suck."

A tension breaker about the old rivalry.

Nick made a nervous laugh without smiling.

Patrick slid him down the hood. "You're clear now."

Nick opened his eyes and swung around, landing on the ground. A small kid for his age, with thoughtful eyes. He wore a hoodie up over his head, the sleeves too long for his arms. The back of the hoodie sported an image of an old king with a scepter and crown, a cartoon take on his school mascot.

As Alex jogged back over to us, Nick stomped his feet against the cold. "We have to go," he said. "Now."

"The Hosts," I said.

It took him a moment to catch up to the name I used for them. "That's right," he said. "There are *hordes* of them roaming around here. It's like they're guarding the pass. We should—"

The faintest crackling sounds came from the edge of the forest beside the barricade. Twigs snapping. Feet squelching into mud. The cracking of joints.

We stood like a phalanx, breath cold in our lungs, watching. Cassius didn't growl, but his upper lip wrinkled back from his teeth, showing his fangs.

The darkness took shape slowly, resolving into human forms. In the lead a woman wearing a tattered skirt crouched low to the ground. Her hair was still thick enough to cover the holes in the back of her head, so her eyes looked like black coasters.

The others gathered around her, a wall of not-humanity. More Hosts than we'd yet seen assembled in one place, all of them wearing uniforms from the cannery.

They charged.

ENTRY 21   "Over the barricade!" Patrick roared.

Our boots hammered on the hood, over Nick's dead father, across the roof of the station wagon. One by one, we leapt onto the deadfall of pines, grabbing at branches, needles poking our hands. Cassius bounded up and over effortlessly. Nick slipped on the top of the car, and Patrick went back for him, grabbing his shirt collar and tugging him to his feet.

A skeletal claw closed over Nick's sneaker, stripping it off as Patrick ripped him free. The shoe moved back across the throng, hand over hand, held high like some kind of relic. The sea of Hosts pooled at the base of the barricade. In the darkness I couldn't see where they ended.

Nick's sock dangled from the end of his foot. He stared at it in disbelief before Patrick hurled him around onto the stacked tree trunks of the barricade.

"Move it!" Alex screamed down.

I was high on the barricade, straddling the top log, my palms sticky with sap. On the far side, the open road of the pass waited, rising up, clear of Hosts and obstacles.

Patrick scrambled up the face of the logs, side by side with Nick, one arm around the younger boy's waist, practically carrying him.

The Hosts surged over the station wagon, flaring up the jumble of trees like a flame. Fingernails scraped at Nick's feet. Turning, Patrick pistoned a leg down into the face of the Chaser with the tattered skirt.

She plummeted, taking out several Hosts beneath her, but where they'd fallen, six more surged in their place, scrabbling up the trunks like spiders. Nick awkwardly climbed the fallen trees, his bare foot slipping on the wet bark. He nearly fell, but I lunged down and caught his arm.

Behind me Cassius barked and barked, and for once no one hushed him.

As I hauled Nick up, the log rolled between my legs. Patrick kicked and thrashed, freeing his legs from the upthrust hands. A big male Host seized my brother by the calf and started to drag him down.

Gritting his teeth, Patrick swung around, one-arming the shotgun and firing down into the Host's face. I could see blood on his foot. The choke was set wide, and some pellets must have peppered through his boot. The guy rocketed down, taking a dozen other Hosts with him.

It wouldn't be enough. More scaled the wall all around us. Alex swung her hockey stick, knocking a few back, but they kept on, scaling and lunging. It was like an old-fashioned battle from that movie, orcs trying to storm the castle wall.

Patrick shot up toward us, leaping like a rock climber scaling a cliff face.

I stood, the log wobbling beneath me. Unstable. "Step back!" I shouted at Alex.

She hopped away, sinking into a bramble between logs on the back side. Patrick flew up the wall at me, throwing his shotgun before him. It sailed over my head and landed somewhere behind me.

Below, the barricade creaked with the weight of countless bodies. Another few seconds and they'd swarm him. I leaned over the top of the log, praying it would hold, and lowered my hands, screaming, "Jump!"

Patrick bent to leap. For an awful moment, I thought he

was too far below, that it wouldn't be enough, that our finger-tips would brush and he'd fall away into the living mass. Then I remembered the baling hooks that had been dangling from my wrists all this time.

As Patrick leapt, I shoved the hooks down at him, adding about a foot to my reach.

His hands rose to the metal curves, and I clamped down on the handles with everything I had. My chest and stomach ground painfully on the top log. My shoulders popped under Patrick's weight, the ligaments screaming. I dragged him up and over. He tumbled down the back side of the barricade before grabbing hold of a bough heavy with pine needles.

The clamor of hands and feet pounded the barricade below us.

Next to me Nick stared down, his muscles locked up from terror.

"Nick!" I yelled. "Move!"

He pivoted to vault over the top log.

His bare foot slipped on the wet bark.

His arms rose up into the air to grab something that wasn't there, and for a split second he floated right beside me, facing over the barricade at Patrick and Alex, his legs cycling.

Then he dropped.

I grabbed his hood as he fell, but the hands below caught him. There was an instant of resistance. Then they tore him away, screaming, down the canted face of the barricade.

His hoodie still swayed from my fist; they'd ripped him right out of it.

With shocking speed they moved him overhead toward the back of the throng. He was whisked away like a rock star surf-ing a crowd at a concert. His wild eyes found me for an in-stant. Then a gnarled hand gripped his chin and spun him around. Countless hands carried him across the swell until he faded into the darkness.

My throat had closed; I couldn't even yell after him.

The Hosts resumed their upward race, clawing their way to the top of the barricade. Several had reached the apex, arms bent over the highest log, faces rising into view.

I stepped back, dug my heels into the branches behind me, and drove my chest into the wobbling topmost tree. It rocked once on its makeshift bed, aided by the Hosts tugging from the other side, then rolled back at me. When it rocked forward again, I hurled myself into it with all my might. It rose up, up, reaching a tipping point. And then it went.

The tree hammered down the front of the barricade, smashing Hosts, bulldozing everything in its way. It picked up speed, catching one Chaser square in the thighs and launching her so far that she smashed into the overturned bus. Once the tree hit level ground, it slowed until it rolled off the highway into a ditch.

I didn't have time to be impressed with the damage. A number of Hosts still remained down below, picking themselves up, regrouping. I stared hard through the darkness, but there was no sign of Nick. He'd been carried off already. Some of the injured Hosts staggered toward the barricade again. A woman with a caved-in cheek and a missing lower jaw. A man with his collarbone spiking through his uniform shirt.

We couldn't wait around.

When I turned, I saw Patrick and Alex looking up at me. I was still holding Nick's Stark Peak Monarchs hoodie. I reached over the top of the barricade and let it go. It fluttered down out of sight.

Then I started hopping down the back side of the barricade. At the bottom we circled up. Cassius stuck his wet nose in my palm, and I stroked his soft head.

"I should've left him to hide in the car," Patrick said, and walked away.

Alex shot me a frustrated look and then followed. The road up was empty. No abandoned cars we could take. We made the choice to stick to the woods beside the pass, hiding under cover as we started up. Sure enough, the few Hosts we saw came stumbling down the middle of the road. They were smart to do so; the terrain was brutal. We went from mud to boulders to brambles to granite faces that we had to help one another scale. Treetops blotted out the moonlight, making the climb even harder.

Through the trees we kept an eye on the road for vehicles but spotted nothing except a Subaru upended in a roadside gully. We hiked until I felt like my hamstrings might snap, until my hands were raw and my calves on fire. At last we broke free of the pines, standing in an open patch near the top of the pass. Looking back across the valley, we saw only darkness. Crisp air usually meant that from high on the pass we could spot the flare of lights marking Creek's Cause, but not today. Not anymore.

We topped a cracked hump of stone, pulled ourselves to level ground, and lay panting on the cold dirt. Above us rose a solemn ring of Douglas firs. A stone's throw away, the highway forked into two dirt roads, one winding up to dead-end at Law-renceville, the other rising to a plateau on the north before starting its corkscrew descent into Stark Peak. At either side crevices fell away treacherously, sheer drops without bottom.

"Let's rest here a bit," Patrick said.

I about collapsed with relief. He and Alex started clearing pine needles to make a space to lie down. Taking the hint, I got Cassius, moved a brief ways off toward the road, and cleared my own makeshift camp.

Patrick with Alex.

Me with my dog.

I sat down, my muscles complaining, my lower back stiffening. It had been a grueling climb. I stared at the stars and breathed the air, as clean up here as it was anywhere on earth. Was it free of spores? This far away from Creek's Cause, it *had* to be.

Cassius lay against me, the ridge on his back pressed to my side. As I scratched behind his ears, I noticed that he'd grown into some of the extra folds of fur. The shape of his face had changed, too, losing some of its puppy softness. Sometime over the past few days, he'd become a young dog.

I supposed whether we liked it or not, we were all growing up.

I took out my notebook and leaned against my backpack. Resting my flashlight on the ledge of my shoulder threw enough of a glow for me to write by.

From across the clearing, I could hear murmured voices.

". . . have to send help back for the others," Patrick was saying.

I had to strain to hear them.

"We will," Alex said. "But we don't have to worry about your birthday anymore. About your turning into one of *them* next week. We can let adults worry about fixing everything. That's supposed to be their job anyways."

"Then what?" Patrick asked.

"Then we can do whatever we want."

I felt a gnawing at my stomach. It took a moment for me to recognize it for what it was. Loneliness.

Patrick and Alex were going to move off into a new life together, and I was going to be left behind.

I pictured those windshield pebbles spilling from Mom's purse, red like rubies. How they'd bounced on the floorboards at my feet. How alone I'd felt downstairs with the purse and my dad's cracked watch. How the smell of lilac had flowered all around, taunting me. The darkest despair I'd ever felt until Patrick had found me. *I got it from here, little brother.* He'd held me tight, so I knew that even if the world had come apart, he'd be there.

Would he be there now?

Falling asleep felt like an escape.

———

A hand clamped over my mouth.

My eyes flew open. Dead of night. Skeletal branches over-head.

I bucked, but the grip was too strong. Cassius lay at my side, not growling but watching silently. I put it together an instant before the whisper came in my ear.

"Quiet. It's me." Patrick reached past my head where the flashlight had rolled when I'd dozed off. His hand pulsed around it, the thin beam vanishing.

I'd tensed from my heels to my face, but I forced myself to relax and melt into the ground. Then I heard it.

Wails and cries.

Tires crackling over the dirt road.

Very slowly, I turned my head. We were mostly hidden by a net of leaves, but through the gaps we watched a procession of flatbed trucks roll by.

Each loaded high with cages.

Each cage filled with a kid.

The sounds were the worst part. Hacking and gagging and rent-open sobbing.

They looked like chicken trucks brimming with hens stuffed into little cubes. Except hens didn't have fingers that clutched the bars. They didn't plead and sob. They didn't thrash violently, making the metal jangle.

The trucks kept on, the tires less than ten yards from where Patrick and I lay flat in the dirt, protected only by the mesh of branches. To avoid the barricade, they must've backtracked, then circled all the way around to Bristol, a six-hour detour through several towns in the low valley—too dangerous an option for us. Then they must've refilled their tanks somehow and driven up the southern shoulder.

Now we watched the trucks veer up toward Lawrenceville at the top of the pass. The turn was abrupt, the tread throwing up pebbles.

A cage slid free of the straps and plummeted down the sheer rock face, a girl's scream growing fainter and fainter. The cage pinged once off the stone and vanished into the abyss. The other cages on the top level shifted around, a few more sliding off, bouncing against the lip, and plummeting into space.

I can't describe the sounds those kids made as they fell.

Though I didn't dare look over at Alex, I could hear her muffled sobs.

Finally the procession ended. As the last truck chugged upslope, I caught a glimpse of the crates in the very back. Crammed into a battery cage, Nick stared out at the kicked-up dust on the road, his face blank, his eyes as black and lifeless as those of a Host.

That last truck rumbled off into the darkness. We stayed perfectly still until the final vibration of the engine faded from the air. Then we dragged ourselves out of the clearing, raw from what we'd witnessed.

"They just kept going," Alex said. "Those kids fell off . . . into the . . . and they just kept driving."

Patrick put his arms around her.

"We gotta move," I said.

On stiff legs I headed north, toward Stark Peak.

After a moment their footsteps pattered behind me. The incline steepened, my thigh muscles aching. I bent into the rise, cutting through a stand of pines to get us out of plain sight. Cassius trotted at my side.

"Good boy," I said. "Good, good boy." He grinned up at me, unconcerned. Taking his kid for a walk.

Crossing my arms in front of my face, I forged through pine needles. Something hard came underfoot, and I opened my eyes just in time to find myself on the brink of a granite ledge, staring at a drop that seemed to fall forever.

I halted sharply, the tips of my boots tapping a few pebbles that floated down and down. "Guys, wait—"

But Patrick collided with me from behind. My head and torso rocked over the edge, my boots holding on the lip, my arms pinwheeling through empty air as I tried to keep my balance.

Patrick's hand shot out, steady as ever, and locked down my wrist. I was tilted over the edge, nothing around or beneath me. We stayed like that for a moment, too scared to move. Exhaling slowly, Patrick reeled me in over my boots. I took a few steps away from the edge, joining Alex back near the tree line. Then, finally, I let my muscles unclench.

She pointed past me. "Look."

I turned. Spread way down below like a scattering of jewels were the lights of Stark Peak. Streetlamps and windows and the giant spire atop city hall, glowing orange and yellow for the coming fall festival. Life in ordinary motion.

I'd never seen such a welcoming sight.

A different weather system, like Alex had said, devoid of spores.

"We did it." Alex smiled. "We *did* it. We'll find a car on the way down. And even if we don't, we'll make it on foot in what—four, five hours?"

"Less," Patrick said.

"We can send them to save the kids at Lawrenceville. And to our school. They can finally start putting the world back together."

We came together in a victory huddle of sorts, arms around shoulders, a tiny hard-won celebration.

A boom rent the air, loud enough to vibrate my ribs. Pinecones dropped from the branches all around us, plopping on the ground. Cassius yelped and shot in reverse into the forest.

The granite ledge spiderwebbed. We leapt back as it went to pieces and crumbled away.

Another boom sounded. Then another. So loud I hunched and covered my ears.

"Oh, no," Alex said. "Oh, God, no."

I looked at her, but her gaze was elsewhere, fixed on the sky. Patrick's was, too.

Rising slowly, I drew shoulder to shoulder with them.

Hundreds of asteroids streaked through the night air, rocketing for Earth. Alight with flames, they slanted toward Stark Peak, Lakewood, Springfield—more cities than I could name, more than I could even *see*. Too many to count, they filled the sky.

The asteroid over Creek's Cause wasn't the problem.

It was the prelude.

ENTRY 22   It wasn't the grueling hike down that wrecked us, nor the half-day wait at the base of the pass for nightfall. It wasn't the two hours we spent huddled behind the barricade for the horde to disperse so we could boost the Silverado, nor the long, silent drive across the valley. It wasn't even the jarring off-road route we were forced to take as we neared Creek's Cause, having to dodge the town that once belonged to us.

It was the weight of despair.

We hadn't failed just in our mission; we were coming back to a far more chilling reality. It wasn't just Creek's Cause that was compromised—or the valley itself.

It was the whole state. Or even the continent.

And Patrick turned eighteen in four days.

After leaving the truck in the woods outside town, we circled the school and came in from the barren plain to the west, sneaking to the left-field fence of the baseball diamond. Patrick had switched the locks on the bullpen gate himself, and so after a few twists of the combination dial we drifted onto the outfield grass and crept toward the school just as dawn started to lift the cover of night.

Finally we came up on the back door near Dr. Chatterjee's biology room. Before Patrick could give a tap with his knuckles, it swung open.

Ben Braaten's wide, broken face peered out at us, chewing a Slim Jim, a lookout canteen looped around his neck.

He took our measure, then stepped back to let us in. "All hail the rescuing army," he said.

———

We entered the dark gym, worn out and exhausted. Some kids were sleeping, but there was a surprising amount of activity. JoJo and Rocky tossed the Frisbee, the fluorescent green disk zipping back and forth. JoJo had set Bunny on the bottom bleacher so that those half-marble stuffed-animal eyes could watch them play. JoJo spotted us first, gave a shout of delight, and ran over, wrapping her arms around me. Her sweeping brown hair had been cut short, sticking out at jagged angles. I guess the two-minute showers had made it too hard to manage. It looked terrible and adorable at the same time.

We walked over to the storage room to turn in our supplies and weapons. Eve had fallen asleep at her desk, her cheek resting on her arms. I shook her gently.

She lifted her sleepy head. At the sight of me, a smile seemed to catch her by surprise. "Chance. I wasn't sure you were coming back."

"Uh, *we're* here, too," Alex said with a knowing grin.

"Right." Eve looked embarrassed as she took our stuff. "Glad you're okay."

Most of the others had noticed us by now, the kids on the cots rousing as news of our return rippled through the gym. Over on the bleachers, Dr. Chatterjee was frowning down at the carbon monoxide detector. He looked up and threw a salute in our direction.

"What happened?" he asked, the others quieting down at his voice.

"You guys really don't know?" Patrick said. "You didn't hear?"

"Hear what?" Ben asked.

"The booms in the sky?" Alex said.

A hundred blank faces looked back at us.

Then Marina Mendez bolted upright. "The explosions we heard," she said, prodding her twin sister.

"Yeah," Maria added. "We thought the Hosts were blowing up gas lines in town or something."

Dr. Chatterjee found his feet and stood shakily, his face blanched with concern. "What were they?"

"Asteroids," Alex said. "There were more of them."

"How many more?" Chet asked.

Alex walked to the bleachers, slid out the TV, set it on one of the benches, and turned it on. The kids swept around onto the gym floor as if drawn magnetically.

A panicked newscaster clutched her papers in her sweaty fists.

"—meteorites scattering the eastern seaboard—"

Alex turned the old-fashioned dial, clicking through the channels, every fresh bit of news as unsettling as the last.

"—confirmed reports of strange stalks sprouting up—"

"—pods splitting open—"

"—afflictions from Los Angeles to Seattle—"

The images were even worse.

Times Square, empty except for trash blowing around and a few Mappers walking their spirals.

A woman with a swollen belly pulling herself atop the hovering disk of Seattle's Space Needle, lying like Snoopy on his doghouse, and bursting, scattering spores far and wide.

Two men harnessing themselves with climbing gear to the main towers of the Golden Gate bridge, leaning back into the great wide-open, and exploding.

And the small towns, too. Gym-ready housewives on church steeples. Accountants in suits scaling transmission towers. Streets filling with Hosts. Screaming children, fleeing and bloody, like something from the Vietnam documentaries Mrs. Olsen used to show in history class. Everything narrated by the panicked voices of reporters until the cameras, too, shuddered and fell, lenses cracking, screens turned to snowy white. As the broadcasts went down, Alex bit her lower lip and kept clicking through the remaining channels, chasing the thread of civilization. We watched in shock, glued to the images.

Dr. Chatterjee paced, rubbing his head. "After the meteorites hit the soil, the stalks took a *week* to grow in McCafferty's field before they burst and infected him."

At the mention of her father, JoJo stiffened. Rocky took her by the shoulder and said, "C'mon. You don't need to see all this. Let's play catch."

Chatterjee removed his glasses and polished them on his sleeve, though at this point his shirt looked dirtier than the lenses. "It's happening so much faster now. The process is accelerated. Why?"

My throat felt scratchy, the words coming out hoarse. "They found what they're looking for," I said. "Here at Creek's Cause. We were a test case, maybe. For all we know, there were a thousand test cases on a thousand planets. But this one worked. And now they don't want to waste any more time."

"Doing what?" Chatterjee said.

"Taking over."

"You're talking about *aliens*?" Ben said. "You think they sent asteroids from outer space?"

"As opposed to asteroids from Wichita?" Alex said.

"I'm afraid Chance could be right," Dr. Chatterjee said. "With the deliberate mapping, the directed actions of the Chasers, that squirming eye peering out of Ezekiel . . ." At this he shuddered. "It seems that they're seeding Earth." He placed his smudged eyeglasses back on his face. "Preparing it."

He returned his solemn gaze to the television. As the rest of us stayed there, mired to the gym floor, the younger kids tossed the Frisbee around, wiping tears from their cheeks in between catches.

A bad throw bumped off Ben's back, and he turned sharply. "*Stop* that," he said. "We're trying to watch the invasion."

"Come on, Ben," Patrick said. "Let them play if it distracts them."

Ben didn't reply. He kept his gaze on the television. After a cautious pause, the young kids resumed their throwing.

The rest of us couldn't *not* watch the images on-screen. Throughout the day and evening, destruction swept across the globe.

Chasers ravaging the beaches of Melbourne, rolling young kids in their own beach towels and spiriting them away.

People shuddering on the floor of the Tokyo stock exchange, ash drifting from the spaces where their eyes used to be.

Factory workers buckling themselves to construction cranes thrusting out from half-built skyrises in Shanghai.

Mappers pacing through Red Square.

Sheikhs and their wives lying on the roofs of luxury high-rises in Kuala Lumpur as if suntanning, their ripe bellies exploding beneath the Southeast Asian sun.

A shoeless investment banker scaling the Tower of London.

Chasers storming the Louvre, hijacking a field trip of uniformed schoolchildren.

A man with a huge gut roping himself to one arm of the giant Christ statue in Rio de Janeiro.

The world was a very big place. We were finally getting to see all of it.

Just after nightfall we were down to the last channel.

Live footage showed Chasers wading into a grand fountain in Caracas, yanking children out from where they hid beneath the arcing water. The camera toppled over, giving a tilted view of the atrocities.

Then it went to static.

Alex clicked the dial frantically around and around, but there was nothing left to see. We had lost the outside world. Everything we knew had shrunk to within the four walls of the gym.

Alex sank to the floor and pressed her fists to her chin. The static kept on, a white-noise roar. Ben clomped up the bleachers and settled on the top bench, staring through the open windows at the darkness beyond.

Patrick moved to Alex, rested a hand on her head. "Alexandra," he said.

She didn't respond. He reached over and turned off the TV. The sudden silence felt even scarier than what we'd just seen.

The only remaining sound was the whoosh of the Frisbee as the young kids tossed it around. JoJo's throw went wide, drifting up to Ben. He caught it and said, *"Enough."* Then he flung the Frisbee through the open window.

JoJo cried out and scampered up the bleachers. She rested her hands on the sill and watched, then crumpled to the top bench. "It went over the fence," she said. A few wisps of hair that the scissors had missed fell down past her eyes. "You threw it over the fence."

"This ain't no time for kid games," Ben said. "We got bigger concerns right now."

Dr. Chatterjee rose, facing up at Ben. "What does that accomplish? It's cruel, yes, with the added advantage of being foolish. The younger kids are quiet when they play."

"The time for playing is over," Ben said. "We should be training these kids to kill Hosts."

"That is not what we're going to do."

"And why not? You can't defend us. Not as a cripple. Who's

to say I don't just take over and run things the way they need to be run? That's the problem with your vote earlier. You *say* you're the leader. But you got no way to enforce it."

"*I'll* enforce it," Patrick said.

Ben looked over at him and gave a thoughtful nod. "For four more days, maybe."

"Ben," Chatterjee said. "Come down here right now."

Ben looked at him. Then folded his arms. "Or what?" he asked.

Chatterjee had no reply.

"That's the problem," Ben said. "You can't enforce anything. You have no authority. There's a new order we have to recognize, Dr. Chatterjee. The old rules don't apply. If I decide not to play along, who's gonna do anything about it?"

A tense silence settled over the gym.

Alex stood first.

Then I did, too. Eve was next.

Others starting rising, one after another, until about two-thirds of the kids were on their feet. The rest sat glaring up at us, making clear they were Ben's allies.

"Okay." Ben gave a nod and started down from the bleachers. He stared at those of us standing against him. "But you should realize, guys. It's only a matter of time." His footsteps padded across the court, and then he took up his usual post by the double doors.

JoJo was still crying, so I climbed up to her. "Don't worry," I said. "I'll get it back for you."

"When?"

I peered past her through the window. Her Frisbee stood out, a fluorescent green dot in the middle of the street across from the school's front lawn. In the driveway just beyond, a Chaser crouched on her haunches atop a Volvo, facing away.

"Later," I answered.

From below, Alex said, "What are the readings?"

It took a moment for Dr. Chatterjee to catch her meaning, and then he raised the carbon monoxide detector to the dim light. He shook his head. "It's gotten worse. There are more of the unknown particulates in the air than before."

I looked over at Patrick and saw him swallow. Alex reached across and gripped his hand.

Chatterjee said, "I'd hoped that there would be a period where the air was fertile—infected, that is—and then it would pass. But no. It seems that the air composition itself has been altered."

"Maybe it's permanent," Rocky piped up from the back. "Like when a supervolcano erupts and changes the air for like a million years."

"One great Dusting," Chatterjee said.

A strangled sound rose out of the bleachers. "I'm dead, then." Chet lowered himself to one of the benches and let his face droop into his hands. His voice came out muffled through his fingers. "I'm dead." His shoulders shook, but aside from a few wet gasps he was silent.

No one knew what to say.

Ben finally spoke up. "You're right. We gotta call it like it is. Come tomorrow, it's over for you."

"Do you remember what time you were born?" Dezi Siegler asked.

Chet lifted his face, smeared with tears. "A minute after noon. Since I was so . . . big, the delivery took a long time. My mom used to joke that my birth was a high-noon showdown."

"So you have till midday tomorrow," Ben said. "Then I'll put you down. I'm sorry, Chet, but it's gotta be done."

Chet looked around from kid to kid, appealing for some kind of help, but there was none to give. I'd never felt so helpless in my life. And that wasn't even the worst part. Scratching at the back of my skull was an even more terrifying thought: *Four more days till we'll have to do the same to Patrick.*

Dr. Chatterjee made his unsteady way to Chet and sat beside him. Chet tilted into him, sobbing into his shoulder. "I'm sorry, son," Chatterjee said. "I'm sorry I can't protect you. If there was any way it could be me instead of you, I would make that trade."

Chet cried for a long time. When he started to wheeze, Dr. Chatterjee told him to slow his breathing down, to take deep, measured inhales. Finally Chet looked up.

"Is there anything you want?" Patrick said. "For tonight? Tomorrow morning?"

"Like a last meal?" Chet's laugh turned into a stifled sob. "No. I think I just want to look at the view, maybe. Breathe some fresh air."

Patrick nodded. "How 'bout the roof? You could go up there."

Chet rose and made his way down the bleachers, pausing on his sturdy legs. "Will you come with me, Patrick?"

"Of course I will."

As they headed out, Ben called after them, "Careful you don't get spotted."

Patrick and Chet were gone for a long time. The two oldest kids in our party. The two closest to death. I don't know what they did, but I imagined Chet sitting up there staring at Ponderosa Pass in the distance, trying not to count the ticking seconds. Our air was crisp, the view clear, and I hoped every breath was a reminder of the good things his life had held.

They came back in for dinner, and all the kids went out of their way to be extra nice to Chet, offering him their dessert, making sure he had the most comfortable cot, the best pillows.

But even after night fell, he didn't sleep.

If I had only a few hours to live, I wouldn't be able to sleep either.

He sat on his cot, rocking, his arms wrapped around himself.

Everyone tried not to look at him, but he was the center of attention—even the air seemed to pull toward him there in the middle of the cots.

I lay in my own bed scribbling in my notebook, doing my best not to stare. But I couldn't help shooting looks over at him now and then.

Morning passed in a crawl. Now kids kept their distance from Chet, who moved through the breakfast line sluggishly, his face heavy with dread. He sat at a table alone in the corner of the cafeteria, chewing his food, his eyes lowered.

I picked up my tray and went to join him. We didn't speak. There was no point. Nothing could make him feel better. I just didn't want him eating his last breakfast alone.

Back at the gym, Chet sat in the bleachers, his head hanging low.

The clock crept to ten, then eleven. Finally the minute hand inched its way up toward noon.

Ben stood, tugging the stun gun from his belt. "It's time," he said.

The Mendez twins burst out crying and ran to hide behind the bleachers.

"Where do you want it done?" Ben asked. "Want me to take you somewhere private?"

"No," Chet said. "I don't want to be alone. I want to be here with all of you. If that's okay."

"Of course it's okay," Patrick said. "You get whatever you want."

Alex said, "You're surrounded by friends here."

Ben strode over and said, "I'll wait for you to start to turn. Then I'll do it. You won't feel a thing."

Chet nodded, his cheeks wobbling.

Ben raised the stun gun and pressed it to Chet's forehead. "Ready, Chet?"

Chet closed his eyes.

ENTRY 23   It felt like there was no air in the gym. We watched stiffly, our bodies tensed, waiting for the clack of the stun gun firing through Chet's skull into his brain.

Ben's fist tightened around the handle.

Chet's eyes flew open. "Wait!" he said, stepping back. "Wait. I don't want to. I can't. I don't want to be dead."

"Sorry, Chet." Ben glanced at the clock. "You're down to a few minutes. We have to do this."

"Just . . . just let me go. Please. I'll go out there."

"You want to turn into one of *them*?" Alex asked.

"What if there's a cure someday?"

"There are holes bored straight through their skulls," Ben said, stepping forward again with the stun gun. "There ain't gonna be no *cure*."

Chet held up his hands defensively.

Patrick grabbed Ben from behind. "It's his choice," Patrick said.

Ben shoved him off, whirling around.

"If he wants to turn instead of die, it's up to him." Patrick looked across at Dr. Chatterjee. "Right?"

Chatterjee nodded.

Ben's jaw shifted left, then right, redness creeping along the lines of his scar. "You got a minute and a half to get him off school grounds," he said.

Patrick took Chet's arm, and they bolted. Alex and I ran after them. We made it to the front and crouched behind a row of bushes as a Chaser flashed by in the street, sprinting after something. She vanished around the corner. For a moment the coast looked clear. We sprang out from cover, running for the gate. Patrick's hands fumbled at the combination lock.

Moans escaped Chet's mouth. "I'm scared," he said. "I'm so scared."

The chain fell away, and the gate creaked open. "I'm sorry," Patrick said. "But you have to go."

Chet took a shaky step forward, then another. He was moving too slowly, and Patrick had to give him a little push. The gate closed behind him. Patrick looped the lock through the chain.

"Wait." Chet's chest was heaving, each breath coming with a rasp. "Please can you just . . . just wait?"

Alex's eyes were wet. "I'm sorry," she said. "We have to go before you turn and see us here. We have to hide from who you're gonna be."

"I don't want to be out here alone. I don't want it to happen to me."

I couldn't make my legs move. Patrick grabbed me. "We have to go, Chance. We have to leave him."

"Wait, please," Chet said. "I'm just a kid. I'm a kid like you."

I stumbled after Patrick and Alex. We ran through the open doors, Chet's cries carrying behind us.

When we got back to the gym, a lot of the kids were crammed on top of the bleachers at the windows. They parted as we climbed up and took our place at the sill.

Twining his fingers in the chain-link, Chet looked up at us, his face lit with terror.

I pressed my palm to the window. I would've done anything for him not to feel so alone. Next to me Alex wiped her cheeks and said, "Damn it. *Damn it.*"

Chet's face suddenly went blank, as if something had washed through his features beneath the skin. His hands dropped to his sides.

Then he shuddered.

A current of emotion passed through the kids around us. Many turned from the window; some leaned closer.

Chet's eyes blackened, and then the ash blew away. We ducked further beneath the sill, barely peering over.

He turned and began walking a straight line, his head lowered to the ground. Then he turned again, walking past JoJo's Frisbee. As he continued his pattern, the kids drifted away from the casement windows, one by one, until only me, Patrick, and Alex remained.

Chet's legs carried him across a front lawn and into an alley between houses. We watched until he disappeared from view.

———

Late that night I was awakened by a wet slurping on the side of my face. I turned my head into a gust of dog breath. Wrinkling my nose, I sat up as Cassius whined.

"Okay, okay," I said. "I'll take you out."

I crept from the gym and down the dark corridor, nodding at the lookouts. Cassius hustled along with me. We veered toward the humanities wing, stepping out into the sheltered picnic area, which I'd designated as his bathroom spot. Since the wings of the building folded around the benches, it was the outside zone most hidden from the surrounding streets.

As Cassius did his business in the flower bed, I leaned against one of the trees, blinking sleepily.

That's when I sensed movement beyond.

My hands clutched instinctively at my sides, but my baling hooks were back at the supply station. I was defenseless. And yet Cassius wasn't growling.

I leaned around the trunk, Alex and Patrick coming slowly into view. She was sitting up on one of the picnic tables and he was standing, leaning into her, holding her face.

His voice carried to me. "—not sure exactly when, but Dr. Chatterjee said it was one A.M. Or a little after. He didn't deliver me, but he was there with my dad."

It took me a moment to understand that he was talking about when he'd been born.

Alex's voice came sharp and angry. "So we only have one hour of the last day. It's not a day at all."

"Hey," he said softly. He tried to tilt her chin up so she'd look at him, but she fought it, blinking back tears. "Hey," he said again.

She shook her head. "There has to be *something*. There has to be some way to . . . to . . ."

"I could stop breathing," he said, "but that probably wouldn't help me much either."

She didn't laugh. "Forty-eight hours," she said, still not meeting his eyes. "That's what we have. That's *all* we have."

Finally she let him turn her face upward. He said, "Then let's spend it the best we can."

She nodded. "Okay. You're right. I'm sorry."

They embraced.

I knew I was watching something I wasn't supposed to see, and yet I couldn't stop.

"You have to take care of Chance," he said. "He's tough, but he's still just a kid."

The words felt like a slap.

Alex nodded, rolling her lips over her teeth and biting

down, trying to fight off tears. They hugged again, squeezing each other tight.

Cassius finished, and I pulled back quietly from the flower bed and headed inside, filled with more feelings than I could make sense of.

Lying on my cot in the darkness, I realized what the worst part was.

It was that Patrick was right.

I *was* just a kid.

Sometime later my brother crept between the cots and stood over me. His face looked hard, even angry. "When I start to change, you take me out right away. Understand? I want it to be you."

"Patrick, I—"

"You don't hesitate. You do it."

"You won't change." I could hear the desperation in my voice, and I hated myself for it, hated him for being right about what he'd said out there. "You *can't* turn into one of them."

"Chance," he said. "We gotta deal with reality. Now, promise me."

I swallowed around the lump in my throat. "I promise."

———

Thirty-six hours till Patrick died.

The next two days passed like torture, the hours dragging like claws across my skin.

The food was going stale, the sheets getting dirty, and the lookouts reported regular Host activity beyond the fences. They'd mapped the surrounding streets already, sure, but they kept wandering around as if on patrol. Now and then we'd hear a scream carry to us on the wind, and we'd know they'd discovered another holdout somewhere in the neighborhood. Some poor kid dragged from a cupboard or an attic into the open and carried off in a cage.

Bits of the conversation I'd overheard by the flower beds played endlessly in my head.

You have to take care of Chance.

I could stop breathing, but that probably wouldn't help me much either.

That's all *we have.*

I tried to get some sleep but wound up tossing and turning. I looked at Patrick's back facing me from his mattress and struggled not to think of the clock ticking down. Alex was crammed next to him in the tiny cot, his arm draped over her. They were determined to spend every final minute together.

Twenty hours till he died.

I don't know if I slept at all, but I do know that when sunlight streamed through the windows, I didn't feel the least bit rested. I ate breakfast with Alex and Patrick, all of us chewing our food silently, alone with our thoughts. Only Cassius didn't know what was going on, slurping his food out of his bowl with relish.

We stayed together for Patrick's afternoon lookout shift on the bleachers but found even less to say. Alex sat one bench down from Patrick and rested her head in his lap. As he gazed out the window, he stroked her long, long hair. Cassius had scaled the bleachers with me, and I was petting his neck until I noticed the parallel and felt stupid enough to stop.

Nine hours till he died.

I cleared my throat. "They were taking the kids to Lawrenceville," I said. "Maybe we could go there. We could confront the Hosts, find some solution."

"Chance," Patrick said in that parental voice he barely ever used with me. "We won't make it in time. You know that."

"And there's no *confronting* them," Alex said. "They don't exactly show reason."

I said, "It's better than staying here and just . . . *giving up.*"

"I'm not giving up," Patrick said. "But the little time I have left I want to spend with Alex. And with you."

JoJo came up and tugged at my sleeve. "You said you'd get my Frisbee."

"There are too many Hosts out there right now."

"But you *promised.*"

My nerves were so worn that even JoJo was bothering me. "Look, I'll get it when it's safe. I'm not gonna risk my life for your dumb Frisbee."

The moment I saw her reaction, I regretted what I'd said, but she slinked off before I could apologize.

Patrick just looked at me. It was enough.

"Come on, Little Rain," Alex said.

I wheeled on her. "Stop *calling* me that."

She recoiled. I didn't realize how cutting my tone was until I saw her expression.

Even from his post by the doors, Ben overheard, his gaze tilting up. I wanted to be alone, to hide where no one could see me. I stomped down the benches and headed to the bathroom. After splashing cold water on my face, I stared down my dripping reflection in the mirror.

When I came back into the gym, I plopped down on my cot rather than be a third wheel and disrupt the lovebirds. I tried to rest, tried to calm myself, tried to stop the flood of my thoughts.

Six hours till he died.

Over by the dry-erase board, Ben set about rabble-rousing, gaining more followers. As I jotted in my notebook, his voice rolled across the gym floor. "We gotta stay alert and dig in here."

"And then what?" one kid asked.

"We don't need Chatterjee's rules. Having no adults is the only *good* part of this. Of course we stay alert, stay ready. But when we're *not* on lookout, we can do whatever we want. Eat ice cream all day, play floor hockey in the gym, practice fighting."

Finally his talk got too much for me. I threw down my notebook and stood up. "What happens when we run out of ice cream?" I said.

"We raid the supermarket and get more."

"There's no electricity there. You know, to keep ice cream cold."

"We'll get cookies."

"And when *those* run out?"

"We'll worry about that then," he said. "We're all gonna die anyways. Why not enjoy ourselves while we're here?"

"So you just want to give up also?"

"It's too big, Chance. It's everywhere. It's the *air we breathe.* You can't give up if you've already lost. Might as well enjoy the ride."

"We can't just sit around and wait for them to come get us. We have to *do* something."

"What? Fix the entire world?"

Now Ben was laughing at me, and his lackeys were, too. I looked around for Patrick and Alex, but they had left. My brother's shift had ended. Alex was on lookout next in the math-and-science wing, so off they'd gone. They'd even taken Cassius.

"You gonna do that, Little Rain?" Ben continued. "Beat all the adults in the world and an entire alien race or supervirus or whatever? You can barely go to the *bathroom* without your big brother holding your hand."

I got up and stormed out before I said something that would

get me into trouble I couldn't get out of. Eve shook her head, as annoyed by Ben as I was.

"Without big bro backing you up, you'd *better* walk away," Ben called after me. "And you'd better get used to the feeling, too."

I stopped before the double doors, fists clenched, my heart banging in my chest. Then I turned. I ran at Ben, yelling, and though Eve and Chatterjee stood up, no one could get to me in time.

Unlucky for me.

I tackled Ben from the side, knocking him down. He rolled over, swinging with his elbow and clipping my temple. I smacked into the base of the dry-erase board, and then he was on me, punching me, snapping my head against the floor. Pain flared in my eye.

Chatterjee hurried toward us. I saw his hands clamp Ben's shoulders, and then Ben whirled and shoved him. Chatterjee fell down hard, his leg braces clattering against the floorboards.

All at once everything stopped.

Ben was still on top of me, his fist drawn back, his other hand tangled in my shirt. Blood trickled from my nose, and I could feel my eye swelling. Dr. Chatterjee rolled to his side and then sat up, wearing a pained expression. His legs stuck out awkwardly before him.

Ben let go of me. "Dr. Chatterjee," he said. "I didn't . . . I'm really sorry."

He went to help Chatterjee up, but the teacher pulled away from him angrily. "I don't need your help."

Chatterjee adjusted his orthotics and pushed himself carefully onto his feet. Straightening his grimy shirt, he limped back to the bleachers.

Eve rushed up to me. "Chance, your eye—"

I ran across the gym and shoved through the double doors. I stormed through the corridors, heading for the math-and-science wing. In Mrs. Wolfgram's room, I found Patrick and Alex sitting on a raft of desks shoved together, keeping watch over the back fields. Cassius lay curled up on the floor, traitorously content.

I couldn't keep the rage from my voice. "Where *were* you?"

Patrick took one look at my face and stood up. "Who did that?"

"Ben. And he shoved Dr. Chatterjee over, and you weren't there."

Patrick went to check me, and I pushed him away, knocking off his cowboy hat.

"You weren't there. You weren't there. You weren't there." My face was hot, and then I was crying.

Patrick hugged me like he had the night Mom and Dad died. "You're gonna be all right without me."

I pulled back and wiped at my face. "No," I said. "I'm not. No one is."

I walked out. I went to my old desk in Mr. Tomasi's room and sat there and pretended that everything was like it used to be. Patrick and I would drive home from school soon and do our chores, and the dogs would be waiting for me. We'd help Uncle Jim with the cattle and Sue-Anne would have a hot dinner on the table for us, and then I'd go to sleep in the room I shared with Patrick, and we would both wake up and go to school again, and I'd sit here at this very desk and talk about books and heroes and imaginary worlds.

Sitting at my old desk, I watched the sun lower beneath the horizon. Shadows lengthened, creeping across my desk, my hands, my arms, until darkness claimed the whole room, the whole world.

Four hours till Patrick died.

I squeezed my eyes shut, because there was nothing out there that I wanted to see anyways. I knew that Patrick and Alex were combing the school looking for me, but I didn't care. In a few minutes, I'd get up and spend my brother's last hours with him. But right now I had to be with myself and get ready to say good-bye to him.

Three hours.

Now two.

One.

Still I couldn't rise. I couldn't face Patrick any more than I could face the world without him.

Again I thought of that private conversation I'd overheard between him and Alex in the picnic area.

Let's spend it the best way we can.

There has to be something.

I could stop breathing, but that probably wouldn't help me much either.

The first part stuck in my mind: *I could stop breathing.* An idea was there just beneath the surface, glittering like a half-buried jewel.

It sailed through the jumble of my thoughts, and I grabbed it. My eyes flew open.

I knew how to save Patrick.

ENTRY 24   I barreled up the empty corridor, my footsteps echoing off the lockers. Skidding on the tile, I swung onto the stairs and took them down three at a time. I shouldered into the nurse's office so hard that the door flew back and clipped my hip.

Some of the cabinets and drawers were open, most of the basic medical supplies already moved to the supply station.

But I wasn't looking for basic medical supplies.

I searched the remaining cabinets, dug through the closet. My swollen eye started throbbing, but I paid it no mind.

Twenty-three minutes.

Twenty-two.

Panic clenched my chest when I didn't see it. What if it was gone? What if it had been used up already or Chet's mother had taken it back home?

I hurled an empty cardboard box over my shoulder, and there it was, hidden in the back of the closet. When I yanked it out, it clanked against the floor.

The portable oxygen tank was heavier than I'd imagined. The mask hung from the valve, its clear tubing coiled up neatly. The meter showed full, the needle pegged at the limit in the green zone.

Chet's oxygen for his asthma attacks.

Hefting the tank, I sprinted out, slipping on the slick floor. Back upstairs, my boots pounded down the hall, my blood racing as fast as I was. The front-door lookouts raised their heads in unison, their faces pivoting as I flew by toward the gym.

I kicked through the double doors, shouting for Patrick. Kids popped up from their cots and looked over from the bleachers.

"Quiet," Ben hissed, coming off his chair.

"Where is he?"

"Out looking for you."

Of course.

"But don't worry," Ben said. "He's due back any minute. He swore it to Chatterjee. So we can handle him before he . . . you know."

I set down the tank and mask. "Keep this here. Do you understand?" My wild gaze found Eve. "Keep this right here until I get back."

She nodded.

I sprinted back out, passing the lookouts. "Patrick—have you seen—where is he?"

Dezi Siegler flicked his head toward the corridor. "He said he was gonna look for you in the picnic area."

I took off. My breath burned in my throat, but I didn't slow down. One long hallway. Another.

The door came up, and I knocked it open with the heels of my hands.

Patrick, Alex, and Cassius moved frantically through the flower beds. Patrick's head snapped up. "Chance! Where the hell did you go?"

He ran over, snatching me up and hugging me so tight I couldn't breathe. Or talk.

I shoved him off.

"You're still mad at him?" Alex said. Her red-rimmed eyes showed that she'd been crying. "You're gonna waste his last ten minutes alive being *angry* with him?"

I was still panting from all that running. "Not angry . . . No time to explain. . . . Just . . . *come*. . . ."

Patrick said, "Chance, we don't have time for—"

"I have a plan!"

Something in my face must have convinced them, because they ran back with me. Cassius galloped next to us, tongue lolling, tail wagging. He probably thought it was some kind of game.

Seven minutes.

Six.

We careened into the gym. I leaned over, hands on my knees, trying to catch my breath. I pointed at the mask. "Put it on."

Ben stood behind the tank, his burly arms swaying at his sides, the stun gun glinting in his waistband. "This'll never work. And besides—"

"Kindly shut up, Mr. Braaten," Chatterjee said.

While we were gone, Chatterjee had connected the tube to the tank.

Patrick looked at me. "Is this your idea?"

"Just do it."

"What do we do when the tank runs out?" Alex asked.

"One thing at a time," I said. "Get it on."

Four minutes.

All the kids were up now, forming a giant ring around us.

"How will I eat?" Patrick asked.

"We'll figure it out," I was practically yelling. "Just *do it*."

"If I put that mask on, I won't be able to take it off," Patrick said. "Not ever."

"That's right." I grabbed the mask from Chatterjee and shoved it into Patrick's chest.

Patrick looked from me to Chatterjee to Alex. Then he slid off his cowboy hat. Something about the gesture made him look humbled, defeated. Taking the mask, he pulled it over his head. It was transparent like the ones football players use on the sidelines. Thick straps, firm seal, a one-way valve to clear exhaled breath without allowing any outside air in.

Patrick looked trapped inside it, and I couldn't blame him.

Three minutes.

"Wait." Alex's eyes were brimming.

Patrick looked at her. Understood. Sliding the mask up onto his forehead, he pulled her in. They kissed. For the last time. Eyes closed, her hands pressed to his chest, his arm looped around the small of her back. She was on her tiptoes, face tilted up to his.

I could feel the emotion radiating off them like something physical, and I knew everyone else could, too. It might as well have been the last kiss in the history of the world.

I couldn't help but wonder what it felt like to have someone kiss you like that.

They parted. Alex took a half step back, stifling a sob.

Patrick slid the mask back into place.

Chatterjee twisted the valve open, set the dial to eight liters per minute, and said to Patrick, "Take a deep breath. And blow out."

Patrick did. Then he inhaled.

"You are now breathing only from the tank," Chatterjee said.

"Just in case," Ben said, raising the stun gun and resting it on Patrick's forehead. "For everyone else in here."

One minute.

The bag bullfrogged beneath Patrick's neck, expanding and collapsing with each breath.

The seconds counted down.

I plucked the Stetson from the floor and put it back on

Patrick's head. I couldn't stand for him not to have it on right now.

He had Alex's hand, their fingers intertwined. He reached for me with his other hand.

Fear shone from his eyes. I'd never seen him look like that.

I clasped his other hand.

We stood there bracing ourselves, Alex and me on either side of Patrick, Ben before him, that wicked steel rod pressed right between his eyes.

And everyone else watching.

Ten seconds.

Five.

It was one o'clock.

Patrick exhaled, his shoulders lowering a good two inches.

"We don't know the *exact* time," Ben said. "It's sometime after one. So let's not celebrate yet."

He lowered the gun from Patrick's head but kept it at the ready.

We stayed like that, breathing hard, for five minutes and then five more. A short time later, Chatterjee looked at his watch and said, "He was born by now. I'm sure of it. The time frame has passed."

Ben shoved the stun gun back into his jeans. "You're only putting off the inevitable," he said. "How much time'll that tank buy him anyways?"

Chatterjee crouched and checked the readings. His face changed. He rose unsteadily. Ben leaned over and read the dial.

"This only gets you five hours," he said.

"I only need five hours," I said.

For once Ben looked taken aback. "For what?" he asked.

ENTRY 25   At the edge of town square, Patrick and I bellied down beneath an ambulance, facing the hospital, watching shadows move in the first-floor windows. He wore his mask. His cowboy hat scraped against the undercarriage, so he kept his chin low to the ground. At one side lay his oxygen tank. At the other his shotgun.

Getting here had been hell.

Not because of the Hosts—we'd actually been pretty lucky in that regard. But sneaking around in the night hauling a compressed-air tank and waiting for a Chaser to flash out of every shadow had frayed our nerves to the point of snapping. We'd crept from bush to tree to alley to car, our hearts racing every time we dashed across the open. Though we'd tried to be cautious, we'd been forced to take risks to save time, all too aware that every breath Patrick drew meant one less breath in the tank.

Our lookouts at the school had noted decreased Host activity along the southern fence line by the teachers' parking lot, so we'd slipped out there. That gate also put us closest to the building itself for our return. Since we'd be lugging back as many super-heavy oxygen tanks as we could, any saved distance helped. Alex stood watch at the gate now, with Cassius at her side; when we got back, she'd signal us once the coast was clear. As strong as she was, she wouldn't be able to manage the heavy tanks as well as Patrick or I. We'd asked for volunteers, of course, but none of the bigger boys had stepped forth. They were either scared or—like Ben—unwilling to risk their necks.

I was unarmed. The amount of loading and hauling I had to do required full use of my hands, so I couldn't have my baling hooks dangling around my wrists. I felt naked without them.

Worse yet, Patrick was getting weird on me. First he joggled his head from side to side. Then he waved a hand in front of his face, wiggling his fingers.

"What?" I hissed.

"Everything's blurry," he said. "And I'm light-headed." He pushed his palm to his forehead. "My head hurts. And feels good at the same time." He offered me a goofy smile. "I think the oxygen's making me loopy."

"Great." I reached for his tank and slid it toward me. I couldn't read the dials, not in the dark, and even if I could have, I had no idea which way to adjust the oxygen concentration. That would have to wait for Chatterjee.

So I was stuck in the middle of the town square, heading into a deadly mission, with my brother acting like a drunk.

He took a few Darth Vader breaths. "Luke, I am your father."

I smacked his arm. "Pull it together."

He furrowed his brow. "Okay, okay." Then he grinned. Then he tried to be serious again.

I rolled my eyes and returned my focus to the hospital.

I had to admit, part of me was relieved to see him smile. Patrick wasn't exactly jokey to begin with, but ever since the Dusting he'd been like a pallbearer. Maybe he thought that smiling showed a lapse in discipline. Like the rest of us, he had plenty to be serious about. Right now he had even more to worry about than we did.

Before we'd left the gym, he and Alex had taken some

time together on the bleachers, trying to adjust to his new life with the mask. Everyone—me included—gave them distance as they sat together, her hands cupped in his, murmuring privately to each other. As I passed, I made out only a snatch of their conversation, Alex's whisper carrying over as she told my brother, "We will make this work." It was hard watching them try to adjust, their expressions holding so many different emotions at the same time. Barring a miracle, that mask was now a permanent part of him. My plan had saved Patrick for the moment, but at a pretty steep price.

As I'd gathered my gear and walked over to get him, I'd heard them playing their old game, her words quiet in the crowded gym.

"—cross raging rivers for me?"

His smile, locked behind the mask, looked as sad as it did happy. "I would."

Her eyes glimmered. "Would you climb mountains?"

I could barely make out his voice beneath the mask. "If they were between me and you, those mountains I would climb."

She'd blinked, and her tears had fallen. "How 'bout that mud, Big Rain? We still on for the mud?"

He nodded.

She'd put her forehead to his, their faces close, his breath fogging the mask from the inside, hers from the outside. You could see the aching in their eyes, how badly they wanted to kiss. But they couldn't.

They'd never be able to again.

I shook off the image of them on the bleachers, training my gaze back on the hospital. Hosts still milled around the ground floor. What were they doing in there? I'd assumed that they'd have to leave soon—to patrol the streets, to help in the church, to search out other kids to grab—but it struck me how little we really knew about them. Maybe they'd stay holed up there the whole night.

In which case we'd be in all kinds of trouble.

I risked a quick click of the flashlight so I could read the dial on the oxygen tank. An hour and a half of air left.

We'd gone from one countdown to another.

I alternated between watching the hospital's ground floor and the pressure gauge on the oxygen tank. The shapes kept moving inside. The dial accelerated toward empty. Soon enough, panic sweat plastered my shirt to my back. With each passing second, my fear grew. We couldn't keep waiting, and yet we couldn't make a move. I was brimming with stress, and to make matters worse, Patrick seemed as content as could be, drunk on oxygen.

Once the dial got into the red, I realized we had to make a move.

I reached over and shook him. "Patrick. *Patrick.*"

He blinked at me sleepily. "Huh?"

"We gotta do something. Now. We're down to twenty minutes. Look. No, look over here."

His wobbly gaze found the dial. "Hmm."

Then I did something I never thought I'd do. I slapped him across the face. Hard. Of course, I made sure to miss the mask and the straps.

He shook his head. "Thanks," he said. "Okay. Twenty minutes. What do you want to do?"

"Remember when Andre Swisher ran out into the square?"

He nodded.

"I need to create a diversion. Draw them out. I'll run across the lawn and loop back."

That made his expression sharpen at last. "No way. We are not risking your life to save mine."

"You got a better idea?"

He blinked hard, scrunching his eyes closed as if trying to squeeze his thoughts into place. Then he opened them. "Yeah," he said.

———

With its siren screaming and lights flashing, the ambulance bulldozed across the town square, turning a bench into a spray of tinder. The tires left muddy tracks through the grass. The ambulance smashed into the central fountain, upending in a pile of rubble, stale water sloshing across the grille.

It wailed and wailed.

For a moment nothing happened. Then a handful of Hosts flashed out of doorways around the square. Four Chasers pried open the ER doors and bolted through, their ragged shoes flying right past Patrick's and my noses.

We were hidden beneath a Buick Enclave in the front lot. We'd rigged up the ambulance, turning it on, then jamming a crutch between the gas pedal and the headrest. From outside the vehicle, I'd reached in and yanked the transmission into drive, the screeching vehicle nearly taking off my arm before I could pull it free.

As the Hosts pursued the wailing ambulance, Patrick and I rolled from cover and slipped through the ER doors. Patrick held his portable gas tank in one hand, the shotgun raised in the other.

Even in the dark, the ground floor sparkled, as spotless as ever. Gurneys and rolling privacy curtains, half-open doors and nurses' stations—a lot of hiding places to keep us on edge. We poked around the emergency room, searching the cabinets and storage areas.

No oxygen tanks.

"I don't see any," Patrick said, his voice distorted through the mask. "Where are they?"

I jogged over to the directory by the elevator, passing a big window looking out at the square. A dozen or so Hosts encircled the smashed ambulance, a pride of lions zeroing in on their wounded prey. Even from here I could make out the quick puffs of air as they breathed.

I ran my finger down the directory, stopping at RESPIRA-TORY CARE—FLOOR TWO. I felt my stomach sink.

"We have to go upstairs," I said.

"Then let's go." Patrick hoisted the tank in one hand and followed me to the wide stairs, being careful not to let the tube tug the mask away from his face. Any snag in the line could mean death.

We took each corner slowly, pausing at the landing. I risked a glance at Patrick's tank—the dial even further in the red.

He shook his head again hard, as if trying to jar something loose inside it. In the distance I could hear the siren wailing away. I wondered how long it would hold the Hosts' attention.

When we stepped out onto the second floor, it looked dark and still. Blue and red flickered in the window at the corridor's end, the ambulance's lights still flashing through the darkness. An overhead sign directed us down a corridor. Side by side, we eased past one doorway, then another.

The squeak of a wheel broke the silence.

We froze.

A crash cart rolled slowly out from one of the patient rooms. It stopped in the middle of the corridor.

We stared at it there, about ten feet away, blocking our path. Patrick's breath fogged the mask quicker and quicker, burning oxygen.

From deep in the room came the tick-tock of shoes against the floor. Then that awful shallow panting.

A Host dressed in ripped nurse's scrubs emerged calmly, her gaze forward, her head twitching. Psychiatric restraints—thick leather cuffs lined with padding—swung from her drawstring. Seemingly she hadn't heard us; she'd just bumped the cart as she'd moved around in the room. She wore clogs with slim heels that flexed her calves. From the side she looked almost normal.

When Patrick set the portable tank down, it gave the faintest clank.

Her head pivoted to face us.

I didn't recognize her. Much of the hospital staff came in from Lawrenceville or Stark Peak for two-day shifts. Fluffy blond hair floated around her defined cheekbones. In another life she might have been attractive. But the holes bored through her eyes caught the shadows, giving her face a skull-like appearance in the low light.

Patrick raised the shotgun.

"Wait," I said. "The noise'll draw the—"

She leapt at us, swatting me to the floor, one hand reaching for the restraints at her drawstring. Patrick jabbed the shotgun butt at her, putting a dent in her forehead, the swinging motion straining the plastic tubing to the breaking point. As if it were happening in slow motion, I saw the mask start to pull away from his face. He leaned forward, trying to give the tubing some slack. Then the Chaser sprang onto my chest, her knees pinning my arms to the sides. The back of my hand knocked the tank, and it toppled and started rolling on the tile. As it spun away from us, I saw the dial rotating around, the needle well into the red zone.

Patrick lunged toward the rolling tank, leading with his mask. If that tank rolled too far from his face, the tube would rip off.

I bucked violently and wrestled with the Host. She stank of sour sweat and grime. I smacked her head to the floor, but she only bounced back stronger on top of me.

Over the frayed shoulder of her scrub top, I saw Patrick on all fours, still scrambling after the tank, keeping the faintest dip in the tubing. He dove for it, but before I could see if he reached it, the nurse's hand slapped down over my eyes. Nails dug into my forearm, and I felt a restraint start to encircle my wrist.

I flailed, freeing my hand and trying to claw at her face, but her grip was too powerful. Her hand slid from my eyes and covered my mouth and nose. I tried to breathe around the reek of her sweaty palm, but my air was cut off, my vision starting to go spotty. It had just begun to haze over when I heard a clank, and her head snapped to the side, bent at an impossible angle on her neck.

She fell away, revealing Patrick behind her, mask intact, gripping the portable tank he'd just used to nearly unseat her skull from her shoulders. At my side she jerked on the floor, dots of static fizzling across her eye membranes.

Patrick took a knee, exhausted from the exertion, the oxygen intake messing with his stamina. Groaning, I turned on my side to face the tank, squinting at the dial.

Nearly on empty.

"Patrick, we gotta go." I stood, picked up his tank, and hoisted him to his feet. He grabbed his shotgun from the floor and stumbled along beside me, his arm around my shoulders.

The Respiratory Care Department turned out to be a glorified suite at the back of the second floor. Three beds, various equipment piled on carts, a hanging privacy curtain in the rear.

I scanned the suite—no tanks.

Patrick looked at me, his eyes wide above the mask. "Chance. You need to get ready." He spun the shotgun around and held it out to me.

We'd come all this way to find nothing.

But I wasn't ready to give up. A last hope flickered as I charged forward and raked aside the privacy curtain.

Behind it a dozen oxygen tanks, gloriously lined up like missiles.

Nearly three times as large as Patrick's portable tank, they were labeled "H," marked as containing 6,900 liters of oxygen. Each one would buy him a day and a half.

I went weak with relief.

Grabbing his arm, I jerked him around the bed and through the curtain. Lifting his tank, I checked the dial. The needle was practically touching the "empty" peg.

"Take a breath," I said. "A deep, deep breath. And hold it."

"Chance." He reached behind himself and leaned weakly on the bed. "I can't think so straight."

"Then listen to me. Take a deep breath now. Just *listen to me*, Patrick."

He sucked in a deep breath. I tore the tube off the portable tank just as the dial clicked to empty.

Holding the end of the transparent tube, I spun to face the nearest H tank. I ripped off the white plastic ring serving as the protective seal, exposing the oxygen outlet.

I stared in disbelief at the barbed nozzle.

It was the wrong size for the tubing attached to Patrick's mask.

ENTRY 26   Patrick's face turned a deeper shade of red. He gestured emphatically with his hands. I unstuck my body, which had gone into a panicked lockdown, and started yanking drawers open, looking for who knows what. Bag valves, syringes, tubes filled with weird solutions.

Patrick's hand clamped down on my shoulder. The butt of the shotgun slid past my cheek. He was trying to give me the shotgun.

To kill him.

I ignored him, ripping open a cabinet door.

Inside, a stack of oxygen masks. More heavy-duty than the one he wore now, with wider straps, like something a fighter pilot might wear. I fumbled the nearest one off the shelf, a coil of tube spiraling open below it. It was wider—a match for the nozzle.

I nearly cried out in triumph.

Whirling toward the H tank, I knocked aside the shotgun, tossing Patrick the mask.

I rammed the thicker tube onto the barbed nozzle and opened the valve. Oxygen hissed up the line and out the mask, clearing out the old air. "Now!" I shouted.

With his cheeks ballooned, Patrick looked like he might explode. But he tore off his mask, flipping it aside, and secured the new one over his head.

"Breathe out, hard," I said.

Patrick blew out so hard that flecks of spit dotted the inside of the mask. He panted, sucking in oxygen as I adjusted the airflow.

He was fine. We'd done it.

I set the dial to eight liters per minute because that's where Chatterjee had set the old one. Though my focus was on the knobs, I could hear Patrick's breathing start to even out.

"I think we're okay," I said, and looked up.

The nurse Host was standing behind him.

Her head was torqued to one side as if some of her vertebrae had shattered. Her eyeless gaze seemed focused.

She seized Patrick, crimping his tube, and ripped him back over the bed. The tube strained on the H tank, almost pulling off the nozzle.

Patrick's giant eyes found mine. He was trying to hold his breath in case the tube tore off, but her bear hug was crushing his chest. She whisked him out into the corridor so fast that his legs flew up in the air. The tube pulled taut. I flipped the H tank over the bed onto its side, sending it rolling after them. It clattered as it went, miraculously clearing the doorway, the tube barely holding on.

Hurdling the bed, I took off after them. Patrick swung an elbow, clipping the nurse's damaged forehead, but she didn't let go. They fell together, banging into the crash cart and knocking it over, one defibrillator paddle springing out on its cord and snapping back like the tongue of a frog.

As the tank hit its outer limit, the tube went piano-wire tight, yanking the mask straps and Patrick's head forward. I braced for the tube to pop free, but it didn't. Instead the rolling tank switched direction, curving in an arc across the tiles, somehow staying tethered to Patrick's face. Given the weight of the tank, the tube wouldn't hold it long—it was like having a swordfish on ten-pound-test fishing line. I dove on my stomach and swatted the tank toward them, putting slack back in the line.

She was choking Patrick out now, one arm locked across his throat, the other flailing to cuff his wrist. How could I get her off without tangling in the tubing or knocking it loose?

A glint to their side caught my eye.

The defibrillator paddle.

I lunged for it, sweeping it up and yanking its companion free. I thumbed the charge button on the portable defibrillator. The unit turned on with a whine. It made a series of short beeps and then a long one. I slammed the metal paddles onto the nurse's head and pulled back on the discharge buttons.

The reaction was unlike anything I'd seen in movies or TV. The nurse jerked back so violently that it looked as though she'd been lassoed. She landed in a sitting position. Electricity fizzled across her eye membranes, sparking, and then they ignited, giving out whooshes of flame. She fell back, her head smacking the floor, and lay still. Wisps of black smoke tendriled up from her eyeholes.

Her momentum had knocked Patrick across the floor. He spun like a hockey puck over the tile, his mask and tank clattering with him. He wound up on his belly, facing me. We looked at each other.

"Sorry," I said.

He mumbled something I couldn't make out.

I scrambled over to the tank. The tube had been tugged to the very edge of the nozzle, a millimeter away from popping off. I secured it tightly and looked up. "You okay?"

He nodded, but I could see he was foggy. " 'Okay' might be an overstatement."

"We made a lot of noise, so we'd better move it before they get here," I said.

I helped him up, and then we hustled back to the Respiratory Suite, Patrick hugging the hundred-pound H tank as he walked. He was having trouble moving well. I couldn't count on his helping me much.

After we checked out the tanks—there were ten more big ones—I saw something in the back of the suite that spelled even better news. A beige machine the size of an industrial copier. Block letters on the side spelled out OXYGEN TANK FILL SYSTEM.

We now had a sustainable plan.

Whether we came back here for future missions or figured how to get the entire machine and its filters back to school, we had a way to keep him breathing.

With a simple push-button setup, the unit was surprisingly easy to figure out. It had a plug in the back but also a toggle for an internal backup generator, one of the benefits of emergency medical equipment. I inserted the lighter portable tank into the system and started filling it.

We wouldn't have time to wait around.

"Can you carry another tank?" I asked.

Tucking the shotgun beneath his arm, Patrick swept up another tank with ease. Sometimes even I forgot how strong he was. I grabbed two tanks myself, staggering under the weight, struggling to keep them from dragging loudly on the floor. We hurried back into the hall.

Patrick led the way down the rear stairs, and I scrambled after him.

He shouldered through a door onto the ground floor, and we shot gazes up and down the corridor, but no Hosts were in sight. From the square we could still hear the scream of the ambulance siren. I prayed it had drowned out the commotion of our battle upstairs.

Sliding glass doors let out into an alley behind the hospital. "Let's go," Patrick said. "We can't carry more than these."

I looked frantically around the corridor, then saw what I was searching for up against a wall.

A gurney.

I ran over, heaving the heavy tanks onto the mattress. Patrick set his on there, too, then leaned on the railing with both hands, panting hard. Sweat ran from his hairline into his eyes as he struggled with the effects of the oxygen.

"I'll run to get the rest," I said. "You're too weak. We can't risk you dragging that tank up and down with you."

He started to shake his head, but I left him there anyways.

I scrambled back up the stairs, stepping over the sizzled corpse of the Host, and grabbed two more tanks. I made it back down okay.

Patrick had stacked the tanks on the gurney and was readying the thick nylon straps to hold them in place. I set the two down by his feet and ran back up. Every time I turned a corner or put my back to the dark hall, fear licked at the nape of my neck. Somehow I made it through two more trips, grabbing the refilled portable tank on my final leg. Since the gurney was overflowing, I decided to leave the last two tanks behind.

Patrick secured the load, cinching the straps to pin the pile of tanks to the mattress.

He leaned his weight into the gurney, starting it rolling toward the rear exit. "Let's go."

"Wait," I said. "We need IV bags and needles."

He looked at me, blinking, fighting for clarity.

"To feed you," I said.

"Hurry, Chance," he said. "Just . . . hurry."

I sprinted back upstairs, my steps pounding down the dark corridor. I'd clocked the big refrigerator behind one of the nurses' stations. When I arrived and tugged open the door, a puff of cool air greeted me. Thank God—the seal had held.

I had to shove aside an EKG cart so I could swing the door wide. The cart wobbled off up the hall on creaky wheels. Grabbing a giant organ-transplant bag, I eyed the IV bags inside the refrigerator. There were solutions with saline and dextrose, minerals and vitamins, but I had no time to figure out which I needed, so I swept every last one from the shelves into the bag. Then I dug through the drawers behind the station, looking for the equipment that Dr. Chatterjee had told me to get. Catheters, tubing, large-bore needles. I loaded them up, zipped the bag shut. I crouched to slide the strap over my shoulder, then rose unsteadily, using my legs so I wouldn't throw out my back.

I wobbled a few steps, passing the front stairs, heading for the rear of the building. I sensed movement in the unlit landing by the stairwell.

The door creaked open.

A shadow filled the doorway.

I could see straight through its head.

I dumped the bag and did the first thing I could think of, which was to kick the Host right in the stomach.

He flew about halfway down the dark stairs, then seemed to stop, floating in midair, his arms spread to the sides.

It was impossible.

Something lofted him back onto his feet, and I saw that he hadn't been floating at all.

He'd been propped up by the Hosts beneath him.

They filled the front stairwell.

Like a rising tide, they surged up at me.

ENTRY 27   Blood rushed to my head, so intense I thought I might pass out. I wheeled around, searching for something, anything, to use as a weapon.

The EKG cart I'd kicked aside was a few steps away. I dashed for it and grabbed the edge, using all my might to swing it around toward the door.

I felt the impact shudder the cart before I saw what it had struck—the Host, already past the threshold. The metal edge had hit him in the gut, doubling him over the equipment. The doorway behind him was packed with reaching arms and blank faces. Though my thighs screamed, I put all my force into driving the cart forward, shoving him into the others, through that doorframe, and onto the stairs.

The momentum of the heavy cart packed him and the others back through the doorway. Roaring, I gave a final shove, the cart flying away from me, hurtling through the frame.

Then gravity took over.

The cart seemed to fill the walls of the stairway, blasting down the steps, smashing everything in its path. Meaty crunches and wet gasps.

I didn't wait around to admire the damage.

Swinging the bulging bag up onto my shoulder, I sprinted for the rear stairwell. I didn't have time to be cautious—I just threw open the door and staggered inside, pulled by the weight of the bag. If the Hosts had made it into the rear stairwell as well, there wasn't anything I could do about it. My breaths rang off the walls, loud panting that sounded like the breathing of a Host. In fact, the echoes made it sound like there were Hosts all around me.

At last I reached the ground floor and pushed the door open, barely keeping to my feet as I tumbled forward.

Patrick waited in front of the loaded gurney, his mask tube trailing back to the H tank, now stacked with the others. His shotgun was raised and aimed at my head.

"Chance," he said calmly. "Hit the floor."

I was too exhausted to argue or even ask. I let my muscles go slack, let the heavy bag tug me down until my chest slapped the tile.

The shotgun exploded overhead, and I rolled to my side to see three Hosts behind me fly back, ripped to pieces by the expanding spray.

Those breaths in the stairwell hadn't been my own, echoing back at me. They'd been the Hosts right behind me, their outstretched hands inches from my back. Sprawled there on the cold tile, I shuddered.

For a moment we stayed perfectly still. The echo of the shotgun rang up the stairwell and through the building, making it—I hoped—impossible to source. We waited until it died away, then sprang back into motion.

Fighting to my feet, I slung the bag onto the gurney. The corridor still empty. The rear sliding doors just behind us.

With both hands I slammed into the gurney, getting it moving toward the rear exit. It was too slow, and I was too weak. It clipped a doorway, and one of the giant oxygen tanks bounced off, clanging on the floor, the loudest sound I'd ever heard.

Patrick and I halted. Our eyes met.

A moment of breath-held silence.

Then we heard the shuffling of dozens of feet. A moment

later a wall of Hosts swept around the corner at the end of the hall. They'd reversed course from the blocked front stairwell, tracking the sound.

Patrick rushed back and pried open the doors to the rear alley. They parted. I propelled the gurney toward the opening, risking a look behind me.

They were almost on me. It was too late.

Patrick reached past my face, grabbed a fistful of my shirt at the rear collar, and hurled me up onto the stacked tanks. My momentum started the wheels turning. I rode the gurney out through the rear doors.

Inches from my face, the end of his tube popped off the H tank. I reached for it, but it flew away like a fly fishing line as I rolled clear of the building on the gurney.

Twisting, I stared back at Patrick in time to see the shotgun rise.

But he wasn't aiming at the Hosts.

He was aiming at the floor.

I realized what he was doing an instant before it happened.

The shotgun roared, the shot striking the end of the oxygen tank. It rocketed forward, lifting off the floor and impaling the lead Host right through the stomach. The tank bore a massive dent but somehow it hadn't exploded.

That was about to change.

Patrick shuck-shucked the shotgun and fired again. The tank exploded, wiping out the Chaser it was embedded in and the wall of Hosts behind it. The fireball filled the corridor. Patrick hopped back through the doors into the alley as flame blossomed out into the cold night. Heat billowed over us and then flowed up and away.

I slid off the gurney, groping on the cold ground, finally coming up with the tube. My hands chased it to the end. Patrick waited for me, his breath still held.

I shoved the tube back over the hissing nozzle. Patrick pulled his mask away from his face until the oxygen shot up the line, fluttering his hair. Then he snapped the mask into place, blew a big exhalation through the one-way valve, and started breathing again.

I started breathing, too.

We didn't pause to celebrate.

He took one side of the gurney, and I took the other. Side by side we hurried up the alley, wheels rattling like crazy over the bumpy asphalt.

As we neared the edge of the alley, Patrick said, "Slow up, slow up."

I shot a look behind us and willed my legs to slow down.

"Chance," Patrick said, his voice a bit wonky from the oxygen and the mask. "They're gonna hear us."

I forced myself to slow even more. Finally we eased to a stop and peered around the corner. We had only a slice of a view past the pharmacy. The ambulance was still there in the middle of the town square, but there were no Hosts around it anymore. They'd rushed the hospital—or at least I hoped that was where they were.

The siren was still shrieking. Somehow I'd drowned out the sound in my head, turning down the volume on all background noise as we'd run the gauntlet of the hospital. I was glad to hear the wail piercing the night, shrill and steady. That would cover the sound of our movement through the neighborhood as we headed back toward school.

We set out down an unlit street, pushing the gurney across the sidewalk, one wheel squeaking intermittently. We stopped every few driveways, using parked cars for cover.

We heard movements inside some houses and on the nearby streets, but we chose our path well, weaving through the neighborhood one cautious block at a time.

We were halfway there when Patrick took a knee behind the special van that the Dubois family kept for Blake and his wheelchair. Breathing hard, he held up a finger to signal that he needed a second to catch his breath. Sweat trickled from his hairline, and his face looked washed of color.

"Sorry," he said. "Oxygen. Fuzzy."

I eased him down so he could lean against one big tire, then sat next to him. In the darkness the combination of the mask and his cowboy hat made him look pretty scary. For a time he tried to catch his breath. Then he made a fist around the tube trailing up to the H tank on the gurney. Was he so loopy that he was thinking of ripping it out?

"What do we do when the tanks run dry?" he asked in a hoarse whisper.

I couldn't take my eyes off his fingers tensed around that tube. "We go back to the hospital and fill them up again."

"How 'bout when the IV food is gone?"

"Dr. Chatterjee said he thinks he can figure out some kind of system to make more."

Patrick gave a slow nod, but his face didn't hold much hope. "And what about when the *next* kid turns eighteen? Or Alex? Or you?"

"Let's worry about that later," I said.

His fist tightened around the tube. "It sucks living like this. A mask clamped over my face. Being fed through tubes and needles. *Forever.*"

I watched his fingers turn white as he squeezed the tube, then released it.

"Actually, *not* forever," he added. A bitterness I didn't recognize had crept into his voice. "Just till the mask slips some night when I'm sleeping. Or a tank malfunctions. Or I sneeze wrong and blow the tube out."

"Look," I said, "we just bought you more time. For the particulates to dissipate."

"For a miracle," he said.

"Yeah," I said. "For that."

He squeezed the tube again, kept it compressed. His eyes looked hazy, his gaze loose, though whether from the oxygen or not, I couldn't tell.

I stood up and offered him a hand. "Alex is waiting for you."

He looked at me for a long time. Then he released the tube and took my hand.

I knew that would do it.

Our progress felt like torture, every rasp of our boots against asphalt amplified tenfold, every creak from a shadowed porch amplified a hundredfold. But even with that squeaky wheel, even pushing a gurney loaded with seven giant tanks and one portable one, we made it through undetected. At last we came up on the edge of the teachers' parking lot, halting behind a row of hedges.

Leaving the gurney, I crawled through the hedges and signaled at the front gate with a blip of my flashlight. Then I waited for Alex's signal that the coast was clear.

No signal came.

I waited and waited and then flickered my beam again and waited some more. Only darkness stared back through the bars of the gate.

I crawled out to where Patrick crouched by the gurney. "No signal," I whispered. "Maybe Alex took a bathroom break."

"No," he said. "She'd be there. Something's wrong."

Carefully, he lifted his H tank off the gurney. "Let's head for the gate. We'll come back for the other tanks later."

We slithered through the bushes to the other side, cast

glances around us, then bolted across the parking lot. Panting, we reached the gate.

It was locked.

We looked around frantically, Patrick's biceps bulging under the weight of the hundred-pound tank. Once again I clicked my flashlight through the bars toward the building.

Something glinted in the grass.

I lowered the beam.

It was Alex's jigsaw pendant glittering among the blades.

Beside it, grooves gouged the grass, trailing out through the gate.

Finger marks.

The beam wobbled in my hand. I didn't dare look over at Patrick, but I could sense him staring where I stared, seeing what I was seeing.

A voice from the darkness startled us. *"Chance. Patrick."*

A girl ran up to the gate, fumbling with Ezekiel's giant key ring.

It was Eve, not Alex.

Her hands were shaking even worse than mine.

"She's gone." Eve unlocked the gate and stepped back, letting it creak inward. "They got Alex."

ENTRY 28   As Patrick and I staggered into the gym, the others rose to their feet as one. I couldn't tell if it was a show of respect for Patrick since his girlfriend had been taken or if it was some kind of perverse curiosity, that they wanted to see our reactions.

Cassius ran up, put his front paws on my chest, and licked my face. The display of affection felt out of place considering the news we'd just received.

Ben regarded us with something like awe. "You made it," he said. "You actually made it."

Setting down his tank, Patrick collapsed against the nearest wall. Dr. Chatterjee ran over to him.

"The oxygen levels are playing games with him," I said.

Chatterjee checked Patrick's eyes, then began adjusting the dials. "Please talk to JoJo," he said to me over his shoulder. "Behind the bleachers."

JoJo's stuffed animal had been left over by the base of the wall. I couldn't remember ever seeing her without Bunny.

Rocky appeared at my side. "She won't even talk to *me*," he said.

I rested a hand on his black curls. They were matted and dirty. No one around to tell him to wash his hair, behind his ears.

"I'll see what I can do," I said.

I scooped up Bunny and squeezed behind the bleachers. JoJo had wedged herself into the darkest, tiniest corner, and she was clutching something with all her might. I headed toward her, ducking, then crawling, until finally one of the benches crowded down on me so I could go no farther.

"JoJo, I can't get to you," I said. "I can't help you from here."

Her tear-streaked face tilted toward me. "I don't care," she said. "I don't deserve to be helped. It's my fault."

"What do you mean? What happened?"

"I got scared after you left. And I wanted my Frisbee. It's the only thing that makes me think about other stuff besides . . . *everything*. So I snuck outside, and . . . and . . ." She trailed off, crying some more. "I squeezed under the fence by the oak tree."

"You went out there *alone*?" I felt my body temperature rising.

Guilt. I thought about my broken promises to get that Frisbee for JoJo. How I'd dismissed her before we'd left.

And so she'd gone to retrieve it herself.

She nodded. "And I ran over to get it when . . ." A few quick breaths. "When *he* started to come for me. Alex yelled out, 'cuz she was on watch for you. I tried to run away. I tried. But she came out and hit him. With this."

She shifted, and I saw that the shadowy item she was clutching was Alex's hockey stick.

"Where was Cassius?"

"The gate swung back after Alex ran out to get me, and he was stuck behind it. He ran up along the fence away from the gate to bark at us all. And then Ben dragged him inside so he wouldn't make more noise."

"So Ben just *left* you and Alex out there?"

"Yeah. Alex grabbed me and ran back to the gate. But we'd just gotten inside when . . ." JoJo sucked air a few times, her bottom lip trembling. Her rough-cut hair was all blunt edges and stray shoots. "He grabbed her. And she fell. And dropped me. And her hockey stick. Even while he was carrying her away, she was screaming at me to lock the gate. To lock her out. So I did. I did."

Fresh tears rolled down JoJo's cheeks. "And it was *him*." She looked up at me, and I could see the horror on her face. "It was her daddy."

Squashed beneath the bleachers, breathing dust, I took a moment with that one.

It had been awful being there when Patrick killed Uncle Jim and Sue-Anne. But I couldn't image how much more awful it would have been getting *snatched* by them. Dragged off. And caged.

"It's not your fault," I said when I could find my voice. "Any more than it's Ben's fault for throwing the Frisbee out the window. Or mine for not getting it for you like I promised."

But it is your fault, Chance, a voice in my head said. *It is.*

"Now will you please come to me?"

She shook her head.

I thought for a moment, and then I said, "I've got Bunny here, and we're stuck. I'm too big to be under here, and I need your help. Will you help us?"

She stared at me for a while. Then, slowly, she crawled over, Alex's hockey stick clacking on the floorboards. She gave me a shove, and I pretended to roll free. We squirmed through the space beneath the bleachers, brushing dust from our knees. I held out Bunny. "Trade you for the hockey stick?"

JoJo took the deal.

I walked over to where Dr. Chatterjee was still working on Patrick. My brother lay on his back, weak and pale. His shirt was peeled open, and one of the big needles I'd grabbed from the nurses' station was rammed in the crook of his arm and secured with white medical tape.

Chatterjee looked up and said, "You did great, Chance."

Patrick lifted his head and blinked drowsily. "But saving me cost us Alex." He sagged back against the floor, his Stetson falling off to the side.

"We have to get fluids in him." Chatterjee nosed through the organ-donor bag. "Since we don't have a central line, we're limited in what we can give him. It's good you grabbed the bags with ten-percent dextrose, because anything much higher than this will wreck his veins." He gestured at the needle jammed into Patrick's arm. "This is the access port for the peripheral IV. Give me a minute to get him online here. With the oxygen adjusted, once we push some nutrients, he'll come around."

I wasn't used to seeing Patrick vulnerable like that. I backed away, then headed out to retrieve the tanks. Though running to and from the gurney in the night would be scary, it felt less scary than seeing Patrick so feeble.

Besides, I had to get those tanks moved before daybreak.

As I passed Ben at the lookout post, I said, "Real courageous, Ben. The way you helped Alex and JoJo."

He shook his head at me. "Courage is overrated," he said. "In that moment I had to make a tough choice. And I realized: I had *one job*. Get the gate closed. Protect the others. The only thing that matters anymore is staying alive."

"If that's true," I said, "then what's the *point* of staying alive?"

I walked past him down the corridor. I'd almost reached the front doors when I heard footsteps behind me. Eve ran up, keys jangling in her hand.

"I'll watch the gate for you," she said.

I appreciated it more than I could say.

As I ran back and forth across the teachers' parking lot, bringing the tanks in one at a time, Eve waited by the padlock for me, signaling when to wait, when to go.

By the time I lugged the last one to the gym, daylight streamed through the windows and I was worn out and ready to sleep. I set the final tank down with the others. Still woozy, Patrick now lay propped up in his cot, needles and tubes threading into him. He looked like someone dying in a hospital.

I thanked Eve, and she nodded and drifted over to her post at the supply station. I didn't want to leave Patrick's side, but it was also hard to look at him like this. I sat next to him and studied my boots. After a few minutes, Chatterjee called me over to the bleachers. Relieved, I went.

"How are the particulate readings?" I asked.

"No better." He rested a hand on my shoulder, and his expression of concern shot a tremor of fear through me. "Chance, you're an amazing and resourceful kid. . . ."

"What's wrong?"

"I just don't want you to think that this is a long-term solution for your brother."

"Why not? We can refill the tanks. You can make more IV food or whatever you call it." My voice was rising.

"Providing nutrition exclusively by IV carries with it big risks, Chance." His sad eyes blinked behind those glasses. "Infections. Deficiencies. Imbalances. And we can't give him enough nutrition this way. We're too limited without a central line."

"Then I'll get you one."

Chatterjee drew a deep breath. "You did a wonderfully smart and brave thing that will give us more time with Patrick. But at some point you're going to have to let him go."

I felt my face harden into a mask. "No," I said. "Not ever."

I went back over to where Patrick rested and lay on my cot next to his. My eyelids grew heavy, and I knew that the minute I closed them, they'd stay shut. So I forced them open.

Right now I just wanted to be near my brother. He was holding up his jigsaw pendant so he could look at it. Alex's matching piece dangled from his other clenched fist, the two parts swaying side by side.

I wondered where Alex was right now. What was happening to her and who was doing it.

It was hard not to notice her empty cot.

It was hard to notice anything else at all.

ENTRY 29   I woke up to the sounds of fighting.

Patrick was on his feet, heading for the exit, dragging the hundred-pound tank behind him, the IV line snaking from his shirtsleeve. Dr. Chatterjee was trying to slow him while Ben, standing at the gym door, looked on.

"This is ridiculous, Patrick!" Chatterjee said. "You stop this instant!"

Patrick bulled on. "I'm going for her."

As I blinked myself awake, the light felt disorienting. It was dusk already? I'd slept all day?

"You're not gonna get farther than the next block hauling that tank around," Dezi Siegler said.

"Where would you even look?" Jenny White cried out.

"The church," Patrick said. "Then Lawrenceville."

"Lawrenceville," Dr. Chatterjee said. "This is insanity, Patrick."

But my brother kept stumbling forward.

"How about food?" Eve pleaded.

"I don't need food," Patrick said. "I'm not leaving her out there."

As he neared the doors, Ben stepped in front of him. "Forget about her, Patrick," he said. "She's long gone."

Off balance from holding the tank, Patrick swung at him weakly. Ben leaned back, the punch missing. Patrick stumbled forward. I leapt up and ran over to them, hurdling cots.

Patrick swung again, and Ben ducked, then shoved him

over. Patrick fell hard on his side, grunting, and Ben jumped on him, pinning him to the floorboards. "Come on, Patrick. You really think you'll make it out there? Look how useless you are."

Patrick was winded. ". . . not . . . useless."

Ben reached down, gripped Patrick's mask, and pulled it away from his mouth and nose.

All movement in the gym stopped.

Patrick stayed tense on his back, one arm raised defensively. I halted in midstep, afraid that if I moved again, it would mean that time would keep moving, too.

There was no sound except the hiss of oxygen escaping from the mask.

"Ben," Dr. Chatterjee said in a shockingly calm voice, "put the mask back on Patrick. You don't want a Host in here any more than we do."

Ben glared down at Patrick. The wide straps strained. Held tight in Ben's grip, the mask wobbled a few inches from my brother's face. Ben looked from Patrick to Chatterjee, then to me. My brother's life in his hands.

The moment stretched on and on.

Finally Ben released the mask, letting it snap back into place hard over Patrick's nose and mouth. Then he climbed off Patrick and stood, his face shifting with emotion, his scar lines pulling into strange new alignments.

Patrick exhaled hard through the one-way valve, then panted to catch his breath, his chest jerking.

"Hell, I was doing him a *favor*," Ben said. "Showing him what it'll be like out there. If *one* of me could do that to him in here, how do you think it'll go down with hundreds of Hosts in the open?"

It took Patrick a few seconds to push himself onto one knee, then find his feet. I wanted to help him up, but I knew if I went over to help, it'd make him angry right now. He picked up his cowboy hat and put it on. Then he adjusted the mask straps and the tube and walked back over to his cot. Every head in the gym turned to watch his retreat. He slumped onto the mattress, still breathing heavily, one hand resting gently on the mask as if making sure it was still there.

Seeing him defeated like that made something inside me break into little pieces and blow away. I swallowed hard. I wanted to pummel Ben's face until those scar lines cracked open again. But as he took up his chair by the double doors, I detected a note of remorse in his face. That's the only thing that stopped me from attacking him and probably getting myself killed.

I walked over to Patrick, feeling everyone's eyes on me. I was about to ask my brother if he was okay when he tilted his head, looking up at me from under the brim of his trademark black cowboy hat.

What I saw in his eyes chilled me through and through.

"You have to go, Chance," he said through his mask. "Go get her. Get her and bring her back to me."

I had a hard time drawing breath. It felt as though I had a rock lodged in my throat. Everyone was still staring at us— from the cots, the bleachers, all around the basketball court. It was like getting tossed in the middle of a rodeo arena, expected to perform some feat I'd never trained for.

I shook my head.

"Ben's right," Patrick said. "I can't go after her. Not with this." He grabbed the tube from the mask. "And this." He tugged up his stretched shirtsleeve to show the line embedded in the pit of his elbow. His eyes glimmered, and for one terrible instant I thought he might cry.

I pressed my lips together to firm them. "I can't do it, Patrick," I said.

"You can."

"I can't do it without you."

"You can. You always could." He lifted his fist. Dangling from the bottom, Alex's jigsaw pendant.

I stared at it. Then I held out my hand.

He dropped it into my palm.

"Please don't ask this of him, Patrick," Chatterjee said. He'd approached, standing a few cots away. "If you do, you know he'll try, and then we'll lose him, too. He's just a kid."

Patrick's eyes never left mine. "Not anymore he's not."

"No one could pull that off," Ben called over. "How's he supposed to do it? Battle all the Hosts and bring her back?"

Patrick and I still didn't break our eye contact. Though there were nearly a hundred bodies in the gym, this was between brother and brother. My heart thumped in my chest, strong and true. What he'd said and how he'd said it had shown me a strength I hadn't known I had.

I said, "I'll think of something."

Patrick's lips pressed together behind the mask. "He always does," he said, his eyes still locked on mine.

I swept a gaze across all those faces. They'd stay here together, sleeping on cots behind the safety of the perimeter fence. For a moment I envied them.

But something in their gazes caught me by surprise.

They envied *me*.

"Bring her back, Chance," Patrick said.

He gestured for me to lean close. Condensation from his breath fogged the mask, and I could see that he was struggling not to cry. He took off his black cowboy hat.

And put it on my head.

I stepped away. Taking Alex's hockey stick, I shoved it into her gear bag and slung the straps over my shoulders so the end stuck up like a sword handle, just how she used to wear it. The gym remained dead silent, all focus turned to me. I did my best to ignore it. Wearing the Stetson low over my eyes helped block everyone and everything out. I heard nothing but the steady rush of my breath. In, out. In, out. To keep the fear from catching me, I just had to breathe and force my body to do whatever was next.

As I headed across the court to the supply station, Eve rose from her cot and walked at my side. When we got there, she went around the little desk, sat, and looked up with a mock-official expression.

"So," she said, "what can I help you with?"

She was trying for a light tone, but I could see how worried she was. I loaded up with water bottles, stale sandwiches, energy bars, and batteries for the flashlight, preserving the perishables in Ziplocs in case it rained. I also encased my notebook in a plastic bag to protect it. Darkness was gathering at the windows. A few minutes more and it would be night.

"You want your brother's shotgun?" she asked.

"Too big for me," I said.

"Just these, then?" she said, sliding my baling hooks across the desk.

I slipped the loops onto my wrists, then leaned over and pointed to one of the shelves. "And that."

Sheriff Blanton's revolver. The one I'd taken from his bedroom back on that endless first night.

"What good is it without bullets?" she asked as she reached for it.

"I know where to find bullets," I said.

She handed it to me, and I clipped the holster to my belt. Then I nodded at her and touched the brim of the cowboy hat, a mock formality to match hers from earlier. She managed a smile.

"Thank you for everything, Eve," I said.

She couldn't help but beam a little.

"You're a good friend," I said, and her smile faded a few watts. I realized too late how my words had cut her. I hadn't meant to hurt her feelings, but I also didn't have it in me to figure out how to fix it right now. I was concerned about a thousand things, and feelings weren't one of them.

I took the gun and turned to leave.

That first time we'd left the safety of the school to head for Stark Peak, there'd been the three of us like always. Me, Patrick, Alex.

The second time, sneaking into the hospital, me and Patrick.

Now it was just me.

As if he sensed my thoughts, Cassius trotted over to join me.

We threaded our way through the cots, heading out. As I neared the exit, my shadow fell before me and crept up the closed double doors. It was tall and broad, topped by a cowboy hat. It didn't look like my shadow at all.

It looked like Patrick's.

ENTRY 30   A light rain pinged the leaves all around me, making them dance. Cassius shook off water, then shook again. Most ridgebacks don't like rain. They're bred for the African desert, and water annoys them.

I stood a few feet back from the tree line, foliage framing my face as I peered at the rear of the church. There were no flatbed trucks or pallet jacks or patrolling Hosts. Aside from the faint patter of rain, everything was still. I couldn't sense movement through the stained glass.

But I knew I had to take a closer look.

After a few quick breaths to steel myself, I put Cassius on a sit-stay and sprinted across the back parking lot, diving over the hedge. I lay there against the base of the building, gripping the baling hooks, listening for any sounds. It took me longer than seemed reasonable to catch my breath. Then it struck me—I wasn't so much winded as afraid.

Though I'd figured it would be scarier out here without Patrick, I hadn't counted on how *much* scarier.

But I had to get up and look inside. I had to see if they had Alex in there, crammed into a crate. And if so, I had to figure out what the hell to do next. I pictured her terrified, her knees drawn in to her chest, and felt anger take hold inside me. I let it give me strength.

Rising to a crouch, I peered through a clear piece of glass in the mosaic.

The inside of the church was empty.

Not a single crate. Not any Hosts. No meat grinder or piles of food.

And worst of all, no Alex.

Just a few left-behind sneakers and what looked like food stains on the floors.

Seeing the church empty was almost as unsettling as coming upon the caged kids in there earlier, but I couldn't say why. My gaze fixed on an overturned Converse high-top. I grappled with the absence of all those boys and girls and what it might mean.

Any hope that this would be a short mission guttered out. The Hosts had probably crated Alex up and trucked her off with the other kids.

I put my back to the wall and slid down again behind the hedges. For a moment I let despair overtake me. But only for a moment.

I pictured Alex again, the way she tilted her chin up when she laughed. How she'd tuck her hair behind her ear when she leaned forward. Her fingernails, chewed to the quick or broken off from hockey practice, not like those of the other girls. Then, for an instant, I let myself remember that look of admiration she'd thrown my way after I helped us escape Jack Kaner's farm.

Wherever she was, I'd find her. I'd get to her. And I'd bring her back.

To Patrick.

Which meant that I had to cross the valley, scale Ponderosa Pass, and make my way to Lawrenceville, where God only knew what waited for me.

As terrifying as it had been to sneak to the church, my journey had barely started.

My hooks and Alex's hockey stick were useful, sure, but

Patrick had saved the day many more times with a gun. To have even a prayer of making it, I'd need bullets.

And there was only one place to get those.

Back in the forest, Cassius's eyes glinted from the darkness between trunks. He didn't move until I jogged up to him and tapped his head to release him. As he trotted at my side, he nuzzled my palm, his way of saying hi. He looked up at me, tail wagging, and I realized that it was more than just a greeting. I made him feel safe. I was his pack. His family.

Since the minute he could walk, he'd stayed at my side whenever he could. Though it was against house rules for a puppy, I snuck him past Sue-Anne into my room most days after school. He'd been an active puppy, chewing up two pairs of my sneakers and an algebra textbook. That's why I knew that something was wrong when he'd turned sluggish at three months. Then the vomiting started. By the time we rushed him to the vet, he was almost dead from parvovirus. Doc McGraw had to keep him overnight to give him IV fluids and antibiotics. Cassius wasn't supposed to live through the night. Uncle Jim let me stay with him even though it was a Tuesday. He probably realized he couldn't stop me anyways. I'd bedded down on an old horse blanket outside Cassius's crate. In the morning Cassius was too weak to lift his head, but when he saw my face at the bars, he'd flicked the tip of his tail once, the closest thing to a wag he could muster.

Even when he was dying, he'd needed to show how happy he was to see me.

That tiny flick of the tail was the best thing anyone had ever given me. I swore then and there that if he lived, I'd make sure he always knew how much he was loved. He'd taught me the importance of that.

The memory made me stop right there in the woods.

I crouched in front of him and dug my fingers into the scruff beneath his collar the way he loved. He panted through his dog smile, that big tail pulling his rear end back and forth, back and forth. "Good boy," I told him as we started off again. "Good, good boy."

Keeping to the pines, we circled the town square, gradually making our way to the bluff behind Bob n' Bit Hardware. No sign of Hosts anywhere. Had they all left with the kids as part of whatever awful plan was going down in Lawrenceville?

If so, that would make the front part of my mission easier but what was coming much, much harder.

Cassius and I scampered down the bluff to street level, careful not to skid out on loose rocks. Then we ducked behind a car. Lowering to my belly, I peered through the tires. Way across the square, a Mapper was walking his paces. I watched until he vanished up a side street, and then I crept from cover toward the rolling rear door of the hardware store.

Orange light flickered around the edges of the door, and when I put my hand on the metal handle, it was warm from the blacksmith forge inside. I eased it aside, just wide enough that I could peer through with one eye.

Melted pistols and rifles were scattered around the burning forge. A few more still lay across the fire, devoured in the spots where the flickering flames touched them. A blackened set of tongs was sunk into the glowing coals, the handles sticking up like rabbit ears. On the anvil lay a revolver, its barrel hammered out of shape. Lumps of metal filled a crate beside the anvil.

Spilled across the floor in heaps like glittering treasure were countless rounds. The piles rose waist-high.

I'd been counting on finding them here.

You couldn't burn bullets. Not without turning yourself into Swiss cheese.

The farthest stretches of the store were dark. Even so, I could see no Hosts. I listened for a moment but heard no movement.

Nudging the door open another few inches, I crept inside, Cassius slithering through with me, tangling in my legs. I fumbled Sheriff Blanton's revolver, a .357, out of the holster, set it on the floor, and started digging through the mounds of ammo. Rounds spilled over my hands and wrists, leading to mini-landslides. As the bullets clattered on the floor, I winced, shooting glances at the dark reaches of the store. The baling hooks were swinging around on their nylon loops, getting in my way, so I slipped them off and laid them aside.

Searching for .357 Magnum rounds among this many bullets was like looking for a particular piece of hay in a haystack, but I found one, then another, plucking them out of the piles. A minute later I had a run of luck, coming upon a slew of .38 Specials. Though slightly shorter, they'd fit the revolver. I grabbed handfuls, shoving them into Alex's bag. They rattled to the bottom. They'd be heavy, but well worth having.

Just a few more seconds until I loaded the gun. Then I'd be way safer out here on my own. But in my excitement at finding the bullets, I'd gotten focused on the task at hand.

Too focused.

The rumble of Cassius's growl made my hands freeze halfway into the bag. Despite the heat of the forge, a cold sweat broke out across my back. Dread pooled in my chest.

I looked over my shoulder.

Looming above me was Bob Bitley. His shirt in tatters, his wispy beard singed. The dancing light of the forge played through the boreholes of his eyes, giving his face a demonic cast. My baling hooks were out of reach on the far side of the ammo heap. Alex's hockey stick rammed through the bag. The revolver unloaded on the floor beside me.

And yet Bob was ready. He gripped a set of roughly hammered shackles, the type you might see in an old dungeon movie, the chain drooping between them. He shifted, and the crate beside the anvil became clear. Those lumps of metal resolved as dozens and dozens of shackles.

He'd been melting down the guns, turning them into restraints.

It might have been less horrifying if there were any emotion at all on his face—rage or wrath or even evil. But the blank slate of his features somehow made him all the more menacing. I'd only known him to be clean-shaven. The messy beard—nine days of growth—was a reminder of the horrors being wreaked on gentle Bob Bitley, his body still functioning even after his mind had been taken offline.

He grabbed the back of my shirt, shoving one of the shackles toward my wrist. I struck at him. With incredible strength, he hurled me away.

It happened to be in the direction of the forge.

I stumbled a few steps, my hands flailing to keep me upright. I managed to halt just in front of the fire, leaning forward to try to regain my balance.

One of the tong handles nearly kissed my cheek. Hot air gusted in my face. My palms inches from the burning coals. Arching onto my tiptoes, I wobbled, swinging my arms to pull my momentum back.

At last I did.

As I whipped around, Bob lowered his head and charged. There would be no avoiding the forge; he was going to knock me straight into the flames. He'd almost reached me when a tan streak shot in from the side, hammering him from view.

Cassius.

He snarled, chomping down on Bob's beard and shaking his head violently.

Bob drew back a massive arm and swatted the seventy-pound dog aside as if he weighed no more than a hamster. Cassius struck one of the heaps of ammo sideways, rounds flying everywhere, raining across the floor.

With a single lurch, Bob hurled himself from his back onto his feet. He spun the shackles around his hand and charged again.

None of my weapons were in reach.

But something else was.

I reached for the blackened handles sticking up out of the forge and ripped the tongs free. As Bob came at me, I raised the glowing yellow tips up to the level of his eyeholes and let Bob's weight carry him onto them. He impaled his face on the tongs, the membranes popping, the hot metal sinking deep, winding up somewhere near the middle of his head. I clenched the handles hard, cinching the tongs inward toward his brain. His eyes fizzled around the hot metal. Black sludge poured into the eyeholes. Noxious smoke drifted from his ears and nose, his mouth foaming.

With the tongs embedded in his face, he fell to his knees and stayed there, kneeling, motionless, his head dipped as if in prayer.

Snatching up Alex's bag, the revolver, and my hooks, I shot for the door, wanting to get clear after all the racket we'd made. Cassius and I ran from the hardware store. I dove across the hood of the same car we'd hidden behind earlier, Cassius bounding around the grille. On the sidewalk I flattened to the ground, peering through the tires, my dog beside me.

Nothing.

Then a set of legs walked past, just on the far side of the car, heading for Bob n' Bit.

I looked at Cassius, put a finger to my lips. He understood

the command. I lowered my head further so the cowboy hat wouldn't poke up into view.

When I looked back, there were two sets of feet shuffling by. Then a flurry more. The parade kept coming, though I could only see the Hosts from the knees down. I lay there, breathing, until the torrent slowed.

A last set of boots trudged by, and then there was quiet for a good long time.

At last I risked a peek through the car windows.

I couldn't see in the hardware store, but the rear door was rolled back, shadows of Hosts thrown about the walls.

I snapped my fingers at Cassius and ran a brief distance up the sidewalk, my baling hooks raised as I ducked into the first doorway.

The general store.

A bell above the swinging glass door clanged our arrival. Flying in, I was immediately attacked from all sides, hands flying in my face, tangling in my hair.

I'd dived right into a nest of Hosts.

I swung the baling hooks wildly. It took a few moments for me to realize that no one was fighting back.

I'd stumbled into the Christmas-ornament display, rows of them hanging from the drop ceiling tiles. As I calmed and lowered my hooks, the ornaments tinkled against one another, throwing off glints of light.

Aluminum Santas and tin reindeer and trees made of pine cones.

Relics from another life.

I thought about all the trees that wouldn't be trimmed ever again. Our birthdays had been turned into something awful, but I hadn't considered that the other holidays were all gone as well, vanished into the sinkhole of this new reality.

I could hear footsteps on the sidewalk, drawn by my loud

and graceless entrance. I ran through the aisles toward the side door, skimming through with Cassius just as I heard the front-door bell clang again.

We scrambled up the slope alongside the general store and onto the roof where Patrick, Alex, and I had stood the first time we'd gazed across the town square and found it overrun.

I could see several Hosts there now, moving about. A herd of them still clustered around the back of the hardware store, lit by the orange glow of the forge like shamans performing some ancient rite.

I raced up the slope into the woods, running through twigs and bushes, banging off tree trunks. Finally I stopped in a clearing, panting. Even Cassius was breathing hard.

I reached over and stroked his head. "You and me, boy," I said, his tail wagging at the sound of my voice. "We—"

A whoosh of air came at me from behind. Something hard cracked me across my shoulder blades, and then suddenly the world flew upside down.

Somehow I was flat on my back. Groaning, I tilted my head in the matted pine needles to catch an inverted view of chubby Chet Rogers walking toward me, his big cheeks flushed as always, holes bored straight through his head.

Gripping a jagged branch like a club, he closed in.

ENTRY 31   I rolled to the side an instant before the jagged end of the branch slammed down inches from my head. Chet wore a coil of calf rope looped over his shoulder.

I drew the revolver and aimed at his face, the barrel wavering back and forth.

Chet's face. Chet, who used to sneak me free soda when he worked at the diner. Chet, who'd driven me to school that week Patrick had the flu. Chet wasn't a grown-up. He was a high-school student like Patrick. Like Alex. Like me.

A bunch of images came at me.

Chet sitting on the bleachers, his face sunk into his hands as he wept.

His fingers gripping the chain-link as he stared pleadingly at us through the fence. *I don't want to be out here alone. I don't want it to happen to me.*

He came at me again, drawing back the branch. The end of the revolver wobbled even more in my hand. "Please don't make me," I said.

Patrick would shoot him, a voice in my head said. *Patrick would've shot him already.*

Chet terrified on the far side of that fence. *I'm just a kid. I'm a kid like you.*

That made it so much worse.

He stepped within reach, and still I didn't fire.

He drew back the branch, and still I didn't fire.

Cassius jumped up and bit his arm, dragging the branch

down. Chet turned and kicked him. Cassius flew across the clearing and lay panting.

My sweat-slick hands bobbled the revolver. Before I could firm my grip, Chet swatted it out of my hands. It glinted as it flew off into a pile of dead leaves.

Chet backhanded me, knocking me down. Then he turned, picked up the sharpened branch, and went after Cassius. He drew the branch back like a spear, the jagged end aimed at Cassius's ribs.

I dove for the gun, groping for it in the dead leaves. I would've done anything to protect Cassius.

As Chet drove the branch down to kill my dog, the trees behind Cassius seemed to explode. Zeus charged through the leaves as if shot from a cannon, the other ridgebacks behind him.

Zeus hammered into the makeshift spear, the point driving through his shoulder, Chet falling back under the force of 110 pounds of rage. Chet slammed onto his back on the ground, the end of the branch embedding in the dirt by his ear. Zeus was impaled on the spear.

But he didn't stop.

Snarling, Zeus drove himself farther onto the spear to get to Chet's face. The tip of the branch poked out of Zeus's side, emerging between his ribs. Still his powerful legs churned the dirt, the branch sliding into him inch by inch, his snapping teeth ever nearer to his target.

Chet raised a hand, and Zeus tore into it, blood spurting, fingers severing. Zeus got to Chet's forearm next and shredded it until it looked as though it had been stuck in a blender.

Chet wiggled back, and Zeus kept on, impaling himself further, grabbing Chet's other hand and mangling it as well. The other dogs had circled up, barking. I had a firm grip on the revolver at last, but no clear shot.

Chet managed to roll free. Tanner and Princess snapped at him as he ran into the woods, pumping his arms, blood drops flying from what remained of his hands. Atticus, Grace, and Deja tore off after them.

Zeus keeled over onto his side.

I ran to him. Breath leaked from his punctured lung, fluttering the fur where the branch stuck out of his ribs. I was crying, stroking his russet head. His face bore the marks of coyote battles past. Even as a puppy, he'd been my biggest, best boy.

He lay still, breathing. Not a whimper.

My tears fell on him. "I'm sorry," I said. "I'm sorry I didn't do it."

He turned his head ever so slightly and licked my palm.

The other dogs returned from the chase and surrounded us. Then I felt a wet muzzle in my ear.

Cassius.

I leaned aside to let him see his father.

Cassius gave a low whimper and ducked his head to Zeus's. They touched noses.

Zeus's eyes glazed, and air stopped wheezing through his side.

Cassius looked at me, then back at his father. He nuzzled Zeus's head a few times, trying to nudge him back to life. Zeus lay there.

Finally Cassius backed up a step and sat.

The other dogs ringed us. Their coats were streaked with mud, their ears tattered from fights. They were wild now.

And yet they looked healthy and well fed.

I bent down and hugged Zeus, burying my face in a fold of fur at his neck. And then I stood, plucked the cowboy hat from the dirt, and put it back on my head.

There were still valleys to cross and mountains to scale and

Alex on the other side. Patrick waited back at the school, breathing down his air supply.

I went around to the others and let them swarm me as I scratched behind their ears and patted their wagging rear ends. Then I started for the stretch of woods off the highway where we'd left the Silverado.

I tapped my thigh once as I reached the edge of the clearing. "C'mon, boy," I said.

But I heard no rustling behind me.

I turned, and Cassius was sitting among the others, imploring me with his yellow eyes and wrinkled brow. He whined once, faintly.

Understanding came, and my heart fell away, a stone dropped into a bottomless pit.

I walked back to him.

"Okay, boy," I said, crouching before him. "Good boy. Good, good boy."

He licked my salty face, and I let him.

I looked as the pack of ridgebacks circled around me, proud and free. Then back at Cassius. I said, "Release."

But he stayed there a moment, blinking at me.

I was finding it hard to swallow. "Go on, then," I said, waving the dogs off.

They bounded majestically away through the trunks. Cassius paused at the edge of the clearing and looked back at me, eyes bright and alive above that black muzzle. Then he turned and was gone, too.

I stood there wiping my face until I could no longer hear the dogs forging through the brush. Then I stood a while more.

As long as they were here, the woods would be a safer place for me. But that didn't make me feel any better right now.

Trudging heavily into the woods, I remembered Patrick's

reply to me before I left, after I'd told him I couldn't do it without him.

You can. You always could.

Maybe Zeus's death had cleared the way for Cassius to grow up.

Maybe it was time for me to grow up, too.

Remembering our run-in with the migrant workers, I gave Jack Kaner's farm a wide berth, slicing north across a wooded ridge. The trees drifted by, an endless scroll. My legs ached. The night air grew thick, streamers of fog floating by. Visibility got so low that I nearly collided with the wrought-iron bars.

Leaning back, I took in the curved sign over the entrance: CREEK'S CAUSE CEMETERY.

Cutting through would save me a good twenty minutes, so I walked beneath the arch. The fog made the air so wet I felt like I was breathing the white wisps themselves. Staying alert, minding each step, I moved past gravestones and plots and a few mausoleums from richer families like the Blantons.

I was so focused on peering through the fog that I didn't notice where my legs were carrying me until I had arrived.

My parents' graves.

Two humble little plots, side by side, with white markers. It had been all we could afford.

It'd been a while since I'd visited. I'd carried anger at them since their car crash, anger that they hadn't been more responsible, that they hadn't thought more about their kids at home before drinking that extra glass of wine. Over the years that anger had loosened from a hard knot in my gut. But I realized now that it had never left entirely. It had just spread out through my body, less obvious, sure, but just as heavy a burden to carry.

I thought about all the ways the world had come undone and everything I had to face now. The loss of my parents, awful as it was, had prepared me for this. I pictured the view over the revolver, Chet's face wobbling in and out of the sights, my finger on the trigger, refusing to pull it. I'd made a mistake, and Zeus had died. I was human and imperfect and doing the best I could minute to minute.

My parents had been, too.

I owed it to them to forgive them. But even more, I owed it to myself.

I crouched before their graves and patted the green, green grass blanketing them. Closing my eyes, I sent them all the warmth from my body, from myself.

When I opened my eyes, the fog had started to thin. Even as I watched, it lifted, billowing up into the treetops and away into the crisp night air.

Something moved to my right. And to my left.

And then all around the vast cemetery.

Mappers.

Still dressed like ranch hands, probably from Billy Joe Durant's two-thousand-head cattle operation to the north. At least thirty of them.

Somehow in the fog, I'd missed them. And they'd missed me.

They walked their patterns in every direction I looked. Their heads tilted downward, they swept through the cemetery like an army of ants, covering every square inch.

ENTRY 32   Standing before my parents' graves, I unfocused my gaze, trying to take in as many of the Hosts as possible. The entire cemetery seemed alive, crawling with them. Their movements were coordinated, the Mappers keeping a short distance apart as they strategically covered ground. I thought about using the revolver, but by the time I'd spent the six shots, the remaining Hosts would've swamped me.

A ranch hand in a ragged denim jacket was closing in fast. He turned crisply on his heel, cutting across the back of a mausoleum. His next pivot would take him directly into me. And anywhere I stepped would be right into the path of another Host. A second Mapper trudged along behind me; others walked spirals to either side of my parents' graves. Beyond the nearest Hosts were layers more, deep in every direction, stretching as far as the darkness and thinning mist allowed me to see.

I dropped to the moist earth before my parents' plots. The grass smelled fresh like summer, like baseball. A few wisps of fog floated through the air.

I had let go of everyone and everything in the world. I was as alone as I'd ever been, as alone as I'd ever be.

A squish of mud signaled the ranch hand's next turn. He emerged from the side of the mausoleum, heading for me, his head scanning the ground just ahead of the tips of his boots.

I grabbed the baling hooks so hard that my knuckles ached. Wet grass slurped at his boots as he moved forward. His eyeless eyes were inches from noticing me. I watched the cant of his head.

And it struck me how I could save myself.

Sliding off my pack, I rolled neatly backward over my shoulders, landing on all fours atop my parents' graves. Somehow the Stetson stayed on my head. The Mapper walked right past me, close enough that the cuff of his pant leg shushed across my cheek.

Easing to my feet, I pulled the pack on again and slid behind him. I kept right on his back, the tattered denim undulating between his shoulder blades inches from my face. I held his pace precisely, put my boots in his footsteps. When he turned, I turned. I could gaze straight through his head from behind, which helped me gauge where we were going. We crossed paths with another Mapper who drifted within spitting distance but did not look up.

Ever so slowly, our turns widened. I stayed on the Host's back, wiping sweat from my brow. Other Mappers marched by on either side, scanning the ground at their feet, the awful boreholes directed just to the sides of my legs. The slightest misstep would alert the Host in front of me or put me into the path of another.

It felt like playing Frogger on the old-time arcade game at the One Cup Cafe, trying to zigzag between cars without getting squashed.

Walk, turn, walk.

A swinging arm whistled by to my right, a massive Mapper stomping past, sending off a waft of body odor.

Walk, turn, walk.

Painstakingly, we spiraled our way out of the inner sanctum of the cemetery.

Walk, turn, walk.

A half hour passed at this excruciating pace. Another. The

Host in front of me halted, and I nearly stumbled into him, my splayed fingers brushing the back of his jacket. He did not turn. Instead he tilted his head up to the sky. A bluish white glow framed the boreholes and the edge of his head as he uploaded his data to the heavens and whatever resided up there. A clicking sound emerged, maybe from his throat, maybe from somewhere else. Staring through the rear boreholes as if they were binoculars, I watched the mapped terrain scroll across his front eye membranes.

The clicking stopped, the glow faded, the head tilted down, and he continued on. Gathering myself, I followed as carefully as before.

Walk, turn, walk.

We ambled over plots, threaded between tombstones, carved around grave markers. It was slow-motion insanity, my life hanging on every tiny motion. I was following the already dead out of the cemetery, like some mythological hero trying to escape the underworld.

At last the fence came within reach. I fought down a panicked urge to spring onto the wrought-iron bars and scale them. We did a final, endless rotation just inside the perimeter and, after what seemed like forever, walked out through an open rear gate. I followed the Host to freedom. Several Mappers remained in view, dispersing across the rolling hills.

I stayed on the Host's heels until there were no other Mappers in sight.

Then I simply stopped walking. I let him drift on in a straight line through the woods. Way up ahead he turned ninety degrees and disappeared through a veil of branches.

I briefly remained as I'd been, clenched and tense.

And then the pent-up terror of the past few hours shuddered out of me. On cue my muscles cramped. I had to consciously unlock my shoulders, draw them down and away from my head.

Bathed by the moonlight, I breathed and shook out my knotted neck. Exhaling long and slow, I continued on my course.

After what I'd been through, the remaining bank of the ridge was a breeze. I broke out onto the dirt road, and there it was, mud-spattered and glorious. The Silverado. I grabbed the keys off the front tire where we'd left them.

Swinging in behind the wheel, I felt a charge of triumph.

I followed the bumpy road down, the ride smoothing out as I lurched onto the highway. The route through the valley was straight and true, and I encountered no real problems. Like before, the abandoned cars were easy enough to dodge and Hosts were few, far between, and easy to steer around. For a while I even rolled down the window and let the breeze riffle my hair.

At the gas station, using the same air tube Alex had used, I siphoned off more diesel from the huge fuel tank of the semi. The bitter taste of the sludge made me gag. Once I'd filled up, I drove to an empty stretch of highway and parked the pickup right on the dotted line. Sitting on the warm hood of the idling truck, keeping a clear line of sight in every direction, I ate a stale sandwich and washed it down with some water.

A picnic for one.

I drove on, Ponderosa Pass coming up, a black mass even darker than the darkness ahead. Remembering the mob of workers from the cannery, I eased off the gas before the barricade and killed the headlights.

As soon as the barricade vaguely resolved ahead, I steered off the road. It was pitch-black here, the mountains cutting off the moon from sight, so I slowed to a crawl. The tires sank in the marshy reeds alongside the road.

The overturned bus from the Lawrenceville Cannery

seemed to leap out of the darkness. I almost smashed into it, managing to wrench the wheel to the side just in time.

After steering around the bus, I parked the Silverado at the base of the pass. The tree line sloped steeply upward here, impossible to scale. I hopped out, my boots smacking wetly into the earth. To start my hike up the mountain, I'd have to climb the barricade once again.

As I pulled my boots from the wet reeds, they made a sucking sound. It was annoying and loud, but there was no other way for me to get back to the road. I continued on, stepping into a boggy spot. My boot sank even lower. When I went to lift my leg, my foot almost pulled out of the boot. I paused to firm my toes inside the boot.

But the sucking sound continued.

Behind me.

Then it stopped. An echo?

I waited, listening for the faintest sound. Nothing. I took another step, and the sucking noise came again in the darkness behind me. I paused, and it paused as well.

I tried to ram my fear back down my throat. If I started sprinting, I'd literally run right out of my boots. Even if I managed to get away, I wouldn't last an hour out here barefoot.

I started up again.

The sucking noise started up.

But now it was in stereo.

Dozens of feet squelching through the reeds.

When I looked over my shoulder, there was only darkness. I swung my head back toward the highway. I was almost there. I could even make out the station wagon smashed beneath the fallen tree at the base of the barricade.

Ten more steps.

The invisible army marched behind me.

Seven steps.

Terror bubbled up from my chest. I swallowed it back down. Three.

At last I eased onto the asphalt, keeping both boots.

I whipped around.

Emerging from the darkness, a band of cannery workers, looking even more ragged than those before. Seven or eight of them. Clothes half torn off. Bushy beards sprouting from the men's faces. The women's fingernails snapped off and bloody.

They broke into a run, their feet kicking up sprays of mud.

I turned and sprinted for the barricade, the backpack bouncing on my shoulders. Their footfalls pounded the highway behind me, closer and closer.

I leapt onto the hood of the station wagon, landing before the dead Host driver—Nick's father. He was still sprawled through the windshield where we'd left him, his head pulverized. I used his back as a stepping-stone to launch me onto the roof, and from there I shot up onto the beaver-dam rise of fallen tree trunks. My hands scrabbled across the wet bark.

The Hosts reached the base of the crisscrossed tree trunks and flew up at me.

They were closing too fast.

I wasn't going to make it.

If I drew the gun, I'd never get off all the shots in time. I dipped a shoulder, let the pack slide into a trough between the logs. I swung the baling hooks up on their nylon loops and seized the handles.

I turned.

One Host bounded onto the station wagon, denting the roof. Only a few yards away. There'd be no running from them or outsmarting them.

Not this time.

Curved steel hooks protruding from either fist, I turned and leapt into the mass.

ENTRY 33   I landed on the roof of the station wagon, the impact sending out a kettledrum rumble, the metal cratering beneath my boots.

Hosts lunged up at me from all sides.

I didn't think.

I just fought.

A flurry of steel and blood, the baling hooks like a part of my body. I sank a tip in one Host's throat, ripping it out even as I pivoted to cave in another's skull at the temple. The first three fell away, knocking down the others trying to scale the sides of the station wagon.

But I wasn't done there.

Rather than let the others come after me, I jumped down into their midst and waded in, both arms swinging. Blood spatter arced overhead. I was screaming not in fear but in rage. A battle cry.

I hurled a hook up through the soft flesh beneath a Chaser's chin, the tip curving through her skull and shoving through her eyehole, popping the front membrane.

—red windshield glass skittering across the floor—

I wrenched the hook free, and she toppled, shuddering.

—Uncle Jim's eyeless face—

Another Host grabbed me from behind, but I spun, raking both hooks, embedding the points in the sides of his head.

—Zeus licking my face, a puppy curled in my arms—

He dropped back stiffly, his body like a plank, his weight yanking his head free of the steel points.

—my brother hooked to tubes—jigsaw pendant in the grass— Cassius whimpering—Chet's face transforming behind the chain-link—Bob Bitley staggering toward me—Patrick's black cowboy hat lowering onto my head—my shadow looming large on the gym doors—

I tumbled out of the storm of memories, coming back to myself, breathing hard. My arms ached at my sides. The Hosts lay sprawled around, twitching and gone. My face and shirt felt sticky with their blood, and my hooks were stained oil-black.

For a moment the silence bathed me.

Eight Hosts, dead at my hand.

With each breath I seemed to inflate, my spine straightening one vertebra at a time, pulling me upright inch by inch.

A familiar sound called my attention to the side of the highway. A few more Hosts trudged toward the barricade, their legs mired up to the ankles in the marshy reeds.

I drew the revolver, waited until they reached the edge of the asphalt about ten yards away. Then I shot them through their foreheads, one after another.

I thumbed the release and let the wheel click open, the hot brass falling away, bouncing at my feet. I climbed up the station wagon again and found my backpack where I'd dumped it on the fallen trees.

After reloading the revolver, I was on my way.

Though there was no sign of Hosts beyond the barricade, I cut off the main road and traveled through the terrain alongside it as we had before. Scaling the slope was treacherous, as was making headway through the underbrush. The heavy backpack tugged at my shoulders, and the hockey stick tangled in branches. My thighs and calves burned. But at a certain point, I fell into a rhythm.

Everything hurt just as much, but I no longer cared. I was separate from the pain and exhaustion, just like the Hosts, observing it as if from some other place. Every time I got hit by thoughts of what might be waiting for me in Lawrenceville, I pushed them aside.

My focus narrowed to a single aim: finding Alex.

For a while I zoned out, drifting in time. It was a few years ago, a night when Alex had called to tell Patrick that her dad had to go out on patrol.

We sneak over to her house and hide in the bushes, waiting for the sheriff's car to pull out of the driveway. Finally Sheriff Blanton steps outside. He pauses on the porch, looking back at her in the doorway. "I don't want those Rain boys over here," he says. "Rain only—"

"—goes one direction," she says, cutting him off. "Down." She shoves his shoulder playfully. "I got it. Now, go keep the peace already."

When Sheriff Blanton turns for his car, she casts a glance over at the bushes where she knows we're hiding and shoots us a wink I feel in my spine.

I know the wink isn't for me. It's for Patrick. But it doesn't matter. I'm close enough to her, to them, that some of her glow touches me, too.

As soon as the car's taillights disappear, we sneak across the front lawn and Alex lets us in, giving Patrick a kiss I can hear even though I don't look over. We make root beer floats and head outside. Like old times, we cram into the hammock together to peer up at the stars, slurping our drinks, swaying, and picking out the constellations.

"I think I see Man Throwing Up," Alex says, pointing at a spray of stars.

"Is that Greek?" I ask, and she laughs.

I'm nestled against her side, her bare arm pressed against mine, and it is warm and soft.

"What do you see, Patrick?" she asks.

"It's just north of the Big Dipper," Patrick says. "It's called Your Dad Tossing My Butt in Jail."

"Ooh," Alex says. "That's an exciting one."

"Exciting?" Patrick says, and I can hear the grin in his voice. "I think it's more scary than anything."

"Well"—Alex turns her face to Patrick, her hair drifting across my cheek—"I hope it's worth it."

"It's worth it," Patrick says.

The hammock rocks hard as my brother climbs out. "I need another root beer float," he says, and pads into the house.

Alex and I lie there for a moment alone. It feels like floating.

"What do you see, Chance?" she asks.

"The Little Bear," I say.

"Where?"

"There."

"I thought that was the Little Dipper."

"It's called that, too."

I hear her rustle on the hammock as she turns to me. "How do you remember all this stuff?"

I can feel her breath. We're that close. I don't dare look over. I shrug. "I don't know."

She turns back to face the night sky. "Is there a Big Bear?"

"It's called the Great Bear. It's formed using the Big Dipper. See, there? The hindquarters. Then the rest of him."

She leans her cheek against my shoulder, peers up the length of my arm.

"It's much more obvious than the Little Dipper," I say. "Higher in the sky and way huger. It dominates everything."

"Hmm," she says. Her cheek stays against my shoulder, and I

don't want to lower my arm, not if it means she'll move away. "But the Little Dipper has the North Star in it, doesn't it?"

I feel my blood quicken a bit at the playful note in her voice. "Uh-huh."

"Isn't that the most important star? The one sailors navigate by? The one all the other stars rotate around?"

I finally lower my arm and turn. Our faces are so close that our noses almost touch. Her green eyes are luminescent. It's such a perfect moment I almost forget to be self-conscious.

"Know what I think?" she says. "I think the Little Bear shouldn't underestimate himself."

My breath catches in my throat.

Before my whirling brain can fix on a reply, the hammock dips again and Patrick spills into the netting beside us. His arm slides beneath Alex's neck, pulling her into him. He's big enough that if he dangles one leg off the hammock, his foot can touch the ground, and he rocks us, rocks us in the quiet of the night.

Alex has turned her face back to him, sure, but she keeps her arm pressed alongside mine.

We sway for a long, long time.

A splash of bracing cold water brought me back into my body there in the wilds of Ponderosa Pass. A lip of dirt had crumbled away, sending me stumbling calf-deep into a river.

The current was strong, pulling one of my legs out from under me, the weight of the backpack spinning me around.

I lost my footing, found it again, my boots scraping across the mossy bed. Cold water rose to my thighs, but I kept my chest and head out of the water. I bulled my way to the far side and clawed at the clay of the opposite bank, dragging myself up out of the water. For a time I lay there panting and freezing.

Alex's voice came to me from afar: *Would you cross raging rivers?*

I would.

I forced myself to my feet and checked the backpack. It was still mostly dry, the plastic bags protecting the perishables and my notebook. Something tingled at my calf, and I tugged up my pant leg. A dark slippery oval clung to my flesh.

A leech.

I scraped it away, leaving a smudge of my blood. I found two more on my other leg and flicked them back into the river. If I wasn't lost, I was certainly off course, which meant I'd have to find higher ground to regain my bearings. I continued upslope, damp pants clinging to my legs, the pass growing steeper and steeper until I had to lean forward and use my hands to pull myself up a rocky rise.

Would you climb mountains?

If they were between me and you, those mountains I would climb.

At last I reached the top, tumbling over the lip, landing in a mud wallow. My muscles gave out under the burn, and I sprawled there panting in the soothing wet.

It felt so pleasant lying here. It would be so easy to rest, to drift off, to give up.

Would you crawl through mud *for me?*

I shoved myself up to all fours, shook my head hard, drew in a deep breath.

If mud needed crawling through to get to you, I would.

I stood, sludge caking my hands and knees. Staggering with exhaustion, I drifted into the thickening pines. The branches drew denser and denser, needles crowding in on me from all sides until it felt like I'd be skewered alive. Finally I broke into a clearing, scratching at my aching arms.

At first I didn't register where I was. Then I saw the ring of Rocky Mountain Douglas firs around me, the forked road beyond, the three cleared spaces on the ground.

The spaces where Patrick, Alex, and I had slept that night we'd made it to the top of the pass.

Though I'd taken a different route up the rock face, I'd wound up in the right place after all.

North and down to Stark Peak.

South and up to Lawrenceville.

I took a moment there at the fork, staring up the dirt road winding to the very top of the pass. I cast a glance at the two rectangles in the pine needles that Patrick and Alex had cleared.

If ever absence had been made visible, it was in those patches of dirt where my brother and his girlfriend had slept just last week.

Stepping from the ring of trees, I peeled south up the fork to Lawrenceville. As my legs carried me onward, a pulse beat in my temple. I realized the obvious: I was terrified of what I might find there.

It turns out I wasn't terrified enough.

ENTRY 34   I moved cautiously up the south fork, weaving through the trees to the side of the road. As I neared Lawrenceville, I came aware of a suctioning noise.

First the smack of some sort of impact. Then a moist yielding.

I froze in my tracks and listened.

A moment later it came again.

Thump. Squelch.

The noise, arriving at regular intervals, drew me through the night like a beacon. It grew louder as I neared the outskirts of town, passing by occasional rickety cabins that had gone to seed when the cannery started busing in workers and the local economy collapsed. It grew louder yet as I came up behind the factory, threading through mud-caked backhoe undercutters and construction rigs parked in clearings among the trees.

Thump. Squelch.

An industrial wasteland nestled in a dip in the landscape, the Lawrenceville Cannery stood out from the surrounding trees even in the darkness, a vast cleared patch of shadow.

Moving from tree to tree, I crept into position above the little valley.

The sounds kept coming, but I could see nothing below.

Thump. Squelch.

Thump. Squelch.

Curiosity burned in me, but fear burned brighter. Whatever those noises were, they weren't good.

The darkness lifted just enough for me to see the rough shapes of the buildings below. I sensed movement around the facility but couldn't make out more than that. Dawn threatened at the eastern horizon, the black sky beginning to show blue.

Thump. Squelch.

I could make out only the shapes closest to me. The storage warehouse just below my perch. Beside it a yellow bulldozer bled through the gloom, parked by a roof-high pile of gravel. Rolls of fencing were stacked like Lincoln Logs. Rectangles of sheet metal rose at irregular intervals across the hillside. Construction must have been under way when the Dusting had hit.

Thump. Squelch.

The sky lightened another degree, the parking lot showing just barely through the haze. I sensed movement on it. Hosts on patrol?

Thump. Squelch.

The noise seemed to be coming from the factory itself. The giant building emerged slowly, like a mighty ship from the fog. The huge doors had been rolled back, venting heat from the factory floor. I could sense a bustle of activity inside, but what it was, I couldn't say. I strained my eyes, trying to see what was going on in there.

Thump. Squelch.

The top of the sun finally broke the horizon, a pinprick of glowing yellow.

I saw through the open doors.

I really wish I hadn't.

ENTRY 35   The Hosts moved in synchronicity, each bent to his or her task. Watching them work was like observing the insides of an intricate cuckoo clock. It might have been fascinating if what they were doing weren't so gruesome.

Hosts crawled like worker bees over the equipment, reconfiguring the compound into a torture camp of sorts. Kids were strapped at intervals to the conveyer belt, bound at the ankles, thighs, chests, and foreheads so they could barely wiggle. Industrial-strength plier clips secured the straps to ridges on either side of the belt. The belt jerked along in lurches and pauses. It snaked around the expansive factory floor before exiting through a freshly sawed opening in the building's side that allowed it to continue on. I guess they needed more room. Crates and cages rose in a giant wall lining an entire side of the cannery, each filled with a sobbing kid. Worming fingers, mashed faces, the glint of shattered eyeglasses—it was almost too terrible to look at. In front of this backdrop of bars and flesh, Afa Similai pulled kids squirming from their crates. With the help of several other Hosts, he bound them to the starting point of the belt.

Once a kid was secured, Sheriff Blanton hit a red button and the belt slid forward one stop before halting again. The lurching belt movement must have been calibrated for filling batches of cans or bottles.

I'd known most of these adults. Afa and Sheriff Blanton, Mr. Tomasi and Gene Durant. I remembered their faces when they held not just blank focus but human emotion. They'd been subverted and overridden, their brains hijacked. But that didn't make any difference to me right now. Watching them do what they did made me hate them anyways.

Thump. Squelch.

I couldn't see the end point of the assembly line, only where it disappeared into the hatch cut into the side of the building.

Thump. Squelch.

I had to walk around to see where that conveyer belt continued. Where it ended. And what was happening there.

Mindful of the Hosts patrolling the compound's perimeter, I lowered into the scratchy brush and crawled down to the storage warehouse below me. I kept my head beneath the yellow weeds, pushing the Stetson in front of me, moving one cautious foot at a time. For all I knew, Chasers had spotted me and were hurtling up the hill already.

But I safely reached the big pile of gravel beside the bulldozer and leaned against it, catching my breath. A few pebbles trickled over my shoulders. From here I'd be able to see the outside of the building where that belt emerged. Shuffling off the backpack, I peered around the edge of the gravel.

I couldn't take it all in at once; it was too overwhelming. I did my best to make sense of it, to assemble it in my mind piece by piece.

To the side of the cannery, several acres of forest had been cleared and a giant foundation poured for future construction. Before the Dusting the factory had evidently been in the process of a huge expansion. That explained all the supplies stashed around the area. The new foundation was enormous, three or four times the size of the original cannery.

Cratering the corner of the foundation was a massive meteor, cracked jaggedly open around the midpoint. But the inside didn't look like anything I'd ever seen.

It was smooth and perfectly rounded, coated with transparent screens that seemed as if they were made of organic matter like the eye membranes of the Hosts. Various images flashed on the screens, though I could make out little more than shifting bluish lights.

It wasn't just a meteor. It had been co-opted as a spaceship.

Thump. Squelch.

My attention was drawn to where the assembly belt emerged from that roughly cut hatch in the cannery wall. A twenty-foot length of the belt had been reassembled outside so the assembly line could continue to the edge of the new foundation.

Thump. Squelch.

My gaze landed at the spot where the belt ended.

A figure stood there at the receiving end like some kind of high priestess from ancient times. Something about her posture and contours suggested she was female. Everything about her was futuristic, from the sleek black suit to the polished helmet with its dark-tinted sheet of a face mask. No flesh was visible; she was completely sealed in seamless armor, which looked like an astronaut suit from another millennium.

I stared at the perfectly smooth protective suit, shaped like a human. It seemed to be airtight. No gaps between gloves and sleeves. No break at the neckline below the helmet. Just one flexible cover adhering to the shape as if poured on, unbroken from torso to waist to boots.

Was there a human beneath it? An eyeless Host? Or was this another creature altogether, shaped like one of us? Her movements inside the suit were oddly fluid and robotic at the same time. Like the eye membranes, the suit seemed to be formed from some sort of biological technology.

The next kid lurched into place before her, strapped to the belt, bared sacrificially. It was Andre Swisher, the track star we'd seen snatched by Chasers in the town square. Even from where I was, I could hear Andre's weeping. The black sheet of the helmet's face guard reflected back his terrified expression.

The figure smacked a sleek glove to Andre's chest, pinning him in place.

Thump.

And she lifted the other arm.

Which didn't look like an arm at all.

It looked like a giant stinger, tapering to a point rather than a hand. The end had numerous small bumps on it, and it squirmed around like a tentacle. Its sharp tip had a hole in it, like an enormous, living needle.

The stinger shot down as if of its own accord, burying itself in Andre's belly and rooting around.

Squelch.

I watched Andre's eyes go white. He rattled on the assembly belt, but the straps kept him from moving much. It looked like he was having a seizure.

Then he stilled.

Several Hosts released the straps from Andre's body and tossed them into a big crate brimming with them. Another Host carried the crate back into the building to the beginning of the assembly belt so the straps could be recycled, used on a fresh lot of kids.

For a moment Andre lay atop the edge of the assembly belt.

The figure removed the stinger from his belly, the end squirming again, those sensory bumps wiggling.

Then something even more impossible happened.

The figure pulled over a rectangle of sheet metal to the edge of the assembly belt.

But it wasn't connected to anything. It floated in the air like a blow-up raft in a swimming pool. With a faint touch, the figure guided it across, lining it up so it served as an extension of the belt. When the belt lurched forward again, the tread rolled Andre onto the floating slab of sheet metal, clearing the way for the next bound child to slide into place beneath the writhing stinger.

With her gloved hand, the figure gently pushed the slab away, and it glided across toward the far side of the foundation. I followed it into the last sheets of morning mist, and what I saw there made me cover my mouth so I wouldn't gasp.

Andre's slab joined an army of others arranged in neat rows. Hundreds of kids lying motionless on their backs, hovering above the ground on their slabs.

Most of them showed bulges in their stomachs. The closest ones looked bloated. But as I peered into the far reaches of the concrete plain, I saw that the farther away the kids were, the more pronounced the bulges were. At the far edge, the boys and girls showed humps protruding almost a foot, filling the space between their waists and their chests. I noticed now that these kids and the others strapped to the assembly line all looked older—at least twelve years old. Where were the younger kids? Being fed at some other center, aged up like cattle?

Making the rounds through this perverted harvest were several more figures wearing seamless space suits like the high priestess, but they were shorter and more muscle-bound. Males? Parading around on autopilot, bent to a single task, they reminded me of drone insects. Their suits were black as well, though less shiny than the female's armor.

I had to remind myself to breathe. I was confronting odds so impossible I couldn't even imagine a version of success. Even if Alex *weren't* already lost and even if I *could* spot her, it would be impossible to sneak into the compound, dodge the Hosts and Drones, free her, and get out.

Thump. Squelch.

The sound made me wince. My cheeks were wet; I hadn't even realized that my eyes were watering from the sight.

I forced myself to exhale. And then draw another breath.

Thump. Squelch.

The figure, she was impregnating them.

Using the children of Earth as pods to incubate . . . *something.* Probably her offspring, which would hatch up out of the kids.

The cannery resembled nothing so much as a beehive.

And the sleek, suited figure was the queen bee.

Or *a* queen bee.

Remembering all those asteroids raking through the night sky a week ago, I wondered how many scenes just like this one were being played out around the planet right now.

Again I told my mouth to draw air, forced my lungs to inhale.

A scream drew my attention back to the cannery. As Afa dragged the next girl from the cage, she thrashed and fought, a shimmer of blond hair flying up over her face. She twisted free and ran, but only got two steps before colliding with Sheriff Blanton's chest. He seized her thin wrists, torquing them painfully, guiding her back into Afa's arms.

Together they strapped her to the assembly belt's starting point, bending over her, their broad flexed backs blocking her from view.

Thump. Squelch.

As the next victim drifted off across the foundation, the belt lurched forward, bringing the girl into view.

It was Alex.

ENTRY 36   The bulldozer hurtled down the graded hillside toward the cannery, blade raised, motoring through boulders, snapping tree trunks, bouncing violently as it reached even ground. It skipped over the curb, took out a length of chain-link fence, dragging it along, and plowed into the corner of the factory.

Chunks of the walls collapsed around it, rubble raining down.

Though the assembly belt kept lurching along, the Hosts flew from their positions toward the crash site. Others swarmed the grounds, the previously perfect mechanics of the operation turned to chaos. It was as though I'd poked a stick into an anthill.

They dug at the sharp rubble to unearth the bulldozer cab, their hands bloodying with the effort. As they worked, the assembly belt kept on, moving the strapped-down kids along toward the Queen.

Thump. Squelch.

One of the Drones had moved over to her side to help with the straps. The show would go on.

The Hosts closed in on the bulldozer, then climbed on top of it, coyotes hungry for the kill. They pried at the rubble, unearthing the machine. At last the final chunk of concrete tumbled away to reveal the cab.

It was empty.

I wasn't in it.

I'd taken advantage of the distraction to sneak down to the factory from a different direction, using stacks of sheet metal and rolls of fencing for cover. In a half crouch, I'd run across the brief open stretch of the parking lot and dived inside the factory floor.

With the Hosts busy at the bulldozer, I'd crawled beneath the assembly belt. It was lifted off the floor by spaced brackets, the cramped crawl space providing access to the belt's underbelly for repairs or adjustments.

On my hands and knees, I scurried beneath it now, the path steering me all around the factory floor as if I were a rat in a maze. When my head or shoulders lifted too high, the belt sanded my skin painfully. Fortunately, I'd stashed the cowboy hat on the hillside with the backpack.

I couldn't see where Alex was, but I knew she was somewhere above me. I could have passed her already. One turn took me toward the far wall, and a chorus of voices erupted beside me.

Turning my head, I saw countless faces peering at me through bars—kids trapped in their cages at the base of the giant stacked wall.

"Hey, kid—please help me!"

"Over here! Over here!"

A young girl was curled up in a ball, weeping.

It was horrible, and yet I had to keep moving.

I couldn't save them all.

I couldn't.

Tearing my eyes away from them, I risked sticking my head out and peering down the assembly line. Nothing. I looked the other way, behind me. There Alex was, twenty yards up. I'd passed her, all right. She'd been the last kid strapped to the belt before the bulldozer diversion. I could see the soles of her shoes lurching away from me.

Relentlessly, the sounds carried in from outside.

Thump. Squelch.

I reversed course, scrambling beneath the belt back toward Alex. When I peeked out to gauge my position, I saw one of the plier clips pinning her down up ahead. The Hosts had moved off the bulldozer now, resuming their duties, their legs sweeping past me in both directions. Raspy breaths filled the air all around me. Despite the pauses in the belt's movement, I was having trouble catching up to Alex. It was hard to move through the narrow space, and the hard floor hurt my hands and knees.

Thump. Squelch.

Ignoring the pain, I hurtled forward.

I was making headway. Closer, closer—

Then I collided with the wall. I'd been so focused on rushing that I'd forgotten to look up at where I was heading.

I'd reached the point where the belt continued through the wall to the foundation outside. I watched helplessly as Alex lurched out of reach. The plier clips binding her to the belt passed through the hatch over my head.

Thump. Squelch.

The lip of the wall beneath the rough-cut hole left little room under the assembly line, squeezing the crawl space even more. Thrusting my arms through the narrow space like a diver, I launched with my legs. The belt bit into my back and shoulders, scraping them. As it jolted ahead, it shoved me backward until the edge of the wall cut into my gut. Then the belt paused.

I was stuck.

Thump. Squelch.

The next movement was going to rip me apart.

I had a moment of blind panic.

I closed my eyes. Heard Patrick's voice.

You can. You always could.

I thought of Alex up there, three kids from the end of the line. And I thought about what the Queen was about to do to her.

I blew my breath out all the way, shrinking my chest, and pulled my stomach taut.

The belt juddered backward again, tugging me the wrong way. With everything I had, I shoved against it. The wall ground across my ribs and stomach, the belt moving in the opposite direction above, threatening to skin me. For a second I thought my hips would catch and the bones simply snap.

But then I shot through.

I landed under the belt outside, pain screaming through my body.

Thump. Squelch.

Alex was two kids away from the Queen.

Pulling the folding knife from my pocket, I jerked it open and bit down on the blade, clenching it between my teeth like a pirate. Then I shot toward Alex and the end of the line. The Queen's slender sheathed legs came into view alongside the thick calves of her Drone.

I didn't have time to be afraid.

The boy ahead of Alex lunged into position beneath the Queen.

Thump.

I could hear the stinger uncoil wetly. Then the conveyer belt shuddered under the impact, dust raining over me.

Squelch.

Alex was next.

I was directly beneath her. I could hear her crying above me. A drop slid off the side of the belt, tapping the ground beside me.

A tear.

The next movement of the belt would bring her into position.

Rolling onto my back, I rammed the knife up through the bottom of the belt, wedging it between two of the powerful metal rollers.

The belt went to lurch again.

The machinery groaned above me. It seemed it would just power through the blade.

But then the conveyer snapped somewhere farther back on the line, the belt rippling like a sheet of paper jammed in a printer. Heavy rubber folds fell around me.

A moment of silence as dust swirled in the air.

Then the Drone trotted off to check on the trouble, his legs vanishing from view. The seamless, bootlike feet of the Queen's suit remained right there by my face. I could have reached out and rapped her toes with my knuckles.

I waited, holding my breath.

Finally one boot pivoted away. Her knee bent slightly.

A moment passed. Another.

Then her feet moved off, heading toward the building.

I didn't wait long. I couldn't. I wormed my torso out, slid my aching hips through, and crouched beside Alex.

Her green eyes, wet with tears, turned to me disbelievingly.

"Chance," she said.

It was just my name, but it was all the payment in the world.

I didn't answer; I just undid the plier clips from the ridges, the straps springing free. We were mostly alone out here. The other Drones patrolled the floating slabs way across the foundation, and the Hosts and Queen were inside the cannery trying to figure out what had gone wrong. More Hosts scoured the hillside, examining the bulldozer's path, searching for whoever had loosed it. The metal slabs of the kids who'd just been implanted glided away across the vast foundation to join the others.

The slab designated for Alex hovered right off the end of the assembly line.

"Slide up onto this," I said.

She scooted herself onto it.

When I crawled beneath the floating slab, I felt an intense energy in my joints and bones that made it hard to breathe. It wasn't completely unpleasant, but it forced me to fight for focus. When I touched the underside of the slab, it responded easily, sliding like a puck across ice. I scuttled under the slab, using it for cover, guiding us to the edge of the foundation nearest the tree line.

For now Alex looked like another fertilized kid drifting to join the others, but soon it would be evident that we were off course. From my squashed position, I watched the legs and feet in the distance. Hosts and Drones everywhere.

And then the Queen's slender boots exited the cannery, rounding the corner to head back to her spot.

Alex and I reached the edge of the foundation. When I rolled out from beneath the slab, the heavy pull on my joints lifted away. I grabbed Alex's arm. "Let's go," I whispered, and she slid off next to me.

I tapped the slab, sending it back toward the others. It re-entered the stream heading to the far side of the foundation.

I could hear the clamor of the kids inside. One girl's keening rose above the din. I felt emotion welling up beneath my face. "I have to . . ." My voice cracked. "I have to go back for them."

"Those things in armor," Alex whispered. "There are *hundreds* of them. We've only got our fists." She looked frail, her face white and bloodless. "I doubt we'd even *make* it to the kids, but I'm willing to die trying if you are."

Her legs were trembling, and not from fear. She was spent. I'd never seen her so fragile.

I remembered the unspoken promise I'd made to Patrick. Had I come all this way just to get Alex killed in a pointless charge to the death?

I tried to drown out the chorus of cries from the cannery. Alex was looking at me, doing her best to keep her feet, waiting on an answer.

I shook my head.

No point in killing ourselves today.

We broke for the woods. A bunch of the Hosts were north of us, crawling all over the trail of wreckage from the bulldozer.

Alex moved weakly, though from fear or exhaustion, I couldn't tell. She seemed to be favoring her left leg. We reached the massive hollow tree where I'd stashed the backpack. The inside was deep and dark, stretching back several yards. We fell to our knees before it.

That's when I heard the crunch of a pinecone behind me.

I barely had time to turn before Sheriff Blanton lifted me off my feet.

ENTRY 37   Sheriff Blanton had me by the shoulders in a vise lock. It felt as though he might pulverize my bones, turn them to dust. I kicked and twisted uselessly. Then I slammed my head back into his face. I heard his nose break, but his grip didn't falter.

I'd lost sight of Alex, and for an instant I thought she'd deserted me.

Then I heard a click.

Sheriff Blanton must have heard it, too, because he turned, still holding me up before him.

Alex stood in a shooting stance just outside the tree hollow. She'd crawled in and fished her dad's revolver from the backpack. One hip was cocked, her bangs sweeping down across an eye. From my perspective it looked like she was aiming the gun right between my eyes. I could find no air to breathe. She flicked her hair from her face and steadied her aim.

"I love you, Daddy," she said, and pulled the trigger.

I felt the heat of the bullet—it couldn't have passed more than an inch from my cheek—and then there was a wet smack. Sheriff Blanton's head snapped back. The lock on my shoulders released, and I tumbled to the earth.

He toppled back and lay still.

Smoke drifted up from the revolver. Alex hadn't moved, not since pulling the trigger.

I shot a quick glance down the hill. Through the branches

the compound was visible below—the tilelike slabs hovering above the foundation, the Hosts repairing the damage, the Queen waiting in position at the assembly line's end for her duties to resume. A few Drone helmets were raised, scanning the hillside.

"Alex," I said. "Alex. We have to go. The noise of the gunshot. *Alex.*"

At last she snapped into motion, sticking the revolver in her waistband. I grabbed my baling hooks. When I pulled the backpack on, she whipped her hockey stick free and twirled it expertly in her hands, the familiar little move bringing me relief I hadn't expected and didn't fully understand.

We ran.

I can't tell you how long or how far, but eventually we heard no footsteps or crackling branches behind us. By the time we slowed, we were miles away, past the fork in the road and heading down the steep terrain of Ponderosa Pass.

Alex leaned against a tree and then slid to the ground, clutching her left leg. "I'm sorry. I need to rest. I was in that cage for two days. . . ."

I went back to her and gave her some water. Breathing hard, she sipped and sipped again. Then she lowered the bottle.

"You came for me," she said.

"I did."

I reached into the backpack, pulled out the black cowboy hat, and put it on. It made me feel closer to my brother. I felt like it might give me some of his strength, too.

Alex studied me, the hat. "Patrick," she said. "Is he . . . ?"

I realized she was taken before we'd returned from the hospital. "He's okay. We got the oxygen tanks. He's waiting for you."

She tilted her head to the tree trunk and pointed her face at the sky, her eyes closed. "Thank God. And thank God for you." When she opened her eyes, the relief was gone. "Chance, they were gonna *implant* me. Use my body as a shell."

I'd never seen her look so young and lost, not even after her mom up and moved away.

"Why are they doing it?" she asked.

The sun worked through the pine needles, making the back of my neck tingle. I pictured those space suits that sealed up the Queen and the Drones from head to toe. Not an inch of exposed flesh.

"Maybe they can't breathe on Earth or handle the environment here," I said. "So they need to birth a new generation that can."

She gave a faint nod, her eyes glazed. "Like there were two generations of Hosts. First the ones like Hank McCafferty who infected everyone else. Then the Mappers and Chasers."

"Their plan keeps evolving step by step."

"And they used our parents—my dad—to help. The people who are supposed to take care of us." Her voice trembled. "They're trying to live through us. Turn us into something else." Anger burned in her green eyes. "Turn us into *them*."

"Your dad," I said. "Alex, listen—"

"I don't want to talk about it," she said, standing up brusquely.

Even though she was limping, she kept pace by my side as we headed down the pass. It was gonna be a long, hard way to the bottom. After a while we fell into a trance. We came around a bulge of granite, and I heard footsteps crunching fallen leaves up ahead. I stopped and pulled Alex behind a tree trunk. My chest pressed into her shoulders, her head drawn back so our cheeks touched. She started to protest, but I put a hand gently over her mouth. We waited.

A moment later a Mapper emerged from the brush and headed right for us. Alex's body tensed against mine, but I held her firmly, willing her not to move. I was watching the angle of the Mapper's eyeholes, a trick I'd picked up in the cemetery, and they were pointed a foot to the side of us. Sure enough, he passed by, his shoulder brushing against the bark inches from Alex's face.

Once he'd disappeared into the foliage, I released her. When she turned to me, her look held something different in it, though I couldn't say what.

"We should find somewhere to hide until night," I said. "Traveling in daylight's too risky."

"You're right," she said. "I think we've pushed our luck enough today." She raised her arm, pointed past my cheek. "How 'bout there?"

I turned, seeing nothing at first. Then it came into view. A cabin a half mile away, obstructed by trees.

We headed for it. As we neared, it emerged from the forest. Aside from a small barn a stone's throw away and a generator shed covered with solar panels, there was nothing man-made in sight.

We circled the cabin once, peering through the windows, and paused at the front door. Alex raised her hockey stick, and I firmed my grip on the handles of the baling hooks.

"Ready?" she asked.

"Ready," I said.

She busted in, and we turned, back to back, scanning the place.

No Hosts.

Truth be told, it was sort of cozy. Queen-size bed with a quilt, potbellied stove, kitchenette. A gun cabinet against the wall showed off a hunting rifle and several boxes of rounds. A framed photograph on the side table captured a couple in their sixties sitting at a poolside table somewhere, his arm around her shoulder. Behind them a tropical sun glowed through scattered clouds.

Alex sagged to the bed.

I dumped the backpack from my shoulder and dug through it, tossing her an energy bar. She caught it in front of her face.

"Thanks," she said. "I'm starving."

Shoving a browning apple into my mouth, I moved over to the gun cabinet and tugged open the glass door. I pulled out the rifle. It was a basic Ruger M77 Hawkeye .308. In my hands it felt like home. It was too big to carry back with us, but I loaded it and leaned it into its slot. Even if we were only staying until sundown, I liked knowing that it was there.

When I glanced at Alex, she was turning the bar over in her hands, looking at it but not peeling the wrapper.

She spoke slowly. "You saw that solar-powered generator outside, right?"

"Mmm-hmm," I said around the apple.

She rose and crossed to the refrigerator. When she opened the freezer door, cool air wafted out. Inside, frozen cuts of venison and elk.

"Maybe we can live like humans again," she said. "At least for a few hours."

She lifted a finger and swiped it across my cheek, her print coming away dark with grime. "Shower off. You're filthy."

"But—"

"I have a hockey stick, a revolver, a hunting rifle, and I just shot my own dad through the head. So I think I'll be able to protect us for a few minutes while you clean up."

I nodded dumbly.

She rooted around in a bureau, found some clean clothes roughly my size, and tossed them at me.

Dropping the Stetson on the bed, I went into the bathroom. The shower stall was tiny, but the hot water felt amazing. Dirt ran down my legs, pooling around the drain. It was hard to believe how much muck came off me—I must've looked like a wild animal.

I scrubbed until I was clean, then scrubbed some more. After I toweled off and dressed, I spent a little more time in the mirror than was necessary. Through the tiny window, I saw dusk coming on strong, the mountain air turning grainy.

A delicious scent reached me—cooked meat. After so long eating stale sandwiches and energy bars, I'd almost forgotten what real food smelled like.

When I walked out, the front room was dark. Alex had drawn all the curtains and lit candles on the kitchen table—a smart move to avoid giving us away. As I stepped closer, I saw that she'd put together a full meal with plates and settings and everything. She was already seated, waiting for me.

It was like a romantic dinner.

Except, of course, it wasn't.

She pointed to the chair opposite. "Sit."

"Gladly."

We dug in. Elk in a pepper sauce, rice with cilantro, water with actual ice cubes—I couldn't remember ever tasting anything so delicious. For a while there was only the peaceful sound of flatware clinking against plates. I sat back and wiped my mouth.

"Nicely done, Blanton," I said.

She looked around. "It's a shame we have to get moving soon. But we're still high on the pass and we got a long way back to town."

"That's right. The good news? 'Rain only goes one direction—'"

"'*Down*,'" we said together, and laughed.

She set her fork next to her plate. Her expression shifted, and I could tell she was thinking of her father.

"He had a thing with your mom in high school, you know," she said. "They were sweethearts."

It took a moment for me to process that one. "You're kidding."

"I'm not."

I tried to picture Sheriff Blanton with my mom when they were younger, but my brain wouldn't compute the image. "There's no way."

"Oh, yeah. They were gonna get married, have kids, the whole thing. Then Dad broke up with her after graduation. I don't know what it was. Cold feet, fear, whatever. But he never forgave himself for it. Or her."

My face burned with indignation. "He never forgave *her*? That doesn't make any sense."

"The heart doesn't make any sense, Chance. Its *job* is to not make sense."

I looked across at Patrick's black cowboy hat where I'd dropped it on the bed and kept my mouth shut.

She stood. "I'm gonna indulge in a shower before we go."

She searched through the bureau some more but only came up with a man's undershirt and a pair of boxers. She shrugged. "I'll take what I can get and put my dirty clothes on over it again."

When she disappeared into the bathroom, I poked around the cabin, trying to process what she'd just told me about my mom and her dad. That explained why Sheriff Blanton had disliked me and Patrick all these years. Why he'd hated our family name so much.

I found myself drawn back to that photograph of the older couple. How content they looked sitting there, umbrella drinks in hand. What was it like to grow old with someone that way?

To know the other person was by your side. Not just for the big romantic moments but the day-to-day stuff, too. My mom and dad had it like that. Uncle Jim and Sue-Anne, too.

It didn't seem like something I'd ever have.

I set down the framed picture, then went to do the dishes. It seemed important somehow, a gesture of respect for the folks who'd owned the place, who'd once taken a trip to enjoy each other's company in the sun.

Alex came out, dirty clothes over clean, toweling her hair.

She paused by the bed, leaning a hip against the mattress, still looking a bit weak from her ordeal. "You cleaned up the kitchen? Why?"

I finished wiping down the counter. "I don't know," I said.

It seemed too hard to explain. But she nodded as if she understood anyways. She didn't move from her spot by the bed.

"What did you go through?" she asked. "To get to me."

I looked down at my boots.

"Tell me, Chance," she said quietly.

So I did. I gave an abbreviated version of the empty church, of Chet's attack and how Zeus died. The cemetery and the barricade, the climb up the pass and how I'd waited for dusk to come on, the terrible sounds of the assembly line carrying to my perch in the hills above the cannery.

She didn't say a word, not even after I finished. Her lips were pursed, her eyes glimmering. It looked like she might be about to cry, but I wasn't sure why. We stood in the silence a moment.

Then I remembered. I dug in my pocket. Came up with her jigsaw pendant.

"Patrick told me to bring this to you," I said.

She seemed to realize she was still holding the towel, and she dropped it on the quilt next to the cowboy hat.

She reached back and took up her wet hair, exposing her

slender neck. The whole time her eyes held mine. "Will you put it on for me?"

Blood rushed to my face. I looked down at the silver piece in my hand. That chain pooled in my palm, the tiny, delicate links. I willed my legs to move, but they wouldn't listen.

"C'mere, Little Rain," she said.

Keeping my eyes lowered, I walked over to her, my boots creaking the floorboards. I was standing right in front of her. We were about the same height, and I wondered when that had happened—she'd always been a few inches taller. Her neck was right there before me, an arc of wet hair floating just off the skin. I was looking at her jawline, her mouth. I didn't dare lift my eyes to meet her gaze for fear of what they might reveal.

I reached up, the pendant dangling between my hands. My fingers grazed her neck. Her skin, so smooth. Her hair, cool against my knuckles as I fumbled with the clasp.

At last I got it.

She leaned forward.

And kissed me.

My heart stopped.

Her lips were as plush and soft as I'd ever imagined.

She pulled back, plucked the cowboy hat off the quilt, and seated it on my head. The room felt hazy to me, my thoughts and emotions swimming. Words drifted out of reach.

She gave me a sideways smile and brushed past me toward the door. "Let's get going."

Yanking on the backpack, I stumbled out after her, still unable to speak.

Alex's limp was more pronounced. Though we'd just had a rest, her shoulders sagged with exhaustion. I wondered how we'd make it all the way down the pass. We headed off the porch, passing the little barn, forging into the trees.

That's when we heard it.

Something moving inside the barn.

Something very big.

I paused, and we looked at each other. I knew she was thinking what I was thinking, that she held the same hope for what it might be.

But there was a risk, too. If I rolled back that barn door, a swarm of Hosts could spill out.

Alex staggered weakly to the side, setting her weight on her strong leg. I thought about how tired she was and how rough the terrain before us was.

It was worth the risk.

Reversing course, I moved back toward the barn, and she did nothing to stop me.

My fingers curled around the metal handle. Something shifted inside again, the wood creaking. I hesitated, staring at the flaking wooden door.

Then I slid it open.

ENTRY 38   A shiny black Andalusian stallion loomed in the single stall. Seeing us, he threw back his head, exposing a white star on the left side of his chest. I pushed back the stall door, and he pranced out. With massive hindquarters and powerful hocks, he must have been seventeen hands.

At my back Alex leaned against the tack wall, the reins clanking behind her.

"It's like he's not real," she said.

I put my hand on the stallion's flank, felt the muscle and heat. Stacks of hay remained in his stall, a nearly empty bucket of oats, and a trough half filled with water. Though he'd been nourished, he was agitated from being pent up. He was ready to run.

That was fine by me.

———

I tapped my heels into the stallion's ribs, pushing him from a two-beat trot to a lope. We rode bareback straight down the asphalt strip of Ponderosa Pass, his hooves like thunder against the tarmac. I leaned forward, gripping the reins, Alex's arm looped around my waist. Her other hand swung free, gripping the hockey stick. Just in case.

Sure enough, a Chaser darted from the tree line ahead of us. I yanked the harness to the right, and Alex nearly lopped off the eyeless head as we cantered past.

The road gleamed with night dew, a black river leading us

down to the barricade. We floated above the world, high enough to be safe, fast enough to soar. Alex's body felt warm and tight against mine. She leaned into me, resting her cheek against my back when she got tired.

We made great time, the ride way easier than the brutal off-road hike we would have had to make. The rhythm of the horse beneath us was hypnotic, the crisp night air intoxicating. We encountered few Hosts on our descent. Two of them Alex dispatched with her hockey stick, and a third I trampled right over.

At last the eighteen-wheeler came into view where it had plowed off the road, crashing into the forest and starting the cascade of trees. We reached the rear of the barricade and slid off, Alex's legs wobbly beneath her. I propped her up. The stallion was in full lather, breathing hard, and he looked regal, even godlike. His shiny black coat made him nearly invisible in the darkness, save for the white star.

I stroked his muzzle and thanked him. Uninterested, he turned and trotted off.

Once the mist folded around him, it was as though he had never existed.

As I helped Alex up and over the fallen trees, I realized that she was even weaker than I'd thought. Though she was toughing it out, it was clear that the past two days had taken a serious toll.

We peered over the top of the barricade to check for Hosts, then picked our way down the logs. I set my hand on an upthrust branch, and it felt soft, wrapped in fabric of some sort. When I looked closer, a cartoon of an old king with a scepter and crown became visible. It was Nick's Stark Peak High Monarchs hoodie, snared there where I'd dropped it after he'd been snatched away by the horde.

I kept moving.

When we landed on the roof of the station wagon, Alex took note of the corpses splayed around the vehicle. She glanced over at me. "You did this?"

I nodded.

Again she gave me a look I couldn't interpret. I hopped down, then eased her off the roof. She landed gingerly, trying not to put all her weight on her sore leg.

We rushed off the highway in the direction of the Silverado, our feet squelching in the marshy reeds. It seemed wetter down here; there must've been a good rain on this side of the pass last night.

A few steps farther, when I started to sink to my calves, I sensed we might be in trouble. Once we reached the truck, I pulled up short, dismayed.

It was sunk to the bumper in the boggy reeds, the tires lost from view.

No way I'd be able to drive it out of here, not until the land dried.

The nearest vehicles were fifteen miles away at the gas station. On foot across the open plain of the valley, Alex and I would be picked off easily. I doubted she could make it fifteen more steps, let alone miles.

For the first time since I'd left the school, despair settled through me.

To have come all this way to be defeated by a simple rain.

How stupid of me to park the Silverado out here on soft ground.

As wetness crept through my socks, I leaned against the truck. Then my temper snapped. I banged the hood with my fist, then tried to kick the side panel, though I could barely yank my boot free to do it.

"Chance," Alex said.

I felt her hand on my shoulder.

"I don't care," I fumed. "I don't care if they hear me."

Part of me wanted the Hosts to come so I could take out my rage on them.

I tried to kick the truck again, a poor effort.

"Are you done?" Alex asked calmly.

I turned, hooks dangling around my wrists. "I think so."

"There *is* another car we could use."

"What are you talking about?"

But already she'd started sloshing back to the highway, her feet making sucking sounds as they pulled from the earth. Alert for Hosts—maybe I *didn't* really want them to show up—I followed.

She reached the station wagon, its tailgate smashed beneath the last tree trunk in the barricade. Opening the driver's door, she reached in and unbuckled the seat belt from around the dead Host's thighs. Then she nonchalantly yanked him out and dumped him on the ground.

Nick's father. Killed by Patrick. Now just another dead Host lying among others.

She climbed in and stared at me through the shattered windshield. Streaks of blood marred the hood, along with those fingernail scrapes. "Well," she said, "get in."

"Alex. The car is *crushed* under that tree."

"Just the back."

"Not a prayer."

"Fine," she said. "Out of my way, please."

I stepped to the side.

The engine coughed as she turned it over and then died. On her second try, it coughed some more but finally caught. The transmission clanked as she jerked the car into gear, and then she stomped the gas pedal.

The motor roared, the tires spinning, throwing up smoke. The station wagon went nowhere.

I didn't think it could get louder, but it did.

Bent over the wheel, her face set with determination, Alex gave the engine more gas.

The car remained in place, pinned down by the tree.

"I told you!" I shouted.

Alex either ignored me or couldn't hear.

I cast a glance at the darkness behind me. A few floating white ovals resolved—faces of Chasers. Then bodies came visible beneath them, making slow progress through the reeds. Some of the Hosts were sunk to their knees, but still they drove themselves on.

The wheels screamed against the tarmac.

The station wagon's front bumper lifted an inch. The tree made a faint crackling sound against the crunched metal of the tailgate. Perhaps the slightest shift.

The frontline Chasers were now only a few steps from the highway. Legions more appeared behind them.

"Alex! We don't have time for this!"

She didn't so much as look up.

All at once the station wagon shot free of the tree, the massive trunk slamming into the ground behind it. The car bolted past me, then screeched to a halt. My mouth gaping in amazement, I watched as Alex leaned over and flung open the passenger door.

"Coming?" she asked.

The closest Chaser pulled her foot free of the muck and set it on the edge of the highway, the others waddling behind her. She was near enough that I could see stringy hair flicking behind the holes bored through her face.

I sprinted over and hopped in. Alex pulled out, the car rattling like crazy, a rear tire whining against the collapsed wheel well.

Alex shot me a little smirk.

She pegged the speedometer at sixty, the car shuddering like it might come apart. After a few miles, smoke started drifting up from the hood. The whine from the back grew louder and louder until the stink of burning rubber filled the car.

After another stretch of highway, we heard the rear tire flap free, the car resettling on its chassis. By some miracle Alex kept us going another few miles on three tires and a rim, sparks flying out behind us. Surprisingly, we spotted no Hosts alongside the road.

Just as we coasted up on the gas station, the engine sputtered and quit. Alex hopped out by the pumps and gave a little bow.

"I gotta admit, Blanton," I said. "That was impressive as hell."

We edged into the parking lot, strolling among the vehicles like a couple of car shoppers.

"Well, dear," she said, taking on a housewife's demeanor, "the minivan has more room for groceries and is much more sensible, but then again . . ." She halted by a Mustang and regarded me over the low roof with a wicked smile. "I've always thought 'sensible' was overrated."

Seconds later we vroomed out of the gas station, 420 horses rattling our bones against the seats. Alex rolled down her window, sticking her arm out in the wind, and I followed suit. We must've looked like some kind of crazy earthbound airplane. We averaged well over a hundred across the valley, slicing past the occasional Mapper, barely slowing until Alex veered onto that dirt road outside of town. Snaking back into the forest, we parked where we'd left the Silverado after our last journey, our tires settling into the same ruts in the mud.

We climbed out, and Alex regarded the woods nervously, her fists clenching around her hockey stick. "Think I'll be okay on this leg?"

"Do we have a choice?"

"I'm pretty tired, Chance."

I could tell it was hard for her to admit.

"Slow and steady," I said.

We pushed into the branches, heading toward town, toward school, toward Patrick. Alex leaned on her hockey stick, using it like a crutch. We hadn't made it ten steps when we heard a crackling of branches, something moving swiftly toward us.

The sound of a body crashing through underbrush.

I stepped protectively in front of Alex. The crackling grew nearer, nearer.

Chet's hulking form emerged, shredded clothes swaying about him. One of his hands was gone, the other mangled by Zeus. Bite marks raked his torso and face, and yet he still came at us, drawing back the nub of his arm to strike.

Stepping forward, I swung a baling hook straight down through the top of his head, sinking it a half foot deep.

The weight of the blow sent him to his knees. I kicked him, and he collapsed to the side. Then I set the tread of my boot on his lifeless cheek and ripped the hook free of his skull.

It surprised me how little I felt.

Alex was behind me, drawn back against a tree, her chest rising and falling from the scare.

"You okay?" I asked.

Again she regarded me with that expression I couldn't quite read.

"Why do you keep looking at me that way?" I asked.

"You're not who you were," she said.

I wiped the bloody hook across my jeans. "None of us are anymore."

She pushed herself off the trunk, balancing on her good leg.

"These woods are full of Hosts," she said. "You ran into so many on your way to me. I don't know that I can outrun them."

"Don't worry," I said. "We've got friends here."

"What do you mean?"

I put my fingers in my mouth and gave a sharp whistle. Nothing.

I stared through the branches, waiting.

"Chance?" Alex looked at me like I was crazy. "What are you doing?"

But already I heard them charging through the foliage, churning up dirt. Alex didn't have time to get scared before the pack of ridgebacks exploded through the trees, surrounding us, nipping at our hands and butting into us, fighting for attention. Cassius jumped up on me, setting his paws on my chest, licking my face. Smiling, I settled him down.

The others swarmed Alex, who laughed, delighted.

"Come on, boys," I said. "We need a fanged escort through the woods." I clapped my hands once. "On guard."

They folded around us, burying us in the pack as we stumbled toward town. Alex looped an arm over my neck so I could help her limp along. Bypassing the town square, we charted a course that kept us in the trees for as long as possible. If it weren't for the dogs, we would've been in trouble hobbling through the dark woods, but they were amazing. At one point we heard shallow panting from the foliage to our left. Deja, Princess, and Tanner charged off. When Alex and I peered through the branches, we saw our former history teacher on her knees, being yanked to and fro like a rag doll.

These dogs were bred to hunt lions.

The thing that had been Mrs. Olsen didn't stand a chance.

The dogs came back to us, their snouts bloodied, and we heard nothing more from beyond the branches.

We kept on peacefully for a time, making progress, Alex guarding her hurt leg. Halfway to town the dogs heard something we didn't, and the whole pack shot off through the underbrush. There were snarling and ripping sounds, and a brief time later they emerged, ears perked, tails wagging. We never even saw the Hosts. The ridgies surrounded us again, their brown eyes flashing alertly, and picked up right where they'd left off.

But that only highlighted how vulnerable we felt when we reached the edge of the woods, halting before a row of un-fenced backyards that signaled the start of the neighborhood around school. Though there were no visible Hosts, the sight of all that open ground before us made my stomach lurch.

Firming my grip around Alex, I stepped onto the Wood-rows' back lawn, veering past the barbecue by the side of the house. Then I noticed that the dogs were no longer with us. Hesitating back in the tree line, they whined. Some pack instinct must have told them to stick to the forest.

When we turned, we saw only their eyes glinting in the dark spaces between the trunks. Set by set, they pulled back, vanishing. One pair of eyes remained a little longer, floating there. I knew they were Cassius's. Then those, too, drew back and were gone.

Suddenly the night seemed much lonelier.

Alex and I moved silently alongside the Woodrows' house and up their long driveway. A few blocks ahead, the big shad-owy block of the school loomed, barely visible in the first rays of dawn.

Home. Or at least as close a thing to it as we had left.

The streets looked empty, but even so we made our way carefully from hiding place to hiding place. Alex stumbled, slipping from my grip, holding her injured leg and wincing. She leaned against a pickup truck.

Nervously, I watched a seam of light nudge the horizon, the glow bringing the street into clearer view.

"C'mon, Alex. Just one more block."

"Sorry. Gimme a hand." Biting her lip, she grabbed around my neck and let me hoist her to her feet.

Looking past me, she gasped.

I glanced up.

Barely visible in the predawn glow, a wave of movement swept around the corner between us and the school.

ENTRY 39   I had no time to think.

Lifting Alex off her feet, I dumped her in the back of the pickup, then hoisted myself up and slid in next to her.

We lay curled into each other so our foreheads touched.

Her whisper was so quiet I could barely hear her. "What if they saw us already?"

"It's still mostly dark."

Dozens of feet rasped across pavement toward us.

"But what if they *did*?" she said.

"We'll find out soon enough."

Closer. Closer. Then I sensed shadows flicker past us on either side. The group of Hosts had split around the truck. If any one of them paused or looked to the side, they would see us there, holding our breath and hiding in the bed of the truck.

But they didn't.

Being single-minded had its advantages.

But also its disadvantages.

Alex dipped her face into the hollow of my neck, and I held her, breathing the smell of her hair. The wave of Hosts kept coming and coming, split by the prow of the truck.

Finally the stream thinned, and a brief time later we heard nothing at all.

A spill of light came from the east, making the treetops glow.

"We should go," Alex said.

"We need to wait, give them time to get a few blocks away," I said. "We can't lead them into the school."

"Okay. Okay."

I could feel her breath against my throat. Somehow our arms had wound up around each other.

"When I was four," Alex said, "I got lost at Disney World. There were people everywhere. But I could only see their knees. And then, through the crowd, I saw my mom's skirt. But I couldn't get to her. People kept walking between us, and I'd lose her and lose her again. There were people all around, but I was so lost." Her voice caught. "It was like that at the cannery. When they had us in cages, when they strapped me to that assembly line, I was surrounded by kids but completely alone. I might as well have been the only person left in the world." She lifted her face to mine. "And then there was you."

Her lips, so close. I thought about what might have been between us in some alternate universe where I was the older brother instead of Patrick.

I tore my gaze from her green, green eyes and looked at the lightening sky. "We should go before it gets too bright," I said, and she nodded her agreement.

Cautiously, I eased to the sidewalk, checking the street, and then helped her out. Leaning on each other, we rushed toward the school. We reached the gate at the northeast corner, and I spun the combination lock, opening it. Then we ran for the building.

It wasn't until we'd reached the shadows that I allowed myself a full exhale, seating the Stetson more firmly on my head. We kept close to the building until we got to the door by the picnic area. I gave a tap.

The lookouts, two of Ben Braaten's crew, let us in.

"Man, you guys look like hell," Mikey Durango said.

We ignored him, hustling through the halls, eager to see

Patrick. Alex stopped leaning on me. As we neared the double doors, she straightened up until she was limping on her own two feet. She took my hand. Gave it a squeeze.

Then let go.

We burst through the doors.

Everyone looked sluggish, just stirring in the light of the new day. Dr. Chatterjee stood by the dry-erase board, writing down the latest unidentified particulate readings. The numbers hadn't gone down, not at all.

JoJo and Rocky jumped up and waved at us. JoJo ran over and clung to Alex's side. JoJo's eyes moistened as she hugged Alex, her guilt melting away. Eve peered over the rows of cots at us, her arms crossed, wearing a half smile of relief. Atop the bleachers Ben stood lookout, the early rays catching in the scars on his face. He turned at our entrance, his features falling back into shadow, conveying a quiet menace.

My eyes swept the gym for Patrick.

Chatterjee looked up and saw us. "Chance! Alex! You did it!" His initial expression of delight was quickly replaced by regret. "You just missed Patrick."

All the air whooshed out of me, leaving me deflated. I'd never felt so tired in my life.

"What do you mean we *missed* him?" Alex said.

"The extra oxygen tanks you got, turns out they were empty," Dr. Chatterjee said. "Only the portable one you refilled at the hospital was good."

"No," I said. "I checked them. They were all in the green."

Rushing over to the stack of H tanks, I looked at the meters. Every needle was pegged in the red. The valves had been loosened ever so slightly. A drumroll of fury started up in my gut.

"He only discovered it this morning," Chatterjee was saying. "He was down to his last hours. So he took the portable tank to make a run for the last tanks at the hospital."

"By *himself*?" Alex limped over to the nearest cot, but before she could get there, her left leg gave out and she collapsed onto the floor. "None of you would go with him?"

In the back Rocky stepped out from behind the other kids. His voice came, high-pitched and young. "I *wanted* to go. But Patrick wouldn't let me. He and Dr. Chatterjee said I couldn't."

"Nobody but a ten-year-old?" Alex said. *"Nobody?"*

A shame-filled silence.

"Not in broad daylight," Ben called down from the bleachers.

"He'll be killed," Alex said. "He'll be killed before I see him."

"Probably," Ben said. "But he was gonna die anyways once that tank ran out. So he didn't have much of a choice, really."

I glared up at him. "These tanks were tampered with."

"Come on, Chance," Ben said. "Who would want to do that?"

"You."

He looked directly at me. "I didn't touch those tanks."

"Then you had your lackeys do it."

"I will talk to my guys, and if any of them messed with those tanks, they will answer to me."

"Liar!" Grabbing her hockey stick, Alex tried to get up to charge Ben, but her leg wouldn't hold her weight anymore. She fell over, the stick clattering away.

"If I was you," Ben said, his eyes never leaving mine, "I'd go help your brother. And fast." He turned his face to the window again. "Doesn't look like he's doing so hot out there alone."

My rage boiled over. Firming my grip on the baling hooks, I started for the bleachers.

Eve stepped in front of me, her hands planted on my chest. "Patrick needs you."

Every fiber in my body was pulling me up those bleachers to add to Ben's scars. But she was right.

I turned and ran out, hammering through the double doors, darting past the lookouts, grabbing a key from the windowsill. Charging through the front door, I jumped over the steps, unlocked the padlock, and slipped through the gate. There were no Hosts nearby, but even if there had been, they wouldn't have stopped me.

The sky brightened as I sprinted through the teachers' parking lot, hurdling the hedges. Heading toward the hospital, I scanned the front yards for movement. Though a few weeks ago running down a street in broad daylight would have been normal, it felt bizarre now. Exhaustion and stress dragged on me. My chest was heaving, but I kept on.

I was driven by love, sure. But also by guilt.

I hurdled a flower bed, ran across the Everstons' porch, and leapt over a tricycle on its side. Above the rooftops I could see the rise of the hospital. I shot through a side yard, darting beneath a carport, knifing my body so I wouldn't slam into a silver Airstream trailer parked in the front driveway.

Squeezing between the trailer and a row of trash bins, I popped out into the front yard.

I heard movement behind me.

When I glanced over my shoulder, three Chasers flew out of the shadows beneath the carport. I must've sprinted past them without even noticing.

They'd caught me off guard. As I twisted around, raising the baling hooks, my feet tangled, spilling me onto the ground.

They barreled at me, muscles straining through their skin. There was no time to get up and fight. I crossed the hooks protectively over my head. It was the only thing I could do.

All of a sudden, footsteps hammered overhead.

I squinted up to see a figure flying across the roof of the house, backlit by the rising sun.

Between the portable tank rigged onto his back like a scuba tank, the shotgun angled across his chest, and the heavy-duty mask erasing his features, he looked like a superhero.

The shadow took flight off the roof, passing directly over the heads of the Chasers, swinging the shotgun around so it aimed straight down between his legs.

Thunder.

The scattered buckshot blew the Chasers to pieces on the driveway before me.

The form continued overhead, landing on the Airstream with a thump, cratering the metal.

I was on my back, my arm raised against the morning glare.

"Chance." My brother's voice was distorted through the mask. "Get up here now." Leaning over, he stuck his hand out for me.

Scrambling to my feet, I grabbed it, and he hauled me up.

"Back onto the roof of the house," he said. "Before others come."

I ran down the length of the Airstream, dodging the open sunroof, gaining momentum to leap across the gap to the top of the carport. I made it easily. I turned to watch my brother.

The weight of the tank pulling down on him, Patrick sprinted across the Airstream after me. Just as he was about to leap, a clawlike hand shot through the sunroof, grabbing for his ankle, tripping him.

He stumbled, kept his feet, his force carrying him to the end of the Airstream. Somehow he managed to jump across the gap, but he landed hard, rolling over his shoulder.

One of the straps snapped, the tank spinning away from him. The mask pulled free of his mouth, yanked down below his chin, exhaling a hiss of oxygen. The tubing popped free. The tank rolled and rolled toward the edge of the carport roof.

Then it went over.

A second later I heard a clang as it hit the driveway below.

Patrick was holding his breath, his cheeks already turning red, veins standing out in his throat. The collision had knocked the air out of him. I was a few feet away, standing over him, paralyzed.

It was all happening so fast.

I saw his lips part.

Then he pulled in a breath.

ENTRY 40   We were frozen there atop the carport, me on my feet, Patrick knocked over.

He breathed the infected air again.

I didn't know if we had two seconds or two minutes before he transformed.

"It's okay." He tugged the mask off over his head and tossed it to the side. "I can't do this anymore."

Anger and grief and denial crushed in on me, all mixed together. "But I got Alex," I said. "I got her home safe."

He gave a faint, sad smile. I could read the relief in it. And so much more.

"I know how you feel about her," he said.

He *did*? I was shocked.

But my surprise was nothing next to what we were facing.

"Take care of her," he said. "And make sure she takes care of you."

He flipped the shotgun around, extending the stock to me.

"Now," he said. "Are you ready?"

No.

I couldn't get my mouth to answer.

"Chance," he said, firmly. "This is gonna happen any second now. Are you ready?"

No.

I took the shotgun. He put his fist around the end of the muzzle, held the bore to his forehead, and looked up at me.

Our eyes locked. I watched his lungs fill and contract, fill and contract.

I waited for that full-body shudder.

But nothing happened.

A minute passed. And then another.

Patrick let the shotgun bore slip from his face. "This is weird," he said.

I coughed out something like a laugh. "This is *impossible*."

Noises drifted up from below us, and we peered over the edge of the carport. Hosts were moving up the street from the town square, drawn by the blast.

Patrick stood, swiped the shotgun back from me, and hopped onto the roof of the house, heading back toward school. "Either way," he said, "let's get the hell out of here while we can."

———

We entered the gym quietly, slipping through the double doors. The kids sat in rows on the basketball courts, the cots cleared to the side for the day. Alex sat on the lowest bleacher, having just finished talking to them all. Judging from the mood, it was clear what news she'd related.

The kids' faces were as blank as dolls', as blank as those of the Hosts themselves. Shock hung like a cloud in the room. It was so much to come to terms with, especially for the younger ones.

But they deserved the truth.

They deserved to know what was in store for them at the Lawrenceville Cannery if they were ever caught.

No one noticed me and Patrick standing at the back of the gym.

At last the spell broke. A few of the kids started crying.

JoJo sat between the Mendez twins, trying to comfort them, but they were inconsolable.

"I don't understand," Eve said. "Why would they do this?"

Dr. Chatterjee rose unevenly on his braced legs, his hands clasped before him. "If these beings are indeed implanting off-spring as Alex suggests . . ." He paused uneasily, cleared his throat. This was obviously difficult for him to talk about. "Then young specimens would provide the best . . . nutrients . . . for the growing offspring. Children have a lot of good healthy tissue for the offspring to . . ." He forced out the next words. "Feed off." A deep breath. "As for the bones, the epiphyses—the growth plates—are most active in children, which could serve to accelerate maturation for a parasitic entity." Seeming to lose his train of thought, he stopped briefly, his mouth wavering. "I'd hypothesize that the older kids are being used because hormone levels are highest during puberty, which would best support growth. . . ." He took off his eye-glasses, wiped them on the hem of his shirt. For a moment he looked lost.

Then he did something that caught us all off guard. He lowered his eyes into the fold of his hand and wept. We remained silent while his sobs filled the gym.

"If you can't handle *this*," Ben said, hopping up onto the bleachers and walking behind Chatterjee and Alex, "then you're in serious trouble. Because kids getting implanted isn't what we should be worried about right now."

"What *should* we be worried about?" Dezi Siegler called out.

Ben took his time and looked at the crowd. The heel of his hand rested on the butt of his stun gun. "You should be worried about who's gonna protect you when those things *hatch*."

A chill of fear rippled through the kids.

Patrick broke the silence from the back of the gym: "Know what *I'm* worried about?"

Every head turned; every face lit with amazement.

There my brother stood, without a mask. Breathing real air.

"I'm worried about who loosened the valves on my tanks and let all the oxygen out," Patrick said, striding forward. "I couldn't have this conversation with you before, Ben. I was in too much of a rush to save my life. But turns out I don't need the tanks after all."

Ben looked shaken. Forgetting he was in the bleachers, he tried to take a step back, the bench behind him catching him at the calves. He sat down hard in the footwell.

At the sight of my brother, Alex stood, bearing most of her weight on her good leg. "Patrick? How are you breathing?"

As my brother threaded his way through the kids, they gazed up in wonderment. He reached the bleachers, and Alex threw her arms around his neck, squeezing him hard. They kissed.

I stood to the side, doing my best not to look.

Patrick and Alex broke apart, and he turned to face the others, his arm around her. Everyone clapped. I could feel heat rise to my face; I only hoped it didn't show.

"I'm lucky to be alive," Patrick said. "And I'm even luckier Chance is my brother." He dipped his head, a rare show of embarrassment. "Thanks for bringing Alex back."

Everyone's attention swung to me. Eve watched me very closely.

I gave a dumb little wave because I didn't know what else to do. Then I took the black cowboy hat off my head.

And put it back on Patrick's where it belonged.

ENTRY 41 Moths swirled in the shafts of light falling through the windows of the biology lab. Once Dr. Chatterjee had examined Alex's leg and prescribed ice, Advil, and rest, she'd curled up on her cot and fallen asleep. Then he'd asked to meet with me and Patrick privately. He'd led us to his old classroom. Sitting behind his dusty desk now, he played with a DNA model made of rubber.

"The unidentified-particulate readings haven't diminished since your eighteenth birthday, Patrick," he said. "Not one bit."

"Do you think he might have passed some window of vulnerability or something?" I asked.

"I don't think that's likely."

"Why not?"

"Because so far everything about these spores, these . . . beings, has been maximally aggressive and effective. A brief infection window is neither. Plus, Occam's razor dictates that the simplest solution is often the correct one." Chatterjee spun the rubber ladder in his hands. "Which in this case would be genetic immunity."

"If I have it, then Chance has it, too," Patrick said. "I mean, these things are hereditary, right?"

The hope in his voice was so clear. As was the desperation.

"We won't know for two and a half more years," Chatterjee said, "when Chance turns eighteen. But I don't think it's as likely as in . . . other families."

Watching that genetic model rotating in his hands, I felt my heart pounding. "What do you mean?" I said.

Patrick drew himself upright. "What are you *talking* about?"

"Your parents wanted to keep it all quiet for some reason. I counseled them against it, but I couldn't say anything due to medical confidentiality. But now I don't really see the point anymore, since everyone's gone. You're the only ones who . . . who . . ."

"Dr. Chatterjee," Patrick said, his teeth clenched. "Will you please get to the point?"

Chatterjee set the DNA ladder down on his desk, finally looking up at us. "Your mother had some fertility issues. For a time she thought she couldn't have kids. But your parents wanted children very badly. And your mother wanted to be pregnant, to carry you both. They kept trying to find a way. And finally they did." He took a deep breath. "You were both born by embryo transfer."

You could have knocked Patrick and me over with the tap of a finger.

The bags beneath Chatterjee's eyes made clear what a toll these past weeks had taken on him. Bad news piling on top of bad news, and him the only adult in sight.

"So that means . . ." My brain was still a half step behind. "Patrick and I might have had different biological mothers?"

"Yes," Chatterjee said. "If the genetic code that makes Patrick immune is from the maternal side—"

Patrick looked crestfallen. "Then Chance wouldn't be immune like I am."

For a moment silence reigned.

I thought about how much bigger than me Patrick always was. Stronger, too. The way everyone joked about how little family resemblance we had. And our personalities also had been different from the gates. Our interests and talents seemed to pull us in different directions from the beginning.

"Wouldn't you know if the egg donor was the same?" Patrick asked. "I mean, you were our doctor. You delivered us. Wouldn't that be in a file somewhere?"

"I'm afraid *that* information was kept confidential even from me. It resides somewhere in a computer system at the donor bank."

My head felt heavy, filled with smog. I thought about what Alex had told me in the cabin about her father and my mom: *They were gonna get married, have kids, the whole thing. Then Dad broke up with her after graduation. I don't know what it was. Cold feet, fear, whatever. But he never forgave himself for it. Or her.*

He'd broken it off with my mom because he'd found out she couldn't have kids. Or at least she'd *thought* she couldn't.

When I came back from my train of thought, Dr. Chatterjee was staring at me, looking dismayed.

"Okay," I said, trying to keep the disappointment from my voice. "Thanks for telling us."

"I'm sorry to drop this bombshell on you in the middle of everything else," he said.

"That's what the world is now," I said. "One bombshell after another. We might as well get used to it."

Patrick turned to me. "If I could trade places with you and give you my immunity, I would."

"I know," I said. "But I wouldn't take it."

He put an arm around my neck and tweaked me into him, hard. It hurt and felt good at the same time.

Dr. Chatterjee rose, and we started to head out.

"What are you gonna do about Ben?" I asked.

Chatterjee halted, his leg braces clanking. "We don't know that he loosened those valves, Chance."

"Yes," I said. "We do."

"You're making accusations without evidence. We can't act on that. We can't *live* like that. Think what this community would deteriorate into without rules in place."

"Ben said it himself," Patrick said. "There have to be *new* rules. The old ones won't work anymore."

His face long with sorrow, Chatterjee put a hand on the ledge of my brother's shoulder. "I'm sorry you feel that way, Patrick," he said.

He trudged out ahead of us.

———

Over the next few days, Alex rested up, but something was working on her thoughts like an infection. I watched her chewing her lip at night, staring up at the ceiling, at nothing. During the days she worked on her injured leg with a vengeance, stretching it out on the bleachers and doing deep knee bends. Every morning and every afternoon, she'd turn on the TV and give the dial a twirl all the way around.

I don't know what she was hoping for, but every channel still showed static.

When I dreamed, I saw the faces of those kids in their cages at the cannery. The Queen's stinger, poised to descend. Children floating on metal slabs, their bellies distended. I didn't sleep for long, waking up in starts, drenched in sweat.

One night I jerked awake to find JoJo tugging at Alex's sleeve two cots over. Alex shifted up on her pillow, and Patrick stirred as well.

"What is it, sweetheart?" Alex said.

Over the thudding of my heart, still on overdrive from the nightmare, I barely made out JoJo's fragile whisper. "Alex?" she said. "Tell me it's gonna be okay."

Alex's eyes ticked over toward my brother, and they shared a look through the darkness. I wasn't sure what it meant.

Alex's expression shifted into something hard and unrecognizable. She looked back at JoJo. "I can't," she said, and rolled over again.

She sounded angry, but I could hear the heartbreak beneath the words.

JoJo's shoulders pinched up, and she shuffled away a step, stunned. I rose quickly and came to her side. "C'mon, Junebug. Let's get you back to sleep."

She lifted her arms to me the way she did when she was upset. Picking her up, I carried her over to her cot and tucked her in.

"Are they gonna get me, Chance?" she asked.

I thought about what I'd be willing to do to protect her. "Not so long as I'm around," I said.

Her smile glinted in the darkness. "Then I'll always be safe," she said. "'Cuz nothing would ever happen to you."

Content for the moment, she snuggled into Bunny and closed her eyes.

The weight of the promise pulled at me. From her perspective I must have seemed big and invincible.

Just like Patrick always seemed to me.

I couldn't go back to sleep that night.

I used the following days to catch up on rest and bring my journal up to speed. The sixth night we were back, Alex finished stretching and then started running up and down the bleachers—a drill that Coach Hanson used to make us do in PE when we weren't paying attention.

It was clear that Alex was training for something.

Chatterjee stood and watched her, his forehead grooved with furrows. He seemed worried.

In between lookout shifts, Patrick paced around the school grounds. There was a building sense of anticipation, of unease. I sensed that something was coming, a storm brewing inside him and Alex, inside even me, but I couldn't grasp what it was.

That night a hand shook me gently from sleep. "Okay, Junebug," I murmured, rolling over. "Let's get you back to—"

But it wasn't Junebug. It was Eve.

She crouched beside my cot, her eyes wide with concern. "When you and Alex were gone, it was awful," she whispered. "Patrick did his best, but he had the mask on and the tank, so he could only do so much."

Her gaze lifted past me, and I turned to follow it across the gym. By the double doors, Ben sat watch, alert as ever, a shaft of moonlight falling across his eyes. When I turned back, I was surprised by the fear in Eve's face.

"Chatterjee couldn't control Ben," she said. "He's getting worse and worse. What's gonna happen to the rest of us if all *three* of you are gone?"

"What do you mean?" I asked. "Where are we going?"

Disappointment flickered across her eyes. "Oh, Chance," she said. "You really can't tell?"

"No."

"You're so amazing sometimes, but then you're also so . . . *young.*" Eve leaned forward and gave me a peck on the cheek. Before I could respond, she scurried off toward her cot, keeping her profile low to the ground so Ben wouldn't spot her.

My cheek tingled where her lips had touched. I lifted my fingers to the spot, my thoughts churning. It took half the night, but I finally worked out what Eve was talking about. Perhaps I'd known all along.

Alex said it first.

It was the next day. She, Patrick, and I were on northeast-quadrant lookout in Tomasi's room. Alex hopped off the desk, landing strong on her feet. She stretched her left leg to the side and pulled it up, testing the muscle.

"I'm not gonna let happen to them what almost happened to me," she said.

Patrick bobbed his head in agreement. I wondered if it was something they'd discussed or if it was something they didn't *have* to discuss. Maybe it was one of those couple things where one just knew what the other was thinking.

Then Patrick said what we always said: "We got work to do."

"The kids at the cannery?" I asked.

Alex didn't respond; she just kept testing that leg, her gaze far away. I thought about my hushed conversation with Eve last night and the worried expression Chatterjee had been wearing more and more often. It seemed he also knew he'd be unable to keep control once we left.

"What about the kids here?" I said. "If we go, Ben'll take over."

"Do we protect a few kids from Ben here?" Alex said. "Or all the kids out there from having unimaginable things done to them?"

It wasn't a question. It was an argument.

I said, "What are you proposing?"

When she looked at me, her gaze was alarmingly steady. "Kill the Queen."

My throat felt dry, so I forced out the word. "How?"

"Remember what we found in that cabin?" she asked.

I did. I remembered the polished walnut stock. The perfect balance in my hands. The mounted scope.

I nodded.

"If we go," I said, "we might be taken ourselves. Or killed."

"That's right," Patrick said. "But what does it mean about us if we *don't* go?"

"We can't just stand by and do nothing," Alex said.

"It's probably a suicide mission," I said.

Dezi Siegler and another of Ben's lackeys sidled into the classroom, relieving us for the next shift.

Alex slid past me on her way to the door. "I'm okay with that," she said.

———

After darkness fell, I crept through the cots and shook Eve awake just as she'd done to me the night before. She stirred, looked up into my face, and smiled. Then she saw that I was fully dressed and her expression shifted.

"You have to keep an eye out for JoJo," I whispered. "You're the only one I trust."

She rubbed her eyes. "Of course I will," she said.

"Tell her I talked to you, that I knew you were the best one to look out for her."

Eve nodded. "What about Dr. Chatterjee? Is he okay with this?"

"Patrick talked to him. He said he can keep Ben under control until we get back."

She pushed herself up and reached for me. I leaned into her, and we hugged, her arms extra tight around my neck.

"What if you *don't* come back?" she whispered, her lips right at my ear.

I kissed her on the cheek and pulled away. Across the gym I could see Patrick and Alex waiting for me.

For some reason it struck me that it was Halloween, a time for ghosts and ghouls, sugar buzzes and scares. I thought about how much fun tonight should have been for an eight-year-old girl. And what it was instead.

I said, "Take care of JoJo."

ENTRY 42   It was worse than we thought.

Two nights later, after a grueling journey, Alex, Patrick, and I found ourselves perched in the tree-studded hills above the cannery, gazing down at the compound with shock.

The factory had been repaired using the construction materials stacked around the area. The walls had been built out thicker and a security fence erected. The Hosts progressed with their grisly work on the assembly line, feeding bound children through the hatch in the factory wall to the Queen beyond.

But that wasn't what was alarming.

What was alarming was the number of Drones patrolling the perimeter. After my raid to free Alex, they must've been called in from all over the area.

Or from somewhere else.

With the hunting rifle from the cabin snug in my hands, I crouch-walked backward, vanishing through a screen of foliage. On either side of me, Patrick and Alex eased back as well, melting into the underbrush.

We reconvened in a low clearing by an abandoned backhoe undercutter.

Thump. Squelch.

I'd hoped to take a shooting position at the tree line below, a football field's distance from the Queen. But there was no way we could penetrate the new perimeter to get me that close. Not without a much bigger plan. We were outnumbered, overpowered, and outgunned. Alex ducked her head into her hands, made fists in her hair, and gave a low growl of frustration.

"With the new fences and the patrols, I'm not even gonna get close," I said. "We're looking at a four-hundred-yard shot now."

"You got a bolt-action Ruger M77 Hawkeye in your hands," Patrick said. "I've seen you hit smaller from farther."

"Not with Drones patrolling around trying to kill me," I said.

"We'll create the diversion once you get off the shot," he said. "Draw them after us like we talked about. You just get in as near as you can, take her out, and hunker down somewhere to hide out until it's safe to move."

We'd gone over the plan a dozen or so times in the past forty-eight hours. From a position much farther away, Patrick and Alex would make a lot of noise in the wake of the gunshot, broadcasting their position immediately while I tried to hide. The Drones would have much more ground to make up to get to them. At a certain point, Patrick and Alex would split, confusing the Drones even more.

Leaning the rifle against my leg, I slipped the nylon loops off my wrists and handed Alex my baling hooks. It felt like letting go of a part of myself.

Just me and the rifle now.

Patrick turned around so Alex could unzip the pack he was wearing and slide my hooks in. My own backpack held only food, water, my journal, and ammo. With all the crawling I had in front of me, it had to cling tight to my back, so I couldn't take anything bulky.

Patrick pivoted to face us again. "We'll reconvene at the cabin tomorrow." He cleared his throat, and I could see in his face that he didn't think there would *be* a tomorrow, any more than I did.

We shifted, avoiding eye contact. Before seeing the compound, we'd figured we were probably on a suicide mission. Seeing the number of Drones around the place had removed any doubt. Patrick had his shotgun, Alex the revolver, and of course I had the rifle. We'd never made the vow out loud—we never had to—but we all knew we'd never allow ourselves to be taken alive.

"Sure," I said. "See you tomorrow."

Thump. Squelch.

Every delay cost another life. The pressure felt like something tangible, smashing in from all sides.

Patrick leaned back, his knees cracking, and hiked the pack higher on his shoulders. Alex stepped beside him.

Here's where we parted ways. Them in one direction. Me another.

Like always.

Knowing that this was probably the last time we'd see each other, I swallowed back any bitterness. I hugged my brother. There was nothing more to say.

Then Alex reached for me.

Patrick started upslope, giving us a moment of privacy. She put her hands on my face and looked deep into my eyes. My thoughts tumbled, catching me in a white-water swirl. There was so much I wanted to tell her but nothing I could say.

She leaned forward and gave me a kiss at the corner of my lips.

"Good luck, Little Rain," she said.

"Bye, Blanton."

Her eyes watered, but she turned quickly away.

I watched as they vanished into the foliage, Alex hurrying to catch up to my brother, her hand swinging to find his. Their part of the mission—making themselves the target of the Drones' wrath instead of me—was just as scary as mine, but

• 330 •

I couldn't help feel a sliver of envy that they'd be together right up until the end.

Thump. Squelch.

The sound called me to the task at hand. I had to decide on a shooting location. Closing my eyes, I exhaled, scattering all thoughts of Alex and my brother to the wind. In my mind's eye, I scanned the terrain between me and the cannery, terrain I'd forged across last time when I'd gone to get Alex. I picked my spot. And my hiding place.

When I opened my eyes, I was ready.

Bellying down in the earth, moving the rifle ahead of me, I crawled through the weeds. I angled toward the muddy ruts beside the storage warehouse where the bulldozer had been parked.

I forced myself to take it slow. I was hunting now. A hunter in a hurry never brought home a deer. I tried to make myself invisible. Just another piece of the land.

The terrain opened up, a break in the trees exposing me to the midday sun and any eyeless faces below. I moved in bursts, crawling a few feet, then pausing, breathing hard. My face pressed to the dirt, I'd strain my ears. If I heard nothing above the breeze, I'd continue. It was brutally slow going. Every ten feet or so, I'd risk a peek to make sure I was staying on course.

Thump. Squelch.

Somewhere on the hillside up above, Patrick and Alex were in position waiting.

And somewhere down below, kids were being killed.

The gravel pile remained ahead, though it was only half the height it had been before. The Drones must have made use of the gravel in their construction or repairs. The sun inched its way up, baking down on me. My clothes felt itchy. The start of a sunburn tingled across the nape of my neck. The backpack straps chafed my shoulders.

It took me two hours to come into range of the storage warehouse, but at last I was safely behind the gravel.

I gave myself a minute to stretch my aching limbs, then peered around the edge.

The Queen was in her position at the end of the assembly line. Her squirming stinger rose, then plummeted into the midsection of the girl secured before her. Though a variation of this scene had been playing through my head on a near-continuous loop for day and nightmare-riddled night, it felt as fresh as a cut. My chest cramped, and I had to concentrate to slow my breathing. It wasn't a sight you could get used to.

Nor was the sight on the foundation.

Countless floating slabs of sheet metal, each supporting a kid's deadweight, now covered the majority of the vast concrete plain. The closer kids, those who'd been more recently implanted with offspring, looked like the ones I'd seen last time I was here. Their stomach and lower chest areas were swollen, the humps ranging in size.

But the kids at the farthest reaches of the foundation, those who'd first been turned into cocoons, were no longer recognizable as humans. The entire front sides of their bodies ballooned upward, in some cases even higher than the kids were tall. Their clothes had ripped, their skin stretching to conceal whatever was growing inside them. Broken ribs floated beneath the skin, visible like sticks pushed through latex. Worst of all, their flesh pulsed erratically.

As if ready to hatch.

Thump. Squelch.

From where I lay, the Queen was at least six hundred yards away, too far for me and the Hawkeye.

I had to move fast. And yet that was the one thing I could not risk doing.

Ignoring the sounds rising to me, I continued crawling

cautiously down and across the hillside. Progress was slow, but I was able to pick up the pace a little as the trees thickened.

At long last I reached the giant hollowed-out tree where I'd stashed my backpack last time.

Thump. Squelch.

I passed it. The earth swelled into a knoll between two trees and then dropped sharply away, providing a clean line of sight down to the Queen below.

I took my position at the top of the rise, setting the rifle in front of me and fishing two extra rounds from the backpack. I placed the bullets on end on a flat rock. If I missed with the first shot, I'd be lucky to get off a second. There'd be no way I'd have enough time to fire a third, but I wanted the bullet right there within reach as a comfort.

Then I set my eye to the scope.

Thump.

The Queen's faceless helmet loomed into view. It dipped forward with a plunge—*Squelch*—then leaned back again, filling the crosshairs.

It took all my control not to rush off a shot.

Reading the wind and my distance, I forced myself to account for drift and holdover. My elbows sank into wet moss. Sweat stung my eyes, and I blinked them clear, arming it off my forehead.

Thump. Squelch.

"I'm sorry," I whispered to the kid floating off across the plain to join the others.

I set my eye to the scope. Closed my other eye. Flicked off the safety.

Thump.

The shiny black mask dipped forward out of sight.

Squelch.

I didn't dare move my lips now, but the words cycled through my heart, my brain: *I'm sorry.*

I eased out a breath through my teeth. Took the slack out of the trigger. Moisture from the moss seeped through my shirt at the elbows.

The seconds stretched out.

The Queen's head reared back up, filling my scope, the world.

I fired.

The bullet rifled past her head.

She paused, looked to her side. Her mask held no expression, but her body language conveyed puzzlement.

Forcing myself steady, I worked the bolt, the empty cartridge ejecting with a faint pop. As I reached for the flat stone, my hand nudged the nearest round, knocking it into the one beside it. The first bullet tumbled off the knoll, ping-ponging down the slope ahead. The other spun at the very edge of the rock, each turn rotating the end out over the open air.

I plucked it up.

Thumbed it into the chamber.

Worked the bolt.

Eye to scope.

The Queen was still reeled back, gazing to her side, that unreadable mask giving up nothing more than a slight air of confusion.

She swung her head back and looked, it seemed, directly at me.

Her head cocked to one side.

I put a bullet through the mask.

Her head jerked back, a stream of black smoke hissing through the bullet hole. Her knees went wobbly, and she seemed to deflate as if punctured. The rush of expelled air grew stronger, pressure blowing out the chink in her mask, shards flying. The hiss turned to a scream. It seemed her whole being was shooting through the widening hole in her helmet. It reached whale-spout velocity, and then, all at once, it stopped.

She crumpled to the ground, limp.

From way up above me and a good distance around the rim of the valley came the sound of a construction truck's engine turning over, then roaring to life. A thunderous crash followed almost immediately, several treetops shuddering conspicuously.

Patrick and Alex, purposefully botching their "getaway."

I turned my gaze back to the factory. All around the assembly line, the Hosts stopped their work and stood in place, as if awaiting orders. On the foundation the young floating bodies looked even more ready to hatch, if that were possible. Stretch marks fissured their flesh, widening even as I watched.

Crashing sounds drew my focus to the bigger scene. From every direction the Drones bounded toward the Queen, a swarm of bees narrowing to enter a hive. More and more black space suits leached into view from the surrounding landscape, drawn to their dead leader. In their quest to reach her, they took giant leaps, smashing through fences, bushes, and even Hosts, destroying everything in their paths.

They formed a protective mass around her. Those at the perimeter faced outward, their helmets pointing at the hillside, masks aglow with blueprint-like renderings.

Assessing the hillsides.

I had forgotten to breathe, but seeing those black helmets aimed in my direction got me moving.

Jerking back from the edge of the knoll, I slid on my stomach across the sleek moss, bringing the rifle with me. I scrambled for the dark mouth of the hollowed-out tree, then crawled inside, brushing away spiderwebs, shoving the backpack and rifle ahead of me. The ancient tree was several yards across. The moist air of the tree's core clung to my skin, the sound of my ragged breaths echoing up the shaft through the darkness.

I leaned against the inner wall, not even caring if I was squashing bugs beneath my back, and tried to calm myself down. Aside from the fall of light from the narrow hole I'd squeezed through, the heart of the tree was pitch-black. The darkness cooled the sweat on my face.

I thought about how the Queen had crumpled to the dirt, dead. All the kids she'd never hurt now. The master plan would go on, that seemed certain, but we'd managed to throw a wrench into the works. For that I allowed myself a flicker of pride.

My brother and Alex were high in the woods above me, running for their lives, and I took a moment to send all my hope to them across the distance.

I also said good-bye.

No matter what happened to us now, we'd done it. We'd killed the Queen, fired the first shot in the revolution. Maybe after we were gone, that would inspire other kids to take other measures.

I inhaled deeply and held my breath, listening for any sounds from outside.

A furious insectoid screeching carried up the hillside.

It compounded, rolling across the valley in stereo. I'd never heard such rage. Or such menace. I was glad to be hidden here inside the dark core of the giant tree.

Moving of its own volition, my hand dug in the backpack for another round. I wanted the rifle loaded in case they closed in on me. If I had to take myself out, I'd be ready.

Another series of screeches split the air, and I started, the round slipping through my sweaty fingers. Setting the rifle aside, I leaned forward, groping around in the dirt.

Across from me something glowed bluish white in the darkness.

A mask.

Belonging to a space-suit helmet just like those worn by the Drones.

An arm sheathed with metal flew out at me, a hand clamping over my mouth before I could scream.

ENTRY 43   The mirrored glass of the Drone's helmet threw back my terrified reflection. The glow from the mask illuminated him sitting just like me, directly across the tree's hollowed core.

A computerized rendering of his view blipped up on his mask, which appeared to me in reverse. It was similar to the one I'd seen in Ezekiel's eye membrane. Except now the thing being outlined was *me*. Strands of my hair. The contours of my face. My cells pulled apart and analyzed.

"We have found you, Chance Rain," a digitized masculine voice said. The mask flickered with the words, a blue fizzle for each consonant, like amplitude waves. "We finally found you."

My brain whirred into overdrive, but unlike whatever program ran in his mask, it was offering no analysis. I was stunned, my body awash in adrenaline.

The figure spoke again. "Do not cry out," he said. "You will give away our position."

Beneath his armored glove, my mouth remained open in terror, the scream sealed in my throat. I managed to clamp my jaw shut. Then I gave a nod.

The hand released me.

He came clearer now in the bluish light. I blinked a few times, my night vision kicking in, helping the picture resolve.

He looked a lot like a Drone, but a closer examination revealed some differences. His space suit was charcoal rather than black, matte instead of shiny, and it looked scuffed and battle-worn. His powerful appearance may have been en-hanced by the flexible armor that formed his suit. His position, slouched against the inside of the tree, one hand pressed to his gut, indicated that he was hurt. And he *sounded* hurt, too, light bars flickering with each labored breath, altering the volume of some of his words.

My breathing couldn't have sounded much better, my chest still lurching from the scare. It took a moment for me to find my voice. "Who are you?"

"My name will make no sense to you," he said.

As I watched the amplitude bars flicker, I understood the helmet to be translating.

"Where are you from?" I asked.

He raised a sheathed arm and pointed through the hole in the tree toward the dagger of blue sky. "Same as the Harvest-ers. But we oppose them."

I shook my head, half expecting him to disappear as if he were a hallucination. "So you're, like . . . *rebels?*"

"You can call us that."

"How . . . how did you get here?"

"We travel by asteroid. Like them. And, like them, we have to prepare the way." The glow from his mask flickered. "We are not as good at this nor willing to be as ruthless."

"How do you know who I am?"

"We are capable of mapping and identifying—"

"No, I mean how do you know my *name?*"

Outside, the screeching started up again, scaring birds from the treetops.

"There is no time for that right now," he said. "Listen to me carefully." The glowing contour lines in his mask fuzzed, then regained their clarity. "You and your brother are the key to everything. Is he alive?"

"Wait," I said. *"What?"*

The words came through the helmet, more intense than before. *"Is your brother alive?"*

"Yes." Even as I answered, I wondered how much longer that would be true.

The head tilted back, a gesture that conveyed great relief. "It was all I could do to try to reach the nearest Hatch site to look for you two amongst the cages. I scanned them and searched the Husks as well."

Husks. The kids floating on slabs, their bodies stretched beyond recognition.

But I was still stuck back on the prior revelation. "What do you mean, Patrick and I are the key to everything?"

"For the planet. For survival."

"We're the *key*? Us and who else?"

"Only you two."

My head buzzed. "What are *we* supposed to do?"

"A mission. That only you or your brother can carry out."

"A *mission*?"

"You have accomplished something extraordinary. You killed a Queen and shut down a Hatch site. That's never been done before—"

"Wait—before *where*?"

"—but that is only the beginning. The next stage is about to commence. After the Hatch nothing will be the same. And it will all come down to you."

I coughed out a laugh. "What are you saying? It's up to us or everyone'll die or something?"

"Not 'or something.'" He leaned forward, his grip tightening around my arm. "If you fail in your mission, everyone on the planet will die."

I had no idea what to do with that information. Not right now. There was too much to consider. So many ramifications.

He continued, "You cannot fall into the hands of the Harvesters."

"Or what?"

"You cannot imagine what they will do to you."

After what I'd seen already, that sent a chill up my spine.

"Be careful whom you trust with this information," he said. "Anyone who knows about you will be tortured if captured. Now that the Harvesters have landed, they will be looking for you and your brother everywhere, to stop you before you can carry out the plan. By now they will have used your adult male population to map your entire planet. They know every inch of your terrain. They had to inspect it to see if it would work."

"If *what* would work?"

"The Hatch." The Rebel's breathing grew more labored. The glow guttered, then glitched. It seemed he was shorting out. "They had to know that they could habitate here."

"Why?" I asked. "Their planet is dying?"

The mask stared at me blankly for a moment. "No," he said. "They just want *more*."

I was shocked into silence.

The wind carried the sounds of marching boots, the Drones taking to the hills.

"Please listen to me now," he said. "There are others like me, searching for you and your brother the planet over. Of course we concentrated our efforts here near your place of birth, but we could leave no stone unturned."

"How many are you?"

"Now we number merely in the dozens. The Harvesters took over our planet as they are trying to take over yours. They nearly succeeded in destroying us all." The glow fizzled out, then came back online. "They are stronger. But we are braver."

The screeches grew closer.

"I will relay to the others that you are intact and viable," he said. "That there is still hope. They will find you. Or you must find them."

"Why don't you just stay with me?"

He tried to lift the hand from his stomach, but his arm slid limply to the dirt. "I am going to expire soon. My landing was not successful. I was injured in the crash." A glitch appeared in the rendering lines in his mask, then intensified. "We are not well suited for this environment."

"Then why did you come? Why did you all come?"

He reached his other hand forward weakly and set it on top of mine. "To find you."

Again I gazed at my own stunned reflection floating in the digitized lines of his mask.

The sound of footfalls grew even closer. Then there came a loud whirring noise and a thunderous cracking from downslope. I shot a nervous glance through the hole in the trunk and saw a few treetops vanish abruptly from view as if sucked into the earth.

"You have to go," he said.

"I need to hide here—"

"They are taking down the trees and anything in their path."

"How?"

"Listen to me." The glow flared, the digitized voice even louder now.

Outside, more trees vanished. The screeches of Drones echoed through the valley, cries of rage.

His grip on my hand tightened. "No matter what, they must *never* find out who you are. Do *not* let them take you. We will contact you when we can and tell you of your mission. Until then you have one job: Stay alive. At any cost, stay—"

The glow vanished, the mask turned instantly to a lifeless black sheet. His fingers released their grip on my hand. He remained in exactly the same position.

Through the narrow hole in the trunk, I watched another row of trees below shudder and topple. The Drones were literally clearing the hillside. And the tree I was hiding in was right in their path.

I reached for the rifle, then remembered the Rebel's words. I couldn't take myself out, not now. I had to stay free and stay alive. I started for the hole, then paused.

Gathering my courage, I reached for the helmet. And twisted it off.

It was empty.

A wisp of smoke curled lazily from the space suit's neck-hole, floating up the hollow core of the tree. Grabbing the rim of the collar, I tilted the semi-rigid suit forward and peered into the torso. Nothing inside.

Like the Queen, he'd turned to gas.

I didn't wait around to contemplate this impossibility. Charging through the hole in the tree, I yanked on my backpack and shot to my feet. Through the netting of the branches, I saw the nearest pair of Drones hurtling upslope.

Between them they carried a massive whirring blade. It took a moment for me to recognize it as a backhoe undercutter that had been removed and retrofitted to be carried at either end. It was basically a giant chain saw designed for cutting rock and ballast. The armored carbide plates moved in continuous 360-degree rotation. I watched with amazement as the Drones came straight at a tree, the blade held between them. The teeth buzz-sawed through the trunk, and the massive pine slid away. The Drones barely even had to slow their pace.

Bursts of mist shot out of valves around the necks of their

helmets, producing the ear-rending screeches. Were they caused by gas expanding with the heat of rage?

Several more screeches cut through the leaves all around me, leaving me disoriented. I turned in a full circle, assessing my options. Up at the ridgeline where Patrick and Alex had crashed the truck, trees nodded furiously, then dropped from view. Another Drone team must have moved ahead of the vanguard to pursue them. That left me a course to the west.

I ran.

Pine needles whipped across my body. My boots slid through mud, and several times I went down. I ran until my breath fired through my lungs, until my legs almost gave out. Eventually the sounds of crashing trees receded, but I could still hear the Drones among the trees, pursuing me. Several times I thought I'd gotten clear of them only to have a screech fly out of the foliage right beside me, nearly stopping my heart.

I braced myself for the sound of a gunshot signaling Patrick's or Alex's death but heard none. They might have been cornered and taken their own lives already. The screeches would easily have drowned out the noise of a bullet or two.

Somehow I got out of the valley.

Running blindly, I kept to the woods. I didn't stop, didn't slow. Trunks flickered past me, the landscape strobing by. I made it to the fork in the road, barreling into that ring of Rocky Mountain Douglas firs where we'd camped so many nights ago. Leaning over, I vomited twice, then dry-heaved more times than I could count.

I couldn't catch my breath.

I didn't have time.

Wiping my mouth, I kept on, winding my way down toward the cabin. Just before nightfall I saw the straight line of the roof appear through the brush. It took everything I had not to collapse with relief.

Dead on my feet, I staggered through the front door. "Patrick? Alex?"

A sweeping glance told me that no one was there.

Were they dead? Captured?

I remembered the Rebel's words: *You have one job: Stay alive.*

We'd thought it was a one-way mission, but there was so much more at stake now. I closed the door behind me, then drew all the blinds.

I drank down three glasses of water, then kicked off my boots, sat on the bed, and stared blankly at my toes. I stayed that way for a long time, fighting back tears. Patrick could be dead. Alex could be dead.

I could do nothing but wait and wait some more.

Alex had kissed me right here in this very spot. I remembered how she'd leaned in. The softness of her lips.

I wondered how I'd feel if she came back without Patrick. Or if he did without her.

What if they didn't come tomorrow? Or the next day? How long would I wait before heading back to Creek's Cause?

I was too exhausted to sleep. At the slightest sound outside, my heart leapt with hope, but every time I peered through the curtains, it proved to be branches rubbing together or the barn roof creaking.

I tried to process everything that the Rebel had told me, but it all seemed too huge, and it made me miss Patrick and Alex even more. I took solace in the fact that I'd heard no gunshots. What if something happened to me but Patrick remained alive out there somewhere? How would he ever know what he meant for our survival?

Sometime after midnight, sick with worry, I sat on the floor, pulled out my notebook, and started writing.

ENTRY 44   Okay. I'm here. I'm finally caught up, but my eyes are so heavy. It's almost light out now, and at last I might be tired enough to—

I hear footfalls outside.

Patrick and Alex?

The sun is coming up, so I have to be careful when I peek through the curtains.

ENTRY 45   I'm dead.

There are Drones all around the cabin in every direction—above, below, both sides. They don't know I'm here, not yet, but they're walking in patterns through the woods, just like Mappers, leaving no stone unturned. Except this time the spiral's not expanding.

It's closing in.

I see them flickering behind the trees. I hear their boots trampling the underbrush. There is no way to slip through, not this time.

Every second brings them closer.

I won't kill myself. After what the Rebel said, I know I owe it to everyone to try to stay alive as long as I can, but—

I just heard the barn door bang open. They're probably searching the stable now. There's nowhere for me to go. Nothing left to do. My only chance is if Patrick and Alex made it out. If they did, they'll come for me. I know they will.

The problem is I probably can't stay alive until they do.

I can't help but think of the coming Hatch, those pulsing stomachs about to give birth to a new age. All the kids at the cannery I can't help. The others around the world who I've failed. JoJo and Rocky and Eve, back at school, who I can't even protect from Ben.

I've never been this scared.

I'm gonna hide this book now. If you're the one who discovers it, find Patrick Rain. And give it to him. He's the only one besides me who can carry out the mission, and he has to know everything. Pray he's alive. He's the last chance we've got.

Or I should say the last chance *you've* got. I don't know what will happen to me, but judging from those kids I saw floating on the metal slabs, it won't be good. If the Harvesters find out who I am, it'll be even worse.

I can hear leaves crunching just beyond the front door. The Drones, taking their final turn around the house. They're coming. They're coming for me.

I only have time to scribble a warning on the front cover of my notepad. Please read this whole account and read it well.

Good-bye and good luck.

We're counting on you.

EPILOGUE

The document you are reading does not—cannot—exist. If you're reading this, your life is at risk. Or I should say your life is at even greater risk than it was already. I'm sorry to burden you with this. I don't wish you the kind of harm that came to me and the others from Creek's Cause. This is what I've managed to piece together since it all began. I wrote it down knowing that words are more powerful than bullets—and certainly more dangerous. All is probably lost already.

But maybe, just maybe, these pages will give you a chance.

I hope you're up to it.

NEXT: WHO WILL SURVIVE FOR THEIR . . .

LAST CHANCE?

ACKNOWLEDGMENTS

My thanks go to:

—Lisa Erbach Vance of the Aaron M. Priest Literary Agency, for whom I've run out of superlatives.

—Trevor Astbury, Rob Kenneally, Peter Micelli, and Michelle Weiner, my extraordinary team at CAA. What a job they've done for me.

—Marc H. Glick and Stephen F. Breimer, my expert counsel. Twenty years, boys.

—Melissa Frain, my delightful, insightful editor.

—Kathleen Doherty, my publisher, and Ali Fisher and Amy Stapp, also of Tor Teen, for their terrific support.

—Maureen Sugden, my erudite copyeditor, who slays with wit.

—Mark Sullivan, who taught Chance how to get off that shot with a Ruger M77 Hawkeye.

—Melissa Hurwitz, M.D., and Bret Nelson, M.D., for reading early and helping me make the implausible plausible.

—Christi Goodman, for generously helping me color my fictional setting.

—Dana Kaye, my astute and tenacious publicist.

—Delinah, Rose, and Natalie, for making my life outside my stories as vivid, unpredictable, and rewarding as what goes down inside them.

—My parents, for filling my childhood with the ingredients that give rise to imagination.

*No Rhodesian ridgebacks were harmed in the writing of this book, or Simba and Cairo would have had something to say about it. They are loyalty and goodness personified. Pretty impressive when you consider that they don't even have opposable thumbs.